The ELUSIVE ELIXIR

Gigi Pandian

MIDNIGHT INK
WOODBURY, MINNESOTA

FIRST EDITION
First Printing, 2017

Book format by Bob Gaul
Cover design by Kevin R. Brown
Cover illustration by Hugh D'Andrade/Jennifer Vaughn Artist Agent
Editing by Nicole Nugent

Midnight Ink, an imprint of Llewellyn Worldwide Ltd.

Library of Congress Cataloging-in-Publication Data (Pending)
ISBN: 978-0-7387-4236-6

Midnight Ink
Llewellyn Worldwide Ltd.
2143 Wooddale Drive
Woodbury, MN 55125-2989
www.midnightinkbooks.com

Printed in the United States of America

WORKS BY GIGI PANDIAN

The Accidental Alchemist Mystery Series
The Accidental Alchemist
The Masquerading Magician
The Elusive Elixir

Jaya Jones Treasure Hunt Mystery Series
"Fools Gold" in *Other People's Baggage*
Artifact
Pirate Vishnu
Quicksand
Michelangelo's Ghost
"A Dark and Stormy Light" in
Malice Domestic 11: Murder Most Conventional

Short Stories
"The Shadow of the River" in *Fish Tales*
"The Hindi Houdini" in *Fish Nets*
"The Haunted Room" in *The Bouchercon 2014 Anthology*
"Tempest in a Teapot" in *Ladies Night*
"The Curse of Cloud Castle" in *Asian Pulp*

To you, my readers, for your
boundless enthusiasm for a gargoyle.

ONE

THE WOMAN WAS STILL behind me.

She was so close to me on the winding, irregular stone steps inside Notre Dame Cathedral that I could smell her breath. Sourdough bread and honey.

I could have sworn I'd seen her at the *boulangerie* near my apartment earlier that morning. Now her unwavering gaze bore into me. She must have been at least eighty and wasn't more than five feet tall. She didn't fit the profile of someone worth being afraid of. Most people would have dismissed it as a coincidence.

Unless you're someone like me, who always has to be careful.

We emerged from the cramped corridor onto the narrow Gallery of Gargoyles, high above Paris. I shielded my eyes from the sun. A warm wind swept my hair around my face as I looked out through the mesh fencing that covered the once-open balcony.

The gargoyle known as *Le Penseur*, "The Thinker," sat regally with his stone head turned toward the City of Lights, as he had for over 150 years. Unlike my friend Dorian, this gargoyle of Notre Dame wouldn't be stepping off his stone mount.

1

For a few brief seconds, the stunning details Eugène Viollet-le-Duc had added to his chimeras all those years ago made me forget about the woman. The grandeur even made me lose sight of the real reason I was at Notre Dame that day. My quest was never far from my thoughts, but for those fleeting moments, I allowed myself the space to appreciate the splendor of the craftsmanship of generations of artists and laborers.

A girl around eight years old squealed in delight as she noticed a set of smaller gargoyles perched overhead, grinning maniacally at us. Her younger brother began to cry. His father explained in a thick Welsh accent that gargoyles weren't to be feared. They weren't even real, for Heaven's sake! His father was right—in this particular case.

If I didn't get rid of my shadow and get what I needed here at Notre Dame, the Welshman's words would be true for all gargoyles, including my best friend. I followed the tight walkway for a few steps until I saw it. An unfinished slab of limestone where a gargoyle might have perched.

This was the spot.

I glanced behind me. The woman stood a few paces away. In stylish sunglasses with a perfectly knotted silk scarf around her spindly neck, she was simultaneously frail and glamorous. Unlike the crowd of tourists excitedly scurrying past each other on the balcony that was never meant for this volume of visitors, the woman stood stock still. She held no camera. Her gaze didn't linger on the dramatic cityscape or on the unique stone monsters that surrounded us.

She looked directly at me, not bothering to conceal her curiosity.

"May I help you?" I asked, speaking in French. Though the woman hadn't spoken, the style and care of her clothing, hair, and makeup suggested she was Parisian.

She pulled her sunglasses off and clenched them in boney hands. "*I knew it*," she replied in English. "I knew it was you." Her voice was strong, with the hint of a rattle in her throat. The forcefulness of her words seemed to surprise her nearly as much as it surprised me.

My throat constricted, and I instinctively reached for my purse. Empty except for my phone, notebook, wallet, and homemade granola bars packed in parchment paper. I was thankful I'd had the sense to leave Dorian's alchemy book safely hidden far from me. I willed myself to relax. Things were different now. This wasn't a witch hunt. Being recognized wasn't necessarily a bad thing.

I'd flown from Portland to Paris earlier that week. Because of the urgency of the situation, while I was recovering from an illness and too sick to climb the steps of Notre Dame, I'd stayed busy with people I thought might be able to help me, several of whom blurred together in my mind. Librarians, academics, amateur historians, Notre Dame docents, rare book dealers. Still, I found it surprising that I'd completely forgotten this woman. No, that wasn't entirely true. Now that she'd removed her sunglasses, there was something vaguely familiar about her ... And if she was one of the people who worked at the cathedral, that would explain how she was fit enough to keep pace with me on the hundreds of stairs.

"Please forgive me," I said, switching to English, as she had done. "I seem to have forgotten where we met."

She shook her head and laughed. "So polite! We have not met. You're Zoe Faust's granddaughter, aren't you?"

I let out the breath I'd been holding and smiled. "You knew *Grandmere?*"

The woman gave me a curious look, her eyes narrowing momentarily, but the action was so quickly replaced with a smile that I might have imagined it.

"During the Occupation in 1942," she said. "My name is Blanche Leblanc."

"Zoe Faust," I said automatically.

3

The quizzical look on her face returned.

"Named after my grandmother," I added hastily, stumbling over the words. I'm a terrible liar. Personally, I think it's one of my more endearing qualities—who wants to be friends with someone if you never know if they're being honest?—but in my life it's also a most inconvenient trait. "It's lovely to meet you, Madame Leblanc." That was a lie too. I'm sure she was a nice person, but I didn't need this complication.

Three out-of-breath tourists, the stragglers of our group, burst through the top of the winding stairway. While they caught their breath, I led Madame Leblanc away from the crowded section of walkway next to the gargoyles. There wasn't much space on the gallery, but by stepping back a few feet, at least we wouldn't be jostled.

"You look so much like her," Madame Leblanc said, speaking more softly now. "When I was a young girl, my mother once brought me to her shop. What was the name?"

"Elixir."

"Yes. Elixir. Many foreigners left Paris, but your grandmother stayed and helped people during the war. Her healing remedies saved many lives. But then she left. After the fire … "

I returned her sad smile. These days, people think of me as an herbalist. In the past, people thought of me as an apothecary. Not many people have ever known the truth, that I'm an alchemist.

I've never gotten the hang of turning lead into gold, but ever since I was a small child I've been able to extract the healing properties of plants. My ability to heal people was one of the things that made me think my accidental discovery of the Elixir of Life wasn't entirely a curse. But the dangers of living a secret life created a heavy burden. My "grandmother" Zoe Faust is me.

Since I've always been good with herbal remedies, I've been able to help both sick and injured people.

And war leads to far too many of both.

"Yes," I said, "*Grandmere* finally left Paris to help a family that was fleeing with a child too sick to travel."

Madame Leblanc's painted lips quivered. "My first thought was the right one, *n'est pas?*" Her silk scarf swirled in the wind.

"Are you all right?" I asked.

"Don't touch me," she hissed, twisting away from me. "My mother was right. *You are a witch.*"

The Gallery of Gargoyles was loud with the excited voices of tourists of all ages, but suddenly I couldn't hear anything except the beating of my heart. The multilingual voices of the tourists around us dissipated as if sucked into a vortex. It felt like the only two people left on the Gallery of Gargoyles were me and Madame Leblanc. My stomach clenched. I wished I hadn't eaten a hearty breakfast from that *boulangerie.* "You're confused, madame."

"You were in your late twenties then. *You have not aged a day.* There is no anti-aging cream that good. I know. I have tried them all. You stand before me through witchcraft or some other deal with the devil."

I choked. "I'm told my grandmother and I look very much alike," I said, trying to keep my breathing even. "These things happen—"

"I am eighty-two years old," Madame Leblanc cut in. "My eyesight is not what it once was, but my hearing is perfect. Even with the cacophony around us, I would know your voice anywhere."

"I'm told that I sound like her, too—"

"I remember the voice of the soldier who told me that my father was dead." Her words were slow. Crisp. "I remember the voice of the nurse who handed me my healthy baby girl. And I remember the voice of the apothecary named Zoe who saved many lives in Paris— but not that of my mother."

Momentarily stunned by the heartfelt speech, I was at a loss for words. I looked from the woman to the gargoyles surrounding us then out at the Eiffel Tower stretching into the blue sky, Sacre Cour's man-made grandeur, the flowing river Seine, and wisps of smoke from chimneys. Air, earth, water, fire. Elements I worked with and craved.

"I don't know what sort of bargain you made with evil forces to be here today," Madame Leblanc said, her voice nearly a whisper, "but that woman was not your grandmother. She was *you*. I know it is you, Zoe Faust. And I will find out what you are. You cannot hide any longer."

TWO

My heart galloped loudly in my ears. I feared I might be overcome with vertigo high atop the cathedral. This was a complication I didn't need.

"My grandmother always said she felt bad about the people she wasn't able to help," I said, forcing myself to speak calmly. "What was your mother's name? Perhaps she mentioned her to me."

"Oh, you tried to help her," Madame Leblanc said, a snarl hovering on her wrinkled lips. "You gave her a tincture that day she brought me to the shop. But at home, she refused to take it. She said it was witchcraft. She said that nobody's herbal remedies could be as good as yours without the work of the devil."

"I'm sorry," I said. "My grandmother wasn't—"

"Stop lying!"

The breathless tourists glanced our way before edging their way past, giving us as wide a berth as possible on the narrow parapet. Maybe my hope of salvaging the situation was misguided. I looked longingly at the exit, wondering if Madame Leblanc would be as quick on the stairs down as she was on the way up.

"The strong family resemblance has confused you," I said.

"I'm not crazy," Madame Leblanc said.

The ferocity in her eyes shocked me. Had she harbored this grudge against me since she was a child? I felt bad for her, but I couldn't say more. The world wasn't ready to know about alchemy.

"I'm going to find out what you are," she said. "You made a grave mistake returning to Paris."

"Madame—"

I broke off as a security guard approached us. He asked if everything was all right, but his bored eyes told me he was more concerned about moving us through the narrow stone gallery than with finding out what our disagreement was about.

With the distraction from the guard, I wondered if I could make a run for it.

Six months ago, my life had turned upside down. Perhaps not quite as upside down as it had in 1704 when I accidentally discovered the Elixir of Life, but it was the second-biggest shakeup in the intervening 300 years. Half a year ago, I learned that dangerous backward alchemy was real.

Alchemy is a personal transformation. Its core principle is transforming the impure into the pure, be it lead into gold or a dying body into a thriving one. Backward alchemy's Death Rotation skips the natural order and sacrifices one element for another. Backward alchemy takes more than it transforms. Backward alchemy and the Death Rotation are based in death, not life.

I've been running from alchemy for a long time, so I didn't make this discovery on my own. I'd been sought out by Dorian Robert-Houdin to help understand a book of backward alchemy, *Non Degenera Alchemia*, which roughly translated to *Not Untrue Alchemy*. Dorian's fate was linked to that of the mysterious book filled with disturbing woodcut illustrations and strange Latin text. The book was changing, and so was Dorian. He was dying an unnatural death. He would soon be alive but trapped in stone—a fate that struck me as far worse than death. I couldn't let that happen to the quirky fellow who had quickly become my best friend.

Did I mention that Dorian is a gargoyle?

Dorian Robert-Houdin was originally carved in limestone for Notre Dame's Gallery of Gargoyles. He'd been a prototype carving by Notre Dame renovator Viollet-le-Duc, created for the brand-new Gallery of Gargoyles built in the 1850s and 1860s. The statue turned out to be too small for the balcony, so Viollet-le-Duc gifted the creation to his friend Jean Eugène Robert-Houdin, the French stage magician credited with being the father of modern magic. Neither man was an alchemist, but a stage show magic trick went very wrong one day when the retired magician picked up a beautiful alchemy book. The gargoyle statue came to life as the magician read from the alchemy book he believed to be merely a stage prop. On that day in 1860, Dorian the living gargoyle was born in Robert-Houdin's home workshop.

Madame Leblanc and I were now nearly alone with the gargoyles and the security guard. Tourists were divided into groups that the staff sent up the stairs of the cathedral in waves, to prevent an unsafe level of crowding on the gallery. While Madame Leblanc assured the guard we'd be moving on shortly, I tried to ground myself in reality.

In addition to the stragglers who'd only recently reached the gallery, the only other person nearby was a man in a priest's collar who was staring intently at one of the gargoyles. Now there was a respectable fellow. If a living gargoyle came to him for help, I bet it would be a calm, well-mannered creature—not like the opinionated Dorian, who thought of himself as a French Poirot and was constantly getting into trouble. Though my fellow misfit Dorian was dear to me, he didn't listen. Ever.

I clung to the small amount of relief that I hadn't followed Dorian's advice for me to take him with me to Paris. He could shift between life and stone within seconds, so he'd suggested I carry him around Paris in a backpack in stone form. I had no doubt that he would have peeked out of the bag regularly and ruined any hope I had of convincing Madam Leblanc she didn't need to tell the world I was an immortal witch.

The guard left us to scowl at two teenage backpackers who were attempting to reach through the mesh barrier to touch a gargoyle. When I turned back to Madame Leblanc, she was blushing.

"I'm sorry," she said. Her lips were pinched. It was a difficult phrase for her to utter. "I have been foolish, no? I don't know what came over me. I hope you will forgive an old woman. It is only that you look so much like her."

"*De rien*," I said. "Think nothing of it. Good day, madame." I turned away, giving my attention back to the perch I wanted to verify with my own eyes. There was no doubt in my mind that this section of molding had been constructed to support a gargoyle. *It was true.*

Another gargoyle *had* once perched here. Local history held that a group of drunken Parisians had stolen the stone creature 150 years ago. But I knew the truth. A gargoyle much like Dorian had once stood here. *A gargoyle that had come to life and vanished.*

A hand touched my elbow.

"I would very much like to hear your memories of your grand-mother," Madame Leblanc said. She stood uncomfortably close to me in the confined space. "Your fond memories of her will help me push my mother's angry memories from my mind. I do not wish to die with such bitterness. It will also allow me to apologize for my foolishness that must have disturbed you. May I treat you to lunch?"

"It's truly not necessary to apologize," I said. "And I, uh, have a phone call I need to make."

"I insist. I will wait for you to complete your call. You only bought enough bread for breakfast at the *boulangerie* this morning, so I know you haven't already prepared lunch."

I'd been right about seeing her at the bakery next to the apartment I was renting. She must have known where I was staying. It wouldn't be easy to back out of the invitation. And in spite of my discomfort, I didn't want to leave this woman with so much anger over an old misunderstanding.

Taking advantage of my hesitation, Madame Leblanc wrapped her bony hand around the crook of my elbow and led me toward the exit. Her cold fingers tightened around my arm like the brittle fingers of a skeleton, making it impossible for me to break away discreetly.

I didn't trust that her change of heart was genuine. But if it wasn't, I could use this opening to convince her I *wasn't* over 300 years old. I just had to lie convincingly.

No question, I was in trouble.

THREE

WE EXITED THE CATHEDRAL through a twisting metal gate, a modern affront to the majesty on the façade above. I stole a glance up at the limestone carvings that adorned the front of the iconic cathedral underneath the Rosetta stained glass window. Hidden in the Christian imagery were a few alchemical symbols that had been added over the centuries. As an accidental alchemist, I had taken months to brush up on the more obscure alchemical codes in Dorian's book, but the symbols on Notre Dame were straightforward—if you knew what you were looking for.

In a row of saints, a saint was shown defeating a dragon that looked suspiciously like an ouroboros, the serpent who swallows its own tail, thus representing the cyclical nature of alchemy. In a different panel, a salamander was engulfed in flames but not burning, symbolizing how the animal can protect itself from fire, just as Dorian's alchemy book had done when caught in a fire. As we hurried along to reach the quieter side of the cathedral my eyes flicked to an unassuming carving of a simple man holding a book. If you looked closely, you could make out the chiseled letters NON DE-GENERA AL. *Non Degenera Alchemia.* The alchemy book that had brought me here.

In the walled park behind Notre Dame, filled with Parisians walking their dogs, Madame Leblanc deposited me on a wooden bench. She strolled along the path, giving me privacy to make my phone call.

I'd been bluffing that I had a call to make. Yet after being shaken, I had an impulse to call Dorian or Max. I wanted to hear a friendly voice. I scrolled through the photos on my phone of my life in Portland. A hurricane-strength wave of homesickness nearly knocked me from the bench. I hadn't felt the emotion in so long that it took me a few moments to identify it. Homesick? The bittersweet emotion meant that after all these years, I truly had a home.

From my small phone screen, the image of my sort-of-boyfriend Max Liu looked up at me from behind a jasmine bush in his backyard garden. Max didn't yet know everything about me, but we'd come to care deeply for each other since I moved to Portland.

The photo of my misfit best friend was far less personal, because I didn't want to risk anyone else seeing the image of a supposed statue cooking up a storm in the kitchen. Therefore my photo of Dorian was of him standing next to the fireplace in the posed form he took when he returned to stone. I liked this particular snapshot for the mischievous gleam in his eye.

The sun hadn't yet risen in Portland. Max would be sleeping, but I wouldn't be stirring Dorian from slumber. The gargoyle didn't need to sleep, and the predawn hours were his favorites because he could move around most freely. I slipped earbuds into my ears, made sure there was nobody behind me, then hit the button to call him for a video chat.

"I am so pleased you called," Dorian said in his thick French accent. The formal voice didn't match the excited grin on his face. "I have made the most amazing discovery."

"You have?" In spite of the shock I'd received from Madame Leblanc, Dorian's enthusiasm was contagious. "What have you discovered?"

"Avocado!"

"You discovered … avocados?"

"Yes. They are *magnifiques!* Once you are home, we must share this with the world."

I let out a breath and lamented the fact that my dying friend was far more skilled at culinary creations than alchemy. "I'm pretty sure people already know about avocados."

A blur of claws flashed across the screen as he waved away my concern. "*Oui.* But do they know they can use avocado *in place of cream* to make a perfect chocolate mousse, pudding, or even frosting?" He was sitting so close to the screen that his horns bumped into the monitor.

"Is something wrong with the video camera?" I asked. It was mildly disconcerting to have such a close-up view of stone pores.

"*Pardon?* No, I am simply busy baking. I was skeptical of the skinny women on the Internet at first, but the flavors of cocoa and salt are stronger than the flavor of the avocado. It works perfectly! But I am speaking over you. You have something to tell me as well? Have you seen my brother yet? Yes, this must be why you are calling!"

"No, I'm sorry, Dorian. I haven't been granted access to see the stone gargoyle yet."

"Oh. *C'est regrettable.*"

"But Dorian, I found his empty perch at Notre Dame."

"*Vraiment?* This supports our suspicions that he is a creature like me."

"It does. I'll find a way to see him."

He narrowed his liquidy black eyes. "The professors continue to hold him captive?"

I wouldn't have described the study of an unmoving statue quite so dramatically, but he wasn't wrong.

Shortly after the Gallery of Gargoyles opened in the 1850s, one of the stone gargoyles was stolen. It was thought to be a prank, perhaps perpetrated by drunken artists or writers inspired by Victor Hugo's *Notre Dame de Paris* who found a stone chimera not properly secured and therefore made off with it. The great cathedral had been defaced many times before in its long history, so Parisians gave a Gallic shrug and moved on. The gargoyle wasn't seen again for over 150 years—until last month.

A gargoyle that looked suspiciously like the missing stone gargoyle was found on the Charles Bridge in Prague and repatriated to France from the Czech Republic. My friend and I suspected he was another creature like Dorian, who'd been brought to life but was reverting to stone. The Charles Bridge gargoyle had turned completely back to stone more quickly than Dorian. Was he alone in the world without an alchemist like me to help him?

"He's still under lock and key at the university," I said. Since the statue's pose was anomalous, architecture scholars at a local university were studying the gargoyle.

"You will find a way. But … you have other news, no?"

"Why do you say that?"

"Your face. It reads like an open book."

Now that I had him on the line, what was I going to tell Dorian? There was nothing he could do to help, so did I really want to worry him by telling him that I'd been recognized by someone who could expose me?

Furthermore, he would probably *try* to help, which would only make things worse. I could imagine him suggesting I find an underworld contact in Paris who could "convince" Madame Leblanc to leave well enough alone. In addition to being a food snob and a talented chef, Dorian was an avid reader with a vivid imagination. Since he lived a relatively solitary life out of necessity, Dorian had more interactions with fictional characters than real people, and his ideas about real life needed reining in. Frequently.

"I was worried about you," I said. "I wanted to see how you were doing." It was the truth. His backward transformation had been speeding up. Every day his progression back to stone was happening more quickly.

"My arm is not troubling me."

"Your arm? There's something wrong with your *arm* now?"

"I think we have a bad connection," he shouted. "*Allo?* I cannot hear you, *mon amie*. I will sign off and return to my new recipe. I seem to have misplaced my cardamom. *À bientôt.*"

His face disappeared from the screen and I was left alone.

I'd left my Portland home a week ago in order to save Dorian's life. When I moved to Oregon earlier this year I'd been hoping to have a semblance of a normal life for a few years. With its quirky people, respect for nature, and health food culture, the city of Portland spoke to me from the moment I'd rolled into town with my Airstream trailer, thinking I'd stay for a brief time. I'd gotten far more than I'd dreamed. Friends as dear to me as any I'd ever had, a guy I was falling for, and a house that truly felt like a home. I'd put all that on hold to come here. Madame Leblanc had thrown my carefully constructed plan into disarray.

I looked across the park toward the Seine. Parisians strolled with their heads held high, walking dogs, puffing on cigarettes, meeting lovers. An artist with a hat to collect donations was sketching on the pavement in colorful chalk. Next to the surrealist image of pigeons with musical notes in place of eyes, he'd lettered in bright yellow chalk, *Life without art is stupid.*

I wasn't feeling the pull of the romantic City of Lights. Alone in a city that wasn't home, across the world from everyone I cared about, the only person in Paris who cared at all about me was a tenacious woman who could very well expose my secret and prevent me from saving Dorian's life.

FOUR

TEN MINUTES LATER, I found myself seated at an impossibly tiny table squeezed into the darkest corner of a café in the Marais neighborhood, walking distance from Notre Dame. The scent of cigarette smoke lingered in the air, seemingly from ghosts but more likely from centuries of smoke-filled conversations the walls had absorbed.

"There was hunger, fear, and death during the war," Madame Leblanc said, "but it elevated our senses. That's why I remember your grandmother so clearly. She was a flame that burned brightly. Too brightly, some said. That's why they said she was a witch."

I shivered. "She never told me that." I'd been called a witch many times, but until now I hadn't realized people in Paris had thought the same of me. I'd been careful here. Though I owned my shop for decades, I'd only stayed for a few years at a time, leaving the shop in the capable hands of an alchemy student while my beloved Ambrose and I were living in England or traveling elsewhere.

Madame Leblanc kept her eyes locked on mine as she raised a glass of wine to her lips. Her makeup was perfect. I didn't even want to think about what I looked like. I'd been sick in the weeks leading up to my trip to Paris, due to an alchemy experiment gone wrong. I've always been good at taking care of myself with healing foods, tinctures, and teas that I make myself, but understanding backward alchemy was taking a huge toll on me. I never would have left my cozy midcentury kitchen and gotten on an airplane had time not been running out for Dorian.

"Being so young, you would not understand how different things were," Madame Leblanc said. "The war … It's not like in the movies. We weren't living in black and white, or even sepia. It was a more vibrant, heightened state of existence."

I knew what she meant. Being an alchemist is both a blessing and a curse. I've helped thousands of people, but I've also seen many of them die. I've seen more of this wondrous world than most, eating and drinking and laughing and crying with people from cultures simultaneously identical and poles apart. In those travels, I've seen the best and worst of humanity. This was especially so during traumatic times like plague, famine, and war.

But I couldn't say that out loud. I had to check myself before I spoke—it would have been all too easy to reminisce with her. Digging my fingernails into the palm of my hand, I reminded myself that I was twenty-eight-year-old Zoe Faust of Portland, Oregon, who'd been living out of her silver Airstream trailer for the last few years, bumming around the United States after a bad breakup, not my namesake who'd owned a shop in Paris.

I had closed my shop and returned home to America in 1942. Ambrose had died a few years before, followed a short time later by a fire at Elixir. My collection of herbs, tonics, and elixirs was destroyed, along with the *potager* back garden where I grew herbs and vegetables. The alchemy student who'd helped me at the store off-and-on, Jasper Dubois, had already left Paris, so there was nothing keeping me there. The side of the shop with alchemical equipment was spared, which allowed me to stay afloat selling paraphernalia at flea markets across the US. I had put the larger items that survived the fire into storage, wondering if they'd survive the war and whether I'd ever return to Paris.

Instead of answering Madame Leblanc, I took a bite of my arugula salad with roasted chickpeas and potatoes, which I dressed with olive oil and vinegar. Madame Leblanc ate a crème frache and steak tartar tartine. I'd declined sharing a carafe of wine and opted instead for tea. I needed to keep a clear head.

"You appear to be more lost in your memories than I am, mademoiselle," Madame Leblanc said.

"I was thinking of how little I knew of my grandmother's life here. What were your impressions of her and her shop?"

She sat back and inhaled deeply. The lines around her mouth grew deeper as she pressed her lips together. Her hands tugged at the starchy cloth napkin in her lap. I wondered if she was nervous that her recollections might upset me. No, she didn't seem like one to shy away from controversy. I thought it more likely she was craving a cigarette.

"At first," she said, "I didn't know it was your grandmother's shop, because an elderly man was there when my mother first took me. But a few months later, your grandmother appeared. She was much more pleasant, no?"

I smiled. Jasper had been a young man when he began minding the shop for me. He was a student of alchemy. Not *my* student, because that would never do for Jasper. He was a product of the times. Born into a title but no money, he was convinced of the superiority of the French, the bourgeoisie class, and the male sex. I doubt it had ever occurred to Jasper that I could have taught him anything. I discovered alchemy's secrets accidentally and therefore wasn't prepared to take on apprentices, but Jasper had never asked how I found alchemy so he didn't know my transformation had been accidental. He simply appreciated the availability of an alchemical laboratory behind the shop, making it a mutually beneficial relationship. Every decade we would switch places as the proprietor, and Jasper continued to age while he sought out a worthy alchemy teacher. The last time I'd arrived in Paris, I found the shop closed and Jasper gone. I was never sure if he'd found the alchemy teacher he was looking for, or if the war had scared him off.

Madame Leblanc returned my smile. "In spite of what my mother told me that soured my memories, I remember that your grandmother was beautiful, like you. She had gone prematurely gray too. No no, don't be self-conscious. I can tell you haven't dyed your hair white to be *avant-garde*, but the color suits you."

"Thank you," I said simply. It wouldn't do to elaborate. My hair turning white was what had alerted me to the fact that I had indeed discovered the Elixir of Life. It was the one part of me that aged.

"My mother told me your grandmother gave remedies even to those who could not pay, and her *potager* was the envy of the neighborhood. That garden flourished even in winter. It was unnatural. That is what convinced my mother it was witchcraft."

I was about to speak when a police officer appeared in the doorway, his eyes methodically scanning the cafe. His stiff stance and uniform suggested he was with the military branch of the police, the *National Gendarmerie*. Tall, dark-haired, young. Most people look young to me these days, but he was truly a boy, only a year or so out of university, I guessed. His gaze came to rest on my table.

Madam Leblanc waved him over. "My grand-nephew," she said to me, beaming. As she turned to the young man, her smile tightened, shifting from pride to a different emotion. *Scheming.*

"Gilbert," she said, "this is Zoe Faust. I trust you had time to look into what I told you?"

I gripped the table. I was being ambushed.

While Madam Leblanc had considerately given me "privacy" at the park outside Notre Dame, she'd made her own phone call. She called her *gendarme* grand-nephew. But surely he couldn't believe a fanciful tale that his grand-aunt was lunching with a 300-year-old woman, could he? Why was he here? Humoring his auntie?

"*Bonjour, mademoiselle*," he said, bowing his head in friendly greeting as he sat down at the table.

"Is there a problem?" I replied in English. Better to play American tourist Zoe Faust.

"Could I see your identification *sil vous plait?*"

"What's this about?" *Breathe, Zoe.*

He shrugged as if he had not a care in the world. Turning away from his aunt, he gave me a conspiratorial smile. "I expect it is nothing. Your passport please?"

I handed him my US passport. I wasn't too worried. It was a real passport. Every decade I received a new birth certificate from a man who'd been a prop-maker in Hollywood in the 1950s before his career was destroyed by the McCarthy hearings. I'd helped him through an illness when he was destitute, and even though he didn't understand the reason why I needed those birth certificates in my name, he'd always happily supplied them until his recent death.

The smile evaporated from the police officer's face as he looked at my passport. "Zoe Faust? You? *C'est vrais?* This cannot be. *Tante* Blanche?" He looked to his aunt.

"I was named after my grandmother," I explained.

"Ah." A chagrined smile appeared on the *gendarme*'s innocent face. "But of course. Is your grandmother still alive, mademoiselle?"

Madame Leblanc scowled at the young man as he accepted my statement.

"Why are you asking about my grandmother?" I asked.

"It is believed that she has information about a fire in 1942. It killed one ... " He paused and consulted his notes. "Jasper Dubois."

I stared at him. "Jasper?" I whispered. "Jasper died in the fire?" My God. Poor Jasper. I always believed he'd been a coward and had run off when the war began. It wasn't as simple to find people in those days.

"Aha!" Madame Leblanc exclaimed. "You admit you were alive in 1942."

My shoulders shook. "My grandmother mentioned him often. He helped her with the store."

"Yes," Gilbert said. "The shop called ... " He consulted his notes again. "Elixir."

"Yes, that was my grandmother's shop. But I didn't realize anyone was killed, or that the police would investigate such an old fire."

"There's no statute of limitation on murder, mademoiselle."

"Murder?"

"The fire was arson. The person who owned that shop is quite possibly a murderer."

FIVE

A murderer? A murderer. A. Murderer.

My brain was having trouble processing the information. Slipping up and being found out to be over 300 years old, I could understand. But a murderer?

"There must be some mistake," I said. "I—my grandmother, she wouldn't have killed anyone."

"We all think we know people," the policeman said in his heavily accented English, "but we do not truly know the depths of their souls."

What an utterly French thing to say. Under other circumstances, I would have been amused, and perhaps had a conversation with him about Sartre or Foucault.

"You say she is dead?" he continued.

"Yes. Many years ago."

"Where is she buried?"

"What? Buried? No, she was cremated."

"At what crematorium?"

"I have no idea. My mother was the one who handled it."

"Where can we find your mother?"

"She died many years ago too." My head throbbed. "Why do you need that information?"

"We need to confirm your grandmother is truly deceased. You must understand, she has been on the run since 1942. What is it you Americans say? On the lam?"

My mind raced as I willed hazy memories to come into focus. The fire had been an accident, started by someone trying to stay warm, and nobody had died. But what if that wasn't true? What if the fire that drove me from Paris had been deliberately set, and had killed Jasper?

Who would have done that? And why hadn't I known?

It was the fire that had prompted my immediate departure from France in 1942, but I'd been ready to move on. Ambrose, the man I loved, had killed himself several years before, after the death of his son Percy had driven him insane, so there was nothing keeping me in Paris.

I still felt this policeman must be mistaken, but I thought back on that place and time, so different than today. In Paris during the Occupation, the rules of life were different. People looked out for each other on an individual level more than in times of peace, but at the same time, authorities had more pressing problems than sorting out the aftermath of a fire that seemed to be accidental.

After Paris was taken, an underground network sprang up that made it possible to travel to neutral European countries and leave for the United States from there. I'd left with a family that was fleeing Paris with a sick child. One of their daughters, Cecily, was stricken with influenza and shouldn't have been traveling at all, but the family insisted it was more dangerous to stay in the city. Ambrose and Percy were dead and my shop was destroyed, so I took the opportunity to help Cecily and start anew. I'd been so focused on administering to the child and hurriedly packing the intact half of my shop that I hadn't sought out the authorities to make an official report. It wasn't the kind of thing that mattered at the time.

"I'm truly sorry to have distressed you, mademoiselle." Gendarme Gilbert's demeanor shifted. He appeared genuinely distressed to have upset me.

"I know you're only doing your duty." I looked at his young face, which might not have been as young as I originally suspected. As he leaned across the small table, I saw that his skin was drawn and sallow, especially around his eyes. He wasn't sleeping well. I found myself thinking of tinctures that might help him.

I shook off my natural inclinations and got back to the matter at hand. "I can look into the information you requested, but it will take time. I simply can't imagine … Can you tell me more about the fire?"

A shrug. "I do not have all of the details. It was only my aunt's call that alerted me and caused me to make inquiries. I'm not sure how much you know about the French police, but this is not my jurisdiction. I am not with the *Police Nationale*." Another shrug. "But my aunt is a persistent woman."

"I understand," I said, wondering what a Leblanc family Christmas was like.

"The crime did not come to light at the time but was noted after the war. Perhaps it was disguised as a casualty of war by the person who owned this shop." He paused and consulted a palm-sized notebook. "Yes, the murderer had intimate knowledge of the shop. A note was made in *l'ordinateur—comment dites-vous?*"

"She understands French," Madame Leblanc said. "She knows you said *computer*."

"*Bon,*" he continued. "A note was made on the computer decades ago when the records were entered in, but no suspects had been found. *Alors,* it was forgotten. Until my aunt called me today."

"I see."

"In this modern age, forensics can find many things that were once not possible. Again, I am sorry to have distressed you! You look like an honest woman, mademoiselle. You are too young and innocent to have this burden." He shook his head. "If you give me your word that you will send me evidence of your grandmother's cremation, I see no reason to confiscate your passport. But if you do not—"

"Gilbert!" Madame Leblanc cut in abruptly. Her face flushed. "You're letting her *go*? I remembered the dead man found in the shop after she left and called you to exact justice, yet you betray me?"

"*Tante*, what can I do? This woman was not even alive in 1942. She is not responsible for anything that happened seventy-five years ago."

What *had* happened all those years ago? Killing is the antithesis of what true alchemy stands for. It chilled my 300-year-old blood to think I could have been so close to a murder and not prevented it.

Alchemy is about life, not death. Alchemical transformations strengthen and purify the basic nature of both inanimate objects and people. Corrupted metals being transmuted into pure gold and mortal people stopping the deterioration of their bodies. The Philosopher's Stone and the resulting Elixir of Life are found through rigorous scientific study and focused pure intent.

We alchemists aren't immortal. It's an oversimplification to say the Elixir of Life is a path to living forever. We *can* be killed; we simply don't age in the same way as normal people. It's a science that the world hasn't proven ready to embrace. Those of us who've gone public have rarely met with a good end. That's why there was no way I was speaking up now.

I felt the gold locket I wore around my neck, with a miniature painting of my brother and a photograph of Ambrose. I'd always felt responsible for the deaths of my little brother and the man I'd loved with all my heart. Was I responsible for Jasper's death, too?

"This is very serious, you understand. I realize she is your grand-mother, but if we find you are shielding her because she is elderly—"

"I'm not."

"I'm trusting you, mademoiselle."

I nodded in what I hoped was a show of meek acquiescence. One of the advantages of looking young is that people underestimate you. Even when I truly was only twenty-eight, most people had no idea what I was capable of. I was an accomplished simpler—a person especially good with plants—by the time I was a teenager, and I unlocked alchemy's deepest secrets a decade later.

"I am truly sorry about your grandmother," Gendarme Gilbert said. "I hate to see it trouble you so. Remember her for the woman you knew. You are not the same woman as she, not responsible for her deeds."

I stole a glance at Blanche Leblanc. She wasn't convinced.

The world is a constantly changing place. Technological advances made it both easier and harder to hide. Yet I've always found that the best way to stay safe is to hide in plain sight. I was so certain I would no longer know anyone in Paris. It never occurred to me that a *child* would remember me.

I tossed a handful of Euros on the table and fled from the ambush. It took every ounce of my willpower not to break into a sprint as soon as I stepped out of the café. When I turned the corner, I ran.

My chest burned. I was still weak. Too weak to be running across Paris from a threat out of the past.

I was out of breath and wheezing when I unlocked the heavy blue door to my building, pushed on the thick brass knocker in the middle of the door, and used the worn wooden railing to pull myself up the three flights of stairs. My lungs were on fire by the time I reached my apartment. I caught my breath and bolted the door behind me.

In addition to my pounding heart and burning lungs, my ears buzzed. At first I thought it was the stress of the situation taking over my whole body, but then I saw the source of the sound—half a dozen bees circled outside the kitchen window. Though I'd wrapped *Non Degenera Alchemia* well, it wasn't good enough. Its scent was still attracting bees. Not the musty scent of a decaying antique book, but the smell of sweet honey and spicy cloves. It was as if the book was aging *backwards.*

I walked across the main room to the kitchenette. A wood-framed window of thick glass separated me from the bees. I wasn't normally frightened of the small insects. They lived in harmony with nature and were essential to the plant cycle of life. But these bees ... I looked more closely. One of the swarm flew away. I hoped his comrades would follow suit. And then I saw my mistake. The bee that had flown away hadn't given up. He was giving himself space to achieve more speed. He flew straight at the window. I jumped back as he smashed the glass with a splat. His fuzzy body fell to the window sill below.

I looked away and shivered. I didn't want to end up like the kamikaze bee. I hadn't yet found what I needed to in Paris, but how could I risk what would happen if I stayed?

There was no way to prove Zoe Faust from 1942 was dead, because she wasn't. I'd have to fake a death certificate, which was possible but inadvisable. I keep my secret by being careful, and the one man I knew who could forge documents was dead. Plus it would take time I didn't have. If I remained in Paris, I risked bringing my secret into the open. My life would be under a dangerous level of scrutiny, especially with Madame Leblanc and forensic evidence to fuel the accusations.

I lit a burner and set a kettle of water on the stove. Tea would replenish my body, calm my nerves, and allow me to think. As I contemplated my options, a knock sounded on the door.

"I know you are inside, Zoe Faust," Madame Leblanc's voice echoed through the door. "I have the information about your past that you crave. I can tell you what my nephew cannot."

SIX

I FLUNG OPEN THE door and immediately regretted it. Though I was careful about leaving any evidence of alchemy in the open, I hadn't been expecting guests and hadn't taken stock of what was visible at the moment.

"What do you want?" I stood blocking the doorway.

"I want the truth," Madame Leblanc said. "In return, I will tell you what you wish to know."

I gripped the side of the door, hesitating with the door open barely wide enough to see all of Madame Leblanc's face.

"The reason I remember you so clearly," she continued, "enough to know the truth that you and your 'grandmother' are one in the same, is because the image of that man, Jasper Dubois, is seared into my mind. I will never forget it."

"What did you see?" My heart beat in my throat.

"When the ashes from the fire were cleared, my friend Suzette and I played in the ruins. We were five years old. We were the ones who found him."

"I'm so sorry," I said. I meant it. What an awful discovery for a child to make.

She tilted her head in acknowledgment of the sympathy.

"My grandmother didn't tell me that Jasper was still in Paris when the fire broke out," I said. Had he been hiding from me?

"You are either wrong or lying. This is why I called my nephew. Jasper Dubois did not perish in the fire. He was *stabbed to death*."

I didn't have time to react because a precocious bee had squeezed its way through a joint in the thick window frame. It flew straight toward Madame Leblanc. It landed on her wrist. She swore creatively and slapped her hand. The dead bee fell to the floor, but not before it left its stinger in her tender flesh. She pulled up her sleeve and I caught a brief glimpse of a black tattoo on her forearm. Had she been branded by a concentration camp? Was the discovery of a body one of her last memories of childhood freedom?

"Come inside," I said, my mood involuntarily softening. I could never resist helping people when I had the resources to do so. Refusing assistance wasn't in my nature. "I have a calendula salve that should help the sting."

Madame Leblanc gave me a curious look. She hesitated for only a moment, then followed me inside and accepted the salve.

"You should—" I began.

"I know how to apply a salve. I'm familiar with most forms of medicines. Getting old has as many frustrations as it does pleasures. I do envy you."

"My grandmother taught me—"

She snorted. "*Grandmother.*"

"You truly believe in witchcraft, madame? I'm sorry it's disturbing that I look so much like my grandmother."

Madame Leblanc walked to the narrow kitchen window overlooking the courtyard.

"Those must be fragrant flowers in the window sill. I have never seen so many bees." She closed her eyes and swayed.

"Can I offer you a seat?"

"You are still as kind as you always were," she said, refusing the seat and standing as tall as her frail frame allowed. "But this is not over. You may be able to fool the rest of the world, but I know you are the same woman who disguised a murder as an accident. I will be sure Gilbert uncovers the truth about what you did to poor Jasper Dubois. My nephew will figure out what you did—and I will figure out what you *are*."

With that she tossed her silk scarf across her shoulder and turned on her designer heel. "*Au revoir*, Zoe Faust," she called out from down the hallway. "For now."

Standing stunned in my doorway, I wondered where I'd gone wrong. My plan had seemed so simple a week ago. The book that had brought Dorian to life had pointed the way to Notre Dame. It was here I would find the last piece of the puzzle to save Dorian's life.

Only it hadn't proven that simple.

I'd been naïve in thinking Paris would hold obvious answers. I'd been hopeful because I hadn't known about Notre Dame's history with backward alchemists until Dorian's book caught on fire that spring. Instead of reducing the book to ash, the fire had brought forth hidden ink and revealed its connection to the cathedral. The unexpected transformation was significant, I knew, yet I couldn't see what exactly it told me about Notre Dame. I was missing something.

I thought the second living gargoyle might shed light on the solution. Unfortunately because I wasn't an academic, an architect, or a stone carver, I'd been refused access to the gargoyle who was trapped in stone. The university's staff studying the bizarrely posed statue didn't realize a living being was trapped inside, and I couldn't very well tell them. I had to find another way to see the creature. And until now, I thought I'd have time to do so.

I also wondered if there might be other backward alchemists out there. If there were, they might be able to help me. I hadn't been able to decipher parts of Dorian's backward alchemy book, which wasn't surprising since alchemy is filled with secrets, obfuscation, and codes. Most alchemists learn through a combination of personal experimentation in a laboratory and an apprenticeship with a mentor. I hadn't worked with a mentor since studying with Nicolas Flamel nearly three centuries ago, and I'd fled from my training before it was complete. I was only in touch with one alchemist—a former slave, Tobias Freeman, who hadn't studied alchemy formally either, and who didn't know any alchemists besides me. Even among properly educated alchemists, most don't know each other because secrecy and suspicion are so ingrained in our training that we hide the truth from everyone. There was no one to help me.

In other words, my trip had been a bust. And now, on top of everything, there was the murder of Jasper Dubois. What had I gotten myself into by returning to Paris after all these years?

I locked the apartment door and breathed deeply. I closed my eyes, but the buzzing of the bees prevented me from relaxing. Rooting through drawers, I found a roll of tape and sealed the joints of the war-time building's window frame to foil the bees.

I wished I could call Tobias to think through my dilemma. But there was nothing more my one true alchemist friend could tell me about backward alchemy or alchemy's connection to Notre Dame, since he'd had even less formal training than I'd had. It was his non-judgmental friendship I craved.

But I couldn't bring myself to burden him. Not now. Though I knew he'd want to help me, he had his own life-and-death situation to deal with. He was caring for his wife of sixty years, Rosa, who was dying of old age in their home in Detroit. Rosa wasn't an alchemist and had continued to age. Still, Tobias and Rosa had loved each other for more joyous years than most of us get.

Instead I sat down, pulled out my phone, and searched for references to Jasper Dubois online. Millions of hits, but none of them my Jasper. Narrowing the search, I found reference to the 1942 fire in a French library's online newspaper archives. It was only a small article, providing no insights. Much more space was devoted to the war. I wouldn't find answers with the tools of the modern world.

My fingers hovered over the screen for a moment, then typed a search I hoped I wouldn't use until I had an answer about how to save Dorian's life. Flights home to Portland.

The more affordable flights connecting to Portland left in the morning, but Madame Leblanc's nephew would probably look for me the next day. I bought a ticket for the last flight that left that night. I would arrive home in the wee hours after a nineteen-hour journey, but I had little choice.

I opened the floorboard under which I was hiding *Non Degenera Alchemia*. I'd chosen this apartment rental because the building had been around for centuries. I knew it would have little nooks where I could hide things I didn't want anyone to find. Not that I was expecting trouble, but old habits die hard. Now I was glad I'd taken the precaution.

The book was safely ensconced in its hole. In spite of my overzealous wrapping, two now-dead bees had made their way underneath the top layer of plastic. They had squished themselves to death in their quest to reach the book. Bees are a minor symbol in alchemy and they are used even more in backward alchemy. Many of the disturbing woodcut illustrations in Dorian's book showed bees circling counterclockwise above a menagerie of dead animals. Beyond the scent of honey that permeated the pages as it aged, was there something more drawing the insects to it?

I didn't have to open the pages to see the woodcut illustrations. The twisted imagery was unforgettable. My mind saw bees filling the skies in a counterclockwise formation, stinging the eyes of the people and animals that writhed on the ground.

From those unsettling coded images in the book, I'd taught myself how to create an alchemical Tea of Ashes that temporarily stopped Dorian from returning to stone. Superficially, the process looked easy—mixing ingredients in fire that quickly transformed into salt. Much easier than true alchemy, which in addition to basic ingredients involves pure intent, time, and energy. Backward alchemy is a shortcut, a straight line through what should be a labyrinthine maze of discovery leading to true knowledge. Because the shortcuts here were backward alchemy, it was a delicate balance between adding life to Dorian and taking it from me.

Before leaving Portland I thought I'd found the right balance to make Dorian a large enough batch of Tea of Ashes for him to stay healthy while I was gone in Paris. I was wrong. The transformation had failed, and even worse, it left me sick for three full days—too sick to travel and too sick to do anything much beyond lie in bed. I'd lost so much time, and now I was being forced from Paris after less than a week.

But I wasn't giving up. I had five hours until I was due at the airport.

The question was, with five hours left in Paris, could I do what I hadn't been able to do in five days?

SEVEN

Sitting at the edge of the sagging bed in the small apartment, I rubbed a bee sting on my arm that was still noticeable and looked through the small set of tinctures and salves I'd brought from home. Traveling with the preparations was a force of habit, but in this case it was also necessary after I'd been sickened by the Tea of Ashes and stung by bees interested in Dorian's book.

After arriving in Paris I'd taken *Non Degenera Alchemia* to Notre Dame to compare its illustrations to the carvings on the façade of the cathedral. For the record, bringing a book of unknown power to an ancient cathedral to which it's tied is a very bad idea. That experiment led to many stings as I shooed bees away from the book; I used my photocopies for reference after that. I'd also visited many libraries and bookshops in hopes of discovering obscure references to Notre Dame's connections to alchemy that I hadn't been able to find in my own alchemy books or in mainstream publications.

One of the places I'd visited was a narrow bookshop within view of Notre Dame. Appropriately, it was called *Bossu Livres*—Hunchback

Books. It was presumably named for the famous character Victor Hugo's *The Hunchback of Notre Dame*. The bookshop's specialty was the history of Paris, with a large section on Notre Dame Cathedral. The bookseller thought I was a graduate student conducting research for my dissertation, so he didn't bat an eye when I asked about information on any secret societies that used to meet at Notre Dame. I bet it wasn't even the strangest research question he'd received. He was the only bookseller who'd taken my request seriously and spent more than a few minutes looking through his files. Though he hadn't been able to help at the time, he'd told me to check back in a few days.

Hoping to continue the research Madame Leblanc had interrupted that morning, I hurried across Pont Notre-Dame to the small Île de la Cité island where the cathedral stood. Normally I took time to appreciate my surroundings, especially when I was in a city as storied as Paris. But not today. If I let myself slow down, I knew I'd imagine Madame Leblanc and her nephew over my shoulder and the ghost of Jasper Dubois in front of me.

It was a warm day, close to the start of summer, and the scents of Paris swirled around me. Strong coffee, smooth wine, freshly baked bread, and ... something smoky that stirred a memory I couldn't quite place. I glanced upward. The Gallery of Gargoyles was visible from the ground, though the personalities of the stone creatures were left to the imagination at this distance. "What are your secrets?" I whispered.

I pulled my eyes from the limestone façade, once painted brightly but now a natural golden tan, and continued to the narrow street that housed the bookshop. The shop was barely wider than I was tall, probably the same square footage as the interior of the Airstream trailer that was parked in my driveway in Portland. The small space was filled with treasures, stacked from floor to ceiling.

I pushed on the solid door, painted a bright blue. It resisted. The brass handle didn't budge either. I peeked into the window. A ray of sunlight shone over a display in the window of Paris-based poets from the nineteenth century. Aside from that illuminated corner, the interior of the shop was dark. A sign in the window read *Fermé*. The shop was closed.

I leaned against the stone wall and tried to keep my spirits from being completely crushed. At every turn, I faced another obstacle.

I gave a start as the bell jangled and the door of the bookshop swung open.

"I didn't mean to frighten you, mademoiselle," said the man who opened the door.

"It's quite all right. I'm pleased to find you're open after all."

He waved me inside. Only then did I realize it was the same bookseller I'd previously spoken with. A plain man in his forties, he had a forgettable face. The impression was rounded out by thinning brown hair, leathery skin, and the hint of a stoop. If he were to lean against a shelf of his leather-bound books, I had the feeling that he'd blend in and be invisible to customers. He'd told me his name just yesterday, but I struggled to recall it. "It's good to see you, Monsieur Augustin."

"Please, call me Lucien." He turned the sign from *Fermé* to *Ouvert*.

My eyes swept over the shelves as I breathed in the scent of books made over the centuries from various wood pulps and animal skins. These books were decaying as normal books did, with a faint hint of mildew detectable in the older ones and nary a bee in sight. Normally I loved spaces crammed full of books, but the haphazard nature of this room kept me off balance. If they had a filing system, it was unlike anything I'd ever encountered.

"I was wondering if you'd had a chance to look for the book on Notre Dame secret societies you mentioned," I said. "I know I told you I'd check back with you in a few days if I didn't receive a call from you, but I'm leaving Paris sooner than expected."

"Finished the research for your thesis already?" Though he spoke with a French accent, the inflection in the question suggested he'd lived elsewhere for a time. Under other circumstances I would have asked him about it, because linguistic nuances tell you so much about a person, but that conversation wasn't meant to happen today.

"Unfortunately a family emergency came up. I have to leave Paris immediately." I feigned interest in a photographic history of the cafés of Paris to avoid meeting his gaze as I lied.

He frowned. "I'm so sorry to hear that. Because I found something of interest."

My eyes snapped up. "What is it you've found?"

"A slim volume, probably produced in the fourteenth century." He hesitated. "Probably not what you're after. Never mind."

"No, please tell me what you found."

"It's called *The Backward Alchemists of Notre Dame.*"

My breath caught.

"Bizarre, no?" Lucien said. "I didn't think it was what you were looking for," he added with a shake of his head, misinterpreting my expression. "*Dommage.* I thought it was worth a try. It sounded like a secret society. The type of thing you mentioned as a possible interest for your thesis."

"I'd love to see it." Hope welled in me again. It was exactly what I needed. *This could lead me to a backward alchemist.*

"*Bon.* I am glad I requested it. The book is being sent here to the shop from a storage facility. Perhaps if you came back tomorrow morning—"

"I'm leaving Paris tonight." I didn't want to think about what awaited me with Madame Leblanc pressuring her nephew to flag my passport.

"Let me check on the status of the shipment. Maybe we'll get lucky." He disappeared through a door shaped like an embrasure of a castle and nearly as narrow as an arrow-slit. I let my eyes wander across the high shelves crammed full of books in a dozen languages, all related to the history of Paris, but none of them organized with any system I could discern. I picked up a book on unique Parisian architecture from the nineteenth century with a focus on abandoned buildings. I turned the pages, stopping at a photograph of *le Cabaret de L'Enfer*. As was typical of the French, the old nightclub was a complete embodiment of its theme: The Nightclub of Hell. It typified the quirky French ethos.

I knew the famous nightclub. *Le Cabaret de L'Enfer* had been one of Ambrose's favorite late-night clubs in the early 1900s. He was a country lad at heart and always felt most comfortable when we lived in the countryside. But because I could help more people when we lived in more populated areas, we always returned to Paris. After a time, he came to love it as I did. *Le Cabaret de L'Enfer* was one of the places that captured his imagination. He wasn't alone. His son Percy had once thought of opening a similar club in London, but he was a lazy, lazy man, so his talk never turned into action. But more ambitious entrepreneurs had opened a parallel nightclub next door to the Paris cafe: *Le Ciel*. Heaven.

I was stirred from the memory of a bygone Paris by a movement at the corner of my eye. Lucien had returned, shaking his head. "*Je suis desolé, mademoiselle.* No luck."

"Could you mail it to me in Oregon? I'll pay in advance for expedited shipping. Plus extra for your trouble."

"Extra is not necessary, mademoiselle. But you are kind." His eyes turned to the book in my hands. "*Le Cafe de L'Enfer.* You know of this landmark? It has quite a history."

"I've read about it. It's too bad it wasn't preserved."

"I have something you might like. I believe I have an old postcard of the Hell-mouth doorway."

He flipped through a stack of postcards on a stand near the cash register, then drew his hand back abruptly. "*Merde*. Damn these frail fingernails."

I winced as he held his finger, clearly in pain. "I might have something that can help, monsieur."

I wound a finger around my white hair as I reached into my purse with my other hand. I carried a tincture with me that would be good for frail fingernails. It was an herbal remedy that helped me with my hair, which would have been thin and brittle without extra care. Through healthy eating and topical treatments, I was able to keep it looking and feeling similar to how it did when I was young. Though I'd never again have thick, long hair, my hair was healthy enough to fool people into thinking I dyed it white as a trendy fashion statement and that I followed a vegan diet because it was the latest fad.

Lucien gratefully, if skeptically, accepted the tincture. I wrote out instructions for how to use it while he completed my order. I'd just have to hope that the book would provide useful insight whenever it did arrive to me in Portland.

The bell above the door sounded. Lucien's friendly eyes turned dark as the young woman with an overzealous application of eyeliner asked if he had any books containing maps of the catacombs of Paris, the tangled tunnels lined with human bones.

"*Je suis desolé, mademoiselle,*" he said, and the customer departed.

"I think I saw a book on the subject in a pile over there." I pointed to a jam-packed bookshelf. "I bet I can catch her."

Lucien shook his head firmly. "*Moutards*. Maps of the catacombs are not for them. They sneak into the catacombs with complete disregard for their history. They use it as a *bôit de nuit*, their own personal nightclub. As if it were *le Cafe de L'Enfer*. This desecration of the catacombs has become acceptable!"

"Urban explorers," I said.

He narrowed his eyes at me.

"I'm not one," I added hastily. "But I've heard about it. Adventurers, kids staging raves, artists." They seemed harmless enough to me. Kids enjoying their youth in Paris. I was too old to understand the appeal myself. Or perhaps the underground crypts disturbed my alchemical sensibilities. Relics like human bones were to be revered, not made into entertainment. I'd visited the ossuary once, shortly after the underground graves had been opened to the public in the late 1800s, when an appreciation for macabre curiosities turned the rows of skulls and bones into a tourist attraction. I'd never had a desire to return.

The bookseller looked from his dim sanctuary to the vibrant street outside. "I do not know what this old city is coming to."

The wind was picking up as I stepped out of the shop. I turned up the collar of my silver raincoat, touched a hand to my locket, and glanced at my watch. I had time for one more errand. It was time to see a possible member of the family: Dorian's brother.

EIGHT

THE PREVIOUS MONTH, A gargoyle resembling the chimeras of Notre Dame had been found on the Charles Bridge in Prague. There were no witnesses aside from a drunk who slept outside near the bridge. The man swore the five-foot statue had limped onto the bridge by itself as dawn was breaking. Needless to say, his testimony was dismissed as the ravings of a drunken fool.

Authorities thought there must have been at least one other witness, because a half-empty bottle of absinthe was cradled in the statue's stone arms. The liquor had been bottled this year. Yet no witnesses could be found. It must have been a prank, the police surmised. Someone who shared a similar sense of humor with the thieves who were leaving gold dust in place of gold figurines in museums across Europe, offering no trace of how they got in or out.

I knew the true explanation for both of these occurrences. There were no thieves, and there was no prankster. Gold created through backward alchemy was reverting to dust. And this was a gargoyle like Dorian, who was brought to life but was now reverting to stone.

Architectural scholars recognized the statue as being one of Viollet-le-Duc's creations for Notre Dame, and it was quickly asserted that this was the stolen carving that hadn't been seen in over a century.

Only sketches of the gargoyle existed, and without any photographs it was all scholarly speculation. It was determined that more study was needed, and that architects and stonemasons would be the most appropriate people to study the beast.

The Czech authorities readily handed it over to France. Now the gargoyle frozen in stone was under study at a Paris university's architecture department.

In spite of my deferential tone and fluent French, I'd been denied admittance to study the statue by the scholar in charge, Professor Chevalier. I'd been confident I'd win him over with enough time, but time was no longer an option. An idea began to take shape in my mind. One that my young friend Brixton would undoubtedly call "wicked."

As I walked back to my apartment to pick up *Not Untrue Alchemy*, I made a phone call to check with Professor Chevalier's secretary, making sure he wasn't allergic to bees. I claimed to be a nurse who wanted to check how an allergic patient was doing, and the secretary assured me I had the wrong number, because she was certain the professor wasn't allergic to bees. If I wished to hear it from his own ears, I could call back when she expected him to return to his office within half an hour.

Perfect.

I freed *Not Untrue Alchemy* from its hiding place, made sure the book was carefully bundled, and pressed the few possessions I'd brought to Paris into my rucksack. Hurrying down the stairs and into the courtyard, I cast what might be my last glance at the centuries-old building. Would this be the last time I was ever in Paris? Instead of walking toward the university, I made a two-block detour to a spot I'd been working my way up to visiting.

Two minutes later, I stood outside the Auberge Nicolas Flamel, the Michelin star restaurant and oldest house in Paris. It had also once been the home of my mentor.

The plaque that adorned the building began with the words *Maison de Nicolas Flamel et de Pernelle sa femme. Pour conserver le souvenir de leur foundation charitable.* The home of Nicolas Flamel his wife Pernelle, honoring their charitable work.

I ran my fingertips across the rough stone that had stood since they built their home in 1407, and that had served as a restaurant for over a hundred years. His building had stood the test of time much better than the building that had housed Elixir. Because of the fire ... I pushed thoughts of poor Jasper Dubois from my mind.

Alchemical symbols were carved into many of the stones on the Auberge Nicolas Flamel, though I knew for a fact they hadn't been made by Nicolas or Pernelle. The carvings came later, long after they had faked their deaths and abandoned their city home for the French countryside. These symbols hadn't been made by true alchemists, but were instead laymen's ideas of what alchemical symbols would look like, added once Nicolas had become infamous. The decorative letters and animals of the faux alchemists had worn smooth over time, but were still visible. As was a loose stone.

That was odd. In a section of solid stone, nonexistent joints of a brick shouldn't have been able to crumble.

Had someone purposefully defaced the building? Though it hadn't been Nicolas's home for centuries, the violation of the home he'd crafted infuriated me. Ignoring the sharp glare of a waiter smoking a cigarette on his break, I stepped onto the windowsill to see what was going on. The light backpack weighed heavily on my shoulders, reminding me how weak I still was.

On the loose stone was an alchemical carving. A real one. *Could this have been carved by Nicolas himself?*

The waiter muttered about uncivilized tourists as I tugged on the stone that bore the ouroboros. It didn't give. Then I thought about the symbol itself. The ouroboros—the serpent eating its own tail, representing the cyclical nature of alchemy. Following the meaning of the symbol, I gave the stone not an outward tug but a clockwise twist. That set it free.

Behind the ouroboros stone was a faded note on vellum.

Addressed to me.

My heart pounded in my ears and the voice of the aggrieved waiter faded away. The familiar hand of Nicolas Flamel had scrawled a note in old French: *Dearest Zoe. If you find this one day…*

The rest of the note was illegible. *No, no, no.* This couldn't be all there was! With shaking hands, I felt around behind the false brick. Nothing. I grabbed at the edges of the rough stone hole, getting nothing for my effort except a scrape across my knuckles.

I pulled my hand away, ran my fingertips over the soft, faded paper, and willed my eyes to see text that wasn't there. Was there anything left of the ink?

The waiter had brought a compatriot from inside the restaurant, a regal woman with leathery skin. She was at least twice my size and carried a rolling pin in her hand.

I could deal with the note later. I shoved the ouroboros brick back into place, making sure I heard a click, then jumped down from the windowsill and sped away from the house, the note from Nicolas in my pocket.

NINE

I walked to the university in a haze, passing elegant women expertly maneuvering cobblestones in perversely high heels, shopkeepers reminiscent of centuries past closing up shop for the day, and sidewalk cafés radiating the mingling scents of cigarettes, wine, and espresso.

What had Nicolas wanted to tell me? And when had he left the message? It wasn't before I left Paris during the war, was it? I'd visited his home then and hadn't noiced the carving. Yet the vellum looked old. I hadn't been in hiding while living in Paris before the war, so why hadn't he sought me out if he was alive and in Paris? And if he was angry with me for leaving my apprenticeship so abruptly centuries ago, before I completed my training, why reach out to me at all? It didn't make sense.

Reaching the Left Bank, I saw groups of college students dressed up for a night out on the town. Evening was quickly approaching. With my distracted thoughts, I bumped into a young couple with their arms draped around each other. They were stopped in the middle of the sidewalk, a map in their hands. They folded the map and nodded at each other, but instead of walking toward a metro station, café, or bar, they knelt down and pried open the manhole they were standing on. On any other occasion, I would have been curious about a young couple climbing into the sewers, but not today. With a note from my mentor in my pocket and a gargoyle to meet, I continued on my way.

I couldn't stop thinking about Nicolas. If he was still alive, would he be able to help me with Dorian's backward alchemy dilemma? No. Of that I was certain. He'd once warned me of backward alchemy. True alchemy is about personal transformation and requires a personal sacrifice to create the Philosopher's Stone and the Elixir of Life. Backward alchemy, in his eyes, was the antithesis of alchemy's purity. Nicolas wouldn't even speak of it, except to warn me away from it.

I stopped in front of a slanted Linden tree and steadied myself on its trunk. The bark was smooth and comforting under my raw fingers. Being with a small piece of nature in the loud and crowded city took the edge off of the troubling realization that even if I found Nicolas, he would fight me rather than help me if my quest involved backward alchemy. Being the purist that he was, I could imagine him insisting that Dorian was an unnatural creature who shouldn't be alive. He would also be furious that I'd been so careless as to be recognized by Madame Leblanc, who was threatening to expose alchemy.

I reached the university without walking into traffic or crashing into a light post, which was about as much as I could hope for at the moment. When I reached the professor's door, I took Dorian's book out of its three layers of taut plastic.

"*Bonjour, monsieur*," I said from the doorway. "I was hoping to show you the architectural woodcuts in this antique book. I think when you see them, you'll understand why I'm so interested in seeing the gargoyle." I nodded toward the gargoyle standing in the corner of the office. More than a foot taller than Dorian, and with rougher edges, the gargoyle wore a pained expression on his stone face. Dorian had taken to calling him his "brother" ever since we learned of his existence the previous month.

"Chimera," the professor corrected me with a stern frown. "The sculpture is a chimera, not a gargoyle. Let me see this book."

I forced a smile and handed *Not Untrue Alchemy* to the professor. Technically, the term *gargoyle* only refers to a carving that serves as a water spout, with the stone creature's mouth and throat serving as the drainpipe. But the word *gargoyle* has become a general term for a range of stone creatures that perch on buildings. Even Dorian refers to himself as a gargoyle.

"Of course," I said. "The chimera. Do you mind if I open this window?" I moved to open it before he had a chance to reply.

He looked up from the book. "I'd prefer you did not—"

His words were drowned out by another sound. The buzzing of bees. The noise began softly, as a hum, but quickly rose to the level of a biblical swarm of locusts.

At least a dozen bees flew into the room. They circled the professor's hands. He dropped the book onto his desk and cried out as the stinging began. It took all of my willpower to stop myself from rushing to help him. *Deep breath, Zoe. He'll be fine.*

Professor Chevalier swore and rushed from the room. I donned gloves and whisked the book into a plastic bag with an airtight seal. Half a dozen bees were trapped inside with the book. The rest followed the professor.

I closed the office door and locked it. I knew I didn't have much time, so I'd make the most of it. First things first: I left a salve on the desk that would help with the bee stings.

Next I slid *Not Untrue Alchemy* from the bag, careful to keep the bees inside. The book fell open to the page it always fell open to. These were the words that had once accidentally brought Dorian to life, when Jean Eugène Robert-Houdin had read the words as a dramatic addition to his stage show.

I began to read the mysterious words aloud.

Here in Paris, I felt the power of the words so deeply that I was caught off guard. My body began to sway as strongly as when I'd been on a fishing boat during an unexpected typhoon. I braced myself against the wall with my free hand and looked at the gargoyle, hoping he wouldn't begin to shake as much as I was. Then he'd be sure to fall and shatter.

The gargoyle didn't move.

I sat down on a nearby chair and cradled the confounding book on my lap. Reading from an alchemy book alone shouldn't direct so much power toward myself. And certainly not this quickly. Alchemy involves practicing in solitude in one's own alchemy lab, going through the processes of calcination, dissolution, separation, fermentation, distillation, and coagulation.

But this book was *backward* alchemy, where shortcuts abound and one element is sacrificed for another. Alchemy can seem like magic, because we can't see the mechanism of the transfer of energy under a microscope. But it's not any different than theoretical physics. You don't have to see science to believe in it. Alchemists were early chemists, but because of "puffers"—the fools who only saw alchemy as a way to make money and sought favor with kings by transmuting lead into gold for political gains—alchemy was squashed, twisted, and discredited. Across time, whenever true alchemists have tried to come out from the shadows, it has ended badly.

Still feeling like I was seasick, I focused my breathing. *Think, Zoe.* I read the incantation again. The gargoyle again failed to come to life.

There was one more thing I wanted to try. I had a packet of tea with me, leftovers of the Tea of Ashes I'd made for Dorian before coming to Paris to stave off his backward transformation into stone.

I'd saved the remnants of the ash-like substance that I'd created from the living plants in my garden.

The gargoyle's mouth was frozen half open, revealing a dark gray tongue and sharp teeth. I rubbed the ashes onto his stone tongue. The gray powder coated the rough surface, disappearing into the stone pores.

I stepped back. Nothing.

The sound of a buzzing bee interrupted the silence. One of the bees inside the book's wrapping was frantically trying to escape. I shut the book and pushed it back inside. Let the bees have it. It wasn't doing me any good.

The buzzing subsided, but the room wasn't silent. There was now another sound.

Wheezing.

My eyes flew to the gargoyle's dark face. His gray eyes began to water.

"*Peux-tu m'entendre?*" I asked. Can you hear me?

The gargoyle wasn't able to move his stone body, but his eyes were alive. I felt a jolt of pity as his sad eyes locked onto mine. Gray stone lips twitched. I wished I'd been wrong. I wished what the scholars believed was the truth, that this was simply a gargoyle carved by a stone carver with an offbeat sense of humor. Not this— a living soul trapped in stone.

I also wished I'd been wrong about Dorian's book. It had led me to the recipe for the Tea of Ashes and to Notre Dame, but it appeared to have served its purpose. It wasn't a miracle that could save the gargoyles from reverting to stone.

"*Aidez moi*," the gargoyle croaked in a deep gravelly voice. "Help ... Help me."

The last words were barely audible. The wheezing stopped. His lips froze, but for a moment longer his liquid gray eyes bore into mine. He blinked once more, then went still.

TEN

Dorian's black eyes opened wide and he blinked at me.

"*Mais c'est formidable!* It is true I have *un frère—a brother!*—and he is being held captive—" He broke off with a curse that had been popular a century ago and began to pace across the creaking hardwood floor. "*Mais attendez…* your visit to Notre Dame did not yet yield the answers we need, yet you are home."

I hadn't had trouble leaving Paris and my connecting flight had touched down in Portland shortly after midnight. Dorian and I sat in my Craftsman house's attic, which I'd half converted into an office for my online business, Elixir. I hadn't slept at all on the flight. Flying affects my body's natural rhythms more intensely than it does most people, because the planetary alignments go by too quickly. It scrambles my head. I much prefer to travel by car or boat, or on foot. I'd felt so alone on the long flights, fleeing both the country and the prospect of finding my mentor Nicolas, who I hadn't seen since I'd run away from alchemy.

"Did you fear they would arrest you for sending bees after the bad man who is keeping my brother captive?" Dorian asked.

I sat down on a hefty crate I'd pushed into the corner next to the sloping ceiling. How to explain what had happened? "Not exactly."

"She comes home speaking in riddles," Dorian muttered.

Home. That was exactly how I felt. Like I was returning home. I *was* home. I was again reminded that this was the first time in decades that I felt I had someplace besides my trailer to call home. I was simultaneously comforted and terrified. I loved the friends I'd made since moving to Portland several months ago. But if I failed to unlock the secrets of backward alchemy, my newfound best friend Dorian would suffer a fate worse than death. If I failed to convince a man who once believed in magic that believing in alchemy wasn't to be feared, I would lose my relationship with Max, my first chance at love in nearly a century. And now, if I dared return to Paris to finish what I'd started, I'd risk exposing my own secrets and the secrets of alchemy that the world wasn't yet ready for.

With Dorian in front of me, I couldn't bring myself to tell him about the complicated accusation of murder from 1942. Telling Dorian of my own entanglement in a disturbing death from so many years ago wouldn't help anyone. Nor could I tell him that I realized true alchemists like Nicolas Flamel might not understand that Dorian wasn't inherently evil. I didn't want to crush his hopes.

"How bad is your arm?" I asked, watching Dorian's awkward stance as he limped back and forth across the room, his clawed feet tapping on the floorboards with each step he took.

"*Ce n'est rien.*"

"In that case, move your left arm for me."

"I told you," he snapped, "it is nothing." He flapped his wings impatiently. "A kidnapped fellow gargoyle and the riddle of my book are much more important."

"I'll figure it out. I'm closer than ever before, Dorian."

Dorian stopped pacing and studied my face. "What else is wrong? What are you not telling me?"

"Why do you say that?"

He narrowed his liquidy black eyes. "I have known you for long enough to have learned your expressions, Zoe. When you are sad, your shoulders fall. When you are angry yet pretend you are not, you purse your lips. And when you are frightened, you tug at your hair. *You are frightened.*"

Apparently I would be a bad poker player. I put my hands into my lap.

"What has you so scared, *mon amie?*" Dorian asked. "I have faith you will help me. Help *us.*" He hopped up onto the crate next to me—he was only three-and-a-half feet tall—and patted my shoulder with his wing. His wings were heavy stone but simultaneously soft and malleable.

"I'm tired. That's all. I've got killer jet lag."

"For someone so old and wise, have you yet to learn you are a terrible actress?"

"You may recall I did fine on my own before you showed up in my living room."

"Yes. But you do much better when you do not lie."

I couldn't argue with that. Since one of the core tenets of alchemy is purity of intent, that's how I live my life. I don't feel comfortable lying. Whenever I can avoid it, I do. When I bought the crumbling Craftsman house in Portland, Oregon, earlier in the year, I didn't make up a story that I was a renovator or a house-flipper. When you act naturally, it's easier for people to believe what they want to. Real estate agents filled in the blanks that made sense to their worldview. They believed I was a young woman who wanted a bargain and didn't know what she was getting herself into. And my new neighbors assumed I was a good fit for the artsy Hawthorne neighborhood because I dyed my hair white to be trendy. In truth, I'm 340 years old, my hair turned naturally white nearly 300 years ago, and I wanted the falling-apart house so I could build myself an alchemy lab without people wondering what the construction was all about.

"You're an insightful gargoyle."

"*Oui.* I know this."

How could one refuse to answer an insightful, arrogant gargoyle?

"Something happened yesterday," I said.

I gave Dorian a brief overview of the unexpected turn of events that had driven me from Paris, telling him about Madame Leblanc, who'd known me when she was a child, and the murder of my old shop assistant. "Madame Leblanc said that her policeman grand-nephew would figure out what *I'd done*," I concluded, "and she'd figure out what *I am*."

Dorian's eyes grew wide with horror as I spoke. "*C'est terrible.* Of course you made the right decision to leave Paris. You could not risk yourself." He jumped down from the crate and began to shake. A seizure? This was a new development.

"Are you all right? Are you feeling yourself turn to stone all at once?"

He shook his head. "I have had a thought most *horrible*. This woman—she might have attempted to put a stake through your heart!"

I smiled for perhaps the first time since Madame Leblanc had confronted me at Notre Dame.

"It is not humorous, Zoe. If other people fail to take her seriously, she might resort to violent action. You are a pale woman who has been alive for centuries. What was she supposed to think?"

"I'm not that pale."

Dorian crinkled his forehead, causing his horns to wriggle. "All the hair on your body is white. People do not come much paler than you."

"You think she might think I'm a vampire? That's crazy. Vampires don't exist."

"Neither do alchemists, according to most people."

"Fair point. But what was I supposed to do? I couldn't tell her the truth. Besides, she already told me her mother thought I was a witch."

Dorian sputtered. "This is worse! Being burned at the stake would be even more painful. Fire takes longer to kill. Your skin would blister—"

"Hey," I cut in, "nobody is getting staked through the heart *or* burned alive."

"You are the one who said she was after the truth."

"Which isn't much better, I agree, but she doesn't want to kill me—only expose me."

"You did the only reasonable thing by leaving. You cannot help me if you are in prison. Or on the run in France. Or dying with a wooden stake in your chest."

"I get the point." I cringed at my unintended pun.

The gargoyle was right. He was a lovable and infuriating combination of adolescent puppy dog and wise old sage. Madame Leblanc was not someone to dismiss. I'd known people like her in different countries and different times. Women who were too easily dismissed when they should not have been. Some of them suffered in silence. Some of them formed communities of like-minded souls. And some of them took revenge.

"What are we to do?" Dorian asked.

"I've been thinking about that. I need to tell you about the other gargoyle—"

"My brother."

I hesitated.

"Why did you purse your pale lips?" Dorian asked. He tilted his head. "Perhaps you should buy some lipstick. That might squelch the vampire rumor."

"There's no vampire rumor."

"Whatever you say, ashen alchemist. Why were you pursing your pallid lips?"

"It's not good to think of him as a brother. You don't know him, Dorian."

"What is there to know? He is my brother."

He blinked at me so innocently that I felt tears welling in my eyes. "You shouldn't get too attached to the idea of another living gargoyle. We might not be able to bring him back from stone. When I saw him—"

"You *saw* him?" Dorian flapped his wings and wriggled his snout. "You did not tell me this! You said he was being held captive by a mad professor—"

"I'm fairly certain I didn't say that. But it's true, I did see him after I sent a swarm of bees after the professor so I could sneak into his office."

"*Bon.*" Dorian slapped his good hand against his knee. "Is my brother arriving later in a crate? I cannot believe you neglected to tell me of this upon your arrival."

"I didn't mention it first thing because I couldn't get him out of Paris, Dorian. He's more than a foot taller than you—there was no way I could carry him out of the university."

"Why did you go to see him without an escape plan? You caused harm to the professor but not so you could free my brother? This makes no sense. What were you thinking?" He flapped his wings.

"I'm most concerned about you. I needed to test what we thought we knew about your book and the Tea of Ashes."

"A test? You think *mon frère* is a test?" He harrumphed.

"If it worked, it would have helped him."

"Yet it failed." His wings folded around him.

"The Tea of Ashes transformed him for a brief moment. Only long enough for me to know he's still alive in there." I trembled at the memory of the gargoyle's pleading gray eyes.

Dorian peered intently at me. "The great Dorian Robert-Houdin knows what you need. I will bring food. Wait here. I will return shortly. Then you will tell me all about my brother."

I gave Dorian a hug. "I missed you, my friend."

"*Moi aussi, mon amie.*" He cleared his throat. This level of emotion was terribly undignified for a Frenchman born in 1860.

ELEVEN

MAYBE DORIAN WAS RIGHT that I'd have a clearer head after eating something. Especially Dorian's cooking.

Dorian had taken over my kitchen pretty much the day I moved into my crumbling Craftsman. Shortly before his death, Dorian's father, Jean Eugène Robert-Houdin, had the idea to serve as a reference for his adopted gargoyle son. Robert-Houdin explained that his "distant relative" Dorian was badly disfigured and did not feel comfortable being seen in public, but was a good man who would be a great help as a companion to a blind person. Dorian's first job was for the chef who'd lost his sight in a kitchen fire. Dorian learned to cook from the famous French chef. He took to it so well that he'd been a culinary snob ever since.

When Dorian followed me to Portland to seek my help last winter, he was horrified to learn that I eat only plant-based foods. Since alchemists aren't immortal, I learned long ago to take care of my body. I've been following a vegan diet since before the word was invented. I was a "Pythagorean" at one time—the mathematician also preached the merits of a plant-based diet. It's been a challenge at times to live in the United States, England, and France, which is why I always appreciated my sojourns to India. I was hopeful when Sylvester Graham's Grahamite diet caught on in the United States in the 1930s, but was dismayed that while he endorsed vegetarianism, he shunned spices. What good is a long life without some spice?

In the months since Dorian and I began sharing the house and the kitchen, he experimented with how to cook the decadent French foods he loved with vegan ingredients. Cashew cream replaced heavy cream made of dairy. Smoked salts and spices replaced bacon. Mushrooms replaced meat. Though it took him a while to admit it, he loved his new recipes more than his old ones. Before I left on this trip to Paris, he'd already declared himself to be the greatest vegan chef in all of Portland.

I smiled at the thought. Then yawned. The adrenaline that had kept me going was wearing off.

Dorian returned to the attic a minute later with a stack of three containers balanced in his right hand. I again noticed his inability to move his left arm, but I knew that bringing it up again before he was ready wouldn't get me anywhere.

The snacks he carried included a spread of morel mushrooms cooked simply in olive oil and spices, including a black salt sprinkled on top. I scooped up a mouthful with a piece of bread. It was exquisite, as expected. When I took care of myself, I ate well but far more simply than this.

"Brixton found you these mushrooms at the market?" I asked. Our fourteen-year-old neighbor, the only person in Portland besides me who knew of Dorian's existence, had been bringing Dorian groceries while I was out of town. Brixton was also tending to my backyard garden, which was the excuse he gave for coming over to the house while I was gone.

"Not Brixton," Dorian said.

"You promised you'd tell me if you were going to use my credit card again."

"This is what you think of me?" His snout twitched. "*Non*. I have my ways."

"Your ways?"

"A gentleman must keep his secrets."

"Dorian."

He shrugged. "While you were sick and then out of town, I was unable to cook for Blue Sky Teas, since they believe it is you who cooks there. I was bored. I wished to experiment with new recipes— ones that would work with only one good arm. You slept even more than usual while you were sick. It was quite tedious."

"That doesn't answer my question."

"No? Did you not taste the nut bread? It is superb. The perfect texture and the ultimate balance of sweet and savory. What else do you need to know? I have told you everything important that transpired last week—unlike *some* people. You still have not told me of my brother. *Bof*. I am so distracted thinking of my brother that I did not even remember *serviettes* with our snack. You are dripping oil and we have no napkins."

"It's not a long story," I said, grabbing a tissue to serve as a napkin. "Once I got into the office on my own, I read the backward alchemy incantation from the book." I glanced nervously at the book, its sweet scent of cloves and salty scent of the ocean filling the attic. "The words didn't affect him as they did you all those years ago, when Jean Eugène read from his 'prop.' But when I placed the Tea of Ashes in his mouth, he awakened and spoke—"

Dorian gasped.

"Only a few words," I whispered. The pleading terror in his eyes was something I'd never forget. I hoped Dorian couldn't see the horror on my face. "He was only awake for long enough to ask for help."

"*Alors*," Dorian said. "So it is true. This is the fate that awaits me."

"Not while there's an ounce of breath left in me."

Dorian frowned. "I am humbled by the sentiment. Yet you have already lost too much weight in this last month. Soon you will have completely wasted away." He pointed a clawed hand at the decadent snack that would have looked more natural at a sunny wedding reception than the silent shadows of an attic at three a.m. "Eat."

I obliged.

"How's Brixton?" I asked.

"Happy that it is now summer vacation. He is a good boy. He has been tending your garden, as you asked, and also bringing food to both me and Ivan."

"Ivan needs people to bring him meals? He said he was feeling better." I wondered if Ivan had told me that so I would answer his practical alchemy questions instead of telling him to rest.

Retired chemistry professor Ivan Danko had an interest in the history of alchemy as a precursor to modern chemistry. Like most modern-day scientists, he hadn't believed alchemy was real. Ivan suffered from a degenerative illness that left him with a weak immune system and a crushed spirit. His last wish was to finish writing his book before he died. At least, that was his wish before I'd been reckless. I'd accidentally shown Ivan that alchemy was real. I couldn't be a proper mentor to him (unlike Jasper Dubois, Ivan had asked), but because Ivan understood the need to be discreet about alchemy, I agreed to answer his questions as best I could when he set up his own alchemy lab. He was a good man and I wanted to help.

I was far from confident that Ivan would find the Elixir of Life that had consumed and eluded so many intelligent men over the centuries. I would have discouraged him from trying, save for one thing: it gave him *hope*. That hope gave him renewed energy for life. He might yet finish his book before he died.

"I do not trust that man," Dorian said.

"You don't trust anyone who knows the secret that alchemy is real."

"That is not so. I trust you and the boy."

"You trust me because you purposefully sought me out, and you didn't trust Brixton for months."

"This is true. But it is dangerous to trust others—as your trip to Paris proves. Brixton is young and naïve. So yes, the thoughtful boy brought Ivan a meal when he was recently home from the hospital, but this gave me an idea. Visiting Ivan was a perfect way for Brixton to keep him under surveillance during the daytime, when I could not watch him."

"Watch him?" I felt my eyes narrowing. "Why do you need to watch Ivan?"

"To see if he is up to nefarious deeds. Did I fail to mention we have been visiting Ivan?"

I rubbed my temples. "Are you trying to tell me that you and Brixton have been spying on Ivan?"

"*Spying* is a strong word. I prefer to call it gathering intelligence."

I closed my eyes and breathed deeply. "This is a bad idea."

"The boy can move about freely during the day—"

"He's fourteen."

"He did nothing unsafe. What is the harm? You are the one who believes we should trust Ivan."

I rolled my eyes at Dorian. "People don't generally react well when they learn they're being surveilled."

"Have you ever known us not to be careful?" he asked.

I opened my mouth to speak, but he cut me off by saying, "I withdraw the question."

TWELVE

In spite of the late night, I awoke with the sun, thinking of Jasper Dubois, who hadn't simply decided to move on from dangerous wartime Paris but had been killed.

My body is attuned to planetary alignments, so I always awaken with the first rays of sunlight. Alchemists have different strengths—some of us excel at transmuting corroded metals into pure gold, some of us feel the energy of gemstones, and some of us, like me, have a connection to plants—but all of us are affected by nature, from the scents that drift through the air to the rotations of the celestial planets above.

In the light of day, my immediate situation didn't seem as dire. I doubted the French authorities would spend limited resources to follow up on such an old crime, especially since I'd left France and the suspect was most likely dead. Ivan was a good man who would laugh if he learned Brixton was keeping an eye on him. An apprehensive feeling tickled at the edge of my consciousness, but with so many unanswered questions, that was to be expected. Jasper's death was an unsolved tragedy, but he was gone. Dorian was alive and needed me.

Since I'd arrived in the middle of the night, I hadn't yet seen my backyard garden. As a plant alchemist, the garden wasn't simply a hobby; it was an extension of my being and my salvation. Feeling the energy of the plants, from their roots in the earth to their soft, fuzzy, or prickly leaves, touched my soul. When my aptitude was discovered by an alchemist who assumed it was my brother's work, I learned that the alchemical term for creating healing medicines using the ashes of plants was spagyrics. I prefer to think of myself simply as a plant alchemist.

I was apprehensive as my bare feet touched the cool wood of the back porch. Breathing in the chilled air, I saw that Brixton had done a great job. Especially flourishing were the beets, parsley, and an assortment of salad greens. My young neighbor had more of an aptitude for gardening than I'd anticipated. I laughed as I noticed the plant that was doing the worst: nettles. Normally the tasty, healing plant that most people thought of as a pesky weed would grow under any circumstances, pushing out other plants. Brixton was afraid of the stinging leaves, so he must have ignored it. Now that I was home, I'd pour some extra energy into the nettles.

Simply stepping into the sanctuary helped calm my mind, which was still racing with all the confusing facts being thrown at me. The lavender made my head spin in a different way—it made me think of Max. I'd missed him more than I'd imagined I would. I shouldn't have been surprised. We shared so much in common, from our gardens to devoting our lives to helping people, and the chemistry between us was something I hadn't felt in decades. Was it enough to overcome the chasm in the foundation of our understanding of the world that made Max skeptical of anything he couldn't see?

After watering the garden and fixing myself a revitalizing green smoothie for breakfast, I came to a decision about what to do with the illegible vellum note from Nicolas Flamel. As much as I wished to learn what had become of the generous man who'd briefly been my mentor, I couldn't risk what he'd think of Dorian's connection to backward alchemy. I made sure the note was safely hidden away in an empty jar of Devil's Dung in my basement alchemy lab, where nobody would ever look, then climbed the stairs to the attic. The door was latched from the inside, so I knocked.

"I am at the denouement of a book that is giving me a *frisson*," Dorian called through the door. "Come back later, *s'il vous plaît*."

I wondered if it was true he was reading a thrilling novel, or if he didn't want me to see how poorly he was feeling. It distressed me to see my friend in so much pain, and it scared me to watch his body reverting to stone. Dorian used to shift between life and stone as easily as a person would move between standing up and sitting down. But now each time he transformed into stone, it was more and more difficult for him to regain movement. I needed answers. I hoped the bookseller would send me the book on backward alchemists as soon as promised.

Since the garden was thriving, I collected two buckets of parsley and beet greens, then went inside and unlocked the door to my basement alchemy lab. I hadn't had a chance to build a proper alchemy laboratory, just as I hadn't finished construction on my fixer-upper house, but both were holding their own. After things with my contractor didn't work out, my underemployed locksmith had made sure the house was in good enough shape that the neighbors wouldn't complain, and I'd cleaned the basement and made it my own. Both solutions were painfully close to the quick fixes I abhorred in backward alchemy. My imperfect alchemy lab served as my daily hypocrisy check. It was a good reminder that we do the best we can, but life isn't black and white.

I set the buckets of greens down on my work table, feeling an uneasiness creep over me as I did so. Something was amiss. There was nothing obvious, but I knew I wasn't wrong. The *energy* of the basement felt different. I glanced around.

I'd purposefully kept the room sparse, with two simple yet solid wooden tables, alchemy ingredients ranging from cinnabar to gold dust, and only candles and kerosene lanterns to light the space. Those sources of light served two purposes. First, they transported me to the right mental state to begin alchemical transformations. Second, they made sure that anyone snooping would have to take an extra step to cast light on their surroundings.

Had Dorian tidied the room in an attempt to be helpful? Though his body was failing him, he was a helpful little guy. I wanted to make another batch of Tea of Ashes for him. I knew if I told him what I was up to, he wouldn't let me go through with it. That's why I wasn't going to tell him in advance. Besides, this would be a small batch, not like the unwieldy batch that had backfired and made me so ill before going on my trip.

I followed the backward steps, beginning with fire. Extracting the essences of the fresh greens through this backward process left me with ash that wasn't alchemy's true salt, but mimicked it closely enough to work temporarily.

Two hours after beginning the Death Rotation, I had an ash-like substance to dissolve in hot water for Dorian to drink as medicine.

My joints ached as I climbed the steps leading out of the basement. At the top, it took a minute for me to catch my breath. It took all my energy to boil the water to make the tea for Dorian. Luckily, the scent was so pungent that he smelled it from the attic and came downstairs before I began dragging my tired legs up the stairs. He shook his head but accepted the tea.

"I'm going to rest for a little while now," I said. Dorian helped me to the couch. Between his limping gait and my wilting body, we were a sad sight. My eyes fluttered shut as soon as I hit the couch cushions. I felt Dorian place a blanket over me as I drifted off to sleep.

I woke up abruptly, with a gargoyle poking my arm with his claw and waving a bunch of fragrant roses under my nose.

"The roses worked!" he declared.

I rubbed my arm and sat up. My throat was so parched it took me a moment to speak. "I need sleep, Dorian."

"You have slept for many hours. You at least need to drink liquid." He set down the roses and handed me a glass of water. I sat up and drank it, then lay back down and pulled the blanket over me.

Dorian tapped me again.

"I'm serious, Dorian. I need more sleep."

"Zoe." The gargoyle gently tapped a claw on my forehead. "I do not wish to worry you, but you have been asleep for more than a day."

THIRTEEN

AGAINST THE WILL OF my aching body, I sat up. "I slept for a whole twenty-four hours?"

"*Oui.* This is why I needed a strong scent to wake you." Dorian waved the roses in front of my face again. "Your phone rang many times, yet you did not awaken. It was Max."

"Max? Did you—"

"Of course I did not answer. He phoned many times. He must have missed you very much." Dorian frowned. "But the ringing was most distracting. I asked Brixton to tell him you had horrific jet lag and needed sleep."

"A *whole day*?" At least it was one day closer to receiving the book from Paris in the mail. I stretched my cramped neck. My velvet couch wasn't the most comfortable bed. "I slept for an entire day?"

"Is your hearing affected?" Dorian shouted into my ear. "Yes! A whole day!" He raised his arms above his horns to pantomime the rising and setting of the sun.

"My hearing is fine. At least it was until a moment ago."

"Ah, I understand. You were being incredulous at the amount of time you slept."

"Where's my phone?"

Dorian scampered across the room and brought it back to me. Ivan had left me a voicemail asking me to call him because he had something to show me, and my sort-of-maybe-boyfriend Max Liu had sent me several welcome home text messages. In spite of everything else going on, I couldn't wait to see Max. In his last message he said he was working on a case today, so unfortunately I wouldn't get to see him quite yet.

I looked up from the phone and felt a pang of guilt that I'd been thinking of Max and ignoring a problem right in front of me. "Your left arm and leg," I said, abandoning my phone on the coffee table. "The Tea of Ashes didn't work?"

Dorian hopped up onto the couch next to me. "Yes and no. They are easier to bend than before you returned home, yet I still cannot control them very well."

"I'm so sorry, Dorian." I groaned. "I know what must have gone wrong. Brixton was the one who's been keeping up the garden. The plants I sacrificed didn't have much of my own energy in them."

"*C'est rien.* The book will come and you will capture a backward alchemist. Then he will tell you what we need to know to save me and my poor brother."

"I don't know if it will be that easy."

"*Oui.* You will need assistance to get them to reveal their secrets. I have read many thrillers with ingenious methods of torture."

I gaped at Dorian. "We're *not* torturing anyone."

"It is not difficult. And your basement is perfect. Brixton has returned the books to the library, but I can ask him to check them out again."

"Absolutely not. No torture."

"But the professor is probably torturing my brother as we speak! Chipping away at his stone flesh. By the time we rescue him, there may be nothing left of him!"

"The professor doesn't want to destroy the statue—"

"Statue?" Dorian sniffed and stood tall. The dignified stance was only slightly marred by his limp and awkwardly hanging arm. "This is what you think of me? That I am nothing more than a piece of stone?"

"Of course not. All I meant is that the other gargoyle is in stone form right now. And yes, the professor will probably take small samples of stone to test—"

Dorian's good hand flew to his mouth and his black eyes opened wide with horror.

"He'll be fine," I added. "You were fine after your toe chipped off."

Dorian squirmed uncomfortably. "If you would be so good as to ship me to Paris in an express delivery crate, I could stage a hostage rescue."

"The book that I hope will lead us to a backward alchemist should be here any day now—"

"No books arrived in the mail while you slept. Only advertisements. These Americans and their advertisements … " He shook his head. "You are confident about this book?"

"It sounds like a good lead. If there are any practicing backward alchemists left."

Dorian narrowed his eyes. "You suspect there are."

"I do. But until we find one—"

"You are the smartest, bravest person I have ever met, Zoe Faust. Even more so than my father."

"Flattery won't convince me torture is okay."

"No?"

"No."

Dorian muttered something under his breath and hopped down from the couch. "It is almost eight o'clock in the morning. The market will be open. I have taken the liberty of drawing up a shopping list. Brixton was helpful, but he could only do so much."

Dorian used to slip meat products into his lists, hoping I wouldn't notice.

"No bacon?"

He pointed a claw. "Smoked salts are even better."

"No cream?"

"I have five pounds of raw cashews."

"Maybe my hearing was affected after all. I could have sworn you said *five pounds* of cashews."

He beamed at me. "Wait until you taste the new recipes I have created during your absence."

Three pints of lemon water, a mug of healing ginger and turmeric tea, and almond butter and sea salt drizzled on freshly picked fruit gave me the energy I needed to start a nettle infusion and pick up groceries.

Making a full alchemical preparation, with the steps that distill the core essence of a plant into ashes, takes time. To extract energy from my nettles more simply, I poured hot water over a tangle of nettles in a mason jar and left it to steep on the back porch.

I usually walked to the market, but the length of Dorian's list and the heaviness of my legs led me to the truck in my driveway. My 1942 Chevy took a couple of turns of the engine to get started, but I'd taken good care of it over the years and it repaid my love with reliability.

An hour later, I hauled in five bags of groceries. Dorian jumped up and down with glee. With his good arm, he pulled his stepping stool to the counter next to the bags.

"You're happier to see a kitchen full of food than you were to see me," I said.

He pulled his snout out of the bag containing grains and dried beans. "Would it offend you if I admitted to equal amounts of happiness?"

I left him to his food and went to the other room to make my phone calls in private. With the time difference I couldn't call the bookstore proprietor to check on the status of my book delivery, but I could call Max and Ivan. Max's cell went straight to voicemail, so I tried Ivan next.

Though Ivan knew alchemy was real, he didn't know that my interest in unlocking *Not Untrue Alchemy*'s secrets was to save Dorian's life. Everyone aside from Brixton and Tobias believed I owned a gargoyle statue that I liked to move around the house and had an interest in alchemy because of the business I used to run out of my Airstream trailer and now ran out of my attic. Ivan assumed I was passionate about understanding alchemy because I was an accidental alchemist who wanted to understand more. Ivan was a scholar, so that's what made sense to his own worldview. Alchemy was a quest for knowledge.

But I'd been *too* passionate in my attempts to understand the bizarre woodcut illustrations in Dorian's book. Approaching the problem from an academic angle, Ivan had insights that hadn't occurred to me. These insights had helped me understand some of the book's illustrations. I'd subsequently let my guard down and accidentally allowed Ivan to see that alchemy was real.

"*Dobrý den*," Ivan said when he picked up the phone.

"My friend, how are you?"

"Me? Never better." The enthusiasm in his voice came through over the phone. I knew what it was: hope. His realization that alchemy was real had given him hope.

"I'm glad to hear it."

"I have a newfound appreciation for alchemical riddles," Ivan said. "I'm so glad you called. I wish you were back from Paris so we could talk in person, but this will do."

"That's actually why I'm calling. I'm home."

Ivan paused for so long that I wondered if the connection had been dropped. "Where are you?" he rasped. "Can you come over?"

"Are you all right?" I waited for a reply that didn't come. "Do you need me to call a doctor?"

"No, no. I'm fine," he said. But the tone of his voice said otherwise. "Zoe, now that you are home, there's something you must see."

FOURTEEN

BOOKS ON CHEMISTRY, HISTORY, and alchemy filled the giant study in Ivan Danko's house. Had he bought more research books in the month since I'd been here? I didn't remember his library being so labyrinthine.

I maneuvered around a pile of books on Chinese traditions in alchemy that partially blocked the study doorway. I couldn't stop myself from straightening the precarious stack. It wasn't the quantity of books that had changed, I realized; it was their organization. The bookshelves were only half full. Books that were once shelved in a methodical way were now stacked in haphazard piles. I tensed as I stepped over a toppled stack of leather-bound books to enter the room. Pages ripped from a disassembled book lay on the desk.

"Ivan, what have you done?" My heart ached at the sight of the damaged books. As someone who collected antiques before they were antique, I hated to see so much knowledge and craftsmanship treated so poorly. "Practicing alchemy requires you to respect your materials. You've completely ruined this book." I picked up the skeletal remains of what had once been a museum-quality book from the sixteenth century.

He waved off my concern. "The opposite. Quite the opposite, I assure you."

My eyes fell from his sunken eyes to his scruffy beard. Ivan hadn't looked healthy for as long as I'd known him, but his eyes held a desperate tint I hadn't previously seen. His dress shirt and slacks were pressed and pristine as usual. It was only his surroundings that had changed.

Still, this wasn't like Ivan. Forced into early retirement from his job as a chemistry professor in Prague because of his illness, he liked to be in control of other things in his life, such as his library. He stressed the importance of order to properly organize his thoughts for his book on the history of early chemists—in other words, alchemists.

"Is everything all right, Ivan?"

"I'm so pleased you've returned. A photograph didn't capture the necessary nuance, so I thought it best to wait to show this to you." He took a labored breath but grinned as he lifted a hefty book with pages so dark they were nearly black. "Now that you can see it in person—"

"You *burned* this?" The memory of the fire at Elixir filled my mind. The fire that disguised the murder of Jasper Dubois.

"Not burned. I put ashes on the pages, as you did with *Not Untrue Alchemy* to reveal hidden meaning in the pages."

"That book is unique. I haven't come across anything like it in the centuries I've been an alchemist."

"But," Ivan said with fire in his eyes, "you were never looking." He pointed at the charred pages of the sad-looking book.

"What am I looking at?"

"Don't you see?" He jabbed a shaking finger at the blackened page. "The ashes reveal the page beneath, making the flying bees on this top page circle the dragon on the page below. That symbolizes—"

"It's a coincidence, Ivan. Alchemy books are filled with woodcut illustrations. Of course they'll end up on top of each other like that."

"You don't know that." His Czech accent became more prominent as he became agitated. How could I balance helping him feel like all his efforts hadn't been in vain with getting us back on track?

"When I left for Paris to do my own research there," I said, "you talked of reading your books in a new light as a first step on the path to alchemy, not experimenting on them in an attempt to replicate the bizarre codes from my backward alchemy book—"

"You don't have all the answers, Zoe. You said so yourself. You don't fully understand alchemy. If you did, you could help me find the Elixir of Life more quickly. I've done good work to help you understand the strange book in your possession and also to help my quest for the Elixir. What do I care if I ruin books? Even if you're right that I've destroyed them, what good are they to a dead man?"

"But your book—"

"I would rather live on than leave a book behind."

I squeezed Ivan's gaunt shoulder. When it comes to ideas about what's most important at the end of life, comfort is better than words. I've seen people deal with looming death in many ways. Some find consolation in what they leave behind for their children or the world, some wish to surround themselves with loved ones, and some push it from their mind altogether.

"I'd at least like a few years longer," Ivan continued softly, taking my hand. "At this rate, I might not have time to finish writing my book, even if I tried."

"I'm sorry, Ivan," I whispered.

"I know, Zoe. And I know why you have this drive to solve the riddle of this book."

I pulled my hand away.

"Don't be embarrassed, Zoe. I know you feel sorry for me. You wish me to be healthy again, as I do."

I bit my lip. Dorian's existence wasn't my secret to tell, and I *did* want Ivan to be healthy again. He was a good man and a rigorous scholar who could likely unlock alchemy's secrets. But that would take time—more time than Ivan had. The Elixir of Life was something each person had to discover for him or herself. I couldn't do it for him. And while I could play a small part in mentoring Ivan, saving Dorian was my first priority.

"I do, Ivan. I really do. But applying backward alchemy to your own practice isn't going to help you. It's not true alchemy. Backward alchemy takes life in order to give it. That's not right—"

"I understand that," he barked. "My books aren't backward alchemy. I only wish to learn from that book of yours, not to use it. You're the one who brought it to me in the first place."

"Ivan, I—"

"Forgive me. I'm sorry I snapped at you. We can figure it out together."

"*Without* backward alchemy's Death Rotation."

He smiled. "Let me show you the laboratory I set up in my garage."

To the average Portlander, it probably looked as if he was setting up a space to make home-brewed beer. Prominent on one table was a distillation vessel with an alembic retort to distill vapors, a round cucurbit for boiling, and a receiver to collect distilled liquids.

"I never imagined I'd be putting what I read into practice," he said, "so I'm sure I've got it all wrong."

"Not bad at all, Ivan. Not bad at all."

The doorbell chimed. Ivan went to answer it while I studied some handwritten notes in a notebook.

"Thank you, Max," I heard him say from the other room.

"Max?" I hurried from the garage. Max Liu stood in the doorway holding a bag of food truck takeout in one hand and a stainless steel thermos in the other. He dropped them onto the floor and swept me up in a hug. Everything else faded away. I'd missed his scent, his touch, and everything about him. He pulled back from the hug and cradled my face in his hands for a moment. His brown eyes held an intensity that combined delight, regret, and longing.

I'd thought about Max so many times while I was in Paris, wishing he could have been there with me. Even though I knew he wasn't ready to hear the whole truth about my past, I could be myself with him in so many important ways. I hoped he'd be ready to know the whole truth someday soon. But for now, it was easiest if I kept the alchemical part of my life separate. Max knew I was interested in alchemy, but he thought it was because of the alchemical artifacts I sold in my online store.

It had taken me a long time to realize an essential truth: I *could* have connections with people who didn't know I was a true alchemist. Thinking otherwise was a misguided idea born out of self-pity. Most human interaction doesn't take place on the spoken level. Before I'd come to realize that, I kept myself shut off from anything beyond the most superficial of friendships.

I'll never forget the moment I embraced that truth. It was a day that had started out without hope. I'd been lost and was suffering from heat exhaustion in the south of India. A young family took pity on the strange, pale foreigner. They invited me into their modest clay home for a meal. That scorching, dusty day, I learned to cook dosas and poori as people on the Indian subcontinent had done for millennia, grinding the flour by hand, adding spices that killed germs and healed the body, and watching the bread bubble on an open fire. I taught their toddler English nursery rhymes that made him laugh and squeal with delight. I don't think any of us under the thatched roof understood a single word we said to each other that day, other than our names. But I will always remember them.

Max stroked my cheek and drew me into a kiss. As I lost myself in the embrace, I remembered the special evenings we'd spent together that spring, sitting together in Max's backyard garden drinking tea, sometimes talking and sometimes simply reading in the twilight. The important thing wasn't what we talked about, but the feeling of togetherness, easy comfort, and electricity.

Ivan cleared his throat. I opened my eyes and saw him leaning in the doorway, shaking his head and smiling.

Max pulled back from his kiss, but he didn't blush. He kept his eyes locked on mine and his fingers entwined in mine.

"Since Ivan hasn't been feeling well," Max said, "I thought I'd bring him some lunch and tea while I've got a break. I'm so glad I caught you here too. I have to run, and today is going to be a long one for me, but how about dinner tomorrow night?"

"I'd love that."

Max gave me a quick kiss goodbye before departing.

"He brought more than enough for me," Ivan said after he shut the front door. "You're welcome to stay for lunch. Let me clear off the kitchen table."

I followed Ivan to the kitchen but stopped before stepping inside. The kitchen table was covered with more than a dozen alchemy books—each one of them destroyed.

Ivan hadn't experimented on only one book with questionable results. He'd obsessively taken apart at least fifteen antique books. Some had been soaked in water, some smeared with ashes, and some charred by fire.

Ivan had unnecessarily destroyed priceless history on a fool's errand. He was no longer simply a dedicated scholar. He was obsessed.

FIFTEEN

I GAVE IVAN AN excuse and made a hasty departure. I needed to think, and I knew the perfect place to do so. I went on a long slow ramble to Lone Fir Cemetery, named for the single tree growing in the cemetery when it was founded in the 1840s. Since then, nature has become as much a part of the graveyard as anything else, with hundreds of trees creating a serene atmosphere for contemplation.

The Victorians held many beliefs I disagreed with—such as the prevalence of dresses that made it nearly impossible to walk through a room without knocking things over let alone breathe—but their view on cemeteries mirrored my own. A calming atmosphere with well-tended landscapes and remembrances of loved ones provided a perfect setting for a thoughtful walk or picnic. In a cemetery, there was no rush. You could think about people past and present without the burdens of the outside world.

Ivan had clearly crossed the line from passion into obsession. I'd done that myself once, so I couldn't blame him. It was how I'd found the Elixir of Life without realizing I'd done so. I was obsessed with finding a cure for the plague that had afflicted my younger brother, and I'd foolishly wasted his last days. I hadn't listened to Nicolas or Pernelle about what was possible, nor did I heed their warning that I would regret it if I didn't spend time with Thomas making him more comfortable before he died.

I remembered that raw emotion well, so I knew there was nothing I could say to Ivan to make him believe he was approaching alchemy incorrectly and that his time would be better spent with his friends or writing his book.

Jasper Dubois had never listened to me either, but for different reasons. What had happened to him all those years ago?

I'd walked for only ten minutes, but the serene cemetery no longer felt peaceful. Death is one thing, but not knowing what happened to someone was another. Without consciously realizing where I was going, I walked out of the cemetery and found myself heading to Hawthorne Boulevard.

Blue Sky Teas was half full—much less crowded than it had been two months ago. Still the same was the weeping fig tree that stretched to the high ceiling in the center of the teashop, and the thick tree-ring tables that filled the cozy space.

It was partly my fault the teashop wasn't doing the brisk business it had been. I was Dorian's front, so while I was sick and then gone in Paris, he wasn't able to supply home-cooked treats for the teashop. Dorian baked vegan pastries in the teashop kitchen before dawn, but everyone thought it was me who was the chef who got up early to bake while they slept. I can transform herbs into healing remedies, but it's Dorian who's the culinary alchemist, transforming basic ingredients into decadent feasts. When "I" was unable to bake because of illness or travel, there was no way to explain fresh-baked treats showing up when the teashop opened.

The other reason for the drop in business was the fact that the owner, Blue Sky, was in jail for a past crime that we all wished hadn't resulted in prison time. Blue created teas and decoctions that rivaled anything I'd tasted in Munar, delighting the senses and healing the body and soul. She was due out soon, but in the meantime our friend Heather Taylor was running the teashop.

Heather stood behind the counter this morning. Her teenage son Brixton sat at a corner table next to a man with dark brown skin, long black hair, and a tattoo of interwoven metal bars winding up his neck. At first I wondered why Brixton wasn't at school, but then I remembered summer vacation had begun. His wealthy friend Ethan was organizing a fifteenth-birthday trip to London that summer, paying for his friends to attend.

"Zoe!" Heather called out. "Welcome home." The words warmed my soul. It wasn't a one-sided feeling that this was my home. "One second, then I'll introduce you to Abel." She turned back to the customer at the counter, but at the sound of his name, the dark-haired man sitting with Brixton looked up, as did Brixton. So this was Brixton's stepfather. He worked out of town a lot of the time, so I hadn't met him yet.

Abel stood and extended his hand. It was calloused and his handshake firm. "The famous Zoe Faust. Thanks for looking after Brix. He's been telling me all about your garden. I know he started helping you in the garden so you wouldn't press charges after he broke in, but it's been really good for him. Thank you."

Brixton rolled his eyes.

"How could anyone resist the lure of the neighborhood haunted house that someone was finally moving into?" I said. "I don't blame Brixton. If the tables had been turned, I might have broken into your house to see what was going on."

"So can we change the subject or something?" Brixton said. "I didn't think you were coming back so soon from your trip to visit your grandmother's friend in Paris."

I hoped Brixton wasn't paying enough attention to notice the flush I felt on my cheeks. I'd forgotten how close the lie I'd invented for my last-minute trip to Paris was to the truth I'd discovered, though Madame Leblanc couldn't rightly be called a "friend."

"The visit wasn't what I imagined it would be," I said truthfully.

"Well, I'm glad you're back," Abel said. "This way I get to meet you." He moved a banjo from a chair to make room for me.

"Pretty cool, huh?" Brixton said. "Abel brought it back for me. Did you bring me back something cool from Paris?"

Abel elbowed Brixton. "Manners."

"What?" Brixton said. "Isn't that what people do?"

I smiled. I could already tell that Abel was a good influence on Brixton. He wasn't Brixton's biological father, but they held themselves in a similar way. Abel actually looked like he could have been Brixton's half brother. He was in his twenties, a few years younger than Heather, who wasn't quite thirty. Without her then-boyfriend's support or her family's blessing, Heather had dropped out of high school when she became pregnant with Brixton at fifteen. Whenever Heather's flaky behavior frustrated me, I reminded myself that her father had left the family when she got pregnant, never to be seen again. I hadn't seen my own family since I was sixteen, so I knew how difficult that could be.

"Not hungry?" I asked, looking at the half-eaten sandwiches on the table.

"Mom thought of getting fresh herbs for tea," Brixton said, "but she forgot about making sandwiches at lunchtime. So she's making mint and basil baguette sandwiches." He rolled his eyes. "It's your fault, Zoe. Not only were you gone so we didn't get fresh food, but

84

now that I've eaten Dor—I mean, *your* cooking, I can't stand these premade sandwiches she picked up for behind the counter."

Able shifted his position so the weeping fig tree would block him from Heather's view. "We're going to get out of here in a little while to get some real lunch," he said quietly, a conspiratorial grin on his face.

Something was different about the setting. It wasn't just the people and food. Had the tree been trimmed? No. It was the paintings that now hung on the walls. I recognized the style.

"Heather's new art is remarkable," I said.

Brixton shrugged, and a look of pride spread across Abel's smiling face. "She sold two of them the day she hung the series on the wall," he said.

"I can see why," I murmured.

In contrast to Brixton's mom's bubbly personality, she used unusual colors of paint to create dark and deep images. In her latest series, she'd added metallic accents to black, brown, and green forest landscapes. The gold and silver peeked out of the trees like eyes watching the viewer.

These new paintings were close-up studies of women's faces, but there was more to them than portraiture. The reflections in the eyes and the wrinkles on the skin each told their own stories, as if transforming from one meaning to another as the viewer looked more closely. In the painting closest to me, the reflection showed a raven in flight, and a crease on the woman's cheek was two simple line figures dancing.

"I think Mom needs help with the lunch rush," Brixton said to Abel. "Would it be cool if you helped her so I can catch up with Zoe?"

It didn't look very crowded to me, but Heather was taking orders and grabbing premade sandwiches from the display cabinet. Abel tousled Brixton's hair and stood up. "Glad you're not too cool to think of your mom."

Once Abel made it to the counter, Brixton hunched his shoulders over the table and spoke softly. "I didn't really expect you to have brought me a gift from Paris, you know. That was just part of my cover, pretending like you were on vacation with your grandma's friend like you told everyone."

"That's what you wanted to tell me privately?" I whispered back.

"Nah. Did Dorian tell you what's up with Ivan?"

"Yes. About that, it's a terrible idea."

"Why? You don't care about what we learned?"

"I already know that Ivan is obsessed with alchemy. You need to distance yourself from him. Desperate people can change."

"Yeah. Whatever. Fine. But that's not what I'm talking about."

"It's not?"

"No. It's not just me and D keeping an eye on him. There's a creepy guy spying on Ivan."

SIXTEEN

SOMEONE WAS SPYING ON the alchemy scholar? I felt my temple twitching furiously.

"A creepy guy?" I repeated.

"Well, maybe *creepy* isn't the right word. But he was totally spying on Ivan yesterday."

"Dorian neglected to tell me that." Why hadn't he told me? The vein in my temple was now fully pulsating. I knew why Dorian hadn't told me himself: he knew I'd disapprove.

"You need to stop," I said. "Now."

Brixton rolled his eyes. "I have the daytime shift, so it's not like it's dangerous. What? You're friends with Ivan. He, like, helps you with stuff. You said so."

"There's so much going on right now that we don't understand. It's safest for you to stay away from anything that involves spying."

"Whatever. So do you want to hear about the guy I saw or what?"

I glanced at the counter. Abel and Heather had a good rhythm together. They weren't paying any attention to us. "Who was he?"

Brixton shrugged. "Just some boring-looking guy. He was spying on Ivan, like in a movie."

"Define *spying*," I said.

"Did you forget English while you were in France?"

I sighed. "I know what the word means. I want to know why you think someone is spying on Ivan, not visiting him. What exactly was he doing?"

"Looking in the windows. That totally counts as spying, right? When he first walked up to the house, I thought he was some professor Ivan knew. But then instead of knocking on the door, he looked in all the windows, and then flattened himself against the wall to make sure Ivan didn't see him."

That certainly sounded like spying.

My senses tingled. I was experiencing the feeling of being followed myself. Was it real or an overactive imagination? I scanned the tables and the sidewalk that was visible beyond the large front windows, half expecting to see Madame Leblanc hiding behind a potted plant, stealing a glance at me through her designer sunglasses. But that was crazy. The bushes on the sidewalk weren't big enough to conceal a person, even a small one. Besides, she didn't know where to find me. Still, I was uneasy as I watched several people walk past. None of them resembled the persistent Madame Leblanc or anyone else I knew.

"Without making obvious movements," I said to Brixton, "look around and see if you spot the man you saw spying."

"Wicked."

My pulse raced. "You see him?"

"No. He's not here. But we're totally in a spy movie."

"I'm being serious, Brix."

The eye roll. "I'm being serious too. There's seriously a guy spying on Ivan. That's why you need my help. Something is going on."

"When did your stepdad get back?" I asked Brixton.

"Yesterday." He scowled. "You don't think he—"

"No, that's the opposite of what I meant. You want to spend some time with him, right?"

"Yeah. That's not lame. He's really cool."

"I can tell. Spend the time with your family, and with Ethan and Veronica. Forget all about Ivan. Forget all about me and Dorian for the time being too."

"What's going on, Zoe?"

"I'm not sure. That's what worries me."

"You're kind of freaking me out."

"Sorry. Nothing freak-out worthy. You know me. I'm old. I worry."

"You're worried about saving Dorian, aren't you? Why did you leave Paris so soon if you hadn't figured stuff out?"

"I've got a lead." Would the book be in today's mail? "I should go check it out, actually. No more surveillance, okay?"

"Cool."

As I stood up, I fought the urge to tousle Brixton's hair as Abel had done.

On the sidewalk, my skin again prickled. There was no sign of anyone I didn't wish to see, but for a fraction of a second the profile of a man turning the corner reminded me of Ambrose. I felt for my locket. My encounter with Madame Leblanc had brought up too many painful memories. My long-ago lover who'd died by his own hand, my brother who'd been claimed by the plague, and Jasper Dubois, my assistant who'd met a murderous end. Death followed me. Why did I think I could save Dorian?

I hurried home. *Backward Alchemists of Notre Dame* hadn't arrived in the mail. I'd looked up the title after the bookshop proprietor told me of its existence, and I understood why I hadn't found it before. The only reference to it was a footnote in an obscure text I didn't own, according to the comments of one of the many blogs devoted to "the Secrets of Paris." In the modern age, people often assume they can find anything online. They don't realize how far from the truth that is.

I needed to get that book as soon as humanly possible. I'd already paid Lucien Augustin for the book, but it wouldn't hurt to reach out to rare book dealers I knew in the States.

I found Dorian standing on his stepping stool in front of the stove. With his right arm he stirred a fragrant pot of tomato sauce, heavy on the garlic. His left arm hung awkwardly at his side. It was even worse than it had been before my latest attempt at creating another batch of Tea of Ashes. I wondered if I should fix him a little sling.

I crossed my arms and stood over him. "You didn't tell me about the spy."

"Ah. You spoke to the boy." He continued stirring. "I wished to wait until we knew more. There was no sense speaking of it before I knew what was going on."

"I told you everything I know about the other gargoyle, about Jasper Dubois, and about all of my Notre Dame leads, even though I have no idea what's going on with any of those things."

"Using my little grey cells," Dorian said, setting down the wooden spoon and tapping his head with his index claw, "I have taken the liberty of diagraming a chart of possibilities for all of these problems—both yours and mine."

Dorian thought the famous Poirot expression "little grey cells" was especially appropriate to him because his body was gray.

"A chart," I repeated.

"*Un moment.*" He stepped down from the stool and opened the drawer with scratch paper and pens. He rummaged until he found the notepad he was after, then cleared his throat.

I sighed. "All right. What have you figured out?"

"*Bon*. We will begin with Ivan. He is Czech. He has defected, and therefore we can assume he is a spy—"

"Let me stop you right there. What was the last novel you read from the library?"

Dorian frowned. "Do not use the fact that it was a John Le Carré book against me."

"This isn't a spy novel," I said. "I'll let you finish cooking dinner, and then you can tell me what you think might be a realistic theory."

I left him grumbling in the kitchen and stepped through the back door to get the nettle infusion that was waiting for me on the porch. It was ready, so I strained the liquid into a clay mug and took it with me to the basement.

I sipped the energizing liquid as I descended the steps. When I reached the bottom, I nearly dropped the mug. Something was very wrong.

Someone had been inside my alchemy lab.

SEVENTEEN

A SWEEP OF THE room assured me there was nobody besides me in the room, but my heart refused to stop pounding. Because this time, I wasn't imagining that someone had been there. My dragon's blood had been moved from the front of a row of glass jars to the back. I twisted the lid, tilting the jar away from me as I eased it open. The contents were right, so nobody had added anything. I didn't keep a record of measurements, so I couldn't be certain if they'd taken any or simply looked.

Was this the same person who'd been spying on Ivan? How did they get in? And why look through my alchemy lab? Was someone spying on *alchemists*? Was I right after all that Madame Leblanc had tracked me down to expose me?

I abandoned my nettle infusion and raced up the stairs. "Dorian!"

"What is the matter? Is there news of my brother?"

"Someone has been in the house."

His horns twitched in horror. "*Mais non. C'est impossible.* You installed security locks on the doors and windows, and no human can enter via my rooftop entrance."

"You weren't doing anything in the basement alchemy lab, were you?"

"How can you think this of me? I know you do not wish it to be disturbed. What did you detect had been taken?"

I sighed. "Nothing is missing." But I hadn't imagined that the bottle had been moved, had I?

"You have not yet recovered from making the Tea of Ashes. It was foolish of you to make it again. But I forgive you. I will cook a satisfying early summer meal. That will help you think straight." He took my hand and dragged me back to the kitchen.

"*Alors*," he said, "no word of my brother?"

"I'm sorry," I said, wondering what Professor Chevalier's reaction would be if the woman who'd brought a swarm of bees to his office called for an update on his gargoyle—excuse me, his *chimera*—statue. I also wondered how soon a locksmith could get here to rekey the house. With so many unexplained mysteries circling me, I at least wanted to feel secure in my home. I stared at an unfamiliar basket on the kitchen counter.

"Where did these wild mushrooms come from?" I asked.

"The forest."

"You know how to safely forage mushrooms?" Eating poisonous mushrooms was a complication not worth risking. I'd seen the effects on people who'd eaten foraged mushrooms that looked nearly identical to safe varieties. Sometimes I'd been able to help the unlucky people who'd simply been trying to feed their families, but more often it was already too late once the first symptoms appeared.

"Do not worry," Dorian said. "They are safe."

I couldn't imagine a forager taking a gargoyle along with him on a forest walk. "How do you know?"

Dorian looked everywhere in the kitchen except at me. He coughed. "Did I neglect to mention I have a job?"

"A job? You? Without me as your cover?"

He sniffed. "I had many jobs before I met you. I have impeccable references."

"You brought your references to Portland?"

"It was not necessary. You remember Monsieur Julian Lake? Yes, of course you would. You may recall that the elderly gentleman is blind. What you may not have known is that he appreciates gourmet cooking. Unsurprising for someone from such a distinguished family. However, his housekeeper is a terrible cook." Dorian shook his head and pursed his lips. "After Monsieur Lake tasted my cooking, when I was pumping him for information earlier this year, he desired more meals cooked by the great Dorian Robert-Houdin. Monsieur Lake wished to employ the services of the disfigured Michelin-star chef who does not wish to be seen."

"You have a Michelin star?"

Dorian sniffed. "Not officially, no. One needs to be associated with a restaurant to receive the honor. May I continue?"

"Please."

"His invitation was so insistent that I could not refuse without being rude. He would have gone to extreme lengths to find me, had I not accepted. He is a man used to getting what he wants."

"I see. How long have you been secretly working for Julian Lake?"

"It is not a secret."

"You didn't tell me about it, and I had no other way to find out. That makes it a secret." Something seemed fishy.

"I did not wish you to worry."

I thought about that. "I'm not really worried. He's blind and you know how to hide from others. Why would you assume I'd worry?"

"No reason." Dorian became overly interested in brushing dirt from the mushrooms.

"Dorian."

"Yes, all right." He turned from the counter and looked up at me. His liquidy black eyes were imploring. "I did not wish you to think you had been replaced."

"Replaced?"

"*Bon.* I should have known you have a big enough ego that you would not feel threatened. One would hope so, after living for so long."

"You were worried about me being *jealous*?"

"It is a natural emotion, no? And Zoe, if you saw his kitchen! It is a thing of beauty. No, I shall never show it to you. For then you might succumb to a tremendous fit of jealousy. Modern stainless steel appliances including a subzero freezer, a five-burner gas range, and an island larger than your whole kitchen. Of that you *should* be jealous. And of the covered pizza oven near the backyard pool."

"There's nothing wrong with this kitchen. Or my backyard. Modern amenities and square footage are overrated."

Dorian waved his good hand in a dismissive manner. "Yes, yes, I know of Julia Child learning the art of French cooking in her closet-size kitchen. *Peutêtre.* I will grant that you might be right about space not being a necessity. Yet modernity has brought such wonders."

I pointed at the vintage blender that had been my travel companion in my Airstream trailer since 1950, up to the simple copper pots hanging from the ceiling in the cozy kitchen, and down to the glass bottles I'd filled with infused olive oils, vinegars, and salts. "This is the height of kitchen technology right here. Haven't you noticed the resurgence of young people embracing traditional methods?"

Dorian rolled his eyes. He and Brixton were a bad influence on each other. "I do not understand your resistance to modern food preparation techniques," he said. "You embrace modernity when it comes to language. You pick up modern vernacular like a house on fire."

"That's not quite the right idiom—"

"You have proven my point. You understand slang in ways I never could, yet you do not try to adapt your methods of preparing healing foods."

"Adapting to language lets me fit in without raising suspicions." At least it did when my worlds didn't collide. I tensed as I thought about my carelessness in Paris. The city had transported me back to a century ago, and I'd spoken the French that I'd spoken at that time, not thinking how it would sound. "But preparing foods, teas, and tinctures isn't something I do publicly. The old methods are what speak to me."

"*D'accord*. We shall agree to disagree, as always, *mon amie*."

"How did Julian Lake find you in the first place?" I asked. "He didn't come over to the house, did he?" A worrisome thought.

"*Non*." Dorian jumped off his stepping stool and opened the recycling bin under the counter. He pulled out a wrinkled newspaper dated earlier in the month. He opened the pages to the Classifieds section and shook it in front of me. "Modern technology has not completely replaced civilized communication."

"Stop shaking your fist. I can't read what you're trying to show me. Let me guess. Missed connection, seeking a Frenchman who'd visited him with vegan pastries this spring?"

"Close," Dorian said. "Very close. The newspaper advertisement is what caught my eye. Only I never told him the pastries I brought him were vegan. This advertisement offered a modest reward for anyone who put him in touch with the disabled French chef. When I called him, he remembered my voice." Dorian's snout twitched as he gave an indignant sniff. "Can you believe that he gave me a test before hiring me? A test! He did not trust that I had baked the food I brought him."

"Sounds like a smart man."

Dorian chuckled. "He would not accept my suggestion of plant-based cooking. I knew right away he was not a man to lose an argument, so I stopped arguing. Instead, I simply did not tell him I was not using the meats he purchased to use as starters in my soups and casseroles. He declares he has never eaten so well. Between smoked salts, infused oils, and creamy nut sauces, he never had a chance."

"With Julian Lake's setup, I'm surprised you're still doing any cooking in my kitchen at all."

Dorian pointed a clawed fingertip at my midsection. "You are skin and bones, Zoe. What would you do without me cooking for you? When I met you, though you did not cook feasts on par with mine, you ate well. You took care of yourself by fixing yourself smoothies with vegetables from your garden, soups with oils and salts you infused yourself, and an assortment of healing teas you created with the power of the sun and moon."

I twirled my hair around my finger. "I still do those things." Did I, though? I'd let Dorian bring me food while I was sick before leaving for Paris. While in Paris, I'd bought fresh food daily, like other Parisians, but I didn't have my blender, which is what allowed me to make healthy meals easily. And since returning, I hadn't followed my usual morning practice of starting the day with a glass of lemon water, tending to my garden, and fixing either a smoothie of fruits, vegetables, and nut butter or a bowl of slow-cooked porridge with dried fruits, nuts, cinnamon, and sea salt.

"You have not noticed that we are out of half of the flavored salts in the cabinet," Dorian said, "nor that I used the last of your favorite cayenne-infused olive oil."

"We have enough left. My first priority is finding a cure for you."

"*Food is life*, Zoe. I appreciate the sentiment, but you must first slow down and take care of yourself."

A faint buzzing sounded. My shoulders tensed for a fraction of a second before I realized it was my phone. Not bees. I went in search of my phone and found that I'd missed a string of text messages from Brixton, as well as two voicemails.

A fist banged on the front door so loudly that I dropped the phone.

I opened it to find a trembling Brixton. When he spoke, his voice shook as well. "He's dead, Zoe. He's dead."

EIGHTEEN

THE FRAZZLED TEENAGER PUSHED his way past me into the house. He ran his hands through disheveled hair and took several deep breaths. "I've never seen a dead body before."

"Who—"

"It's not like it is in the movies, or even photos of real corpses."

"Brix—"

"I tried calling you, Zoe." He shoved his hands deep into the pockets of his jeans and paced the length of the living room. "When you didn't answer, I called Max. I didn't know what else to do! I didn't want the killer to get away."

Killer? "You *saw* someone murdered? Oh, God, Brixton. Who—"

"I didn't see the actual killing, just the dead guy with a gash in his head." Brixton broke off and flung himself onto the green velvet couch. He put his head in his hands. He brushed off my attempt to put my hand on his shoulder, so I gave him space.

When he looked up at me, his face was calm. So was his voice. "I screwed up, Zoe. I was far enough away that the killer slipped out without me seeing where he went." He punched the coffee table.

I cringed. So much for forced calmness. I'd get him a poultice later to help with the inevitable bruise. For now, an injury was the least of my concerns for Brixton. If a killer had seen him, he'd have suffered a lot worse than a sore hand. "You did the right thing getting away and calling the police. You should have called them first. Why did you call me?"

I dreaded the answer I expected: that it was someone I knew.

"Didn't I say? It wasn't a random dead body I saw. The killer was the same man who Dorian and me saw spying on Ivan."

"Ivan." I sank onto the couch, my legs no longer steady enough to support me. "He killed Ivan?"

Brixton swore. "I didn't mean it's Ivan who's dead. Sorry to scare you. I don't know who the dead guy is. I mean, I kinda thought he looked familiar, but I probably just saw him around somewhere. But Ivan is probably in danger now, right? Since the spy who was spying on him killed someone?"

I desperately hoped Brixton truly had been far enough away that the killer hadn't seen him, otherwise he'd be the one in danger. "You told all this to the police?"

"Yeah, Max was on some other case and said he couldn't just assign himself to whatever case he wanted. But he made sure some cops showed up real fast. I told them everything. They made me call my mom too. Not cool. She totally freaked."

I could imagine. "Brixton. Back up a sec. *How* did you find the dead body?"

"You know we've been following Ivan, right? How Dorian had the idea to figure out what Ivan was doing now that he knows alchemy is real—in case he was going to expose you and D." Brixton's voice shook as he spoke. "So, this dude we saw at Ivan's, we didn't have a clue who he was." Brixton hit the coffee table with his fist again. At least it wasn't as hard a punch this time. "It doesn't matter, really, cuz we know the important thing now—that he's a killer."

"We should get Dorian," I said, surprised he hadn't heard us and come downstairs already. I ran up to the first flight of stairs and called to him. He had to have heard me, but he didn't reply. "Hang on one second, Brix." I continued up to the attic, slowing only on the narrow steps leading up from the second floor to the attic. The attic door was closed. I turned the handle, but it was locked. "Dorian, let me in." I shook the handle. "Dorian?"

"He's not there?" Brixton startled me from the landing below me. "Weird."

"He must have snuck out just now. Now that he has my cape, I think he's getting more brazen." I whirled around. "Don't follow his example."

He rolled his eyes. "Like I'd imitate a gargoyle."

A perfectly sensible response. "Let's go back downstairs. You were telling me how you found the man."

The detour to look for Dorian seemed to have given Brixton the time he needed to collect his thoughts. He was more relaxed when he continued.

"There's this cabin that looks like an old shack. It's in the woods past Ivan's house, in one of those greenbelts in between housing developments. The cabin is boarded up and there are signs saying to keep out. It's where Dorian saw this guy go a couple of nights ago. So I went to check it out during the day today."

"And you stayed, even after you saw there was a dead body? You stayed in the woods with a killer out there?"

"I went far enough away." Brixton rubbed his hand.

Brixton's temper worried me. He was a teenage boy, so some outbursts were to be expected, but I hoped he would grow out of the uncensored temper that had already given him a juvenile record. "All

101

that matters is that you're safe. Next time you see something like that, you get the hell out of there. No, there's not going to be a *next time*, because you're not going to be involved in this. Or anything like this. Ever. Again. Is that clear?"

Brixton rolled his eyes. "I had to see what was going to happen."

"I know a crime scene can seem intriguing—"

"That's not what this is about! The shed, Zoe. God, aren't you listening to me? It wasn't a normal shed. The stuff inside—" He broke off and shook his head. "It's why the killer was following Ivan. What they have in common. It's what *you* have in common with them too."

I felt a cold shiver tickle its way down my spine. The look on his face terrified me.

"It was an alchemy lab, Zoe. The dead guy and the killer, they were practicing *alchemy* in the woods."

I stared at Brixton. This wasn't a joke. "You're sure?"

He nodded "What's going on? I mean, I thought there weren't hardly any of you guys around. There are more alchemists here in Portland?"

"I didn't think so," I said, but I wasn't so sure. My head swam. Had I been drawn to Portland on a subconscious level not because of its welcoming people, splendid food options, and lush greenery—but because alchemists were here? Could that have been the reason Portland felt immediately like home? As a female alchemist, I'd always been an outsider. Only Nicolas Flamel, who thought of his wife as an equal, had deemed me worthy of an apprenticeship. But I'd left abruptly, after a personal tragedy, and had lost touch with him.

"Tell me what you saw." My throat was so dry that my voice cracked.

"Do you need some water or something?" Brixton took me by the hand and led me to the kitchen. His hands were clammy but strong.

I was still in a daze as he poured me a glass of water. It was the people that drew me here to Portland—normal, everyday people like Brixton, Max, and Blue. Alchemists aren't drawn to each other like that. We're not magical beings. We're simply people who've tapped into different energies, performing different experiments than mainstream science.

There was another explanation, but I didn't like it one bit: that alchemists were here in Portland because of me, Dorian, and his backward alchemy book.

I accepted the glass of water from Brixton and drank it in five gulps. The liquid revived me. "I'm the one who's supposed to be taking care of you, kiddo."

Brixton shrugged.

"I'm all right," I said. "I don't know what came over me. Go ahead and tell me what you saw."

"I don't know how to describe it exactly." The frustration was clear in every aspect of the boy in front of me. The expression on his face hovered between innocence and angst, between boyhood and adulthood. "Stuff like in your alchemy lab."

"You haven't taken chemistry yet, have you?"

"No, I just finished freshman year. Chemistry is later. Why?"

I grabbed my phone and looked up a photo of a chemistry lab. I handed the phone to Brixton. As he hesitated, I relaxed. "You've only seen my alchemy lab a couple of times. Come with me."

I unlocked the door to the basement and lit the candles that illuminated the room.

"I still think it looked more like this than the photo you showed me," Brixton said.

"Have you been inside a chem lab?"

"I saw that meth lab before it got shut down."

"And that's it?"

"I'm not making this up. I'm not."

Was he trying to convince me or himself? "I didn't say you were. It must have been really upsetting to see a dead body."

"I'm not a kid, Zoe. I'm not imagining things." His voice broke and he swallowed hard. "I know what I saw."

That's what worried me. If Brixton had seen a murderer, that meant the murderer might have seen him too.

NINETEEN

I MADE SURE BRIXTON had told the police everything he'd seen and extracted a promise that he wouldn't investigate further. I wasn't sure how much good that promise would do, so I insisted on tossing his bike in the back of my pickup truck and driving him home.

From my seat I watched Abel open the door and give Brixton a bear hug in the doorway. Abel mouthed "thank you" to me and waved. I drove home in silence, save for the sound of the engine I'd tended for more than half a century.

I turned off the engine once I reached the driveway in front of my Craftsman house. I sat there for a few minutes, unsure of what to think, feel, or do. This couldn't be Madame Leblanc's revenge on me, could it? It wasn't impossible that she could have tracked me to Portland. But this was far too subtle a way for her to frame me through alchemy. This murder wasn't meant to be discovered so quickly. The discovery in the remote area had occurred because Brixton had been following the killer.

Gripping my keys, I walked over to the Airstream trailer that had sat in the other half of the driveway since I'd moved in. I unlocked the creaking door that needed oil, then lay down on the built-in couch.

Though I'd cleaned out most of the contents of the trailer when I moved into the house, subtle scents from years of love and life lingered. The musty postcards I'd sold at flea markets across the country for decades. The fresh, uplifting mint from the tendrils of lemon balm and peppermint plants that had lived in my traveling window box garden. And the salty scent of the sea—a combination of the flavored salts I used to flavor simple meals and the trailer's long stretches driving across snow-covered country roads and through sandy beach towns.

I wasn't maudlin enough to truly believe that death followed me wherever I went, but I was at a loss to explain the deaths surrounding me. Jasper's death in my Paris shop couldn't be connected to a dead body found in a shack in the woods in Portland—yet they were both connected to alchemy.

I closed my eyes and let the fragrance of salty, musty mint carry me back to a time when life had been simpler. Only that was a false memory. My life had never been simple. From the time I'd been driven from Massachusetts for having an "unnatural" aptitude with plants, to ignoring Nicolas Flamel's warnings about how to study alchemy, to finding love with a man who'd killed himself after his son failed to find the Elixir of Life along with him. Those hadn't been simple times.

The years I'd spent traveling across the United States in my truck and trailer were simple on the surface, but if I was honest with myself, I knew I'd been running away. There was always a cloud lingering over my head, even when I would park my trailer in a nice town and settle down for a year or two at a time.

The quirky friendliness of Portland's residents and the greenery the city insisted on maintaining was an inviting combination that made me think I might finally have a simple life, at least for a little while. Though that illusion had been shattered the day I moved in, I still held onto hope. If I could figure out the last piece of the puzzle to save Dorian, put these unsolved deaths behind me, and spend time with Max—

My eyes popped open.

I was having dinner with Max that evening. The thought filled me with a mix of emotions, ranging from desire to comfort to apprehension. Part of me wanted to cancel, because how could I possibly think of enjoying myself with everything that was going on? But life has always been complicated. I'd seen too many people regret spending their time worrying instead of living. With one last look around my empty trailer, I went inside the house and picked out a dress to wear that night.

———————

I walked to the restaurant on Hawthorne with the sun high in the sky above me. It was the start of summer, but it was also an early dinner. Max knew I wasn't a night owl. Even though he didn't know how closely my body's reactions were tied to the cycle of the sun and the planets, he understood that I felt most comfortable in the earliest hours of the evening.

Max had suggested this restaurant because it served organic vegan food, and as I looked through the front windows, I realized the restaurant was even closer to my own way of eating than I'd imagined. Patrons were being served on wooden plates.

Even as the world moves towards progress, a pendulum is also in play, swinging between different ideas that societies embrace at different times. When I was growing up in Salem Village—not to be confused with wealthier Salem Town—in the late 1600s, we grew our own food and ate off of shared wooden plates called trenchers.

Today's young people had embraced much of what I remembered from my childhood, going back to the land and appreciating slow food, the idea that food should be locally sourced and respected for its traditions and transformative processes rather than thoughtless calories that immediately appear out of thin air at a takeout counter. As a bearded man in the window took a sip of dark beer from a mason jar, I smiled at another parallel. In my day, beer was often drunk for breakfast with porridge. I'm sure today's hipsters would have approved.

A heavily tattooed couple stepped past me. The one with an intricate black dragon wound around his elbow and a fedora on his head held the restaurant door open for me.

Max was already in the lobby. He was dressed in a slim-fitting charcoal suit and skinny silver tie that made me want to reach out and touch it. I resisted the temptation, but Max didn't. He greeted me with a brief kiss that tasted of lemon and rose hips. I pulled back but left our noses touching for a moment. That made him smile.

"I'm glad you're home from visiting your grandmother's friend," he whispered.

If you want a lie to be believable, stick as close to the truth as possible. When I left for Paris, I told Max and most of my Portland friends a believable lie: that my grandmother's dear friend was quite elderly and wanted to see me before she died.

"I'm glad to be home too. Thanks for making sure Brixton was taken care of today. He came to see me after he was done talking to the police."

"Poor kid. He seemed really shaken."

"Does he need protection?"

Max pursed his lips. "Why would he need protection? People used to deal drugs out of that place, but not since it's been boarded up."

The hostess interrupted Max's strange answer and led us to a corner table.

"Are we talking about the same thing?" I asked once we were seated. "He told me he found a dead body and saw the killer. I know he says he hung back far enough and the guy didn't see him, but what if he was wrong? I'm still worried he'll be in danger."

"Brix either let his imagination get the better of him or he was trying to get a rise out of you. I can see him doing that." Max's deep brown eyes softened. I wished I hadn't brought up the murder.

"He wasn't acting, Max."

"The body is at least a decade old, Zoe."

"But Brixton said—"

"I don't know what Brixton was playing at when he talked to you, but the victim has been dead for quite some time. For whatever reason, Brixton lied to you."

TWENTY

"MAYBE IT WASN'T A deliberate lie," Max continued. "Brixton loves dark things, like how he's into Portland's murderous history."

"Not so much anymore," I murmured, thinking of where that interest had led us earlier that year.

"His imagination probably got the best of him. But I'd have thought he'd find it exciting to find a mummified dead body."

"*Mummified?*"

"That's not exactly the right word, but I'd rather not talk about decomposition over dinner. Brix really didn't tell you that? Maybe he was trying to tell a macabre joke that backfired and he didn't know how to talk his way out of it."

I shook my head. Something wasn't right here.

"I'm surprised you kept our date if you thought Brixton was in danger," Max said. "I'm glad you came, and that I could put your mind at ease."

My mind was far from at ease, though. Brixton could be immature, but this wasn't right. "Brixton told me there were alchemical items like the things I sell." I took a moment to take a sip of the water placed on the table, deciding how much I should say to Max. "I suppose you're going to tell me that was Brixton's imagination, too, since he knows I collect healing and alchemical artifacts for Elixir?"

Max swore softly and shook his head. "I'd have thought the guys would tell him not to talk about the case. Don't you want to talk about something else? How was your trip? How was the visit with your grandmother's old friend? Did the boxes she found in her attic belong to your grandmother like you thought?"

"Yes. No. I mean, I don't want to change the subject yet."

Max rested his elbows on the table. "What can I tell you so we can properly begin this meal? At first the guys thought it was a drug lab, but it turns out Brixton got the part about alchemy right."

"*He did?*" Brixton was right about alchemists being in Portland, but not about the state of the dead body?

"It wasn't exactly like the stuff in your shop, though," Max said. "Someone was using it as a lab to practice alchemy. Can you believe in the twenty-first century there are still people who believe in that nonsense?"

My shoulders tensed, and I instinctively reached for the gold locket hanging around my neck. A waitress came to take our orders, so I was saved from saying something I'd regret. If cayenne-spiced bean burgers with a seasonal early summer salad and white wine didn't make me feel better, I didn't know what would.

"I'm glad you ordered some wine," Max said, his eyes lingering on my locket. "You still look tense. Don't worry about Brixton. He'll be all right."

"Your grandmother wouldn't have called alchemy nonsense, Max."

"Being an apothecary is different." He crossed his arms defensively. "That's about healing people. It's like the herbal remedies we both use, but with a different name."

"That's not how you talked about it before." Sometimes it seemed like Max was so close to being open to the ideas I wanted to share with him, but other times he was closed off, as if two sides of himself were fighting with each other.

"I can get fanciful when I think about my childhood. False memories from photographs." He gave me a shy smile and relaxed his arms. "I hope you like the guy in front of you more than eight-year-old Maximilian."

"Not Maxwell?"

"Nope. Now you know everything about me."

I couldn't help but smile. "I doubt that."

The waitress dropped off our glasses of wine, and we raised them in a toast. "To eight-year-old Maximilian," I said, "who saw the world as full of wonder, and who believed anything was possible. May we find him once again."

Instead of laughing, Max frowned. What had gone wrong with my date?

———————

On my walk home—alone—I replayed Max's words again and again. Someone had been practicing alchemy in the woods. That was the relevant fact. But what I couldn't stop thinking about was that Max thought my beliefs were idiotic. Of course, he didn't know they were my beliefs. Not exactly. How could I tell him, especially now? But I had more urgent things to worry about.

I still couldn't quite believe that Brixton had been right. I had to see that shed in the woods.

I climbed the stairs to my attic. The door was locked from the inside.

"Dorian?"

"*Un moment!*"

The door swung open a minute later. A gargoyle with one of his arms hanging limp at his side looked up at me. "I thought you were out on a date."

"I was. It ended. Why did you have the door locked?"

He flapped his wings defensively. "You are the one who says I must be careful."

"Tonight isn't a night to be careful," I said. "It's a night for action. I need you to show me the cabin in the woods."

While we waited for it to be late enough for Dorian to safely venture outside, I made myself a chocolate elixir in the blender, which I needed for energy to stay awake so late into the night.

Two hours later, I doubted the caffeine had been necessary. Adrenaline was more than enough to keep my eyes wide open as Dorian and I snuck across the grass in the no-man's land between two neighborhoods.

From the outside, the cabin in the overgrown section of woods looked abandoned. Though a public path cut across this narrow swath of forest, a sign nailed to the cabin's door marked it as private property. Holes and broken pieces of wood indicated the front door had once been nailed shut, but jagged pieces of wood now hung loosely around the door frame. The door itself, musty and half decayed from years of neglect, pushed open easily.

Stepping through the crime scene tape across the rickety threshold, it became obvious that the disrepair was only an outward disguise. Though the police had taken most of the objects from inside the cabin—presumably why they hadn't left an officer to guard the shack—enough remained to assure me that Max and Brixton were right. This was the workspace of practicing alchemists.

It was the scent that hit me hardest. Honey, charred salt, and ash. It smelled like Dorian's Tea of Ashes.

This wasn't simply an alchemical lab. *This was backward alchemy.*

A branch snapped in the distance.

Dorian's horns twitched. He'd heard it too.

I turned off the flashlight and felt my way to the window on the far side of the cabin. I tensed as a weak floorboard moaned under my foot, but I needed to get to that window. That was the direction from which the sound had come. Dorian shushed me, but I had no choice. I had to see what was out there. Like the door, the window had been boarded shut long ago. Unlike the door, the window hadn't recently been opened. My only view was through the uneven spaces between rotted boards.

Only a small sliver of moon hung in the sky, leaving our surroundings nearly pitch black. But it wasn't too dark for me to make out the shadow of a figure, perhaps fifty feet from the cabin. A man.

"We need to leave," I whispered. "*Now.*"

"What do you see?"

"There's someone out there."

"Let me see. You know I see better in the dark."

"Cover yourself in your cape."

Dorian didn't fight me. I heard the sound of cloth flapping as he flipped the cloak around his wings. He took my hand and remained mute. Thank heaven for small favors.

My eyes hadn't adjusted to the darkness, but Dorian could guide us. He led the way out the front door.

"*Un moment,*" he whispered.

"Don't—"

But it was too late. He'd already let go of my hand.

It couldn't have been more than a minute that I stood alone in the crisp darkness of the cabin porch in the sinister woods, willing my eyes to adjust and for Dorian to return. But it felt like an hour. Every sound made by nocturnal creatures and plants blowing under the pressure of the gentle wind set my senses on edge.

I jumped as a familiar hand took mine. My eyes had adjusted to the dim moonlight enough for me to make out Dorian's cape-shrouded form.

"A man," he whispered. "With my leg, I cannot risk getting a closer look. But you are right. A man is out there. Watching."

Dorian tugged at my hand, pulling me away from the cabin. "If we go this way, the cabin should block us from his view. As long as he cannot see in the darkness as I can, this path should be safe."

I followed Dorian's lead, creeping between the thick groupings of trees on our way out of the woods, hoping the man out there didn't have night vision goggles. At the edge of the greenbelt, we waited in silence for a few more minutes before walking to where my old truck was parked. We didn't need to speak. Both of us understood we had to be sure we hadn't been followed.

"This is bad, Dorian." I turned the ignition, cringing at the sharp sound of the engine revving. No sense in keeping quiet now. I opted for speed instead. The tires screeched as I peeled onto the street and pointed us homeward.

"It will be worse if you are given a speeding ticket."

I gripped the gear shift.

"I wish to hear 'Accidental Life,'" Dorian said.

The cassette was already in the player, so I hit the play button. Tobias Freeman's booming voice filled the car. He'd written the song for his 100th birthday, in the 1950s. After I'd nursed him back to health when I met him in my work on the Underground Railroad, Tobias had discovered the Elixir of Life. His loved ones had not. One by one, he had watched them age and die. It was a lot to grapple with, as I knew well. He'd recorded the track under the moniker The Philosopher. The soulful song by my friend immediately made me feel calmer.

"*Bon*," Dorian said with a grin.

"You asked me to play the song so I'd feel better, didn't you?"

"*Oui.* I know you wish Tobias could be here. Now he is."

Careful to drive the speed limit, I watched the nighttime greenery bounce off my headlights, then give way to houses. "What's going on, Dorian? A long-dead man was found in a backward alchemy lab. Another man, 'creepy guy,' who must have known about the dead body, was following Ivan—possibly the same person followed us back there by the cabin."

Dorian peeked out from the folds of the cape. He was sitting on the floor of the passenger side of the truck. "Do not forget the woman in Paris who wishes to expose you."

The brakes screeched as I came to a stop at a red light. Dorian bumped into the glove compartment. "How," I said, looking down at the scowling gargoyle, "could I possibly forget her?"

"You are upset," Dorian said. "Perhaps we should continue our discussion in the morning."

Feeling the effects of being awake so late at night, I had to agree with Dorian. Talk could wait for tomorrow. But I had one more thing to do before I could sleep.

I dialed the Paris bookseller's shop to check again on the book he was sending. It was early afternoon in Paris, yet there was no answer at the bookshop. As the phone continued to ring, a disturbing thought tickled my brain. Someone was following alchemists. They'd spied on Ivan and they'd broken into my house. Had they also been following me in Paris when I'd visited the bookshop? Had they done something to the bookseller?

What had become of the bookshop proprietor?

TWENTY-ONE

I DREAMT OF A fierce sea.

Dressed in a feedsack dress with scratchy fibers that bore into my skin, I watched from a rocking boat as water serpents gracefully spun their lean bodies through the water, circling each other in an underwater dance. What at first looked like a benevolent action morphed into a scene of battle. The creatures curled their bodies around one another and bit into each other's flesh. Above them, bees circled and toads fell from a dark sky.

A pelican swooped from the air and caught a toad that was about to fall on my head. She nodded at me, then flew back to her nest, where she would give the toad to her offspring. I watched her flapping wings until the bird disappeared in the clouds. These dream clouds weren't the clouds of reality. They were faces of women.

These were the faces from Heather's new paintings, with reflections in the women's eyes. One of the reflections was of a man. Was it her father who'd fled? No, I recognized this man. It was the Frenchman who owned the bookshop, Lucien Augustin. His body was bound in thick ropes, and he'd been lashed to the mast of a ship. The ship that I was on. The raven I remembered from one of Heather's paintings appeared behind him, only the bird was no reflection. The black bird flew out of the clouds and dove straight for me. The ominous feathered being would have crashed into me had it not been for a toad I had assumed dead. The amphibian jumped from the boat at the last moment and caught the bird in its mouth.

I woke up.

The cotton sheets of my bed were tangled around me like tentacles. I was drenched in salty sweat. If I'd been fanciful, I would have sworn the salt came from the sea of my dream.

Sometimes I really hated that Freud was right about our subconscious speaking to us in our dreams. I'd found him to be a terribly arrogant man, but I grudgingly admitted he was a smart one. In alchemy, serpents represent the life force that's exchanged in each transformation, pelicans represent sacrifice, and toads represent the First Matter that both begins and ends the creation of the Philosopher's Stone. My subconscious was definitely trying to work out the confusing events around me.

A sweet aroma brought me back to reality. The scent of fresh apricot tarts told me that Dorian was back from his predawn baking at Blue Sky Teas and had brought back misshapen pastries, as usual. The treats tasted as good, but customers were less likely to buy a lopsided tart, so he brought these malformed treats back to the house … if he didn't eat them first.

I made myself a cup of jasmine green tea from tea leaves Max had given me and sat down with Dorian at the dining table. Built by a craftsman I met in the south of France shortly after the turn of the twentieth century, the table had been in storage during the years I'd lived out of a trailer. It was nice to have a home again, even if I always made sure to keep the curtains drawn tightly so that Dorian could have the run of the house.

Even at the familiar table that had brought me joy from the moment it was handcrafted, with a perfect breakfast and my best friend at my side, I couldn't relax. I was plagued by the troubling idea that the bookseller had been harmed by whoever was following me and Ivan. Could the book he found be more important than either of us thought? Could *Backward Alchemists of Notre Dame* hold a real clue to finding a backward alchemist? And if so, was someone trying to stop me from getting it?

"Breakfast is unsatisfactory?" Dorian asked, his horns twitching in alarm. "I will cook fresh food. I suspected I had gone too far trusting the malformed atrocities. This scone resembles your Richard Nixon, no? It is the chin." Dorian frowned at the scone. "What would you like? Buckwheat crepes? Chickpea pancakes? Almond milk porridge?" He jumped down from his chair, falling onto the creaky hardwood floor in the process. His left ankle was now unbending, solid stone.

"These pastries taste perfect, Dorian." I helped him back into his chair and held my tongue about his stone lower leg. "I simply didn't sleep well."

"If you are certain."

"I am." I took a huge bite of a heavenly apricot tart to prove my point.

"*Bon.* Then we can get to work. My little grey cells have been mulling over this most unusual problem: not one but *two* old alchemy murders. Both of which are distracting you from helping me and my brother." He tapped his claws on the wooden tabletop. "When we have eliminated the impossible, the only thing that remains, however improbable, is the truth to which I will apply my little grey cells."

"I'm pretty sure you're mixing your fictional detectives."

"I am being most serious, Zoe. Murders across time and location, yet they have one thing in common: *you.*"

"The connection," I said emphatically, "is alchemy."

Dorian shook his head even more emphatically. "This week has stirred up two alchemical murders relating to you. You cannot think this is a coincidence."

"Jasper was killed in France seventy-five years ago. The unknown man in the cabin was killed in Oregon around a decade ago. I was careless in Paris and Brixton was snooping in Portland because we want to get alchemical answers to help you. In that sense, you're right: they're connected. But only because of dangers we both stepped into."

"You miss the logical next step, *mon amie*. You being recognized in Paris could have set forces in motion—"

"I can't think straight. Everything seems connected right now. Even Heather's paintings remind me of alchemy."

"*Oui.* She has a vivid imagination. I can see why the themes of transformation remind you of alchemy."

"You've seen the paintings?"

"When I arrive in the café's kitchen at three a.m., before removing my cape I look around to make sure there is nobody there."

"Now you think Heather is an alchemist? *Heather?* The woman who dropped out of high school at sixteen, who can't be bothered to wear shoes for half the year, who's more interested in weaving daisy chains in her hair and finding the perfect shade of green paint than making sure where her son is?"

"I agree, it does not make sense that all of Portland is overflowing with alchemists. I have explored enough to know that is not the case. There is something else at play, Zoe. *You.* You must investigate the unknown dead man to find out his connection to you—"

"The police are already doing that."

Dorian flapped his wings at his side. "But there is a connection to the man who has been spying on Ivan!"

"The only thing I have to investigate is the alchemy that will save you. I'm so close to understanding what's going on, Dorian. So close to saving you." I swallowed hard, willing my eyes not to fill with tears. "As soon as that book from Paris arrives, I'll be able to find a backward alchemist and have the last piece of the puzzle."

"And in the meantime?"

"The book will be arriving soon. Maybe even later today." If someone hadn't gotten to Lucien first.

"*Alors*, the meantime? We are well equipped to solve these past mysteries, you and I."

"I know you're careful, but you can't move your left arm. And your foot . . ." I let the words trail off as I looked at his poor foot. His stone ankle was frozen at an awkward angle. Was it painful?

Instead of protesting, as I suspected he would, Dorian's wings folded as he nodded sadly. "I nearly fell from the roof the other day. No, no. Do not worry. I have since compensated and know how to hold on with one hand and foot. But you are right that I cannot investigate as I once could. Yet I have other skills to assist you. In addition to reading the entire Christie canon, I read Tey's *Daughter of Time*. Twice."

I crossed my arms and stared down at the gargoyle. "Then you should stay in the attic instead of following phantoms. If memory serves, the hero in that novel about solving a centuries-old mystery didn't leave his hospital bed the entire time."

Dorian's snout twitched. "Well played, Alchemist. Well played."

"If you want to play armchair detective, why don't you help me look through online archives of newspaper accounts from 1942 Paris?" I didn't think learning more about Jasper Dubois's death would help, but it couldn't hurt, and it was a safe line of investigation for Dorian. I handed him my laptop.

"I have already done this."

"You have?"

"You thought I would not use my little grey cells to help you?" His shoulders and wings fell. "I searched for clues for many hours, while you slept. Alas, I have not discovered any new facts, only theories. This is why I have not spoken of my findings. As for my brother—"

"The other gargoyle," I corrected.

Dorian narrowed his eyes.

"I should run to the market," I continued. "There's a farmer's market today."

"You are a *très intelligent* woman, Zoe. You knew the one thing you could say that would not cause me to object to ending this conversation."

————

Though it was early summer, an unexpected rainstorm had blown in that morning, though I probably shouldn't have called it "unexpected" since this was Portland. I grabbed my silver rain coat and walked to a local farmer's market. I found myself looking over my shoulder the entire way. Could Dorian be right that the two murders were connected to me? It wasn't possible. Jasper's death might have been connected to me, but I wasn't in Portland a decade ago.

I was so distracted I barely noticed the early-summer fruits and vegetables. I was vaguely aware of a pyramid-shaped stack of apricots, but didn't stop wandering until I reached a stall that sent me back to another century.

The farmer had freekeh, a preparation of durum wheat in which the young green stalks are set afire to stop the process of the wheat aging and to give the grain a smoky flavor. It would be a perfect complement to the green onions from my garden. And I knew Dorian would love it. For a brief time he'd missed the smoky flavor of cured meats, but he'd been delighted to discover a whole other world of smoky spices and grains.

The more I got to know Portland, the more I loved my new home. A stab of frustration overcame me. I was *so close* to having a happy life here. If only I could solve the riddle of Dorian's alchemy book to save him and rid myself of the murderous mysteries that had followed me, I knew that life was within reach.

I was almost hopeful on my walk home. I let myself appreciate the moment, taking in the scents of the smoky freekeh and sweet summer peas in the bag over my shoulder, and the roses and pine from the nature that surrounded me.

I quickened my pace as I approached the house. A package was sticking out of the mailbox. I'd let my imagination run wild in thinking something bad had happened to the bookseller. I tore into the package.

It wasn't the book from Paris.

The book-shaped package contained a bound stack of magazines. I flipped through the pages. All back issues of a vegan magazine Dorian had recently discovered.

It was probably still true that I was jumping to conclusions about the bookseller. An unsettling thought about Lucien crossed my mind: The French police could have tracked me down to the bookshop. If they told the bookseller about Jasper's murder in 1942, Lucien might have decided that he didn't want to help a criminal.

Or worse. If the authorities had traced my movements in Paris, could they have traced me back to my house in Portland?

Dorian had an escape-hatch in the roof of the house; if anyone entered the house with a search warrant, he could make an easy escape. What did it say about my life that I'd already had to think about such matters multiple times this year?

Being traced here didn't seem especially likely, though. The supposed granddaughter of a possible criminal who was most likely long dead wouldn't merit the French authorities sending their American counterparts to follow up with me. But Madame Leblanc cared enough. I tensed as I remembered her high-end clothing. She could very well have the resources to hire a private investigator to look into anything related to alchemy in Portland.

I couldn't sit at home doing nothing, so I walked to Blue Sky Teas. It was early afternoon, but as I drew near I saw that the teashop was dark and the sign set to CLOSED. A little rain never stopped a Portlander. I peeked in the windows but saw nothing amiss.

Is EVERYTHING ALL RIGHT? I texted Brixton.

WHERE ARE YOU? he texted back.

TEASHOP.

MEET ME AT THE MORGUE.

The morgue? This couldn't be good.

TWENTY-TWO

"Mom is supposed to identify the body," Brixton said. "They think it might be her dad."

"Oh God, Brix. I'm so sorry." In the sterile hallway outside the morgue, the astringent scent in the air was stifling. It didn't help that none of this made any sense. *Brixton's grandfather?* Brixton and his mom didn't have anything to do with alchemy.

"Why do they think this man—"

"Unsolved missing persons cases from that time. Mom's dad was one of them. Her mom filed a report after he disappeared."

"I didn't realize. I thought he . . . " What was a nice way to say his grandfather fled instead of sticking around to support his young daughter and grandson?

Brixton shrugged. "Yeah, Mom thought he ran out on the family. You don't have to look so uncomfortable, Zoe. I never knew him." He shrugged again, trying to look aloof but fooling nobody. "Looks like he might have been killed right here in Portland."

And Brixton was the one who found the body.

"All these years we hated him," Brixton whispered.

Abel tried to give him a hug, but the kid shrugged him off, opting instead to shove his hands into the pockets of his hoodie. Abel tapped his foot nervously. Brixton fidgeted and began to bite his fingernails.

Abel straightened and put his hands on Brixton's shoulders. I followed his gaze. Heather was walking down the hallway toward us. Her blonde braids were a mess, her face set in a stoic mask unlike any expression I'd seen on her before.

Heather could be an immature flake, but she was always full of vitality and hope. Until now. This was the first time I'd seen her with a cloud over her face. Even when Brixton had been in trouble in the past, she met the challenge with energy and love. The woman in front of me wasn't the same person. Her face was cold. Defeated. When she reached us, I could see her arms were shaking.

"Was it him?" Abel whispered.

For a fraction of a second, I could have sworn she stared at him as if he was a stranger who had no business talking to her. When she recovered, her reaction wasn't much better. "How could I tell? Tell me, Abel, how am I supposed to know what that *thing* was?"

I cringed. The body had been decomposing for more than a decade.

Abel's muscles tensed. "They showed him to you, even though he was beyond recognition?"

"They thought I might recognize identifying markings."

I would have expected her to shudder or break down. Instead she was emotionally distant.

"Let's get you home," Abel said.

"The teashop," she said. "I have to open Blue's teashop."

"It's okay for it to be closed for a day."

"But there's no need. I don't know who that poor man is." She paused, and I saw the first hint of emotion cross her face. "He didn't have any teeth—they'd all been removed." She shuddered. "Dental records won't work, so they might have to do a DNA test to identify him. They're sure to get an answer. A real answer. Oh, God, Abel. What am I going to do if it's him? All this time, I thought he hated me. But what if, what if he went off and did something dumb, trying to get money for me? What if that's why he never came home? He might have sacrificed himself for us, and I never knew it."

I left the morgue understanding far less than I'd known going in.

Had Brixton and the police been wrong about the old cabin in the woods being an alchemy lab? The person Brixton had seen leaving the shack had been spying on Ivan, and possibly on me, but that man wasn't necessarily here in Portland years ago when the murder took place.

Did we even know it was murder, and not just a recluse who'd died of natural causes? That would be a less gruesome answer for why he didn't have any teeth. Why hadn't anyone found the body before? Had it been hidden until now? Had the man spying on Ivan moved the body?

The more I thought about my unanswered questions, the more my theories fell apart. Was I being narrow-minded to think these deaths were connected to me? Or, at the very least, to alchemy? Guilt at being so self-absorbed replaced my confusion. Heather's dad, Brixton's grandfather, might have been cruelly taken away from his family. Was it him in the morgue? Did he die with regrets, or was he happy to have died trying to provide for his family?

I drove home past the combination of parks and forests, bridges stretching across the river and urban neighborhoods, wondering what secrets were hiding beyond what I could see. The brief summer storm had felled an old tree that had crumpled a small car, and a detour rerouted me onto a different street. If I were to be killed by a falling tree branch, would I die with regrets? I was doing everything I could to help those I cared about. But what about my own life? I was pushing Max away for stupid reasons.

When I got back to my house, a bouquet of amaryllis was waiting for me on the porch in a simple hourglass vase. The red flowers streaked with white were the perfect choice, for the scent was beautiful but subtle. It struck the right balance: heartfelt but not too pushy.

The card read *Peace Offering. I'm cooking a veg curry for an early dinner tonight. There's plenty.* The card wasn't signed, but it was Max's handwriting.

I brought the flowers inside and placed them in the center of my beloved dining table, then picked out a bottle of wine to bring to Max's house. I would have asked Dorian's opinion, because he was the one who created our wine list, but he wasn't home that I could see. Was he cooking at his new employer Julian Lake's house? I couldn't help worrying that he would struggle with his arm and foot while away from home.

I was used to living on my own, so the stillness of an empty house didn't usually bother me. But with the unexplained deaths surrounding us, being in the house alone filled me with apprehension. I walked through my basement alchemy lab and watered my plants, then methodically checked the locks on all of the windows and doors. My locksmith friend had come over as soon as I'd called him. The house was secure. I checked again. And maybe one last time. Third time's a charm, right?

I picked up the bottle of organic Zinfandel and walked to Max's house.

Max opened the door with his black hair spikier than usual, wearing a once-white apron over his black clothes. He grinned sheepishly as he wiped his hands on a clean corner of the apron and accepted the bottle of wine.

I knew a fair amount about wine from when I lived in France, but it was Dorian who forced me to get caught up to the twenty-first century. He didn't believe in using cooking wine or table wine. According to the little chef, the wine used in cooking had to be every bit as good as a wine you'd order to drink. Since Dorian couldn't come to the local markets with me, I photographed the wine shelves and he gave me lessons on which ones to buy for different dishes. I wasn't completely convinced it mattered as much as he thought it did, but there was something to the idea of pairing.

"This wine goes well with spicy food," I said. "From the smell of sizzling cumin seeds and cayenne, I think I chose wisely."

Max sniffed the air and bolted for the kitchen. His modern kitchen was sparsely decorated but simultaneously full of character. Teacups and a kettle from his grandmother gave the room an elegant simplicity that embodied Max. A philosophically decorated room.

"I didn't know I was getting in over my head when I started this curry," he said as he stirred the pot with a bamboo spoon. "It always looked so easy when I watched it being prepared."

"Thanks for the flowers, Max. And for inviting me over."

"When I heard about Heather's dad, it made me realize how stupid our fight was. I mean, it wasn't even a *fight* fight. But I didn't like it."

"I don't even know what we were fighting about anymore." I felt for my locket. My security blanket.

His eyes dropped from my eyes to my neck, where I held my gold locket between my fingertips. "You're holding me at arm's length, as usual. Your actions speak louder than words. I know you're not completely over your ex."

I stopped fiddling with the locket. *That's* what this was about? Jealousy?

"It's supposed to be a difficult thing to work through," Max continued. "We each have our baggage. Plus I'm too old for you."

"What are you saying?" Had I misinterpreted the flowers, and this whole invitation? "Is this a break-up dinner?"

"I said it's *supposed to be* difficult." He set the wooden spoon on the counter and took my hands in his. "But it's not. When I'm with you, the hours pass like minutes. I like being with you. So much. Can we forget about all that other stuff? And just be here in the present?"

Ever since I'd met Max, that's what I'd been hoping for. I was about to verbalize my answer, but as soon as I smiled, Max drew me into a kiss spicier than the curry cooking next to us.

The coconut milk curry and basmati rice pilaf ended up slightly burned, but neither of us cared. The hours passed without me realizing where the time had gone or feeling tired.

When I helped Max clean up the kitchen after dinner, I noticed the recipe. In a wrought iron cookbook holder sat a three-ring binder of recipes. Facing forward was a hand-written notecard behind a plastic sleeve. The handwriting wasn't Max's. Was it his grandmother's? I set down the dish rag in my hand and flipped through the binder. More than half of the recipes were for Indian foods. This binder had belonged to Max's dead wife, Chadna.

I felt my cheeks burn with a small pang of jealousy. I willed myself to push away the baseless feeling. Why was I being so silly? I'd been in love before, too, and it didn't change my feelings for Max.

I set the binder down as Max placed the last dishes into the cabinets.

"That was perfect," I said.

"When did you learn how to lie?"

"I mean it. You make it so easy to relax and enjoy life, even if I only get a few hours' break from it. Thank you for the perfect evening. But I should go. I've got an early day."

"I've gotta be up early too."

I hoped I didn't show my disappointment. Part of me had hoped Max would try to convince me to stay. A big part of me.

"But the thing is," Max continued, "I don't seem to care."

I didn't either.

———————

I crawled out of Max's bed at 4 a.m. I'd remembered to set my phone alarm for the time everyone thought I got up to bake for Blue Sky Teas. I glanced back at Max, who was sound asleep. I sent Dorian an email that he shouldn't worry if he didn't see me when he came home, then crawled back into bed.

My locket felt cool on my chest. I realized I hadn't thought of it all night. That hadn't happened in … I couldn't remember how long. I fell back asleep with a contented smile on my face.

I woke up next as the sun rose shortly after 5:30. I rolled over onto my stomach, enjoying the comfortable warmth of Max's bed. Thin rays of sunlight pushed their way through breaks in the curtains. The top of Max's head poked out from the duvet. He was always so put-together that I smiled at the sight of his sleek black hair askew on his forehead.

I was so contented that I must have dozed off again, because I awoke to the sensation of kisses on my bare shoulder.

"I'm glad you came back after baking," Max said.

"I wanted to be here with you when you woke up."

"I'm glad." He propped himself up on one elbow and ran his hand through my hair. "I always assumed you dyed your hair. I mean, the bright white suits you. It adds to your beauty. But … " He ran his finger down my arm. "*What happened*, Zoe? Every hair on your body is white."

"Life," I said. Honesty is the best policy.

"You told me about the stuff you went through losing your family so young, and I've heard of people getting streaks of white hair from stressful encounters. But *all* of your hair?"

"We all experience life differently, Max." I put a finger to his lips as he tried to speak. "I'm glad I'm experiencing mine here with you. What's up with the skeleton at the end of the hallway?"

"You're changing the subject."

"It's a fair question, considering I spent the night with a detective who might moonlight as a homicidal maniac."

Max laughed and covered his face with a pillow. "I'm not very good at disposing of bodies, though, am I?" he mumbled.

I pulled the pillow from his handsome head. "Maybe you're just a body snatcher."

He grinned and grabbed me. "You caught me. I'm a body snatcher." He ran his hands over my hips. "You're not too tired after getting up in the middle of the night?"

I shook my head. "I'm a morning person."

"Good."

An hour later, I stepped out of the bathroom, drying my hair with a towel, and found Max putting on his shoes.

"I really do have to get to the office to finish the paperwork on this case," Max said. "Want to grab a cup of tea at Blue's before I head on to work?"

Max and I both lived in the Hawthorne neighborhood within walking distance to Blue Sky Teas. The storm from the previous day had passed, and we walked to the teashop under a bright blue sky.

Heather stood behind the counter and waved at me as we walked through the welcoming door of the teashop.

"Here she is," Heather said to a man who stood at the counter.

He turned around. My balance gave way. It felt as if the world was spinning out of control. Max steadied me. My heart raced and my limbs went numb. I grasped the locket hanging around my neck, but I could barely feel it between my fingers.

Though I hadn't seen him in nearly a hundred years, I knew the man. Or at least, I had known my beloved a century ago. Before he died.

Ambrose.

TWENTY-THREE

Noisy voices swirled around me. I blinked and saw blue sky and clouds above me. No, that wasn't right. It wasn't real sky. A dream? No, I was awake. I was looking up at the painted ceiling of Blue Sky Teas. I was lying on my back. A group of people stared at me from above. I struggled to focus on the blurry faces.

"She's coming to," Heather said. "You guys, give her some room."

Max and another man helped me up. A familiar man I'd known a century ago.

"Hello, Zoe," he said in an English accent. "So sorry to have startled you."

Could it really be Ambrose? I clutched my locket as my eyes focused on the handsome face in front of mine. No. This wasn't Ambrose.

"Percy?"

It was Ambrose's *son*.

The Old English accent was more refined than I remembered, as was the man. Gone was the plump insolent man suffering from gout, replaced by a younger, fitter man with a humbler tone of voice.

"It's been a long time," he said.

That was an understatement. Percy had died in 1935.

I closed my eyes. This wasn't real. I was hallucinating. I must have fainted and hit my head after seeing a man who reminded me of the great love of my life. Percy had the same black hair, distinctive nose, and striking eyes as his father. The similarity hadn't been as strong when I'd known them, because Percy's fondness for beer and overindulgence in rich foods had given him a pudgy layer and a ruddy tinge.

Max put his arm around me and pressed a glass of water to my lips. "Do you want me to take you to a doctor? Work can wait."

"I'm all right. I usually eat first thing. Must be low blood sugar."

"Help her to a chair," Heather suggested.

Max and Percy lifted me to a chair. Much more forcefully than was necessary, I thought. I looked sharply at them both as they lifted me off my feet. Were they each trying to prove they were stronger than the other? Percy's flab had been replaced by lean muscle. He wore a leather jacket over a white dress shirt and trendy fitted jeans.

"Let me get you one of your carrot cake muffins," Heather said. "Lot of natural sugars."

I nodded. Even though I was pretty sure it was shock that had caused me to faint, one of Dorian's treats couldn't hurt.

"Max Liu," Max said to Percy, extending his hand.

"Percival Smythe."

I raised an eyebrow involuntarily and hoped Max didn't catch the gesture. I wondered how long Percy had been using that surname. Though the last name he gave was false, he was very real. Rage and regret swirled inside me, feeding each other. Ambrose and I had been told Percy was dead, and Ambrose had bitterly mourned the loss of his son. Our lives would have been more different than I could fathom had we believed otherwise. Ambrose might still be alive today.

Percy had never had the patience and demeanor to become an alchemist. It had been painful for him that both I and his father had found the Elixir of Life while he continued to age, so he'd moved far away from us. Ambrose and I hadn't seen Percy's body, but we had no reason to doubt the news of his death. If only we'd known it had been a lie, Ambrose would never have killed himself.

"So you're an old friend of Zoe's?" Max asked, pulling up a chair protectively close to me.

"Percy is Ambrose's son," I said.

"Ambrose?" Max said. He knew I'd traveled across the US in my Airstream trailer after the man I was involved with died. Max didn't know those travels had stretched over decades rather than just a few years. I could see the unspoken question on his lips. Percy looked like he was in his mid-twenties, the same age I claimed—far too old to be the son of a man I'd been involved with.

"I was hoping we could get caught up," Percy said.

Heather saved me from answering by setting a carrot cake muffin in front of me. "I've gotta get back to the counter, but give me a holler if you need anything else."

I didn't feel hungry, but I forced myself to take a bite. Pecans and cranberries, salt and dates, a sweet and savory blend to awaken my senses while feeding my lightheaded body. Dorian continued to outdo himself.

"You want me to leave so you can get caught up with him?" Max asked. His voice was sharp, and I recognized the emotion. Jealousy. It was a stronger version of the same feeling I'd experienced the previous night when I realized the recipe I'd just enjoyed had come from Max's dead wife. I couldn't worry about Max's jealousy now. My unfinished past trumped my love life.

Percy lowered his eyelids, giving me a hint of the petulant man I remembered.

I had never liked Percy, but I had to talk to him in private, without Max looking on.

"Go file your paperwork," I said to Max. "I'm all right. I'll stay here and catch up with Percy."

His lips set in a frown, Max nodded and left.

"I really am sorry about all this," Percy said. "I—"

"You *died*," I whispered sharply.

"Rumors of my death were greatly exaggerated."

"Very funny. While you were *not dead,* I see you've had more time to become well read. I can't remember you opening the pages of a single book when you stayed with me and Ambrose."

Percy was already a young adult when I met Ambrose. His mother had died in childbirth, and Ambrose had done the best he could. It was far better than most men had been able to do at the time, even the ones who'd been able to maintain custody of their children. But Ambrose had spoiled the boy.

Percy sighed. "I deserve that. But I'm a different man than when you knew me, Zoe. I've turned my life around."

"Where have you been all these years? You discovered the Elixir but didn't tell us? And now, all of a sudden, you decided it was time for a reunion? This isn't the best time—"

"That's not why I came. I'm here because I need to warn you. A dangerous alchemist followed you here to Portland. I believe you met him at a bookshop in Paris."

The plain man from the bookshop? "Lucien? He's an alchemist?"

Percy nodded. "Not just an alchemist. A backward alchemist."

TWENTY-FOUR

I'D FOUND A BACKWARD alchemist and hadn't even known it.

Worse yet, the backward alchemist had turned the tables. While I'd been blindly seeking someone like Lucien, he knew exactly who I was. And he'd followed me to Portland. But why? He'd taken the time to lead me on with talk of the obscure book that could have helped me locate backward alchemists, but it now seemed he never meant to send the book at all.

"Why?" I croaked. "Why is he here?"

Percy seemed surprised by my expression of horror. Had he expected me to be surprised or disbelieving instead?

"I take it you know what that means, to be a backward alchemist," he said, his gaze unwavering. "I didn't figure you for the type to know about that kind of thing."

"What kind of thing?"

"Not untrue alchemy."

Not Untrue Alchemy. The translated name of Dorian's book.

"That's what they call it these days, you know," Percy continued. "'Backward alchemy' is so passé."

"What they practice isn't true alchemy," I murmured mostly to myself. "But it's not completely false either. So they practice not untrue alchemy." He was talking about a *phrase*, I realized, not the name of Dorian's book itself.

Percy nodded. "Lucien Augustin is a very dangerous man."

"Percy, what the devil is going on? A backward alchemist is following me—and you! You let us think you were dead."

"I didn't have a choice—" He started to raise his voice but glanced around the café and broke off. "I know you've got no reason to trust me," he continued in an earnest whisper, "but I want to help you."

"Why? You never made a secret of the fact you despised me."

"Half a century can do a lot for one's maturity. It took me awhile, Zoe, but I've grown up. I may look nearly as young as the day you last saw me, but I've had a lot of time to think. You and I may not have always gotten along—"

"An understatement."

"—but you're the only family I've got."

I, too, had lost my entire family long ago. Aside from my beloved brother Thomas, I hadn't been close with my immediate family. They didn't question the ways of Salem Village and were quick to judge when I was accused of witchcraft simply because I had an "unnaturally good" way with plants. My connection to plants and aptitude for plant alchemy weren't witchcraft. My only "crimes" were helping the vegetables and grains on my family's plot of land grow more robustly than our neighbors.

My brother and I fled the village instead of waiting for me to be condemned to death as a witch, but Thomas died only a few years later. It wasn't until I met Ambrose that I felt like I had a family again.

I looked straight into Percy's eyes. "Ambrose would want me to hear you out," I said. "His love of you was so great." My voice broke. Of all the unexpected things life had thrown my way, I never thought I'd see *Percy* again. And looking so much like his father.

"Once, that didn't mean as much to me as it should have," Percy said. "I know I took Father for granted. And you too. Like I said, I've grown up." He gave me an embarrassed smile before his eyes darted around the teashop again. "Look, is there somewhere we can talk in private? I'll tell you everything, but I'm worried about Lucien. I don't know where he is, and I don't want him to find me here in Portland."

"Stay here. I'll be right back."

"But—"

"Stay inside and I'll be right back."

I rushed outside to call Dorian. My hands shook as I dialed, but I relaxed slightly after getting a good look at the people on the sidewalk near Blue Sky Teas. They were all far too hip to be Lucien, even in disguise.

So Lucien had followed me to Portland. That explained why he hadn't answered the phone at the bookshop. It also meant there was probably no book that would give me the answers to save Dorian. Well, maybe there *was* a book that held answers about people who'd died at the hands of backward alchemists practicing at Notre Dame, but not one that he'd share with me. But why had Lucien followed me here?

I thought that if I could find a backward alchemist he could answer my questions, but I hadn't thought through the reality of the situation. Lucien must have known what I was to follow me to Portland, but he didn't reveal himself to me. He wasn't going to let go of his secrets easily. My grand plan was in shambles.

After completing our special sequence of coded rings, Dorian picked up the phone.

"I'm bringing someone over to the house who shouldn't see you," I said. "Get whatever you need to stay in the attic for a couple of hours."

"Max is moving in?" an indignant gargoyle replied.

"What? No. Why would you say that?"

"He is why you did not come home last night, was it not? Yet you do not sound happy, like people in the movies after they have—"

"Max has nothing to do with what's going on this morning. Ambrose's son Percy is here."

A pause on the other end of the line. "I thought he died many years ago."

"I thought so too. I need to talk to him in private, so I'm bringing him over to the house."

"You can trust him?"

I hesitated before answering. "Not completely. That's why I want you—and *Non Degenera Alchemia*—out of sight."

"Why is there such fear in your voice?"

"I'll explain everything as soon as I understand it myself."

"No matter. I will simply listen through the pipes."

"Fine. Wait, *what*?"

"From the attic, there is a way to access the audio qualities of the plumbing in the house."

"You're telling me you've been able to listen in on downstairs conversations all this time?"

"I only recently discovered it, during the party. And you have been away—"

"What party?"

Dorian cleared his throat. "I misspoke. My English, it is not so good."

"Your English is perfect, Dorian. What party?"

Dorian sighed. "Brixton and his friends wanted to have an end-of-the-school-year party. They were supposed to have it at Ethan's home, while the boy's parents were out of town, but his parents came home unexpectedly. Brixton asked me if they could have the party at your house. He already had a key..."

"Do you realize all the dangerous elements in my alchemy lab—" Was that the reason the items in my basement alchemy lab had been askew when I arrived home? Oh God, if *kids* had gotten in there...

Dorian clicked his tongue. "You think I did not consider this? The basement and the attic were securely locked. The children were only allowed on the first floor. I listened through the pipes to make sure they did not get into trouble."

"How could you—"

"If I had not allowed them use of the house, they would have gone somewhere else—perhaps somewhere more dangerous, like those Shanghai Tunnels they used to sneak into. But... *qu'est-ce que* a 'jello shot' I heard them speak of while giggling? When I cleaned up the last mess that Brixton made, I did not see a dessert mold."

I groaned, but I had more important things to worry about than unchaperoned fourteen- and fifteen-year-olds getting drunk off jello shots. Even though he could be infuriating, Dorian would take care of Brixton and his friends. A trustworthy gargoyle chaperone was better than no adult oversight in the dangerous tunnels under the city.

"Percy and I will be there in a few minutes," I said.

In front of Blue Sky Teas, I looked through the large windows to where Percy sat under the weeping fig tree, with his hands wrapped gently around a mug of tea. My throat tightened. He looked so much like his father.

Were my feelings for Ambrose getting in the way of a rational decision? Was I fooling myself that I could trust a word Percy spoke?

TWENTY-FIVE

"The twenty-first century suits you well," Percy said, resting his elbows on my dining table and tapping his manicured fingertips together. Like his diction, the way he carried himself was more refined than the slovenly man I'd known. "Vegan restaurants are everywhere in this strange new century, you can buy unusual herbs and minerals without being hunted as a witch, and your white hair looks good in this short, modern hairstyle."

"You look good too, Percy. For a dead man."

"I'm sure you've guessed that I found the Elixir."

"Mmm. What I can't guess is how you found *me*."

"This is where things get tricky." Percy pushed the chair back from the table and began to fidget. He tapped his breast pocket, and for a moment seemed surprised to find it empty.

"Recently gave up a smoking habit?"

"Something like that."

"Nobody followed us back to the house. You don't have to be so nervous."

"If you knew what I know, you'd be nervous too."

"You're stalling, Percy. Why don't you tell me what it is you know?"

"You have to hear me out—the whole story—before you pass judgment. Will you do that for me?"

I didn't answer for a moment. What was his game?

Percy jerked backward as my phone beeped, nearly toppling the chair. What was he so frightened of?

The phone was set to only make a noise if one of a few people contacted me. I reached for the phone while keeping one eye on Percy. The phone notification was an email from Dorian. I expected he was in the attic along with my laptop, listening to us through the pipes.

Hear Percy out, Dorian's message said.

"I owe it to Ambrose to give you the benefit of the doubt," I said.

Percy's lip quivered, giving his face the humanity of his father. "I never meant for any of this to happen. I didn't know what I was getting myself into. When I found Lucien, he told me so many wondrous things about not untrue alchemy. Things you and Father never told me."

"Oh, God, Percy." The skin on my cheeks prickled, my mouth went dry, and I felt like I was looking through a tunnel. "What have you done? You found the Elixir through backward alchemy?"

I should have realized it as soon as I saw him. Both because he didn't have the temperament for true alchemy and also because he was *younger* than he was the last time I'd seen him. He hadn't simply stopped aging; he'd reversed the clock. I hadn't seen it at once because of my feelings for Ambrose. I hadn't wanted to believe Percy capable of such evil; I was already subconsciously giving Percy the benefit of the doubt. Ambrose and I had tried to teach alchemy to Percy and failed. But because Ambrose always held out hope, I did too.

"You said you'd hear me out," Percy said, a flash of the petulance surfacing. There was the young man I remembered. "I told you it wasn't an easy story to tell. Please, Zoe. Please let me tell you. Maybe then you'll understand."

I bit my lip and nodded. This was what I'd wanted: a backward alchemist who could explain to me how it worked. What was he going to tell me? Would it be possible to save Dorian's life?

But now that I had a backward alchemist right in front of me, I was frightened of what he might say.

"Go ahead," I said through trembling lips. "I'm listening."

"I know now," Percy said, "that there was a reason you didn't speak of not untrue alchemy. But I couldn't see it then, could I? I never had the same sense of discipline as you and my father. Back then, I blamed Father for spoiling me. Lucien told me I could be more. And that I could achieve it without the years of effort that might not ever pay off. He was so charismatic in how he talked about it—"

"Lucien? Are we talking about the same man? The bookseller at *Bossu Livres*?"

"He might not be charismatic now, but that's only because he's been alive so long that he's begun to lose his humanity. He was different back then."

It was one of the dangers of any type of alchemy. The longer you lived, the easier it was to disassociate from normal people, to begin thinking you were something more. I wondered if that was one of the reasons I hadn't searched as hard as I could have for Nicholas Flamel. He'd been alive since the fourteenth century. If I found him and Pernelle again, I wasn't sure I'd like what I found.

But something wasn't quite right about Percy's analysis of Lucien's change. If an alchemist lost a firm grip on human emotions, it wouldn't have made him less charismatic. Could it be that Lucien wasn't the man I'd met?

"I was young and foolish," Percy continued. "He told me my sacrifice would be cutting ties with the people I knew. Lucien was the one who arranged for the plot in the cemetery and a telegram with news of my death. I didn't want to do it, but he insisted. That's how we've lived without being found out."

"How many of you are there?"

"Not many. Around a dozen at the time of my transformation, but only three of us left that I know of. It seems like a lonely existence, I know. But I believed the stories Lucien told me." He broke off and shook his head.

"How does it work?" I asked. "How do you get a life force back?" This was the moment I'd been waiting for. The last pieces of the puzzle.

"There was a book, and we followed the formulas in the illustrations."

My heart raced. "What's the code?"

Percy blinked at me. "There's no code."

"There's always a code, Percy. We're alchemists."

He shook his head and smiled. "The whole point of backward alchemy is *shortcuts*, Zoe. The founders were lazy, lazy men. Lucien and Olav."

"Who's Olav?"

"A Viking. Exceptionally strong, but very stupid. Like the Vikings were."

I reminded myself this wasn't the time to combat Percy's stereotypes.

"The two of them were complementary," Percy continued. "With Lucien's brains and Olav's brawn, they bullied alchemists into sharing the codes of true alchemy, then used the Death Rotation to cut through the clutter and skip straight to the Elixir."

"But if there's no code in backward alchemy, then what's the secret?"

Percy swallowed hard. He sat back down at the table and reached for his water. After drinking it in one gulp, he slammed the glass down and met my gaze. "Are you going to make me say it? You're a smart woman. You already know, don't you?"

"Sacrifices," I said without realizing I was speaking out loud. "You're talking about the necessary sacrifices. It was *people* you sacrificed, wasn't it?"

Percy nodded gravely.

I'd suspected as much, but I hadn't let myself believe it because I was terrified about what that would mean for Dorian. I'd been able to keep him relatively healthy through *plant* sacrifices that also drained my own energy, but that wasn't enough. Even with the knowledge a backward alchemist could give me, I would still have to go through with a sacrifice.

It was an impossible situation. I could never purposefully take a life. There was no way I could convince myself it was right to sacrifice a life, even if it was to save another.

My phone buzzed. I scooped it into my hand so Percy wouldn't see Dorian's message.

No sacrifice, Dorian's email read. *If it is my fate to live trapped in unmoving stone, so be it.*

I swallowed a sob as I set the phone facedown on the table. Even if Dorian was ready to accept his fate, I wasn't.

TWENTY-SIX

"L<small>UCIEN DIDN'T TELL ME</small> about the sacrifices." Percy's chest rose and fell. He wiped sweat from his forehead with a handkerchief. "Not at first. It wasn't my fault. I was already in too deep when I found out. He started me off performing processes that weren't so different from the alchemy you and Father practiced—except that these processes involve counterclockwise Death Rotations shown in a book, skipping the long, boring steps. So it's not necessary to use a long-burning athanor furnace to cook the vessel that becomes the Philosopher's Stone. Only fire is needed, just like the book illustrations showed. The result is an ash-like substance."

"The Tea of Ashes," I whispered.

"What did you say?"

"Nothing. I'm thinking aloud. Go on."

"The result is Alchemical Ashes." Percy cleared his throat. "Could I get some more water?"

I filled Percy's glass with more water from the kitchen. It gave me a moment to think. Now I knew the real term the backward alchemists used: Alchemical Ashes. But it was the same substance as in the tea I'd been making Dorian: ashes. I'd followed the coded instructions successfully. I *wasn't* missing anything. Only the sacrifice.

"And the sacrifice?" I said as I handed the glass to Percy. I remained standing over him as he accepted the water with shaking hands.

"It's the sacrifice who stirs the transformation that results in Alchemical Ashes." Percy lowered his voice and his gaze. When he continued, he whispered his words to the table. "That's how the energy gets transferred: through an apprentice who gives his life."

"An apprentice 'gives his life.' As in gives *up* his life?"

"Or *her* life, I guess I'm supposed to say, now that it's the twenty-first century." Percy forced a laugh as he again wiped sweat from his forehead. "But as far as I know, it's only been men."

And I thought *my* alchemy apprenticeship with Nicolas Flamel had been difficult. Staying awake through the night to watch the fire burning steadily in the athanor furnace was nothing compared to an apprenticeship that ends with losing your life. "Apprentices *willingly* sign up for this?"

"Well, the thing is … "

"They don't know what they're signing up for, do they?"

"I didn't either," was Percy's indignant reply.

"You killed someone to be here today."

Percy wouldn't look up at me. "*Not* directly."

"That's splitting hairs, Percy."

"It's not, you know." His gaze snapped to mine. "I *couldn't have* killed anyone directly. The boy signed up for it himself."

"Have you ever taken responsibility for anything in your life, Percy?"

"I didn't mean to, Zoe! Please forgive me. I've never forgiven myself, but if you could forgive a child's mistake—"

"You were far from a child."

"When nobody ever treated me like an adult, how was I supposed to grow up?"

I tried to steady my breathing. "I don't want to fight with you, Percy. I want to know why you came to me. I want to know what Lucien is doing here."

"I'm getting there. I told you, you need the whole story if you're going to understand." He nervously tapped his fingers on the table. "I broke off contact with Lucien years ago, once I knew what he was. I was able to stay young through my plant sacrifices—never hurting another person, I swear. You were so good with gardening. I paid attention to that. I learned from you. I've got a garden now, so I make my own Alchemical Ashes every year or so, whenever my life force begins to fade. It's only that first transformation that requires an external sacrifice."

"It doesn't hurt you to do that?"

"To do what?"

"Make the Alchemical Ashes."

"Why would it hurt me?"

I didn't want him to know I had the backward alchemy book and had made the Alchemical Ashes for Dorian, so I had to choose my words carefully. "Based on how alchemy works, I would assume it would be extremely draining."

"It's not so bad."

"No?"

"Well," Percy continued, "it's not so bad as long as you only need to do it once a year. More frequently and you're looking for trouble."

"How do you know?"

"That's what I'm getting to." The petulant boy was back. "It's why I'm here. Even though I broke off contact with Lucien, he kept tabs on me. Several months ago, there was a change that caused our backward alchemy to become unstable. Lucien got in touch with me to see what I knew."

150

"Wait, you mean he *didn't know* what the change was?"

"I don't know either. That's the problem. None of us know. Several of us have already died."

This wasn't how I imagined things would go when I found a backward alchemist. They were supposed to know what was going on. "Nobody knows?" I echoed.

He shook his head. "I don't have the answers. That's what we're looking for. The book I mentioned, it's called *Non Degenera Alchemia*."

I held my tongue, even though part of me wanted to confide everything I knew. I was so close to answers. But I was also close to an unknown danger. Could I trust Percy?

"The book spelled out the secrets of not untrue alchemy," Percy continued. "It was lost or stolen ages ago, but it didn't really matter, because we had other practicing not untrue alchemists to pass down the knowledge. Lucien and Olav created the book at Notre Dame, and after that, a small secret society followed their work, meeting at Notre Dame."

That explained the book's connection to Notre Dame. And how Dorian had been brought to life by accident. He'd been created specifically for Notre Dame. Life forces were linked.

"Why did Lucien need the information in the book if he's the one who created it?" I asked.

Percy shrugged. "Maybe he forgot. That's the reason he wrote the information down, right? So he wouldn't have to remember it."

"But you just said he, Olav, and others passed down the knowledge."

Another shrug. "Maybe there's something special about the book itself."

"You don't know what's special about it, though?"

"I already said that, didn't I?"

I called upon every ounce of my will power to avoid strangling, or at least slapping, the lazy man in front of me. "If you had this book, would it save you? Is there something in there that would stop the shift? Something that doesn't involve another sacrifice?"

"It doesn't matter, because how would we find it? It's been gone forever."

"Nobody looked for it?"

Percy shrugged yet again. "Why would we? We'd already gotten what we needed from it."

I shook with frustration. Backward alchemists and their short-cuts! They didn't see the power of true knowledge. I circled the table. Clockwise. Was I subconsciously trying to counteract the backward Death Rotation?

"But now," Percy said, "our energy is fading. It's fading at different speeds, but fading all the same. Even mine."

"You could have saved yourself a lot of my skepticism if you'd come right out and said you wanted help. That's your real motivation for coming here, isn't it?"

"Lucien really did follow you here from Paris. I'm not making this up."

"I didn't say you made it up. I believe you want to help me too. But it's not your main focus. You want to save yourself."

"Is that so bad? For all of time, man has been interested in self-preservation."

"I'm all for self-preservation. Just not when it involves murdering others."

"I didn't kill anyone on purpose, I swear. And I stepped back from it once I knew. I'm not a bad guy. I didn't have it in me to do it again. It was only Lucien. After the inexplicable shift, he made another sacrifice—"

I gasped. "He killed someone else? Now? This year?"

"The sacrifice didn't work, though. He's still aging rapidly. All of us who are left have been aging quickly for the past few months."

"That doesn't make sense, Percy. That would mean you were, what, twelve years old last month? Or ten?"

Percy smiled. I couldn't believe he actually smiled moments after telling me a man he knew had recently murdered someone. "It's thanks to you that I'm spared, Zoe. I was a few years younger a few months ago, and because of my thriving *potager* garden, I've been able to keep myself relatively young." His smile faltered. "But I've run out of plants. We're all desperate to discover what changed. Lucien thinks the answer is in *Non Degenera Alchemia*."

"What does that have to do with me?"

Percy stood up and crossed his arms confidently. Several inches taller than me, he positioned himself to look down his nose at me. "Why were you in Paris, Zoe?"

"I used to live there, you know."

Percy stood so close to me I could feel his stale breath on my face. Yet I refused to back away.

"You went to Lucien's bookshop in Paris," Percy said, "asking questions about alchemy. You made him suspicious. Lucien now believes you have this book. That's why he's here. He wants that book, and he won't stop until he gets it."

TWENTY-SEVEN

"It's ridiculous of Lucien to think you've got the book," Percy continued. "*Zoe Faust* in possession of a backward alchemy book?"

"Absurd," I murmured. It was my turn to avoid his gaze.

I thought back on all of my interactions with Lucien. I couldn't imagine him as the charismatic leader Percy had described. What had I said to Lucien to arouse his suspicions that I was a true alchemist, let alone that I had his backward alchemy book? It couldn't simply be the interest I expressed in alchemy. There were many people out there like Ivan, who weren't true alchemists but who had an interest in alchemy. That's why there were so many modern books on the subject.

"Why would Lucien even think I have this book?" I asked as casually as I could.

Percy shrugged. "Something you said made him suspect it. He mentioned that you two talked about the Cabaret de L'Enfer, but I don't know why that would mean you had *Non Degenera Alchemia*."

I groaned. "I do. Or rather, I bet I know why he suspected me of being an alchemist. He saw me looking at a photo of a Hell-mouth door that led into the nightclub I once knew well—a hundred years ago. He asked if I knew it. I said I'd read about it, but I'm sure my face revealed the truth." Caught up in those memories, I also might have slipped into colloquial French. Not a problem in and of itself, since many Americans speak fluent French, but my conversational French is from a century ago.

"Lucien didn't realize you were someone I cared about," Percy said, "or he wouldn't have told me he was going to get the book *by any means necessary*. I didn't like the tone in his voice when he said it. I didn't like it one bit."

"He admitted that to you?"

Percy's eyes darted nervously around the house. "He, uh, might have thought I was on his side. Because I, uh, told him who you were. Don't get angry! I didn't mean to do it. He caught me off guard. I hadn't seen him in ages, and he showed up on my doorstep with a photograph of you. He took it on his mobile phone while you were browsing at his crummy little bookshop. I asked him why he had a photo of Zoe Faust … He'd heard of you because you're one of the few women alchemists taken on as apprentices with a master. You can't blame me for that, can you?"

"It's not your fault, Percy," I said, half believing my words.

"I'm glad you can see that. Lucien said you left Paris abruptly. Otherwise I bet he would have stolen the book from you in Paris."

"The book I don't have, you mean."

"I meant he would have *attempted* to steal it from you in Paris. I don't know how he found you in Portland, though."

I put my head in my hands. "I gave him my address."

"I know he can be a charmer, Zoe, but giving a strange man your address—"

"For him to send me a *book*, Percy. He's a bookseller."

"Oh."

"How did *you* find me?" I asked.

"I knew the name of your apothecary shop." He pulled out a cell phone and scrolled for a minute. He held up the web page to my online business, now an "antiques" store as opposed to an apothecary. Brixton's friend Veronica Chen-Mendoza had overhauled the website. The bottom listed my home address. Veronica didn't know I was hiding.

"I came to your house this morning but nobody was home," Percy said. "I peeked into the recycling bin outside and saw a takeaway cup with a stamp that said Blue Sky Teas." He said it like riffling through someone's trash was the most natural thing in the world. "I knew I had the right house, because you've got the oldest car on the block. Is it from the forties? I don't know how you keep it running."

"It's called hard work."

The dig was lost on Percy. "Aren't you worried you might give yourself away with the alchemical artifacts you sell through Elixir and that old truck?"

"Apothecary wares are cool again, hadn't you heard? Hiding in plain sight has been working well for me." *Until last week.* "Let's get back on track, Percy, since there's a madman out there."

"God, I could use a beer."

"It's ten o'clock in the morning."

"It's six o'clock in the evening in England. Seven in France."

"No beer." My phone buzzed. I ignored it. I'd forgotten Dorian was listening to our conversation through the pipes, but I knew perfectly well there was beer in the kitchen for a beer-battered vegetable tempura recipe. "I think it would be helpful for me to understand more about this book."

"You've never come across it over the years, have you? You sell so many antique books. If you and I find it before Lucien, we could use it to help us. Not sacrificing anyone again, of course. But I'm already immortal; I only need to figure out how to stop whatever change happened."

"We're not immortal, Percy."

"Speak for yourself." He flexed his muscles, clearly pleased he had the toned body of a twenty-five-year-old.

"Your cells have stopped aging, but we can both die. You realize that, don't you?"

Percy frowned. In denial, as always.

I weighed my options and made a decision on instinct. I trusted that Percy didn't wish to harm me, but I didn't trust him to keep my secrets under pressure.

"I came across photographs of the book you spoke of," I said. "That's what sent me to Paris to research alchemy's connection to the cathedral of Notre Dame. When overlaid, the woodcut illustrations pointed to the cathedral." Everything I said was true except that I possessed the original book, not only photographs. And that it was fire that had shown me how the illustrations fit together.

Percy nodded vigorously. "That's where the not untrue alchemists used to meet. Where did you find the photos? Do you have them?"

"Not here. They're at a friend's house. He's an alchemy scholar—" I swore.

"What is it?"

"Someone was seen spying on my friend Ivan—the alchemy scholar I mentioned. I'm sure it was Lucien. And you don't know about the murder victim who may have been an alchemist, do you?"

"*Murder?*" Percy flipped his head around. Was he making sure Lucien wasn't hiding behind the couch?

"It's an old murder. A decade old, something like that. But the odd thing is that the body was found in a cabin in the woods with alchemy supplies, and I think Lucien was seen there too. What was he doing there?"

"He's after the bloody book, Zoe. Your friend is in danger, as are we. Even though Lucien can't kill you directly—"

"Of course he could kill me. Especially if he's as bad a guy as you're making him out to be."

"You don't know?" Percy blinked at me. "Of course you wouldn't, since you've never killed anyone." Percy shook his head and spoke as if addressing a toddler. "The Elixir of Life is a transformation of the life force. If an alchemist kills a living being directly, their own life force is taken away. That's what I was talking about earlier, how the sacrifice has to be volunteered. You understand?"

Was he attempting to lecture me on alchemy? Not only was he condescending, but he was completely wrong.

"Percy, that's an old wives' tale. There's nothing stopping anyone on earth from killing another person. Aside from their moral compass. Or fear of being caught."

"No, it's true. That's why Lucien hasn't killed the rest of us. He's a very bad man, Zoe, but he's afraid he'll die if he goes too far. The sacrifices are different, because they're *willing* participants. Unwitting, but it's still their choice to sacrifice themselves."

"Then why do you think Lucien is so dangerous?"

Percy bit his lip. "There are many things that can be done to a person without killing them."

I shivered. It was an absurd theory, but if Lucien and Percy believed it…

"Give me a minute," I said.

I stepped into the living room, keeping my eyes on Percy while I called Ivan. Thankfully he picked up the phone immediately. "This is going to sound strange," I said, "but I need you to take what I'm going to say seriously."

"With you, Zoe, I've ceased thinking of anything as strange."

"There's a man called Lucien who's stalking people and places related to alchemy."

"This man is harassing you? How can I help?"

"Yes, and he might harass you too. And he could be dangerous."

"I'll be careful. What does he look like?"

"He looks like ... " I closed my eyes and tried to think about how to describe such a nondescript man. "Average-looking guy, but don't underestimate him."

When I opened my eyes, Percy was gone.

"I can take care of myself," Ivan was saying, "but I thank you for your concern. I'll be careful."

Percy was a bigger concern, so I ended the call with Ivan. The kitchen door swung open a moment later. Percy emerged with a platter of misshapen vegan pastries.

"God these are good," he said. "Why didn't you cook like this when I knew you? I'm starving after that long flight."

"Where are you staying?"

"Nowhere yet." He indicated the small satchel he'd dropped inside the door.

"That's the entirety of your luggage?"

"I've never understood why people in this century feel the need to travel with so many possessions."

"In some ways you're very much your father's son."

"I'm so sorry about what happened to him, you know." His face was filled with such sincerity that my eyes welled with tears. "I wish—I wish I could take it all back."

I didn't completely trust Percy, but I wondered ... Could we help each other?

TWENTY-EIGHT

Dorian stomped across the tiled kitchen floor. "How could you do it? How could you let him stay here?"

Percy had gone to a restaurant for lunch, so Dorian and I were alone in the house. As tasty as Dorian's pastries were, Percy had insisted there was no way he would eat a vegan lunch. Dorian and I were in the kitchen with the curtains drawn, as always. I was making a summer salad with a bounty from the backyard garden that Brixton had been keeping up, and Dorian was slicing freshly baked French bread for sandwiches.

"You keep talking about the perfection of Julian Lake's kitchen," I said, "and the delicacies he'll order for you. Why don't you stay there for a few days—and take your book with you. I want to keep Percy close and the book far away."

"*Je ne comprend pas.* Do you or do you not trust him?"

"I haven't yet made up my mind. But he's a backward alchemist. We need the information he can give us."

"You do not need to pretend with me, Zoe. I heard every word. I know there is no hope. I will not stand for the sacrifice of an innocent to save me."

"We don't know that's the only way."

Dorian didn't answer. Instead, he selected a paprika-infused sea salt and handed it to me. "This one will be good with the salad."

Though I'm not the cook Dorian is, I've always been intrigued by how salt can bring out the flavors of the simplest foods. Unlike some unnecessary culinary flourishes, salt fulfills a body's basic needs. Throughout history, salt has played an important role in society and culture because of how essential it is for the body. It's why salt, along with sulfur and mercury, is one of the three essentials in alchemy. In that *tria prima*, salt represents the body, and is the child of sulfur and mercury.

As Dorian skillfully tossed a salad using only one hand, my phone buzzed. It was a text message from Brixton, asking if Dorian could prepare a feast for two dozen people—tonight. I called Brixton back to tell him it was bad timing. To my surprise, he picked up his phone.

"I got your message, Brix, but that's awfully short notice. We can't just—"

"Blue's home," he said. "She's out of jail."

I could hear the joy in his voice. It was so innocent and blissful that I nearly forgot the tragedies swirling around me. "That's wonderful. I didn't know she was being released so soon."

"She didn't want to tell any of us in advance. I guess she didn't really believe it was going to happen, until she was actually out. Isn't it wicked awesome news? Especially with Mom so upset about her dad maybe being dead. Blue's sure to cheer her up. Have you noticed she has a way of doing that?"

I smiled even though neither the teenager on the other end of the line nor the gargoyle absorbed in his cooking could see me.

"She definitely does have a way about her," I agreed.

"She showed up at her cottage today. Mom and Abel thought having a welcome home party for all of her friends would be even better than keeping her to ourselves. Is Dorian there? Can I talk to him?"

"He's busy. But I'm sure he'd be happy to cook."

"I am not busy," Dorian called out behind me. He hopped down from his stepping stool and snatched the phone from me. "Allo? *Oui.*
Oui." He nodded thoughtfully. "This is a superb idea. If only Zoe had not banished me from my home—"

"I didn't banish you." I tried to grab the phone back. Dorian shushed me and scurried away. "I'll keep Percy out of the house this afternoon, so you can cook before you move into Julian Lake's house for a few days."

"*Merci.*" He handed the phone back to me.

"I'll make sure Dorian has everything he needs to cook," I told Brixton, "then bring the food to the teashop tonight."

"Cool. This is going to be wicked."

"You're going to be with Blue and your parents the whole afternoon, right?"

I swear I could hear the sound of his eyes rolling. "Sure, probably."

"I'm serious. There's a killer—"

"No, there's not. Those cops told me I was wrong and the guy had been there for years. That's why they think my grandfather—"

"I know. I'm sorry, Brix. But the man you saw spying on Ivan is a very dangerous man. I don't know what he has to do with the man who was found, but he's killed before."

A pause came from the other end of the line, then a swear word I chose to ignore. "Seriously?"

"Seriously. You need to stay far away from him. Don't go anywhere on your own."

After I hung up the phone, I had to figure out how to keep Percy out of the house all day. He was expecting me to pick him up in a little over an hour, so I had time to figure it out.

I drove to the market to get the ingredients on Dorian's shopping list. Usually I walked to local shops or farmer's markets every few days, to supplement the vegetables from the garden and the staples in the pantry, but today I was both in a hurry and needed to buy in bulk. After surviving the fluorescent lights at the supermarket, I dropped off four bags of groceries with Dorian. I was about to head back out to pick up Percy, but Dorian stopped me as he looked through the sacks of food.

"Where is the garlic?" he asked.

"We already have plenty of garlic." I pointed to four heads of garlic, Purple Stripe hardneck, and Western Rose softneck.

Dorian narrowed his black eyes. "I need more for this tomato sauce recipe."

"Are you sure garlic pasta is the way to go for a party?"

He chuckled. "If everyone eats the garlic, they will not mind."

"Remind me to pick some parsley from the backyard to mute the effects."

"Garlic will welcome your friend home with luck."

I paused at the swinging kitchen door. "I didn't realize you were superstitious."

He clicked his tongue. "Not superstitious. Food has cultural significance, as you of all people should understand. It feeds both the body and the soul. Everything I am creating for tonight will welcome Blue Sky home."

I leaned in the door frame and looked over the left half of Dorian's body that was rapidly turning to stone. He didn't dwell on his limitations. "Thank you. That's so thoughtful."

Dorian waved off the comment, and moved his stepping stool to unpack the last bag of groceries. The simple task took longer than usual, since he could only use his right arm to lift the stool.

"I can help when I get back," I said.

"It is unnecessary. I have selected recipes that only require the use of one good arm." Dorian said the words casually, but he didn't look at me. He peered into the grocery bag containing the first tomatoes of the season and shook his head. "I will make do," he muttered, dismissing me with a wave of his clawed hand.

I smiled and left Dorian to the feast preparations. I did a quick walk-through of the house, making sure it was tightly secured and thinking about how different my life had been six months ago. I used to eat for healing and nourishment, with pleasure coming in last on my list of priorities. Since Dorian had come into my life, he'd shown me that delectable foods didn't have to be unhealthy. Which was an accidental discovery.

When Dorian showed up on my doorstep—or, in a moving crate in my living room, to be more accurate—he learned I didn't keep bacon, butter, or cream in the house. Dorian respected my eating habits, but he refused to eat the same "boring" food I ate. I used my flavored oils, salts, and vinegars to season simple soups, stews, and salads, but in cooking with what I had on hand, he showed me how easy it was to turn simple meals into mouthwatering feasts.

I knew why I was thinking so much about food. I was starving. I'd been feeling so anxious I hadn't stopped to take care of myself. I knew better than to disregard my body. I stuck my head back into the kitchen to grab a snack to take with me. The thoughtful gargoyle was one step ahead of me. He handed me a toasted baguette sandwich wrapped in parchment paper.

My friend and I were so alike but also worlds apart.

And that gave me the perfect idea for what to do with Percy. I slipped up to the attic before leaving the house.

————————

I picked up Percy from a local brewery where he was enjoying an extended lunch accompanied by beer and a pretty young woman. She wasn't happy to see me, but she perked up when Percy whispered something in her ear before paying the bill.

"Not too worried about Lucien after all?" I said once we were on the sidewalk.

"I was in a darkened back booth, so I knew I'd see him before he saw me."

I led Percy to the truck. My myrrh air freshener was no match for the scent of batch brewed beer that had ensconced itself in Percy's clothing.

"I thought you lived in the other direction," he said as I pulled onto the highway.

"I need the house to myself to cook for a good friend's welcome home party tonight, so I've got another idea—"

Percy gaped at me. "I'm dying and you're having a party?"

The words bristled. Percy was in much better shape than Dorian. And one of the lessons I'd learned after being alive for so long was that you need to slow down and enjoy the small moments in life. Not only did they make existence more meaningful, but they helped you see things more clearly. I was going to give myself this evening to celebrate life with Blue, Brixton, and Max. I didn't know what would happen the next day, but time with them tonight was a gift I could give all of us.

"I'm going to help you help yourself," I said. "I found the photocopied pages of that book we were talking about." I pointed to my purse that lay at Percy's feet. He lunged for it and greedily scooped up the pages.

"You have it," he said. "You have it! Where did you find these?"

"I used to do a lot of research. I found those pages years ago. You're the one who's the backward alchemist. I'm going to leave you at a library."

"A library? Zoe, are you serious? I can stay out of the way at your house."

"I need to concentrate, and so do you. You can read these pages and see what they tell you."

"But—"

"I'll pick you up in four hours. You can come to the party with me."

"Can we have dinner first?"

"Didn't you hear me? I'm going home to cook for the party."

"But you're cooking vegan food."

Family.

TWENTY-NINE

LONG BEFORE I SAW her, I knew Blue was there. The fragrance of her homemade teas filled the cozy space. I'm sure it was my imagination, but even the weeping fig tree in the center of the cafe appeared to have perked up that night. The illusion was created because the tree-ring tables that normally circled the living tree had been moved aside to make room for the crowd that had gathered to welcome Blue home.

I'd dropped off Dorian's feast before picking up Percy from the library. Unsurprisingly, Percy hadn't gleaned anything useful from the hours surrounded by information.

As Percy and I walked into the party in full swing, everyone was facing the back of the café. The sound of two acoustic guitars strumming with two voices harmonizing echoed through the teashop. Abel and Brixton were performing "Imagine," a perfect choice for the occasion. Their voices blended to create perfectly imperfect harmony. Their arms moved in rhythm on their guitars.

The song concluded. Heather whistled and the crowd applauded. I caught a glimpse of wild gray hair moving stealthily through the crowd, toward Brixton. My heart skipped a beat as I thought about how easy it would be for someone to get to Brixton if they wanted to. Blue snuck up behind Brixton and gave him a hug. He turned nearly as red as the beets in my garden but hugged her back.

I saw another smiling face in the crowd. Max Liu. He must have felt my eyes on him, because his gaze met mine. I felt my stomach give a little flip-flop as his smile grew wider.

"These two are way too good," Blue said to the crowd. "I'm calling for a forced break so you'll all eat this wonderful spread of food Zoe prepared for the occasion. Eat!" She caught my eye and winked.

"First," Max said, "a toast to the heart of the neighborhood." He raised a clay mug of tea. "Blue, you were here for me during a rough time in my life, and you made me feel at home. I can confidently say that every person here feels the same way. Thank you, Blue."

"Hear, hear!" several voices chimed in.

Blue wiped a tear from her eye. "I'm only crying because the food is getting cold." She laughed and cleared her throat. "This is the first place that's ever truly felt like home."

I knew the feeling more acutely than she or anyone else in that room knew. I wished I could have told Blue how much I related.

We all knew Blue Sky as the owner of Blue Sky Teas, the woman who knew how to brew exquisite teas, who'd helped Brixton with his homework at the teashop since he was in elementary school, and who brightened any room with her infectiously relaxed demeanor.

But the woman who let her curly gray hair run wild and lived in baggy jeans also had a past that nobody knew about until earlier that year.

"Thanks for welcoming me back," Blue concluded. "Now eat!" I could barely imagine blissfully chubby and exuberant Blue Sky as Brenda Skyler, a stick-thin workaholic who wore power suits, dieted, and worked for her husband's legal practice, where she unknowingly helped him with illegal schemes. She wasn't culpable for the crimes she didn't know about, but she was guilty of forging documents and faking her own death to begin her new life.

The woman in the teashop that evening was a mix of the two. She'd lost weight in jail, and her radiant face, usually full of natural color from the time she spent wildcrafting outside, was pale.

The party guest list included me, Brixton, Heather, Abel, Brixton's best friends Veronica and Ethan, Max, and a dozen of Blue's friends who I hadn't previously met, as well as Percy, who I'd brought along with me. Ivan wasn't feeling well enough to attend.

The teashop usually closed at seven o'clock in the evening, but tonight it was open for this private party. Two of the tree-ring tables had been pushed together for the spread of food prepared by Dorian in my kitchen that afternoon. I needn't have worried about his infirmity. He'd outdone himself with a freekeh and parsley salad , freshly baked bread with garlic tomato sauce for dipping, bowls of nuts, each home-roasted with a different spice mix, plus a dessert tray of miniature tarts and mousses. Everyone congratulated me on the food.

"How did you get the tomato sauce so creamy?" Heather asked, popping a bite of sauce-dipped bread into her mouth.

"A chef never reveals her secrets," I said. I'd have to ask Dorian later. She was right. A delicate flavor I couldn't place added depth and balance to the flavorful garlic.

Heather had woven a banner out of wildflowers that was supposed to read WELCOME HOME BLUE. But some of the flowers refused to be tamed, so by the time the party started the string of letters read EL ME HOME BLUE. Blue loved it.

The teenagers took photographs of people standing under the sign to share on social media. Percy and I ducked out of the way as photos were snapped.

"It was so much easier before every bloody man, woman, and child had a damn mobile phone," Percy whispered.

During a short break for everyone to fill their plates, I introduced Percy to my friends. Brixton and Abel resumed the live music, with Brixton still on his acoustic guitar, and Abel switching to a banjo. I wished Tobias could have been there to sing, but I knew he was exactly where he needed to be, spending precious last moments with his beloved Rosa.

Max brought me a lemon tart. "Penny for your thoughts."

I took a bite of the tart, giving myself a few moments to think. "The tart is more tart than I expected," I said. *Smooth, Zoe.*

"You didn't taste them at home?"

Damn. "Too many things to sample. I trusted the recipe." *Please don't ask what's in it*, I thought to myself. Although from the flavors dancing on my tongue, I could guess most of the ingredients, the two dominant ones being coconut oil and lemon.

Max nodded and bit into a chocolate mousse tart.

The connection between us from the day before was missing, and I knew why. He kept glancing distractedly at Percy.

"You asked what I was thinking about," I said. "I was thinking about how beautiful it is that so many people came to celebrate with Blue at the very last minute."

"It's lovely," Max said. Unlike our generic conversation. Max stole another glance at Percy, who was on the outskirts of a small group with Blue.

"You never told me the story of the plastic skeleton in your house," I prompted.

"It was Chadna's during med school."

Great. He was jealous of Percy and I'd asked about his dead ex-wife. But instead of the reaction I was expecting, a grin spread across Max's face.

"She refused to tell me why she kept it so long. On each of my birthdays, she'd tell me a little bit more of the story. That way she said I'd be forced to live a long life with her, to hear the end of the story."

"That's beautiful."

The smile on Max's face faded as I felt a tap at my elbow. Percy.

"I'm going to get more food," Max said.

"What's up, Percy?" I asked.

"I'm tired. I thought I'd go back to the house for an early night. Could I have the key?"

"You don't have to lie to me," I said.

"Fair enough." Percy shrugged. "I was trying to be sly about giving you some time with your beau and letting you have fun at the fete."

Maybe Percy had grown up, after all. I gave Percy a key and made sure he remembered how to walk back to the house.

"GPS," he said, shaking his phone at me.

Brixton and Abel amped up the music. Blue began to dance with her friends. I was reminded of my love for Portland when I couldn't tell the difference between Blue's forager friends and the group of lawyers who'd come to her aid. Perhaps they were one and the same. Brixton was busy playing guitar and his friend Ethan was too cool for dancing, so Veronica joined the group of older women and let loose. At fourteen, she was already the tallest woman in the group. Her cascading black hair tossed from side to side in rhythm with the music. The awkward young woman I'd met six months before was slipping away, innocent adolescence sacrificed for a more fully formed young adulthood.

Max pulled me from the corner in which I was hiding to dance with him. Looking into his eyes, my stomach fluttered. Things were starting to feel like they had before Percy arrived in Portland—until Max abruptly stopped dancing.

His eyes narrowed and he walked to the door of the teashop without a word.

Two men in suits stood at the door. Even though they weren't dressed in policemen's uniforms, their stance and Max's interaction with them suggested they were detectives. With the volume of the music, from across the teashop I couldn't hear what they were saying, but Max was shaking his head. *No no no.* Had I dismissed the French police too soon?

The two men were insistent. Max shook his head one last time, then led them around the weeping fig tree in the center of the teashop. Not to me.

To Heather.

With an abrupt jerk of his arm, Abel broke off strumming his guitar. He smiled as he stood and whispered to Brixton to continue playing. I knew that look of bravado on Abel's face was a mask applied for the benefit of his stepson. Brixton tried to argue but ultimately listened to his stepfather.

As soon as the music resumed, people forgot about the interruption. They went back to dancing and eating. Nobody else seemed to notice that the newcomers weren't welcome guests. I followed Max and Abel to the corner where the detectives were talking with Heather.

"It'll be easier if we talk to you both down at the station," one of them was saying to her.

"What's this about?" Abel asked. "Did you confirm the identity of the man Brix found?"

"You are?"

"Her husband."

"It's okay, hon," Heather said, stroking Abel's arm.

"Please step aside, sir," the detective said. I hoped Brixton was too busy on the guitar to see the look the detective directed at Abel, or I feared the impetuous teenager might try to punch the detective.

"You have no right to interrupt this private party," Abel said, his voice rising. Brixton's guitar riff ended with a discordant crash. He flung the instrument aside and ran to his mom. All eyes followed him.

"It's okay, Brix," Heather said. "They only want to talk to us."

"Us?" Brixton asked.

Heather linked her arm through Brixton's, stood on her tiptoes to kiss him on the side of his head, then nodded to the detectives.

"Now?" Brixton said, pulling away from his mom. "They can't just—"

"It's okay, sweetie," Heather said softly.

Brixton looked to his stepfather. With a clenched jaw, Abel nodded at Brixton. Then Max, Abel, and Brixton followed the detectives out the door.

Blue tried to assure everyone that it was a private family matter and nothing to worry about, but the party broke up after that.

I walked home alone, wondering what the detectives had found out about Heather's father. Why wouldn't they answer Abel's question? It seemed simple enough.

Walking up my driveway, my senses tingled. I haven't survived as long as I have without listening to the subtle cues surrounding us that we pick up as intuition. Something was different, but what? I chastised myself. I had a house guest. I must have noticed the subtle movement of him moving behind a closed curtain. I continued walking, but stopped as soon as I passed my Chevy truck and Airstream trailer.

The front door was ajar.

I ran to the door and pushed it open. The living room had been ransacked.

"Percy?" I called out.

No answer.

I ran through the house. The lock to my basement alchemy lab had been broken open. I grabbed a heavy flashlight and crept down the stairs. With each step, my heart pounded more loudly in my ears.

At the base of the basement stairs, Percy lay unconscious on the concrete floor, his hair wet with blood.

THIRTY

"I'm all right," Percy croaked. But he clearly wasn't. Blood covered the side of his head.

"I'll call an ambulance."

"No." He grabbed my wrist. "Too many questions. You know that."

He was right. But he was also in bad shape. In worse shape than my natural remedies could fix.

"All right," I said as Percy struggled to sit up. "Let go of my arm and I promise I'll get supplies, not call an ambulance."

He obliged then sank back to the floor. I rushed upstairs to get supplies.

After I'd cleaned his head wound, I saw he wasn't as badly off as I'd feared. Head wounds tend to bleed a lot, but the gash itself wouldn't need my sloppy stitches after all. I led him to the bedroom he was using, exchanged his bloody shirt for a fresh one, and applied a healing salve that would serve as a natural antibiotic.

"Was it Lucien?" I asked, holding an ice pack to the side of his head.

He nodded and winced in pain.

"I don't suppose you have any Paracetamol? No, I didn't think you would."

"He was after *Non Degenera Alchemia*?"

"It appears that way. I'm so sorry I couldn't stop him—"

"I'm sorry I left you alone. Neither of us should be on our own right now."

A knock on the door sounded from below.

"You'll be all right." I tucked him into bed before running downstairs.

At the front door I found Max. He looked infinitely more frazzled than he had an hour before. Brixton sat on the porch steps behind him, a banjo slung over his back.

"Abel is with Heather at the police station," Max said. "I thought I could look after Brix—"

"I'm almost fifteen," Brixton cut in. "Nobody needs to look after me."

"But I was called into the station," Max continued. "So I can't keep an eye on him. I hate to impose upon Blue the day she's out of jail. Can he hang out here until his mom can pick him up?"

I hesitated for long enough that Max picked up on the delay. At the sound of creaking floorboards overhead, he stepped in front of Brixton and shifted into a combative stance.

"It's fine," I said. "Everything is fine. I just have a visitor. Ambrose's son Percy is staying here."

"Oh," Max said, his voice curt. "I didn't realize he'd be staying with you. We can go. Sorry to have bothered you. I'll figure out something else."

"It's no bother," I said. "Brix, since the party got cut short and you were busy making music, I bet you're hungry. There's a lot of food in the fridge."

"I'm not hungry." Brixton glared at me. "But I'll pretend to eat something so you two can talk." He pushed past us and disappeared through the kitchen's swinging door.

"Smart kid," Max said.

"I don't think he likes being treated like a kid. Come inside. What did you want to talk about?" I took a step toward Max, but he turned away. He strode across the living room and gripped the back of a dining room chair.

"What's going on, Max? Is the man Brixton's grandfather? Why the secrecy?"

The sound of scales being played on a banjo came from the kitchen.

"This case keeps getting stranger," Max said. "The lab guys got things wrong. This isn't an old case after all. Some of those chemicals we found in the shack's laboratory messed with the speed of decomposition. The man Brixton found was killed *this past week*."

Oh no … "That means Brixton *is* a witness to a murder." Had Lucien killed a new apprentice in a makeshift alchemy lab here in Portland? Was that what Percy was hinting at?

Max swallowed hard and nodded.

"Then why," I asked, "were the detectives interested in Heather and Brixton, if it's not Brix's grandfather after all?"

"I didn't say that."

"So it *is* Heather's father? That's why they're questioning her?"

"Not exactly."

"What does that mean, *not exactly*? It's both her dad and *not* her dad?"

"He hasn't been identified yet. There are no teeth to test for dental records, and DNA testing doesn't work that quickly. But now that we know it's a new death, it's unlikely to be Heather's father."

"Then why—"

"Those guys don't have the best social skills. Because of the new information about the probable timing of death, they wanted to get more details from Brixton about what he saw. As a minor, they needed his mom present."

"So it was Brixton they wanted?"

"At first." Max rubbed his eyes. "But Heather's manner made them suspicious."

"So now they're talking more with her alone."

Max nodded. "She wasn't doing herself any favors. The first time they talked with her, she wouldn't agree to a voluntary DNA swab when they thought it was her dad, which could prove or disprove a familial match, since there weren't teeth for a dental match."

"She had every right to refuse an invasive test."

"It's a swab across her cheek, Zoe."

"Which you said was *voluntary*. Of course she'd decline." I feared the day when modern technology would make it impossible for me to keep my privacy. I'd already avoided many educational and job opportunities because I didn't want to be in more databases than necessary.

"Even when it could have helped her learn if it was her dad?" Max said. "Look, never mind. I don't want to have a stupid fight. I get it that privacy rights are important. *I* don't think she behaved suspiciously. But it's not my case."

"Meaning you're going to let them—"

"They're good cops, Zoe. We all want the truth."

"How's Brixton doing with all this?"

"Not great. If he was okay, he'd be fine on his own at home." He glanced at his phone. "Look, I've gotta run. You sure it's okay for Brixton to be here with you while your houseguest is here?"

"Positive." With Lucien on the loose, I wanted Brixton close.

"You two aren't ... " He cleared his throat. "You sure you don't need privacy?"

"He's Ambrose's son, Max."

"Yeah, but he's a lot closer to your age."

"Age is meaningless." I took his hands in mine. I believed the words I spoke, and he must have seen it in my eyes. He squeezed my hand and gave me a slow kiss on the cheek before departing. The fresh scent of citrus lingered even after he was gone. A small piece of his comforting presence remained with me.

———————

In spite of his claims that he wasn't hungry, I found Brixton eating a sweet potato pie straight from the pan.

"I thought you and Max were a couple," Brixton said through a mouthful.

"We are." Maybe. I hoped.

"Then who's the guy singing in the shower?"

"Percy. You met him tonight." From the kitchen, if I listened carefully, I could hear the singing coming from the bathroom above us.

"Your ex's kid? No offense, but he's kind of a tool."

I tried not to laugh.

"See?" Brixton said. "I'm totally right, aren't I?"

"I wouldn't say you're wrong."

"So is alchemy, like, hereditary?"

"It's easier to find out about alchemy if you know an alchemist," I said, "but it's not inherited."

Brixton nodded thoughtfully. He set down the half-empty pan of pie and hopped up onto the counter. Dorian hated it when he did that, but I liked how it made the house feel more like a home.

"I don't want you to teach me, Zoe. I don't want to learn alchemy." He picked up a sprig of spearmint from the kitchen's window box and twirled it in his fingers, looking at the spinning green pinwheel in his fingertips as he spoke. "I know Ivan wants to learn, since he's dying. But I think it would suck to outlive Veronica and Ethan, and anyone else I'll ever care about. I'll probably already outlive Abel and Mom." He squished the mint in his hand, releasing the scent into the air.

"Max told me what the police discovered."

"About the skin under his fingernails?"

"I meant how long the man had been dead. They found skin under his fingernails?" Was that the real reason they wanted Heather to voluntarily give her DNA? I decided now wasn't the time to worry Brixton about his mom. It wouldn't be her DNA under his fingernails regardless.

"I told you I wasn't lying about the body being new."

"We need to talk about something else serious." I lowered my voice. "Quickly, in case Percy is feeling better and comes downstairs. I hate to do this right now, when I know you've got so much else on your mind."

"It's cool."

"Percy came to Portland because he knows the man you saw spying on Ivan. The man's name is Lucien, and he's a dangerous backward alchemist. Percy fell in with him a century ago, and got caught up in backward alchemy, but Lucien is after Dorian's book, so Percy wanted to warn me."

"Whoa. He doesn't seem like the kind of guy who'd look out for other people."

"With everything that's happening around here, I'm glad you've got good intuition." Even though I could hear Percy still singing Spice Girls songs in the shower, I kept my voice low. "You're right. I don't trust him completely, so I haven't told him about Dorian or that I have Dorian's book. He's not the most altruistic of men. He also wants my help. He's suffering the same alchemical fate as Dorian,"

"His body is returning to its original form?" Brixton asked.

I groaned. Brixton's concise summation made me realize I'd made a significant oversight. I knew that with his life force deteriorating, Dorian would be alive but trapped in stone *because he was originally made of stone*. With a *human* backward alchemist's life force quickly deteriorating, they'd transform into their original flesh and bone—as their flesh and bones would have with age.

"Zoe, are you okay? You look like you've seen a ghost or something."

"Something much worse. I think I've seen the truth about a backward alchemist."

"Wicked. What is it?"

"I need you to tell me exactly what happened when you saw Lucien go into the shack in the woods."

"I told you, I saw that Lucien guy, who'd been spying on Ivan, go into the shack and then kill some guy."

"But you didn't see him do the actual killing."

"No."

"You saw Lucien sneak out?"

Brixton hesitated, and I knew I was right.

"I might not have actually seen him," Brixton said. "But it was all loud, like a fight, and then it was quiet."

"You didn't see anyone else coming near the shed?"

"No. I waited a while, and after it was quiet for a really long time, I looked inside. That's when I saw the dead guy."

"A dead man who didn't look like Lucien."

"No, this guy was way older. That's how I knew Lucien must have slipped out the back when I was too far away to see him."

"You didn't see the body until a few minutes after he died."

"So?"

"That means," I said, "that the dead man is Lucien."

"I saw the guy, Zoe. He's not—"

"Lucien was a backward alchemist. His life force was reversing, so once he died, his body would wither much more quickly than that of a normal person. That's what's confused this whole situation. You saw him shortly after he died and thought he was an old man. The police saw him a short time later and thought he'd been dead for a decade."

Brixton kicked a kitchen cabinet. "And the police don't know about alchemy, so once they figured out the body was changing they thought it was the chemicals from the alchemy lab. So, he did an experiment wrong or something?"

I gripped the edge of the counter. "I don't think so. Percy isn't here to warn me. He fooled me, making me think he was being thoughtful tonight when really he wanted time alone in my house. Percy followed Lucien here to kill him and to steal Dorian's book for himself."

And by telling him I had a copy of the contents of the book, I'd pretty much admitted to him that I had it.

THIRTY-ONE

"Whoa." Brixton looked from me to the kitchen ceiling. The singing from overhead had stopped.

"We're leaving," I said. "Now."

I scribbled a note to Percy about having to go to the police station for Heather, so he wouldn't think I'd discovered his secret, grabbed my silver coat, and shoved Brixton out the door.

"The scent in this truck is always so weird," Brixton mumbled as he climbed inside.

"It's not weird," I said as I put the key in the ignition of the truck. "Myrrh is a great air freshener. It works well in toothpaste too."

"I remember. Like frankincense, from the Bible. My life is too weird."

"Frankincense is too strong for an air freshener. Seatbelt."

Brixton rolled his eyes but obliged.

"Is it possible that Lucien was already injured when he made his way to his alchemy supplies in the shed?" I asked, trying the engine again. That's what I got for having a 1942 Chevy. I hated to think that Percy was stealthy enough to get into and out of the cabin without Brixton seeing him.

"Yeah. He was kind of disoriented, but I figured it was because he'd forgotten exactly where the shack was. It's pretty overgrown out there. You think that could explain why I didn't see Percy or anyone else?"

"Because Percy had already dealt him a fatal blow."

The engine of my truck turned over three times before finally starting, just long enough that I wondered if Percy had disabled it. I gave silent thanks as we peeled out of the driveway.

How could I have been so stupid as to think Percy believed the old wives' tale about alchemists not being able to kill people? He'd been trying to misdirect me this whole time. Had I fallen for it because he looked so much like Ambrose? Or because I'd wanted so badly to believe him because of my love for his father? Or maybe it was simply because I wanted to believe in the goodness of humanity.

Percy must have knocked himself out to cover his tracks after he searched my house for Dorian's book. A superficial head wound was a good choice. Even a minor wound in that location would bleed profusely and could easily look more serious than it was. He hadn't left the party to give me and Max space; he left so he'd have time alone to search my house. And I'd sent Dorian away, so I had no way to prove it. At least I'd asked Dorian to take *Not Untrue Alchemy* with him.

"Where are we going?" Brixton asked, gripping the dashboard as I turned a corner faster than was prudent. He winced.

"Is your hand still hurting?" I glanced at Brixton, expecting to see a bruise forming. Instead, I saw a bleeding scrape. "You didn't tell me you cut yourself on the table."

"It's nothing." He wrapped his sleeve around his hand. "And you didn't say where we're going."

"Your mom didn't do anything, so I'm guessing they're going to let her go soon."

"We're going to hang out at the police station?" Brixton rolled his eyes. "I should have brought the rest of that pie with me."

"How can you be so relaxed?"

"That guy Percy doesn't seem like an evil mastermind. You and I could totally take him on. And with Dorian in the mix, he wouldn't stand a chance."

I pictured Dorian clawing at Percy's perfect hair and burst out laughing. It was nervous laughter, brought on by the stress, but it was a welcome release of tension.

"See?" Brixton said. "You sure he could really be the killer?"

"I'm not taking any chances."

———————

I left Brixton with Abel, apologizing for not being able to hang out with Brixton because my houseguest was unwell.

When I got back to the house, Percy had his feet up on the couch with an icepack on his head and a tray of ginger cookies on his lap, watching a sitcom on his phone. He'd found the beer in the fridge. Two empty bottles sat on the coffee table, and a third was open on the floor next to the couch.

"How's your friend?" he asked.

I was done playing things safe. I had to find out what was going on.

"Lucien is dead," I said.

The platter of cookies dropped to the floor, as did Percy's phone. The screen cracked as it struck the hardwood floor. He left it where it lay.

I could have sworn Percy's reaction was genuine. Unlike his sincere expressions of regret from earlier that day, this was true shock.

"You saw him? Where?"

"He's the dead body they found in the woods."

The color drained from Percy's face. "But you said—I mean, how—?"

"I know you lied about Lucien being the one to ransack my attic and basement in search of *Non Degenera Alchemia*. It was you." I yanked the icepack from his head and pulled back his hair.

He howled with pain.

"It's only a scratch," I said. "It stopped bleeding right away. You didn't even bother reapplying bandages after your shower. You also didn't back up your lie by breaking down the door to get inside. You unlocked the door with the key I lent you—which you're going to give back to me. Now. Did you think keeping track of your lies wasn't necessary because I trusted you?"

"How can you—"

"Your most convincing lie was that you believe that silly legend about alchemists not being able to kill anyone." I let go of his hair and let him sink back onto the couch.

"It's true!"

"How can it possibly be true when you're the one who killed Lucien?"

"I would never. I *could* never. It was awful with Father—" Percy stopped himself.

Ambrose? My heart beat furiously in my throat. "What did you say?"

"Nothing." He clutched his head in his hands. "I'm in shock over hearing that Lucien is dead. I don't know what I'm saying."

"*What* was awful with Ambrose?"

"Nothing. Truly. I didn't mean anything."

"Yes, you did. When you tell the truth, you lose the cocky tilt of your head. You did it a moment ago. That means you didn't know Lucien was dead—I stand corrected there. I believe you about that."

"Why are you looking at me like that, Zoe? You're scaring me."

"You believe that old wives' tale from *personal experience*." My pulse raced. "Did Ambrose find out you had turned to backward alchemy, and that's the real reason he killed himself? No ... Oh God, Percy, was your father's suicide the death you needed?" With Percy providing no answers, my imagination began running wild with horrible thoughts. The room spun. I couldn't catch my breath.

"You're unbalanced, Zoe. You always were."

My focus snapped to Percy. The spoiled little man who only superficially resembled his father. The physical similarities were striking, but not their souls. "I've never been more clear-headed," I said. "I've always worked to protect the people I love."

"What does that have to do with—"

"You don't understand everything that's going on, Percy. I'm someone with nothing left to lose."

Percy tried to stand. I pushed him back onto the couch and stood over him. His beautiful eyes, so like his father's in appearance but not spirit, opened wide with fear.

"This is how it's going to go," I said. "You're going to tell me the truth about what happened to Ambrose."

Percy's eyes filled with tears. "I never meant to hurt either of you. I only wanted what you had. Can't you understand that? It was so easy for you. Not for me."

"What happened with your father? And what does it have to do with that stupid superstition?"

"You don't know that it's stupid, Zoe. You didn't believe backward alchemy was real at first either."

"That's different. The death rotation makes sense. It's sacrificing one element for another, or even one living being's energy for another's." I thought of how creating Dorian's Tea of Ashes depleted my own energy. "If anything, killing should make a backward alchemist *stronger*, not kill him." I regretted the words as soon as they left my mouth. But alchemy is science, and that's what made sense scientifically.

"How would you know?" Percy snapped. "Have you ever killed anyone?"

"Of course not."

"Then you don't know. It would kill you—or, if you're strong, only bring you to the brink of death." Percy's lower lip trembled. The shaking spread to his whole body. He truly believed what he was saying; he truly was afraid of something.

"Oh God, Percy. What did you do?"

"Nothing," he said too quickly. "I'm not talking about myself." His eyes didn't meet mine.

"What did you do?"

"I told you—nothing! I didn't mean to do it. It was Father's fault. And yours. The more I think about it, it *was* your fault. You put him in that awful place. That's why it happened."

"Why *what* happened?" I'd had no choice about sending Ambrose to Charenton Asylum. I was worried he would harm himself. The psychiatric hospital was known for its humanitarian treatment of patients, unlike so many other "lunatic asylums" of the time. It had been good for him, even though in the end they hadn't been able to stop him from taking his own life. But that couldn't have been what Percy was talking about.

"I don't want to talk to you anymore. You're a bully. You always were."

I stared at the stranger in front of me; funny how the resemblance to his father faded more with every passing moment. Ambrose had been generous to a fault, never petulant or petty. "I've always showed you kindness, Percy. Always."

"By rubbing my nose in your own perfection? By stealing my father from me?"

"Is that what you think I did?"

"He didn't tell you everything, Zoe. My father is the one who told me about Lucien and Olav. He's the one who told me how I could find the backward alchemists." In my stunned silence, Percy rose and pushed past me.

"No, he would never—"

"You don't know everything." Percy rolled onto his heels and thrust his chin out, the same spoiled mannerism he'd had when he was twenty. Yet, he hadn't regained control of his quivering body. He wasn't nearly as confident as he wanted to appear.

"Sit down, Percival," I said in my most commanding voice. "You're going to tell me exactly what you've been dancing around. What do you know about Ambrose being in the asylum?"

He snorted. "Why would I tell you anything?"

I drew a deep breath and took a huge gamble. I could have played more on his superstitions, but there was a seed of a good man in Percy that I hoped I wasn't mistaken about.

"Because you're not a bad man, Percy. You never were. You're weak, though. Whatever you're holding in is what's killing you even more quickly. The weight is crushing your soul."

"I'm dying anyway, Zoe." Percy closed his eyes. His lips moved, but no sound came out. Was he praying? When he opened his eyes, I caught a glimmer of humility in them.

"I might as well die with a clean conscience," Percy said. "My father didn't kill himself."

THIRTY-TWO

"The story begins," Percy said, "when I came back to Paris to see someone. A woman."

Of course, I thought to myself.

"I didn't visit you and Father," he continued, "because you believed me dead. I had no choice but to let you believe that. They forced me—"

"Stop with the excuses. If you want to die with a clear conscience, you need to own up to your actions."

Percy nodded, but the motion was erratic, as if he was battling himself. "Lucien kept an eye on you and Father when you were in Paris," he said with a trembling voice. "He knew that Father was raving about alchemy after *you* put him in Charenton Asylum. He was going to ruin alchemy for all of us. He shouldn't have been in that asylum."

"I believed it to be for the best," I said through my tightly clenched jaw. "He was distraught when he thought you'd died. He thought he'd failed you as a father, that it was his fault you were so unhappy, even though he'd given you everything he possibly could. He was talking about hurting himself."

"Instead," Percy said, "his actions threatened to hurt all of us."

"They believed him a mad man, Percy. Nobody took his ravings about alchemy seriously. He also talked about how he'd opened the gates of Hell at the *Cabaret de L'Enfer*. Which obviously wasn't true."

Percy grunted. "You thought you were so much better than him because you hated nightclubs."

I clenched my teeth. Percy was the type of man who thought he understood everything, even if he only had a small sliver of the truth.

I had rarely accompanied Ambrose when he went to *le Cabaret de L'Enfer* nightclub. Not because I didn't appreciate the macabre beauty or the dancing, but because staying awake late into the night has always been a challenge for me. Ambrose understood that, and he went out of his way to bring me the joys of the nighttime I otherwise would have missed.

The memory washed over me. One winter morning, nearly a century ago, Ambrose had awakened me a few minutes before dawn with a wicked grin on his face. "I have something to show you," he'd said. "Put on your dancing shoes." He'd discovered how to sneak into the nightclub while it was closed. While most of Paris slept but my own energy was surging, he lifted me onto his shoulders and helped me squeeze through a narrow window with a faulty latch. Once inside, I let him in through a larger door. He lifted two glasses from behind the bar and poured us drinks from the bottle of claret he'd brought with him. Carvings of devils and imps hung from the walls. Like the debated purpose of gargoyles, it was unclear whether the inhuman creatures were there to warn revelers or to tempt them. As the sun rose above Paris, Ambrose spun me around and around on the dance floor we had to ourselves.

"They could have believed his rantings," Percy said, shattering the memory. "He could have revealed everything. That's why Lucien asked me to visit Father and talk sense into him."

I bit back tears. I didn't want to hear the rest of the story.

"We looked alike, he and I," Percy continued. "That's what made it possible. I approached the gates of Charenton, pretending that I was Father and that I'd escaped. I couldn't very well walk in as a visitor, as I was supposed to be dead." Percy ran a shaking hand through his dark hair that was so like his father's. "As I expected, a nurse opened the gates for me, letting me inside. She was such a tiny thing, with a fragile heart-shaped face, I don't know how she could work in such a place. It was easy to administer the chloroform. I didn't hurt her. She was asleep before she knew what was happening. With her keys, I let myself into Father's room. *He* was the one who became violent. Not me. I only meant to talk sense into him."

Percy was pacing furiously now and knocked over the coffee table, but he didn't seem to notice. I barely noticed either. This couldn't be happening. This couldn't have been how my beloved Ambrose spent his last moments on earth.

"He must have been forced to take drugs or something that made him crazed. It wasn't my fault. I did only what I had to do to save myself. He said I was a hallucination sent there by God, telling him to reveal alchemy to the world." Percy's voice shook. His eyes darted around the room, looking everywhere but at me. "It was the exact opposite of what I meant to achieve. I didn't know what I was doing. It was an accident. I was only trying to stop him shouting, blurting out our secrets. My hands went around his neck—"

He broke off in a sob as I felt myself crumpling onto the velvet couch. Instead of feeling soft and comforting, the texture was like razor blades. The asylum had found Ambrose with a broken neck. They told me he'd hung himself.

"When I stopped," Percy whispered, "it was too late. He was dead, and I was nearly dead myself." He continued through hiccupping sobs. "It took all the strength I had to get myself out of there. Lucien had to take care of me while I recovered. I w-w-was lucky to survive."

Percy was bawling by now. My normal instincts to comfort and heal were absent. I couldn't find it in me to forgive the man who'd killed Ambrose. He'd felt such guilt that it sickened him to the point of feeling like he was going to die. He wasn't an evil man, but I couldn't look at him for one more second.

"Get out," I said. "I never want to see you again."

THIRTY-THREE

I was shaking so much that I could barely shove Percy's bag into his arms and lock the door behind him. I somehow got the door bolted before sliding down onto the floor.

I didn't cry. I couldn't. I was too numb from shock. I'd grieved for Ambrose, but this was different. Yet strangely, along with my horror, I also felt a sliver of *peace*.

Ambrose had grieved for his son. He'd lost himself in his guilt over finding the Elixir of Life when his only son could not, and he found it difficult to move on in the months that followed Percy's supposed death. But he *hadn't* been so lost that he'd taken his own life.

I gripped the wallet in my hand. As I'd shoved Percy's bag into his arms, I'd also lifted his wallet. It was done sloppily with shaking hands, but he'd been too upset to notice. There were still many blanks about Percy's current situation, but I couldn't bear to keep asking him questions. I hoped the wallet would provide some answers.

I took several deep breaths and picked up the coffee table Percy had knocked over. The simple action gave me a measure of reality to focus on. By the time I'd collected the books and newspapers that had fallen to the floor, I had mostly stopped shaking. I sat down on the couch and opened the wallet. Percival Smythe had a driver's license from Britain with an address in London, a membership card for a gym in a town in a suburb of Paris, and a library card from Edinburgh. A black credit card and several hundred dollars in cash indicated he was living well.

Two photographs were tucked inside the wallet. The first photograph was of Percy and a glamorous young woman. They sat together at a Parisian café, a cigarette in her hand and a pipe in his. They weren't looking at the camera, but at each other. She looked like a movie star. She reminded me of an actress from a 1930s Charlie Chan movie.

The other photograph was a faded black-and-white picture of Ambrose. The print was nearly worn through in the center, as if fingers had run over its surface many times. Percy had saved the photograph of his father and looked at it countless times. Damn. I couldn't dismiss him as completely heartless.

A tentative knock sounded on the front door.

"Zoe?" The voice was hesitant. "You don't have to look at me again, but I think my wallet fell out. Could you check the couch cushions?"

If it hadn't been for that well-loved photo of Ambrose, I wouldn't have opened the door. But now …

I opened the door and pressed the wallet into Percy's hands. "I hope you find peace before you die, Percy. But never show your face here again."

"I'm sorry," he said softly. "For everything."

By the time I locked the door again, my anger hadn't subsided, but it was a calmer rage. Clarity washed over me, showing me an important fact.

Percy was either one of the world's greatest actors, or he truly felt remorse over killing his father. He wholeheartedly believed the myth that alchemists can't kill one another without suffering grave consequences, and thought it was this old wives' tale that had brought him to death's door, not his own guilt. I would have bet my gold locket that he sincerely believed he'd nearly died from the wrath of a magical legend.

Meaning he couldn't have killed Lucien.

———————

Filled with a confusing mix of fury and anticipation, I couldn't stand to be indoors. I went out to the backyard and stepped into the garden. It was a clear, crisp night. Pinpricks of stars dotted the indigo sky above. Amidst the sorrel, garlic, and nasturtiums, I breathed in the early-summer scents.

A desperate sound escaped my lips, half laughter and half sob. Finding a backward alchemist had been a distraction, not Dorian's salvation. An experienced backward alchemist had died because he came to Portland in search of *Non Degenera Alchemia*, and a less experienced one wasn't able to tell me anything truly helpful. All Percy had done was devastate me.

I lay down in the garden, not bothering to look at which plants were beneath me. I didn't mind that I happened to be in the midst of blackberry brambles. I took pleasure in the pain of the thorns pricking my skin. It was a distraction from the mess of a situation I had to climb out of. I stared up at the star-filled sky.

I'd wasted too much of my life wallowing. Five minutes was enough time to compose myself. I had a gargoyle to save.

I brushed the brambles from my hair and clothes and went back inside to climb the stairs to the attic. There, surrounded by my alchemical and healing artifacts, I emailed Dorian to tell him I'd kicked Percy out.

I can come home? he emailed back immediately. *Tres bién. Julian Lake's housekeeper does not like me. She is suspicious that I will not let her see my visage. I believe she will try to sneak into my bedchamber tonight—little does she know I do not sleep!*

It's not late enough for you to walk across town, I wrote back. *I'll pick you up at the end of his driveway in 20 minutes.*

On the drive across town, I second-guessed everything I'd done not only that day, but since deciding to leave Paris several days ago. If I had stayed in Paris, how would things have played out with Lucien?

I pulled up in front of Julian Lake's estate. *House* wasn't a big enough word to describe the castle-like mansion, complete with stone lions standing guard. I didn't plan on walking up to the house and ringing the doorbell, so I idled the engine and waited with my thoughts.

A hunched figure in a black cape carrying a small satchel sprinted across the lawn. His bad leg gave him a limp, but it didn't slow him much. He looked rather like a hunchbacked Little Red Riding Hood with a book-shaped picnic basket.

Dorian climbed into the truck with *Non Degenera Alchemia* tucked under his arm. On the drive home, I filled Dorian in on what had happened with Percy. He replied with a string of profanities.

"I am so sorry, my friend," he said once he'd exhausted all the profane words he knew in both French and English, some of which I'd never heard. "Never fear. Dorian Robert-Houdin is on the case. I will put my little grey cells to work."

That's what worried me.

THIRTY-FOUR

I COULDN'T FALL ASLEEP that night. My mind was racing and refused to calm down enough for my body to get the sleep it craved. I got out of bed and lit a candle. The natural light of the flame was better to get into the mindset of alchemy, and that's exactly what I needed to do. Through Percy, my life had been connected to backward alchemy for far longer than I'd realized. I rubbed my gold locket, smooth for the decades it had comforted me.

How was everything connected?

The sulfurous scent of the candle and a mug of cashew milk cocoa calmed my nerves and awakened my senses. I unlocked the basement door and followed the stairs to my alchemy lab. As I lit a kerosene lantern and sat down at the solid wooden table I'd used for countless alchemical transformations, I thought through the confusing backward alchemy events that had happened.

I reached for my cell phone. My fingers hesitated for a moment before I sent Tobias a text message. I couldn't help chuckling to myself. When I was nursing Tobias back to health over 150 years ago, hiding in plain sight on a farm that was part of the Underground Railroad network, neither of us ever imagined a future when people could communicate instantly from hundreds of miles away, let alone without wires on a tiny device that fit in the palm of my hand.

It was the middle of the night, so I wasn't expecting him to answer. The very act of sending a message to my oldest living friend was comforting. I gave a start when my phone rang.

"Sitting up with Rosa?" I asked. I thought of Max, allowing myself a brief moment of the hope that that might one day be me and Max. It was a false hope, I knew. But that didn't mean I didn't want it.

"Is mind reading an alchemical skill I should be trying to hone?" Tobias replied good-naturedly.

"No supernatural skills required to know how much you love her. How is she?"

"Why don't you let me take care of you for a change. Are things not going well in Paris?"

"I had to leave."

A pause. "You're back in Portland? But that means it's the middle of the night for you too. You don't do nighttime, Zoe."

"I know." I hadn't thought Tobias would reply, much less call me. Where did I begin?

"I've seen you after you stayed up all night." His voice transformed from concern to anger. "You were no good to anyone after that."

"That night we had to run," I whispered, staring into the flames of the kerosene lantern and remembering the wretched night that left me with scars from harsh thorns and brambles.

"Are you in physical danger right now?"

"Not exactly."

"Then hang up and get some sleep."

"Please, Toby."

A long sigh sounded over the phone line. "What is it that has you reaching out in this darkest hour of the night?"

"I'm drowning. I know less than I did two weeks ago, before I went to Notre Dame."

"If I'm a sounding board, why don't you call me back in the morning?"

"I'm afraid." I clutched my gold locket.

A faint rustling sounded on the phone line, followed by the creaking of a door. Softly in the distance came the hum of crickets. I wondered if the lights of Detroit allowed him to see the constellations.

"I was awake because Rosa was dreaming. She kicked me in her sleep, but when I looked over at her, I couldn't fall back asleep. When she dreams, I see the same young woman I fell in love with over sixty years ago. I can't tell her that, though."

"She'd think you love her less now, because she aged. Even though it's not true." I thought again of Max, wondering if I'd ever be able to tell him just how different I was.

"If anything, knowing it wouldn't last forever has made me cherish her all the more." He cleared his throat. "I'm not letting you stay awake just to get philosophical. Tell me, why are you so afraid?"

After a moment's hesitation, the story spilled out of me. Tobias already knew about the unknown shift that had taken place six months before, when anything and any*one* who'd been helped along their way by backward alchemy began to have their life force reverse, from gold figures in museums turning to gold dust to living gargoyles returning to stone. And he knew about how, five months ago, Dorian had sought me out so I could help him decode *Not Untrue Alchemy*.

I smiled at the memory of my dear friend looking up at me from the wreckage he'd created in one of my shipping crates. I hadn't smiled at the time; I'd been terrified to find a living gargoyle, not to mention quite unhappy that he'd disturbed my carefully packed glass jars filled with alchemical ingredients. Dorian had apologized profusely and explained that he'd been hungry and was looking in the jars for food. When Tobias had visited, he'd been nearly as frightened to meet Dorian, and I hadn't known how to broach the subject of a living gargoyle who wasn't a homunculus to be feared. Since then, the two had bonded.

Now I told Tobias about what'd I'd recently learned of the formal origins of backward alchemy, in which a group of lazy men living in the 1500s, one of whom was Lucien Augustin, had found out how to shortcut true alchemy by using sacrificial apprentices, and had recorded their findings in a book that was meant only for themselves. Since alchemy connects as it transforms, the book took on the properties of backward alchemists, getting younger with age and not responding to fire as science would normally dictate.

In the flickering light of my half-finished alchemy lab, I grabbed the notebook on the table I used for recording plant transformations and began to scribble the ideas I was telling Tobias about.

"Why'd they create a book at all?" Tobias asked. "Sounds like they were selfish men who didn't want to share their twisted miracle."

"They're the laziest of men, Toby." I thought of Percy and snapped the pencil in my hand. "They didn't want to memorize even their most simple alchemical transformations. But they were so lazy they lost track of the book a couple hundred years ago."

"You don't know how it works yet?"

"Sometimes I feel like I'm so close to understanding, and sometimes I think I'm so far away I wouldn't understand it if I lived another three hundred years."

"Notre Dame didn't hold the key? I was so sure there was something it could tell you."

I hated to admit to Tobias how careless I'd been, but why had I contacted him if I wasn't going to be honest?

"Zoe?" he prompted.

"I was recognized. I had to leave before I was done."

Tobias swore.

"That's what started the mess I'm in. I thought at first the elderly woman who recognized me had sent a private investigator after me, but it was worse than that."

"Worse?"

"Two backward alchemists followed me home." I was glad he couldn't see my face as I explained how I'd learned a man I once knew in Paris had been murdered, seen a second stone gargoyle come alive for the briefest moment, and been tricked by Lucien about a nonexistent book that I hoped could lead me to a knowledgeable backward alchemist. I explained how I'd learned that Ambrose's son, Percy, was a clueless backward alchemist who'd killed his own father and that Lucien had died and shriveled inside an alchemy lab he'd set up in an abandoned cabin in Portland. It was all the more personal because Brixton had been a witness and now the police were suspicious of him and his mom, but I was so exhausted I was seeing alchemy everywhere I looked, even in Heather's paintings.

As I rambled, I picked up the shard of pencil and continued writing. Pouring my soul out to both Tobias and my notebook, I kept waiting for something to click. It didn't.

"I can see why you can't sleep," Tobias said.

"None of it makes any sense."

"On the contrary, it makes perfect sense."

"I remember you being a philosopher, not a comedian."

"I'm serious. *You're the one* everyone believes can figure it out. That's why they've all come to you."

"Misguided faith in an accidental alchemist."

"You really believe that?"

"Which part?"

"It wasn't an accident, Zoe."

"I never meant to find it—"

"You never meant to find the Elixir of Life for *yourself*. But you worked all hours to find it to save your brother's life. That's purpose. *Intent*. Not an accident."

"This isn't a problem with my ego. I know I'm great at many things. I can grow a thriving garden under the harshest of conditions, I can use spagyrics to create healing elixirs for an assortment of ailments, and I can fix the engine of just about any car produced before 1985. But I'm a terrible liar, I'm awful at turning lead into gold, and I never finished my alchemical training so I don't know how to decode formal alchemy."

"Do you realize the confusion you've told me about tonight sounds much more similar to listening to plants and putting a broken engine together than to speaking the secret language of some old white men?"

I swore. Why are we so blind to seeing what's right in front of us?

"I believe they're right that you can solve this," Tobias said. "As long as you get some sleep, kiddo."

"Kiddo? I'm almost two hundred years older than you."

"Then start acting like it. Stop thinking of what you don't know and focus on what you do. You know more than you think, my friend."

THIRTY-FIVE

I woke up at dawn, after approximately four hours of sleep, with a furious headache and a dry mouth that felt like it was filled with stinging nettles. Tobias was right—I shouldn't have stayed up. Was he also right that I knew more than I thought I did? With my brain in a fog, I wasn't much good to anyone at the moment.

Dorian saved the day. A breakfast feast was waiting for me. The spread took up half the dining table. Dorian had spent the predawn hours baking for me. He'd created variations on several of my favorite foods from my youth, from creamy almond milk porridge to cranberry nut bread. On the other half of the table, Dorian had arranged a set of notecards, written in his impressive cursive script. I helped myself to a serving of porridge and a slice of bread while Dorian explained the notecards.

"Each card is a piece of the puzzle," he said. "It is similar to the notes you wrote last night. By writing each separate point on its own notecard, we can move these items around in ways that are not simply chronological. My method is much more fruitful than yours."

"You snuck into my room and took my list?" I'd carried the note-book upstairs with me after talking with Tobias, hoping I'd have further revelations during the night. I didn't.

Dorian blinked at me innocently. "You left your door open. This was a sign you wanted my assistance."

It was a sign it had been a warm night, but no matter. "So you've rearranged my notes in a different order so they make more sense?"

"*Oui.*"

I stared at him. "You have?"

Dorian tapped one of his horns and raised a stone eyebrow. "I have cracked the case!" He grinned triumphantly. "Lucien was not an alchemist! Percival has misled you, Zoe."

"We know Lucien is the dead body. Brixton saw him."

Dorian waved away my concerns. "Brixton is an impressionable boy. Yet buried in your notes are dismissive descriptions of Heather, the very woman the police believe to be behaving suspiciously. It is *she* who is our most viable suspect."

I popped a bite of cranberry nut bread into my mouth and thought about how to refute the ridiculous idea. Dorian hadn't had an opportunity to interact with Heather. He could see in stone statue form, so he'd once stood still next to the fire place during a dinner party I'd given, and had observed Heather then. But most of what he knew of people was what Brixton and I told him.

"Heather wouldn't kill anyone." I saw Dorian open his mouth, so I quickly continued. "No, you're right. Anyone could kill someone, given the right circumstances. But for Heather, this doesn't make any sense. That's the more important point. Since you read my notes, you know I don't think those detectives are a good judge of character."

"*Non.*"

"No?"

"It is your own thoughts that betray you."

"My own thoughts?"

"You forget that you and Brixton have both said how strangely she has been behaving of late."

"It's true," I admitted. "But people have all sorts of things going on in their lives. Heather has a teenage kid and a husband who works out of town. That's not easy. But she doesn't have any connection to Lucien."

"How do you know there is no connection?" Dorian asked. "Her paintings at Blue Sky Teas—"

"We're reading too much into those paintings, Dorian. Brixton told her about the things I sell at my shop, and she's really creative."

"You are missing the point, Zoe. The motive could be any number of things we do not have enough information to understand. It is impossible to see into the hearts of men. No, my point is that your notes contain many points in history that are linked to one another in theory, such as the unfortunate coincidence of being recognized by a woman who knew you when she was a child. But there is only one true fact: science does not lie."

While science doesn't exactly lie, it's subject to the same human limitations as anything else. Accepted science in one era is later looked upon as laughable. Bloodletting to restore the balance in a sick body, mercury to treat syphilis, aether to explain light and gravity. Concerning forensics, DNA evidence was evolving as other tools had before it. And science didn't tell the whole story.

"Alchemy is science," I said, "but that doesn't do us any good because they don't understand it—"

"Yes, alchemy may be *foreign* science to these investigators, but they are seeking DNA evidence. You said they have the DNA of the killer, and yet Heather *refused* to submit to the test!"

"Do you remember the Phantom of Heilbronn?" I asked.

"The Phantom of the Opera? Have I told you about the time I snuck into a theater performing the musical and newspapers wrote that the phantom himself had appeared at the show?" He chuckled.

"No. Heilbronn. An example of when DNA science lied. A supposed female serial killer in Europe who killed dozens of people."

"Oh, yes. One of her crimes was committed in France."

"She didn't exist, Dorian. Laboratory results were contaminated with 'sterile' cotton swabs. It was the DNA of a factory worker."

"This is not bad science. It is human error."

"That's my point. It's perfectly reasonable to fear what will become of your DNA."

"Ah, so." He scratched his gray chin.

I looked at the set of carefully placed notecards and thought about how to turn the police onto Percy without revealing alchemy. Percy, whose wounds I'd washed. Aside from his head wound, he didn't have any scratches on his body.

But there was someone else who did. I felt as if the room was spinning around me.

"You are ill?" Dorian asked, his gray forehead creasing with concern. "Your face has gone as pale as a ghost from one of Father's magic posters."

"Yes. No. Where's my phone?"

I texted Brixton: ONCE YOU'RE AWAKE, WE NEED TO TALK.

———

An hour later, Brixton pulled up on his bike.

"I'm not going to get mad at you," I said, "so I need you to tell me the truth."

"About what?"

"I know you didn't want to worry me, which is why you didn't tell me. But you didn't only follow Lucien from afar, did you?"

Dorian gasped. "You cannot mean the boy killed him!"

Brixton and I both rolled our eyes.

"Of course not," I said. "But I think Brixton got closer to Lucien than he wanted to admit, when Lucien was spying on Ivan at his house. He didn't want to admit his mistake."

"Is this true?" Dorian asked Brixton.

Brixton fidgeted but didn't reply.

"Your wrist," I said. "I didn't think there was anything sharp on the table. It's not a scrape from when you hit my table, is it?"

Brixton shook his head but didn't look at me.

"Did Lucien grab you?" I asked. "Is that why you were extra careful to hang back when you saw him again?"

Brixton stared at us. "You mean it's *my* DNA they'll find under his fingernails?"

The air felt heavy and stifling. Brixton had a juvenile record. "Did they save your DNA in juvenile court?"

"I don't think so. That's why they had to ask my mom for DNA for that family match thing."

"At least your mom didn't give her DNA to the police. They won't have any way to match it to you."

"Actually," Brixton said slowly, "she decided to do it. It was killing her, not knowing for sure if it was her dad. When it seemed less likely it was him, that's when she realized how much she cared."

I stared at Brixton. "This is bad," I said. "Very bad."

"What happened?" Dorian asked.

"It wasn't a big deal," Brixton insisted. "He didn't think I was spying on him on purpose or anything. He just thought I was being nosy. I followed him around the side of the house, and he grabbed my arm and told me to get lost."

"It doesn't matter that the event itself wasn't a big deal," I said. "Nobody was there to see it, so nobody can back you up."

Brixton bit his lip and looked at me with fear in his eyes. I knew he was thinking the same thing: he already had a record. Even if a jury wouldn't be told, the police knew.

"They won't believe me, will they?" he said. "Even if I leave out the part that I was spying on Ivan because Dorian wanted to know if he was a trustworthy new alchemist."

"If they're looking at you as a suspect," I said, thinking it through as tendrils of worry spread over my body, "they'll be sure to notice you're lying about *something*. And even if you tell them the complete truth—*especially* if you tell them the complete truth—they'll think you're lying." I didn't add that they might even suspect he was crazy and lock him up somewhere worse than a juvenile detention facility.

"Why are you scaring the boy?"

"He's not a boy," I said.

Brixton was now nearly fifteen, older than my brother had been when he helped me escape from Salem Village. In the modern world, it was easy to dismiss a fourteen-year-old as a kid, and Brixton was indeed immature in many ways, but in important matters like this, I needed to treat him as an adult. He had to understand the full consequences of what was happening.

"What do I do?" Brixton whispered.

"You forget we had this conversation. Concentrate on supporting your mom, and leave it to me and Dorian to figure out what really happened to Lucien in that shed in the woods. Don't say a word about this to anyone, Brixton. Not to anyone."

THIRTY-SIX

DORIAN PACED THE LENGTH of the attic, past the shelves filled with antique books on herbal remedies, around the articulated skeleton of a pelican, steering clear of my set of Victorian swords once owned by a famous English physician. With his chin jutting out, left arm hanging limply at his side, and right arm tucked behind his back, he looked like a Victorian caricature. I sat on the old wooden trunk, my knees tucked up under my chin.

"We must assume that the police have not yet figured out Lucien's identity," Dorian said. "He must have left his identification papers elsewhere, since he was working undercover while he was sneaking around Ivan's home. Yet he was not staying in the shed as his lodgings, so his hotel will soon notice his absence. They will report this to the authorities."

"That's a good point," I said.

"I have many good points." He tapped his gray forehead beneath his horns. His *little grey cells*.

"We might not have much time until his identity is discovered," I said, "but we already knew that. Who knows how quickly the police labs will finish the DNA testing—that's the more important problem. Even if they learn who Lucien is, it doesn't necessarily connect him to Brixton. Lucien was a bookseller from Paris. If anything, that will connect him to me."

Dorian stopped pacing. He nodded his head only once, and the solemnity of his expression made me shiver.

"If it would help," I said, "I would take the blame." If it came down to it, I had no doubt in my mind that I would sacrifice my freedom for Brixton's. But the connection between me and Lucien was based on alchemy. Would anyone believe I was telling the truth, not simply trying to help a young man I cared about?

"I know you would," Dorian said. "Yet you could not do so even if you wished to."

"I might be able to convince them about alchemy. My old photographs. If I could prove my true identity, I'd do it to save Brixton, regardless of what it meant for us."

"I do not speak only of alchemy."

"Then what?"

"You do not know what it was that killed him. A 'head injury' is meaningless. And they are unlikely to tell you the specific method of death. Thus, the police would never believe your confession. No, we must figure out who killed Lucien."

"Maybe I was wrong about Percy. Could he be that good an actor? Maybe he doesn't actually believe the superstition that one alchemist can't kill another."

"Perhaps, though I doubt it. He does not appear to be a very intelligent man."

I steadied myself, pushing away the raw memory. "Who besides me would have a reason to harm Lucien?"

"You could return to Paris and examine his life. While you are there, you could also visit my brother again."

"I *can't* go back to France. The French authorities must have flagged my passport by now."

Dorian frowned. "Ask Brixton's young friend Veronique to hack into his personal life."

"Her name is Veronica. But she's fourteen. And she's a coder, not a hacker."

"It is the same, no?"

"No. Plus, hacking into someone's life isn't nearly as easy as it looks on television."

"Unless one can guess their passwords." Dorian drummed his claws against the side of a shelf containing Chinese puzzle boxes and apothecary jars. "A French alchemist would most likely select passwords in French or Latin, but this does not help us narrow things down."

"Ivan," I said.

"Ivan does not know how to hack into personal records."

"No. Lucien was spying on Ivan. I dismissed him as a suspect because he's too ill to hurt anyone. But unlike Percy, he doesn't believe the alchemy superstition that you can't kill another without killing yourself. Therefore Ivan could have *hired* someone."

"We suffer the same problem as we did with Brixton's mother. *Why* kill Lucien? Even supposing you are wrong about Ivan's quest for true alchemy, and he indeed turned to the dark side of backward alchemy, it makes no sense that he would kill the man who could teach it to him."

"We're missing something," I said. "I should talk with Ivan."

Dorian picked up a hefty glass paper weight from the shelf and handed it to me.

"What's this for?" I asked, turning over the heavy piece of practical art. The glass-blown piece was filled with flower petals, giving it the illusion of being lighter than it was.

"Protection. In case Ivan is a killer."

THIRTY-SEVEN

I BROUGHT IVAN A picnic basket filled with lunch sandwiches, potato salad, and multiple desserts; a thermos full of homemade ginger-turmeric tea; and a garlic tincture.

Yeah, I may have been overcompensating because I felt guilty for suspecting my friend. And also, assuming he was innocent, for ignoring his quest to discover the Philosopher's Stone and the Elixir of Life. But I'd taken the paper weight. It weighed down my purse.

"*Dobrý den,*" Ivan said in greeting as he let me in and ushered me through to the kitchen.

"Sorry I haven't been around much," I said, setting the food on the counter.

"Young love." He winked at me. "I completely understand." He shuffled around his library, tidying up.

I would have told him not to bother with tidying, but at the moment I didn't mind that he was turned away from me. His comment had made my cheeks flush. Was I blushing? Not very dignified for a 340-year-old.

"I'm glad you didn't forget about me for too long," Ivan said. "I have a question for you about how I've set up my laboratory."

We stepped into his garage.

Ivan had done his homework. He'd followed the descriptions in historical accounts of alchemists exquisitely. My little basement lab looked pathetic by comparison.

I hadn't had a true laboratory in more than a century. My goal for buying the dilapidated Craftsman house was to ease myself back into alchemy, one step at a time. Since life never seems to turn out quite as we expect it to, I hadn't had time to build my Portland laboratory, at least not properly. I'd been thrust into solving a much more urgent problem than purifying my own alchemical practice.

As I walked through Ivan's lab, I dismissed my concerns that he might be taking backward alchemy seriously. Since the last time I'd been at his house, Ivan had done a lot more to build his laboratory. He wasn't cutting corners.

I felt like I had stepped into a workshop on Golden Lane from Rudolph II's court in Prague. I wouldn't have been surprised if John Dee or Edward Kelley stopped by for tea. In addition to having alembics, matrix vases, and a pelican vessel, Ivan had a spirit holder. Glass jars were filled with ingredients. As much as I wanted to touch them, I knew I couldn't invade his space with my own touch.

One wall bore instructional posters—the torn pages from the books he'd destroyed. Only here, the destruction made sense. From their placement on the wall, the torn pages were close at hand, looking over him as he worked. A page on the steps of the Emerald Tablet, a map of the solar system with planetary metals, and an enlarged woodcut illustration of the *tria prima*: mercury, sulfur, and salt. The only thing missing was an athanor furnace, needed for cooking the philosophical egg.

"It's perfect, Ivan," I said.

The main thing that had led me to be suspicious of Ivan was that he was becoming obsessed, but was that so bad? Many a true alchemist had focused their obsession into a discovery.

"Not quite complete, I'm afraid. My furnace is being installed in the backyard next week."

"The athanor," I said.

"I won't tell you how difficult it was finding a vendor that had something similar to what's described in these alchemy books."

"A brick pizza kiln wouldn't do it?"

Ivan groaned. "You could have saved me time if you'd simply told me that. That's exactly what I settled on."

"Sorry. I didn't think you were at that stage. But truly, it looks like you don't need my help at all. I told you I never finished my training. At this point, I'd probably only hold you back or lead you astray."

"If I didn't know you to be a terrible liar, Zoe, I would think you were simply being polite."

"Shall we go back into the house?" I asked. "That way we can keep your laboratory strictly for you."

"In one moment," he said. He tapped on his cell phone before returning it to his pocket. "I've hung this Emerald Tablet poster on the wall here. It is my favorite so far, so I'm using it as my guiding model as I create my own."

Every alchemist must create their own fourteen steps of a personal Emerald Tablet to guide their work.

"Isaac Newton's?" I asked, looking over the yellowed page Ivan had taken from an antique book.

"I knew you were good, Zoe."

Working on Ivan's ideas in his library, I lost track of time. I pointed out that Ivan was trying to be too literal, as opposed to letting his intent guide him.

"I used to think these coded woodcuts were charming," Ivan said. "But now I wish to strangle the king and the queen here in these illustrations, and even their child. Look at the smug expressions on their faces. They hold more secrets than Mona Lisa."

I couldn't blame him for the sentiment. The king and queen, representing sulfur and mercury, come together in a marriage that results many months or years later in a philosophical child: salt. The two were sometimes shown as royalty, sometimes lovers, and sometimes as the sun and moon. Regardless of how they were represented in ink, they always hid their secrets.

Frustrated, Ivan declared he needed a break. Wincing as he rose from his seat, he led us to the kitchen. He'd cleaned up much of the mess of books I'd seen the last time I was there. The house was much more orderly, but the hard work had taken a toll on Ivan. He was thinner than he had been just days before.

"I could bring you some groceries," I offered.

"Brixton brought me a big bag of groceries yesterday."

"That was good of him."

"So many people grumble about 'kids these days,' but Brixton and my neighbor Sara are two of the most considerate people I know. Brixton's shopping choices contain more desserts than I'd have chosen for myself, but with all this work I have to do, a little sugar will do me good. Energy to complete the process." The flicker of obsession in his eyes had returned.

Only that's not what it was, I realized as Ivan collapsed into a chair. I rushed to his side, wondering if I had an appropriate tincture I could fix for him. I hadn't been making many lately, in proportion to how many I'd given out, so my supplies were low.

"It's nothing." He waved me off and glanced at the antique clock on the wall. "It's later than I thought. We've been working and talking for longer than my body can handle these days."

"Do you need any—"

"No." His hands shook as he spoke. "Leave me."

"Are you sure you—"

"Go."

THIRTY-EIGHT

HUMAN DIGNITY IS A complex thing. Ivan didn't want me to see his body's failings any more than Dorian wanted me to see his. I wished I could do more for Ivan, but my primary goal was helping Dorian—and now, Brixton.

After visiting Ivan, I was no closer to figuring out who killed Lucien. If I didn't make progress soon, the police would connect him with Brixton. And if I didn't get back to focusing on Dorian's life force reversal soon, his whole body would return to stone.

I could think of only one person who might have been able to help me. Why had I acted so impulsively and sent Percy away? I didn't even know his cell phone number! I'd reacted emotionally, but it was a stupid decision.

Berating myself, I shuffled up my stairs to the attic. The private and cozy space with a rooftop escape hatch was where Dorian and I had set up our research center. Dorian was using my laptop, since his clawed fingers didn't work well on the touch screen of a phone, leaving me to use my phone to go online.

Was Dorian right that I'd made unfounded assumptions? I wasn't so sure. All of the mysteries surrounding me were related to alchemy, so I couldn't help thinking they were connected. Occam's Razor: the simplest explanation was most likely the right one.

While I tried to put together the pieces of the puzzle, was Madame Leblanc working on a plan to get her nephew or a private investigator to find me and expose the fact that I was an alchemist? What would they find when they looked into the murder of my old acquaintance Jasper Dubois?

Because of more pressing matters, I hadn't spent enough time either worrying about Madame Leblanc's vendetta or researching Jasper's death. Dorian hadn't found anything, but I needed to try anyway. I again searched online library archives. As I narrowed my search, so many newspaper articles involved the police that I found myself distracted by thoughts of Max. If only I hadn't been encumbered by the secrets of alchemy, he and I could have had a normal life together.

Normal life …

Damn. There was something else I'd been ignoring. I hadn't checked my business orders in days.

I only listed high-end alchemical artifacts on my website, so I didn't do a brisk pace of business. But when a customer bought an expensive matrix vase crafted in Prague or a set of apothecary jars once owned by a famous Bohemian painter in Paris, they expected good service.

I checked my orders through Elixir and found I'd made a sale two days before. I took a break to pack the item—a handwritten speech by Sylvester Graham. I added a small puzzle box as a gift to thank the customer for the delay in my acknowledging the purchase. Since the activities that had transpired earlier this spring, I hadn't been too keen on having puzzle boxes around me anyway.

There was one more parcel I wanted to send. It was Rosa's heart that ailed her, so I packaged a healing Hawthorn tincture for Tobias. Before sealing the padded brown paper envelope, I stepped outside and clipped a sprig of ivy growing wild along the side fence. Tobias would understand I meant it as a symbol of friendship.

After bringing the packages to the post office, I felt myself compelled to stay outdoors in nature. My sanctuary. I took a long walk. Too many ideas were flitting through my mind, and being outside with the early summer flowers of Portland would help me focus. Dozens of varieties of roses were beginning to bloom in the Rose City. Across time and cultures, roses have symbolized many things. Today, I let myself believe the fragrant new petals represented rebirth and life.

When I came home, I was much calmer. And hungry. I called upstairs to Dorian, but he didn't answer. Since he hated it when I interrupted his reading these days, I let him be.

I ate leftovers for dinner. A small hearty scoop of Dorian's secret garlic tomato sauce remained in the fridge in a glass mason jar, so I slathered it on crusty French bread and sprinkled arugula on top. A perfect combination of spicy and mellow flavors, and sharp and velvety textures, danced on my tongue. I had to remember to ask Dorian how he got the sauce so creamy.

There was enough food in the fridge to feed us ten times over, so I thought it would be nice to bring Ivan something else. I took out a nut loaf and a wild rice salad from the fridge and headed off. If I was honest with myself, it also served as another excuse to go for a walk outside.

Ivan wasn't home. At least I hoped that was the case, and not that he was too sick to come to the door. Our alchemical discussion that afternoon had taken a lot out of him. Had it been too much for him?

I peeked in the window of his library, much like Lucien must have done. I didn't see Ivan, but I saw something else I recognized.

Percy's leather jacket. My throat clenched and I staggered away from the window. The bag of food in my hand dropped to the ground.

Percy was staying with Ivan.

That's why Ivan had glanced at the clock. He wasn't feeling as ill as he pretended; he was expecting Percy to return.

This connection couldn't be good. Using tricks I'd learned from watching Dorian use his claws to pick locks, I tried to pick the lock to Ivan's back door, shielded from view. I failed miserably.

I checked all the windows and found one that wasn't locked. It was a high one, but I was glad to find that slipping into a narrow high window was a skill one didn't forget. Either that or I had enough adrenaline pumping through my veins that I could do anything at that moment.

On Ivan's desk I found a copy of a flight itinerary. Ivan was going to Paris. Was he going with Percy? Why?

I rushed home and up to the attic to share these latest developments with Dorian.

I found my gargoyle friend tied up. His wrists were bound behind his back, rope had been wound around his body to prevent him from flapping his wings, and a handkerchief stuffed in his mouth.

His precious *Non Degenera Alchemia* was nowhere in sight.

THIRTY-NINE

I SHOOK MYSELF AND pulled the handkerchief from Dorian's mouth.

"*J'en ai ras le bol*," Dorian spat. "I have had enough, Zoe! This is too much."

"Who did this to you?" I asked, even though I already knew.

"I knew Ivan was not to be trusted!" Dorian screamed, fidgeting as I worked to untie the rope. "Hurry! We must go after them."

"We're too late."

His shoulder's fell. "*Non.* I suppose you are correct. They were here hours ago. I heard you come home, yet you did not come up when I did not answer you."

"You've hated to be interrupted lately."

Dorian sniffed. "Is a small modicum of privacy a bad thing?"

"No. Not under normal circumstances. I'm sorry. With everything going on around us, I should have checked on you. Ivan tied you up and took your book?"

"*Oui.*" Dorian shook out his wings and rotated his one working arm. "Ivan and Percival."

"They're taking it to Paris."

"You know?"

"I saw the flight itinerary at Ivan's house. The plane already left, we're too late. What happened?"

Dorian chuckled.

"It's *funny*?"

"At least when I spend eternity trapped in stone, I will always have the memory of Percival's terrified face when I came to life and refused to let go of *Non Degenera Alchemia*. He is a most annoying man, Zoe. You have the worst taste in men."

"It was his father I was in love with, not Percy. And what's the matter with Max?"

"He wishes to cook in my kitchen! He leaves things in the wrong place."

"Because he's nice enough to clean up—" I stopped myself and shook my head. "How did we get off track? You're *not* going to be trapped in stone for all eternity, Dorian. You're going to tell me what happened, and we're going to fix it."

"*D'accord*. The two men, Ivan and Percival, forced the lock to the attic. They must have had a key to the front door, because I did not hear them until they opened this one. By then it was too late for me to flee. I could only turn to stone and hold my book tightly. Yet with only one working arm … "

"You couldn't hold on tightly enough."

"Nor put up a fight. If I was at full strength, they would not have been able to tie me up. That Percival wished to chip me into little stone pieces. He is a very bad man, Zoe."

"You're all right?" I looked him over, terrified I'd see pieces missing beyond his two toes that had chipped off earlier that year.

"Ivan stopped him from hurting me."

Dorian looked at me thoughtfully. "Ivan was less surprised than Percival when I began to move. It is as if nothing else in this world can surprise him."

"He's dying. He has nothing left to lose."

"Yet he did not wish to kill me. He is the weak link. It is Ivan who has not yet gone too far."

"I need to figure out why they're headed to Paris."

Dorian blinked at me. "You said you knew."

"I knew they'd booked tickets to Paris. But what are they going to do there?"

"*Merde.*"

"What is it?"

"I wish you already knew. Then I would not have to tell you."

My heart thudded. "It's bad?"

"They spoke of a backward alchemy lab in Paris. A powerful one used by all the backward alchemists throughout the ages. It is where they perform their sacrifices. Ivan and Percival plan to use the book to bring back backward alchemy."

"Percy didn't tell me there was an alchemy lab like that."

"Of course he would not. He left out many things when he brought you into his confidence. He has done the same thing with Ivan. Percival is leading Ivan to his doom."

"And you to yours," I said, "unless I stop them."

FORTY

I WAS TOO LATE. The next flight to Paris wasn't until the next day. But even if I could have purchased a ticket and boarded a flight, what would happen when I entered France on my own passport? Would there be a flag on my passport that I was a criminal? The man who'd helped me with IDs for decades was dead, so I needed to find someone to forge me a new passport.

It was shortly after seven p.m. and the teashop was closed, but Blue was still there cleaning up. She opened the door for me. Her gray curls gave the impression she'd been struck by lightning. With the smile on her face, it was a magical lightning bolt of happiness.

"Have you heard if Heather is all right?" she asked.

"I haven't heard anything."

"I'll put on some tea."

I shook my head. "I'm afraid this isn't a social visit. I need to ask you for help."

Blue gave me a crooked smile. "Trying to help me feel at home since Brix is at an age where he's too cool to ask for help?"

"I need a fake passport," I blurted out.

Blue choked. "Honey, we definitely need to put on a pot of tea. A relaxing blend." She locked the front door and led me to the area behind the counter.

"I wouldn't ask if it wasn't an emergency."

"I figured that part out."

"Do you still know the people who helped you change your identity?"

"Tea first, criminal activities later."

Blue brewed dandelion tea that was both calming and invigorating.

"I've always said you were an old soul, Zoe," Blue said as I sipped the tea out of a solid curved mug like the kind found in 1950s diners. "But you're taking it too far. You look like you haven't slept since I left. And if I'm eating and sleeping better in a jail cell than you are here at home, I know something's wrong."

The tea warmed my hands and belly, but with Brixton and Dorian in danger, the comforting sensation didn't reach my soul. I pushed the mug away. "When you faked your death and started a new life, you knew people who helped you set up that fake identity."

The blank look on Blue's face made me wonder if I'd misunderstood how she started over here in Portland. But then she smiled and took my hands in hers. They were calloused but full of vitality. "Whatever you're running from, doing what I did isn't the answer. Trust me, I know."

"Then you do know people. People who can work quickly."

"I'm not going to ask what's going on. It's up to you to decide whether you're ready to tell me. But I will say that however desperate you feel, it *can* get worse."

Not the reassuring words I wished to hear. "I thought you'd tell me it'll get better."

"Ha. That too. But it won't get better if you go this route."

"You don't understand what I have to do."

"I would if you'd tell me. No?" She let go of my hands and ran her fingers through her curly gray hair that was as untamable as a ferocious storm. "All right, Zoe. If you're sure."

"I'm sure. I know what I'm doing."

"I hope you're right, sugar. I do hope you're right."

———————

I stared at the number for Blue's contact, wondering if I should call. It was so late at night that it was difficult for me to think clearly. Dorian had gone on a nocturnal walk to work out his own tension, along with living up to his nightly responsibilities at Julian Lake's house and at Blue Sky Teas. I'd made too many mistakes. I needed to get some sleep to make the right decision.

When I woke up at sunrise, I saw that I'd missed several calls from Max from the middle of the night. Because I'd wasted precious energy staying awake longer than I should have, I'd slept through the phone calls.

I called Max back. It took several rings for him to answer. He must have been sleeping. Understandable, since his calls had come in only hours before.

"Is Brixton staying with you?" Max asked.

"No. Why would he be with me?"

Max swore. "He missed dinner with his parents last night. They thought he was out with his friends, but when Abel checked Brixton's room before going to bed at around midnight, he found some of Brix's clothes missing, along with the passport they just took out of their safety deposit box so he could go on a summer trip with his friends. Abel and Heather called Ethan and Veronica and woke them up, but Brixton isn't with them. Last I heard, he still wasn't home."

No, it couldn't be …

"I'd better check with his parents again," Max was saying. "He's run off for the night before. It's the missing clothes and passport that make this case different. Zoe, are you there?"

I couldn't speak. This was far worse than I had imagined. Brixton wasn't only implicated in a murder—he might become a murder victim himself.

Brixton knew about alchemy. He trusted Ivan, and he'd been bringing him food to help the dying man. Ivan likely didn't know that an alchemy apprentice would give his life when he performed backward alchemy's death rotation.

Brixton had gone to Paris with Ivan and Percy to be the latest unknowing victim of backward alchemy.

FORTY-ONE

IF ONLY I'D HEARD my phone during the night, I would have known Brixton had gone with Ivan and Percy. We could have alerted the authorities in Paris that they should meet the flight on the other end to find a kidnapped child. Max put me on hold while he looked into the flight.

We were too late. The flight had already landed. Brixton was gone. In Paris.

Max said he'd be right over to my house to talk in person, after he told the authorities what he knew. I hung up the phone and ran to the attic. The door was locked.

I pounded on the door. "Dorian, let me in. I know you need your own space, but this is an emergency. Brixton has been kidnapped."

The door flew open. "Kidnapped?"

"Yes. No. Sort of. Effectively, yes."

Dorian cocked his head and wriggled his horns. "You are delirious, *mon amie.* Come inside and sit down." He took my hand and led me to a steamer trunk we used as a bench.

I breathed deeply as Dorian hopped up onto the trunk to sit next to me. A drop of a dark red substance clung to his bottom lip.

"Oh, God," I said. "You're bleeding. I didn't think you could bleed."

"I'm bleeding?" Dorian whipped his head around and flapped his wings. One of them hit my shoulder and knocked me off the trunk. "*Pardon*." He scrambled off the seat and helped me up.

"Your lip," I said. "It's your lip." I held my breath. His health was worse than I thought, with a new symptom.

"Ah. Only tomato sauce."

It didn't look like tomato sauce. Was he lying to shield me from how close he was to death? But as awful as it was, Dorian's unnatural death wasn't this morning's priority. "Brixton left for Paris with Percy and Ivan."

"Along with *mon livre*. Perhaps he wishes to be a superhero and is attempting to retrieve my book."

I shook my head. "Brix doesn't know it was stolen. I've been trying to keep him out of this."

"Then why would he go with them? They are very bad men."

"He doesn't know that! He's friends with Ivan. Ivan now believes in alchemy, and if he's working with Percy, he believes what Percy has told him."

"Backward alchemy," Dorian whispered.

"Which requires a sacrifice."

"*Mais non!* Why would the boy agree to such a thing?"

"I'm sure Percy lied to Ivan and Brixton, like Lucien lied to Percy to trick him into the lazy route of becoming a backward alchemist. Ivan doesn't realize what Brix would be doing to help him."

The doorbell rang, and I moved toward the door. Dorian put his one good arm on his hip. "Max Liu?"

"I'll talk to him in the kitchen so you can hear us, okay?"

In the kitchen, I explained to Max that Ivan had grown delu-sional as his health deteriorated, and that I thought he'd stolen a valuable alchemy book of mine because he thought alchemy was real. I theorized that Ivan had convinced Brixton to go to Paris with him, because that's where a certain type of alchemy supposedly draws its power from.

"Why didn't you report the theft?" Max asked.

"I didn't want to get Ivan in trouble. I thought I could get it back once he came to his senses. I didn't realize he'd go so far."

Max checked with passport control and found that I was right. Brixton had arrived in Paris earlier that day. He'd used his passport to visit his stepdad before; a well-traveled teenager accompanied by two respectable-looking adults hadn't been questioned.

Max wanted to go through the proper channels, but I knew there wasn't time. Besides, it would be impossible to explain to the authorities where they should look for Brixton, especially since I wasn't sure myself.

There wasn't time for me to get a fake passport, either. If I wanted to save Dorian and Brixton, I had to get to France today.

FORTY-TWO

I HAD NO TROUBLE clearing customs in Paris with my own passport. Madame Leblanc's nephew must not have moved forward with the cold case.

With my adrenaline pumping, I set out to search Paris for the trio. I tied a white scarf over my hair and put on sunglasses, hoping to deter the eagle-eyed Madame Leblanc if she happened to cross my path.

I started with Notre Dame, the center of backward alchemy. I waited impatiently in the line of tourists that snaked across the courtyard. Many of the visitors carried umbrellas to shield themselves not from rain but from the spring sun. It made it difficult to identify individual people in the crowd. I listened for voices instead. Chinese, Spanish, Italian, and English with accents ranging from Australian to the American South. Nothing that sounded like Brixton, Ivan, or Percy.

Inside the cathedral's sanctuary walls, I showed a photograph of Brixton to every guide and worker in the cathedral. With the heavenly stained glass above casting a glowing light throughout the stone church above us, they all shook their heads.

Unlike many cathedrals, Notre Dame didn't contain a large crypt beneath its floors. The "official" crypt was a tourist attraction located across the courtyard from Notre Dame. Through miniature displays and audio recordings, it told the story of Paris. When construction of Notre Dame had begun in the 1200s, Paris wasn't yet known as Paris. The bishops had wished to build a monument to God in a spot where people from across Europe had gathered, and the cathedral quickly became a pilgrimage site.

As for the crypt that contained bones of bishops and other important Frenchmen, many were entombed on the street level inside the cathedral, leaving only a small crypt—and it was off limits. I gave a generous "donation" to the same security guard who had given me access to the crypt the previous week.

Brixton wasn't there.

Before leaving the Île de la Cité, I stopped inside the tourist crypt. Just for good measure. Again, nothing.

What was I missing?

I was run-down both physically and emotionally. I stopped in a café in the shadow of Notre Dame for a glass of Perrier for hydration, *pain au chocolate* for energy, and a cup of tea for my spirits.

A siren sounded, but I couldn't see where the sound was coming from.

A crowd of people rushed to the edge of the Seine, and I realized why I couldn't see the vehicle with a siren—it was in the water.

I tossed coins on the table and rushed through the crowd. From the edge of Pont Neuf bridge, I watched helplessly as the emergency boat came to a splashing halt in the river. The text on the side read SUCCURS AUX VICTIMES: SAPEURS-PUMERS DE PARIS.

Divers jumped from the boat and swam toward a still figure.

A shiver like shards of glass covered my body. I couldn't breathe. Was I too late? I imagined Brixton dumped unceremoniously into the Seine once he was no longer of use.

The first diver reached the body. And there was no question that it was a dead body, not a living person. The diver turned over the body. It was a young man, but it wasn't Brixton. I looked on in horror.

It was the police officer who had interviewed me the previous week. Madame Leblanc's grandnephew.

I was sure I was going to vomit over the side of the bridge. I felt claustrophobic in the crowd of people surging forward to catch a glimpse of the dead body. I held my head and pushed my way through the throng, also trying to push away the thought barreling through my mind: *Death follows you everywhere you go, Zoe Faust.*

Who had killed Madame Leblanc's police officer nephew?

I raced down the stone steps that led to the riverbed, but Gendarme Gilbert's body had already been pulled onto the boat. Its engine revved. From the edge of the river, I called out in my most authoritative French for them to stop.

To my surprise, it worked. Sort of. They didn't change course, but they paused for long enough for me to call out a few words to them.

I told them how sorry I was for the loss of one of their own, and asked what had happened.

"You are mistaken, mademoiselle," the officer answered, then motioned to his colleague to continue onward. The boat stirred up a froth of dark water and disappeared down the Seine.

I was mistaken? What did that mean? Did he differentiate between the branches of the police and not feel bad when a man from another division was killed? Or was I mistaken that Gilbert was dead? No, that wasn't right. I'd seen enough death to know what I was looking at. Was it possible it wasn't Gilbert? Could my mind be playing tricks on me?

I jumped as a hand pressed against my elbow. I was standing too close to the Seine. The strong hand pulled me back.

"*Je suis desolé, mademoiselle,*" he said. "I did not mean to frighten you. You seemed so distressed, I did not wish you to fall. Yet I have made things worse."

I studied the newcomer. His eyes were sharp and he spoke in polished French, but he wasn't dressed with the effortlessly put-together fashion sense one imagined such a man to have. In spite of the warmth of the day, he wore layers of ragged clothing and carried a dirty backpack over his shoulders. Two newspapers, *Le Monde Diplomatique* and *La Tribune Internationale*, poked out of his torn coat pocket, and a beaten-up book of Victor Hugo's poetry rested in the side pocket of the backpack.

"No harm was done," I said. "Thank you for your concern, monseiur."

"You knew poor Gilbert as well?"

I hadn't been imagining things. The body floating in the river was indeed the police officer who'd driven me from France.

"Please," he said, "There is a bench just here. You must sit."

"How did you know Gilbert?" I asked, letting him lead me to the bench.

"I am in between residences." He chuckled. "Being outdoors much of the time, I meet many people. Gilbert was one of the better ones. He often brought me a croissant when he took walks here."

"On his rounds as a police officer?"

The man cocked his head and laughed again. "Gilbert? He was not police."

"Not the National Police. A *gendarme*."

He shook his head. "Gilbert was an actor."

"An actor?"

Madame Leblanc's nephew who had told me about Jasper Dubois's murder all those years ago wasn't a police officer at all.

Everything I thought I knew was a lie.

FORTY-THREE

WITH THIS NEW PIECE of information, reality snapped into focus on a different plane. A slight shift in the lens I was using to examine all the facts gave everything a new perspective.

Gendarme Gilbert wasn't affiliated with the police.

Had Madame Leblanc hired an actor to impersonate a police officer to scare a confession out of me? I thought that through. It was a weak plan. If she truly believed I was an immortal Zoe Faust, surely she wouldn't think I'd so easily confess. There also hadn't been time for her to coach an actor with so many facts. He did consult a notebook, though. Even if I granted he was a good improvisational actor, why had he been killed?

"Are you all right, mademoiselle?" the homeless poetry connoisseur asked.

"His death is a shock. I'll be fine. I just need a moment."

I tugged at the ends of my hair and watched the ripples of the Seine. Gendarme Gilbert hadn't been the only person acting.

I hadn't stopped to think about how implausible it was for Madame Leblanc to have such vivid memories of her childhood. Finding a dead body would leave an impression and be hard to forget. But the rest? She could very well be acting.

That meant an unknown person had hired two actors—an old woman to impersonate someone who knew me in the 1940s, and a young man who could play a rookie police officer. Why? The only answer that made sense was to convince me that I should leave France.

So not Lucien. He'd wanted me to stay so he could steal Dorian's book, and it had inconvenienced him that he'd had to follow me to Portland. Who else was there? It had to be an alchemist.

That only left one person: Ambrose's son Percy.

But why kill the actor? Was he a loose end? Was the woman who played Madame Leblanc next? Was there any way I could find the actress to warn her?

"Monsieur, did you see where exactly the police found Gilbert's body?" I spoke before realizing how odd the question must have sounded. "I mean, I'd hate to think about the indignity of him floating in the river for a long time. I hope he was found quickly."

"A woman walking her terrier saw him floating in the river right here, under the shadow of Notre Dame. I cannot imagine he was in the river long. Between the tourists and the locals, it would be impossible to miss him. Rest assured, mademoiselle. I will not be so philosophical as to assert he is now in a better place, but his dignity is intact and he will be adequately mourned by his friends."

"*Under the shadow of Notre Dame*," I whispered. "Beneath the city."

I now had an idea what I was looking for. The actor's body had washed up not only next to Notre Dame, the very place connected to alchemy and Dorian's book, but *beneath* it.

I looked around but didn't see any obvious entry points. But although I didn't know how to find it, I had an answer for how backward alchemists could have a space connected to Notre Dame without being observed as being part of it. The perfect place to hide a backward alchemy lab that needed to be close to Notre Dame. Not only a basement, but truly underground. A secret space where a backward alchemist could perform a transformation.

But where? Invisible to the city above were an assortment of catacomb passageways, bunkers that had been built during World War II, metro tunnels, shafts for water and sewage, and quarries that had been mined for limestone and gypsum for centuries, causing many a cave-in. Those cave-ins were much more common when I'd lived in Paris decades before, causing me to be wary of climbing beneath the surface of Paris.

"I hope, mademoiselle, that you are not looking to venture beneath the city to avenge Gilbert's death. People have died down there, after they've gotten lost and not been able to find their way out."

"I have a young friend," I said. "Just a boy. I think he might be with the same people who did this to Gilbert."

"Even if this is true, your death would not help him."

"There are people who know the city's underground well," I said, thinking of how it was now a trendy thing for artists to stage art shows or dance parties underground.

"You'll never find them."

"Who?"

"The Urban eXperimenters. That's who you're going to try to find, yes?"

"That's what they call themselves?"

"One of the groups. And I've tried. Believe me, I've tried. They don't like to reveal their identities. I once thought the underground might be a good place to stay during winter, but it is not what one would expect. I wish you good luck finding your young friend. But heed the words of an old man who has seen where such folly can lead. Following your heart is beautiful in the pages of a book, but in life, remember to think before you descend."

I thanked my new friend with a handshake while surreptitiously tucking a few Euros into his Victor Hugo book with the sleight-of-hand skills I'd learned from Dorian, then ran down the riverbank.

He was right: I couldn't find Brixton alone, but I now knew how to get the help I needed. I ducked into a quiet square filled with Honey Locust trees to make a phone call to my secret weapon: a fourteen-year-old.

"Hi, Ms. Faust," Brixton's friend Veronica said.

I'd never get used to the fact that people could see your name when you called them.

"I need your help finding Brix," I said.

"Mr. Liu and Brix's mom already asked me. I don't know where he went. My dad even searched my room. Like he'd be hiding in the closet! Can you believe that? I really don't know where he is."

"I think I do. But I need your help."

"You do?"

"I need to get a message to the Cataphiles of Paris."

"Paris? Brixton is in *Paris*? How did he get to Paris? I mean, I knew he had a passport cuz he went to visit his stepdad somewhere a couple of years ago."

"Veron—"

"But I always thought the two of us would go together, you know? Backpacking before college. He knows how much I wanted to go. The City of Lights. The—"

"Veronica. Please listen. He's not here on vacation."

"*Here?* You mean you're in Paris, too?"

"He's in trouble."

A pause. "Really? It's not just a crazy idea to get to Europe before Ethan?"

"I promise I'll explain everything as soon as I can. But first, I need your help."

"Okay. Um, what's a Cataphile?"

"People who like to explore underground. Sort of like what you, Brixton, and Ethan did when you explored Portland's Shanghai Tunnels."

"That was different. There aren't *graveyards* underneath Portland, Ms. Faust. That's who you mean, right? The explorers who sneak into creepy old tombs underneath Paris to walk through old bones and things? I saw the creepiest photos online from an art show and pop-up kitchen set to candlelight in Paris."

"That's them—"

"Oh, you should totally do something like that in the Shanghai Tunnels, where it's cool without being weird with all the skulls and things, you know? Is that what Brixton is in Paris for?"

"Sort of. But because what these groups do is illegal, they don't like to be found by people who aren't part of their group."

"You want me to post a message to this online group?"

"I know it's a lot to ask," I said, "but I think it'll help me find Brixton. I don't know how else to find them, but I thought if you tried you might—"

"Sure."

"What?"

"While we've been talking, I found them. Um, I've only had one year of French, though. Can you tell me whatever your message is *en français*?"

FORTY-FOUR

An hour later, I sat at a crooked wooden table scarred with key carvings in the back room of a Left Bank café with Constantine and Emma, who insisted they would only use their first names. That was fine with me, since I wasn't going to reveal more than my first name to them. Yet we huddled together like old friends, speaking in low voices as we constructed our plan.

Veronica had posted a message that a boy had been kidnapped and taken to the tunnels, and that the police hadn't followed up on the tip. Anyone who wanted to help me could meet outside a café near the entrance to the catacombs. I knew the tourist attraction wouldn't be where we descended, but with urban explorers hiding their discoveries almost as well as alchemists, I couldn't think of a better place for a group of people to meet.

The eight others who'd shown up had departed as soon as they realized this wasn't a piece of performance art. They had wanted to be part of a murder mystery-themed game like a similar one staged in a newly discovered section of the catacombs the previous month. Constantine and Emma were different. They were hardcore Cataphiles who'd taken Veronica's note seriously and come prepared. They arrived in thigh-high rubber boots and carried small backpacks filled with maps, lights, and other items they didn't reveal to me. I guessed they were brother and sister, for they both had tiny bodies, ginger hair, and a familiarity that I remembered from long ago.

The first words out of Constantine's mouth, after listening to my plea and extinguishing his cigarette, were, "You were right to contact us."

"Below ground," Emma added, "we will be of far greater help than the police."

I'm not a perfect judge of character—as my misjudgment of Percy and Ivan reminded me—but in spite of their youthful arrogance, the thing that told me I could trust Emma and Constantine in this situation was their healthy skepticism of the authorities. They hadn't once asked me why I didn't try again to convince the police. Instead, they followed me to a private corner and quizzed me for details of Brixton's disappearance so we could construct the best plan of attack.

"This is our best way in," Constantine said, using his index finger to circle a hand-drawn mark on a wrinkled photocopy of official blueprints.

Emma clicked her tongue. "*Non*. That passageway is always muddy."

"But it gets us close to Notre Dame," I said. "That's what matters."

Emma's pale cheeks turned scarlet.

"Emma brings up a good point," Constantine said, his eyes not leaving the map.

"I'll pay your laundry bill," I said, not caring about the naked desperation in my voice. "I'll pay whatever you want. You know the life of a child is at stake here. *Please*."

"You misunderstand," he said.

"The *reason* for the mud in that tunnel is the problem. I forgot there's a blockage there, after another section collapsed. We might not get through."

"Can't we climb down in a big tunnel you know isn't blocked, and go from there?" I asked. This was taking too long. What had become of Brixton?

"This attitude is why people have died down there," Emma said derisively. "It is not as easy as looking at a map. There are not only side tunnels, but different levels and many underground landslides we don't know about. There's a whole world beneath Paris."

"She exaggerates," Constantine said, "but not by much. Here." He jabbed his finger onto another spot, not far from the first. At least I thought it was close by. I wouldn't have been able to read the map without them.

"*Oui*," Emma said. "That will work."

Constantine gave a single curt nod. "*Bon*."

"Are you ready?" Emma asked me. Without waiting for a reply, she stood and tucked the tightly folded map underneath her shirt.

I tossed coins onto the table and chased after them.

———

When we reached the rusty metal grate that was to be our entrance, Emma handed me a hat with built-in flashlight and an extra set of gloves. I looked down at my own green ankle boots, gray cotton slacks, and black cardigan. Even with my guides, I was far from prepared for this. All that mattered was that I reach Brixton in time.

Willing myself to forget about the people who'd died during tunnel cave-ins of previous centuries, I took a deep breath or five and climbed into the darkness below.

We walked for what felt like an eternity, passing through lime-stone and gypsum corridors that had been mined in the Middle Ages, and passing near the more modern Metro, sewer, and water tunnels. In many of the tunnels, empty plastic water bottles and other trash was strewn about. I stepped on more than one long-dead glow stick from the parties that must have taken place here. The trash gave me hope, though. It meant we were traversing where others had recently come. We weren't going to end up as a statistic, another stupid explorer who starved to death underneath Paris.

At a crossroads, they stopped and consulted a map. After only a few seconds, they pointed to the left path.

"Why that way?" I asked. "It's going away from Notre Dame. It looked like we were almost there."

"You will not find them there," Emma said.

"But that's where I think he's been taken. That's why we're here."

Constantine exchanged a look with Emma before speaking. "Nobody goes there."

"Why not?"

"Perhaps it would be best to call the police now," Emma said softly.

I put my hand on her grimy shoulder. "They can't help," I said. "I need to go."

"You don't," Emma said, gripping my hand. "If this is where your young friend has been taken, you won't find him."

"Why?"

Emma didn't answer.

"Death," Constantine said. "Only death awaits down that corridor."

A mixture of panic and hope welled inside me. That had to be the right way.

"I'll pay you for a map and headlamp," I said, hoping they could hear the desperation in my voice. I didn't care if they asked me for all the money I possessed. "I need to find him."

The two communicated wordlessly for a few moments. I think I held my breath for every second.

"No money," Emma said finally. "But you must be safe. Take these breadcrumbs." She pressed a map and what looked like a bag of plastic sticks into my hands. No breadcrumbs in sight.

"Glow sticks," Constantine explained. "At every turn you take, break one and leave it there. You'll be able to find your way back."

Breadcrumbs to find my way out of the dark forest.

———

My solitary route took me through catacombs and crypts of bones as I continued the search for Brixton. It was a disheartening image that reminded me too much of the very real possibility that I could be too late to save his life.

I remembered to leave a glow stick at each turn, though in these tunnels the curves were deceptive rather than clear cut. I hoped I'd used enough.

The sound of a man's voice speaking made me stop in my tracks. A moment later, I breathed in a familiar scent that blended metallic and sweet. I ran forward, slowing only as a sliver of light cast its glow in front of me. I forced myself to slow down and approach with caution.

I found myself in an alchemy lab like no other I'd ever seen before. Instead of the complicated assortment of dozens of glass vessels, hundreds of ingredients, and countless books, a cozy armchair took up more space than the single table of alchemical apparatuses and ingredients. Candles illuminated the 50-square-meter space that looked more like a child's playroom than a serious alchemy lab.

And a child *was* there. Brixton's body was sprawled on the cold stone floor.

He wasn't moving.

A lone man stood next to Brixton. He clutched Dorian's book in muscular hands. The man turned, and I saw his face. Ivan.

FORTY-FIVE

Only ... Was I mistaken? The hands that gripped *Not Untrue Alchemy* were too strong to be Ivan's. His face and his body looked different as well.

"You don't have to do this, Ivan," I said.

"Zoe? How—"

"Why don't you come over here?"

"What? Oh, Brixton isn't hurt. He's sleeping."

"He's not sleeping, Ivan." A ferocious anger welled up inside me. "He's dying."

Ivan looked hesitantly at Brixton, then shook his head furiously. The motion startled me. Ivan normally moved slowly. Not any longer. That's why he looked different. A vigorous middle-aged man stood before me. There was no way I could take on this new Ivan physically. If it had only been me, I would have risked fighting him. But with Brixton unconscious beneath him, I had to be smart. I had to reason with Ivan.

"The apprentice sacrifices their life," I said. "I know Percy kept the truth from you. That's how backward alchemy works. That's how it begins."

"No. That's not how it works. You're lying."

"It's Lucien and Percy who lied to you."

"Lucien? Did he find you? Where is he?"

"You don't know?"

"I now know of backward alchemy's true potential. You lied to me, Zoe. You said it was dangerous, you said *he* was dangerous. That's why I didn't embrace backward alchemy sooner. If only—"

"Lucien is *dead*, Ivan. He's the man who was found in the shed in the woods last week."

"You're trying to confuse me. That man was Heather's father."

"No, it wasn't. Backward alchemy changes how quickly a body deteriorates. It misled the police. It was Lucien. And if Brixton survives—" I swallowed hard and looked at his unmoving form on the cold floor. *Don't look, Zoe.* I couldn't let myself break down. "If Brixton survives, he's going to be implicated as a murderer unless we find out who killed Lucien."

"This is madness. The boy is simply exhausted from the Death Rotation. And there's no reason for the police to suspect him."

"Lucien caught Brixton following him and grabbed him. Brixton's skin cells ended up under Lucien's fingernails."

"You're trying to distract and confuse me. Nothing you're saying makes any sense. Can't you see backward alchemy's potential? Look at what I've become. When Brixton wakes up, he'll be stronger too."

"You don't understand—"

"You weren't honest with me, Zoe. How can I believe you now?"

"You're right. I'm sorry. It's hard for me to open up. But I'm ready to talk now. To share everything I know. Why don't you come over here and we can talk about it?"

A pained expression crossed Ivan's face. "I see what you're doing. You think I wish to hurt Brixton. How little you know of me. I would never do that."

"I don't think you would do so intentionally." I spoke as calmly as I could manage. "It won't hurt to get him medical attention, will it? Now that you're done with the transformation, we could—"

"We're not done. Not yet."

I said a silent prayer. There was hope for Brixton. "This isn't you, Ivan. I know you're a good man. You don't know what you're doing. You've been lied to."

"Only by you. You twisted the facts so I didn't believe what Lucien had to tell me."

"You spoke with him?"

"He wanted my help. He saw that I had a vast library of books on alchemy and wanted to know if I had *Non Degenera Alchemia*—the book that you've so desperately wanted to understand. You've been lying to me since we met. You never wanted to understand that book for the sake of knowledge. Percival told me the truth. It was to save that creature who lives in your attic." His eyes were pleading. "You could have trusted me, Zoe."

"Because you're showing yourself to be so trustworthy," I snapped before I could stop myself.

"This is your fault," Ivan boomed. "Not mine. If only you'd been honest with me, I could have had the Elixir of Life so much sooner."

I looked at Ivan from head to toe. Was he as strong as he now looked? "How do you feel, Ivan?" I asked quietly.

He frowned and smoothed his wild hair. "Percy said I would feel decades younger immediately, but—" He shrugged. "It must be because there's more to the process."

I thought back on my own true alchemy transformation. I had discovered the Elixir of Life while searching for a cure for my brother, who was dying of the plague. I was so grief-stricken that I didn't realize what I had become until I saw that I wasn't aging.

But true alchemy was different from backward alchemy. The shift in true alchemy was more subtle, because it wasn't a quick fix. From what I'd seen of backward alchemy, the effects were visible and immediate. Ivan did look much healthier than I'd ever seen him, but the full power of backward alchemy was being diminished by the shift that had taken place six months ago. No matter what Percy claimed, Ivan wouldn't be able to experience the full effects of backward alchemy until that fissure was fixed.

"There's indeed more," I said, "but not in the way Percy told you. Did he tell you that a shift occurred six months ago and that everyone who'd been granted an extended life through backward alchemy began to die?"

"It was because you were hoarding that book! That's why he and the others had to make and smoke Alchemical Ashes, to fight for their lives. He had run out of his supply."

"It's not the book, Ivan. The book contains the secrets of backward alchemy and is tied to Notre Dame, but it has nothing to do with why the power is fading."

"You're still lying. I should have believed Lucien when I had the chance."

"What happened when he came to you?"

"Seeing that I was a scholar of alchemy, he confessed to me that he was a backward alchemist who had been alive for centuries. He suspected you had stolen a book that was his. But I trusted you. I foolishly trusted you, Zoe. He wanted me to steal the book from you, as he said you had done from him. He became angry when I refused. I shoved him out the door."

"You shoved him?"

Ivan snorted. "You have always thought me a weak old man, but Lucien was weaker. It was not difficult to push him out of my house. He fell down the front steps."

I gasped.

"It doesn't take much strength to hurt a frail man," Ivan continued, "as I know all too well."

"It was you. It was you who killed him."

"No, he was not dead. I told you—"

"Did he hit his head when he fell?"

Ivan narrowed his eyes that were no longer tired and blood-shot. "He might have, but he got up and left."

"To go back to his makeshift alchemy lab to try to make more Alchemical Ashes. He died before he succeeded."

On the floor, Brixton groaned. Ivan jerked back, startled.

"Brix?" I said, rushing to his side. "Can you hear me?"

His eyes were still closed, but he moaned again. Sweat coated his body.

"Ivan, please," I pleaded. "We've got to get Brixton help."

"He's not supposed to be hurt," Ivan whispered. "He must be faking it. Yes, that's what's happening. He's an attention-seeking kid."

"He's not faking it. And he's going to be arrested for murder."

"I would never let that happen," Ivan said. "You think so little of me? If it comes to that, I'll tell the police what happened."

I recoiled when Ivan's shoulder touched mine as he knelt over Brixton.

Ivan cried out. "This isn't right." He shook Brixton's still shoulders.

"He's not pretending."

"He's cold," Ivan murmured. "Too cold. We must help him."

"Let me call an ambulance."

"No."

I squeezed my eyes shut. I'd been so sure I'd gotten through to Ivan.

"We can't call an ambulance," Ivan said. "They'll be back soon. We have to get Brixton out of here ourselves."

I opened my eyes and saw the good man I'd thought of as my friend.

Ivan handed *Not Untrue Alchemy* to me. With his newfound strength, he lifted Brixton into his arms and carried him out of the backward alchemy lab beneath Notre Dame.

In the darkness of the tunnel, Ivan swore. "I don't know if I can find my way out without them."

"That," I said, "I can help with." I turned him towards a faintly glowing light. The glow sticks Constantine and Emma had brought were the perfect breadcrumbs to make our way out.

As I watched Ivan carry Brixton's limp form from the subterranean gloom out into the summer sunlight, I was filled with two of the most conflicting emotions I'd ever experienced together. The all-encompassing relief of having found Brixton in time was weighed down with the realization that the only remaining hope I had of saving Dorian's life was the backward alchemy transformation I'd been denying: a sacrifice.

I now knew, with all certainty, that I would have to sacrifice my own life to save Dorian's. And I knew that I would do it.

FORTY-SIX

THE HOSPITAL CALLED BRIXTON's family, explaining that he'd been found unconscious and dehydrated, but was stable.

I hated hospitals, with their overbearing astringent scents that assaulted my senses and my memories of the horrors of medicine of past centuries, but I didn't want to be far from Brixton. Ivan stayed with me. We hadn't yet talked about what had transpired, but he'd been the one who carried Brixton's body from subterranean Paris, and he spoke to the hospital staff so I could keep my name out of it.

There was another reason it was difficult for me to talk with the staff. I was so thankful Brixton hadn't died like the actor who played the policeman that it was difficult for me to speak. My eyes kept welling with tears of relief.

Ivan and I sat together in an outdoor courtyard waiting room. People had recently been smoking here, but the scent was far better than the sterilizing chemicals and strong medicines inside. Neither of us could sit still. I paced the length of the courtyard, and Ivan prodded the newly regenerated muscles of his arms. How long would it last? I couldn't let myself begin to feel sorry for Ivan. His blind selfishness had nearly killed Brixton.

"Would you sit with me for a minute?" Ivan asked. "I see your hesitation to be near this monster, but I wish to apologize. And to understand."

I joined him on a wooden bench, not wanting to hear his apologies, but wanting even less for the other visitors to hear what he had to say.

"If I'd performed the Death Rotation experiment properly," Ivan began, then faltered. "If I—" He cleared his throat and looked up at the wispy clouds above. "If I'd done it right, the boy would be dead?"

"If you'd finished the transformation," I said. "Brixton only survived for as long as he did because of his own strength."

Brixton had survived for the same reason that my own backward alchemy transformation *hadn't* worked well the last time I'd tried it to make Dorian's Tea of Ashes. He'd lived for the flipside of the reason I'd been sickened.

"Brix was tending to my garden," I explained. "He has a green thumb, and the garden flourished. His energy gave strength to the plants he tended, and that energy flowed back into him, giving him strength and protecting him."

"Alchemy doesn't create something out of nothing," Ivan said. "You tried to teach me that, but I wouldn't listen."

"Alchemy transforms, and the power of the transformations is tied to the practitioner and their materials."

"You can tell them the truth," he said. "Max and the beast. I can see on your face that you want to call them."

"He's not a beast," I said. The man sitting next to me was much more of a beast than Dorian would ever be. "And what could I possibly tell Max?"

"The truth. I was blinded by my desire to live, so I believed a hoax. I put Brixton's life in danger with a desperate plan."

"You're owning up to this?"

"Of course. I'm mortified by my actions, and thankful alchemy isn't real so I didn't harm Brixton."

I nodded. He understood we couldn't explain alchemy to the world. I stepped to the quietest corner of the courtyard and called Max. I kept an eye on Ivan, who wasn't interested in me. He flexed his fingers and stood on his tiptoes. It must have been a strange sensation to have one's body transform within hours.

My call to Max went to voicemail, which I was thankful for since it would be easier to stick to the somewhat truthful lies if I kept to the script I'd rehearsed in my mind. Next I called Dorian. Even with the coded timing of rings he insisted we use, he didn't answer. Where was he? With me gone, he knew he shouldn't be baking at Blue Sky Teas.

Frustrated, I hung up the phone and looked up at the sky for a few seconds. When I turned my attention back to the courtyard, Ivan was gone.

In his place on the bench was a torn piece of paper. Caught in the gentle breeze, it fluttered to the ground. I ran to it and snatched it in a tense hand. The handwritten scrawl read *I'm sorry.*

I crumpled the note in my hand and rushed inside but caught no sight of him. I asked everyone I saw, down every hall I could find, but nobody had seen him. The hospital appeared to be more labyrinthine than the catacombs.

I wasn't giving up. I looked from room to room. As I finished searching a hall of patient rooms, a news story on the television in the waiting room caused me to stop my search. On the screen was a face I recognized, one that still bore the marks of bee stings. Professor Chevalier, the scholar studying the gargoyle statue, was being interviewed by a reporter. I turned up the volume.

Professor Chevalier was explaining the mystery of the curiously posed gargoyle statue thought to be stolen from Notre Dame in the

1860s. There had been a break-in at the university, and thieves had ransacked the whole Architecture Department. The reporter asked the professor how he first noticed the theft.

"No," Professor Chevalier protested. "It was not thieves who stole the chimera. The stone creature came to life."

The reporter abruptly ended the interview and the camera switched back to a reporter sitting at a desk with a plastic smile frozen on her face. But she wasn't able to hide the flush filling her cheeks.

Was it possible? The Death Rotation Ivan and Brixton performed must have also enlivened the gargoyle. Perhaps because I'd left the Alchemical Ashes in his mouth, the nearby alchemy had woken him enough that he could swallow the ashes and escape.

If I were a gargoyle who once stood atop Europe's most famous cathedral, where would I go? I left the hospital and headed for Notre Dame.

———

People see what they expect to see. They believe what already makes sense to their understanding of the world. Therefore it didn't surprise me when the tourists I spoke to said they'd seen a disfigured man. They assumed him to be homeless because he wore only a sheet and carried a bottle of liquor. They pointed in the direction they had seen him go.

I thought I was going to lose my mind as I waited in line to climb to the top of Notre Dame, but it was the only way to gain access to the stairs. I used the time to look up a few things on my cell phone. Now that Brixton was safe, I felt guilty that I hadn't found the actress who played Madame Leblanc, to warn her that her colleague was dead and she might be next. I found the *gendarme* actor's website. He didn't have any affiliation with an actress who looked like Madame Leblanc.

A tap on my shoulder alerted me to the fact that the line was moving. It was time to climb the winding steps of Notre Dame once more. I hadn't heard any screams from above, so I wasn't entirely certain my theory was correct. But I had to try.

The first place I looked—near the famous Gallery of Gargoyles—was a bust. But while the guard was dealing with two people blocking the way with banned selfie sticks, I slipped into an off-limits area near the bell tower.

A scuffling sound startled me.

"*Allo?*" I said softly, hoping it wasn't a cathedral worker.

A burp broke the silence. I stepped forward and saw a lumpy sheet in the corner. The sheet moved.

"Do you remember me?" I said. "I tried to help you last week."

"*Va t'en!*"

"I'm not leaving. I can help you."

The gargoyle poked his head out from underneath the sheet and glared at me. "*T'es conne.*"

Great. That was all I needed. A drunk gargoyle telling me to get lost and calling me dumb.

"Are you drunk?

"'It is the hour to be drunken! On wine, on poetry, or on virtue, as you wish.'"

"You've only been *awake* for an hour … But if you've already found liquor, I suppose you don't need this." I held up a bottle of absinthe, the same brand that had been found in his frozen hand in Prague.

He lunged for it. I put the bottle behind my back, hoping he wouldn't tackle me. This gargoyle was more than a foot taller than Dorian, almost five feet tall.

"Only if you talk to me," I continued. "What's your name?"

He chuckled. "Leopold. *Je m'appelle* Leopold."

Now that he was standing before me, I got a better look at him. Leopold did look like he could be an older brother to Dorian. Since he'd once stood with the other stone creatures on the Gallery of Gargoyles, he was larger than Dorian in both height and girth. His body was a similar gray color, but his eyes were gray, not black like Dorian's. His horns were larger than Dorian's, yet he had no wings.

"I'm a friend," I said. "An alchemist."

Leopold blinked at me. "Your name is Alchemist?"

"No. My name is Zoe. I'm an alchemist."

He shrugged. "*D'accord.*" Did he not realize alchemy had brought him to life? This was too big a conversation to have a few meters away from the tourists atop Notre Dame.

"Myself," he continued, "I am a *poète.*"

A gargoyle poet? I supposed it was no stranger than a gargoyle chef.

"You have another friend, too," I said. "Another gargoyle, like you."

He drew his horns together. "You mock me, mademoiselle."

"Let me call him, so you can see." I dialed Dorian for a video call. "I think you'll feel more comfortable talking to him."

A moment later, Dorian's beaming face appeared on the screen. An amazed Leopold grabbed my phone.

The two gargoyles spoke rapid Latin to each other, so I wasn't able to follow most of what they said. But when they switched back to French, they told me they'd agreed Leopold would accompany me back to Portland. I hadn't thought that far ahead, but who was I to stop two living gargoyles on a mission? We quickly constructed a plan where Leopold would turn to stone in a completely different shape than he'd been found in on the Prague bridge, so nobody would suspect he was the gargoyle "stolen" from the university.

"Now we need to get you out of here," I said.

Using his sheet to disguise himself and his drunken state as an excuse to keep his head down and lean on me, Leopold and I wound down the Notre Dame stairs and away from the cathedral as quickly and quietly as possible.

Leopold spent the evening in our small rented room alternately drinking the bottle of absinthe I'd offered him and reciting poetry to it.

I flew back to Portland the next day with two special deliveries. Heather had authorized me to accompany Brixton home after I went to the hospital first thing in the morning. The doctors had determined he was suffering from dehydration and severe jet lag but was otherwise healthy, so they wanted to discharge him as soon as possible.

Brixton and I traveled with a special piece of luggage: a storage crate containing a statue I claimed to have found at a flea market. Also in the crate was a case of absinthe. It was meant to last our new friend a month, or at the very least a week. When we arrived at PDX, the bottles were empty.

FORTY-SEVEN

Back at home in Portland, Brixton was safe; that was the most important thing. But I couldn't rest easy. Brixton was still recovering and not yet back to his usual self. Ivan and Percy's whereabouts were unknown. And I hadn't figured out how to cure the deterioration of backward alchemy with anything short of the ultimate sacrifice: giving my own life.

Further down the line, I worried what would happen with the police investigation into Lucien's murder. They hadn't yet discovered his identity, but it was only a matter of time before they connected him to Brixton via the boy's DNA under his fingernails.

In spite of his partial backward alchemy transformation, Ivan hadn't lost his humanity. At least not yet. It was a small silver lining, but I was willing to take it. Even though he hadn't yet come forward to confess that he was responsible for Lucien's death, he'd helped Brixton escape the tunnels in Paris and had accepted that he'd been misled by Percy. I hoped he'd come through before the police got their DNA results back.

In the meantime, I had my hands full dealing with two gargoyle roommates.

I came home from visiting a subdued Brixton to find a smoky scent permeating the house.

"It is his fault," Dorian said as soon as I came through the door. "He distracted me and the bread burned in the oven."

"It's all right, Dorian. So … where's Leopold?"

Dorian frowned. "Taking a nap in the attic. I do not understand, Zoe. He does not need to sleep."

"Maybe he's just lazy."

Dorian and I climbed the stairs to the attic and found Leopold curled up on a stack of pillows on the steamer trunk. The pillows looked suspiciously like the ones from my bed.

"He's not asleep," I said, sniffing the air. "He's drunk."

Dorian gaped at Leopold. Our gargoyle guest stretched luxuriantly and sat up.

"Where is the art in this mansion?" Leopold asked. "Your walls are quite barren. Monsieur Robert-Houdin informed me this is a new abode for you. Have you not yet finished unpacking?"

"I collect books and other alchemical items, not art."

Leopold's gray eyes grew wide. "*C'est vrai?*"

"It is true," Dorian answered. "I have already explained to you that Zoe is an alchemist. This is how she understands how you and I were brought to life. We have not yet discussed the intricacies—"

"No art?" Leopold said, again completely ignoring the reference to alchemy. "*Quelle horreur!* I may as well return to stone."

I wouldn't have believed a gargoyle could be more dramatic than Dorian if I hadn't seen it with my own eyes.

"Without art, what do you do for amusement?" Leopold asked Dorian.

"Before you stated your strong desire to take a siesta," Dorian said, "I was showing you my kitchen—"

"Cooking? This is your idea of fun? I believed you to be joking. This is women's work, no?"

Dorian puffed up his chest. "I am a chef of great distinction."

Leopold giggled. Then burped. "*Pardon.*"

"Perhaps," Dorian said in his most diplomatic voice, "if you have now recovered from your journey, you will tell us of your life."

The gargoyle rolled off the steamer trunk and clasped his talons together. "'How little remains of the man I once was,'" he said softly, "'save the memory of him! But remembering is only a new form of suffering.'"

"Baudelaire," I said. "You're quoting Baudelaire. You quoted his poetry when I first met you too. You said you were a poet. So you enjoy Baudelaire's poetry?"

"*Enjoy?* Is this the right word to describe the influence of the great man? To handle language so skillfully is to practice evocative sorcery!"

"You knew him," I said. Dorian remained speechless.

"*Oui.* Monsieur Charles Baudelaire brought me from the shadows."

"*Bon!*" Dorian chimed in. "I, too, had a great man teach me. Jean Eugène Robert-Houdin. Surely you have heard of—"

"The stage magician? *Pfft.* A common entertainer."

Dorian sputtered several words, none of them intelligible.

"You have more wine?" Leopold asked. "Or hashish?"

————

Dinner that night was a tense affair. We learned that Leopold had been taken in by a group of Bohemian artists and writers who were loosely affiliated with Victor Hugo's romantic army. Critic and poet Charles Baudelaire was the man Leopold was closest to, and upon his death, Leopold mourned him tremendously. Much poetry was written during those dark days. Leopold claimed that some of Baudelaire's last works were ghostwritten by Leopold himself. I was disinclined to believe him. Then again, Baudelaire had been drunk when he wrote many of his famous poems.

Dorian cooked a classical French feast in honor of his newfound brother, sending me to buy expensive wine in addition to a short shopping list to supplement what we already had at the house. The menu consisted of marinated olives, spinach and walnut terrine, and lentil pate for appetizers; Breton onion soup for a starter; cider casserole for a main dish; and apricot tarts for dessert.

Leopold drank nearly all of the wine himself but barely touched his food. "A man can go without food for two days," he declared, "but not without poetry."

———————

After dinner, Leopold didn't offer to help with the dishes. I began to help Dorian, but he said it would be easiest in the small kitchen for him to take care of the dishes himself, even with only one good arm. I didn't argue. It was difficult for me to talk with him alone, knowing the sacrifice I was getting ready to make. He would never agree to it, so I had to keep it to myself until the preparations were ready.

Once it was late enough, Dorian left for Julian Lake's house to prepare food for the following day, after which he'd go to the tea-shop kitchen to bake pastries before dawn. It felt strange to follow such a simple daily routine after the crazy events of the past few days and weeks, but there was really nothing else to be done.

I made my rounds through the house, making sure it was tightly secured. As I passed back through the first floor, I found Leopold passed out. In the middle of the dining room table.

FORTY-EIGHT

THE NEXT DAY THE Portland police declared Brixton well enough to talk with them about what had happened with Ivan. He told the police that Ivan had gone crazy and started to believe all the historical alchemy books he was studying. Brixton also said that Ivan had convinced him he needed his help to save his life. Of course he'd wanted to help. But Brixton swore he didn't know what Ivan had in mind. Max knew him well enough that he might have picked up on the fact that Brixton wasn't telling the whole story, but with the detectives on the case, Brix played the role of an innocent, gullible, and slightly selfish kid to perfection.

The police thankfully hadn't yet gotten the results of the full DNA testing, so they hadn't connected Brixton to Lucien's dead body. As soon as I was sure Brixton was truly safe, then I'd be ready to make my sacrifice for Dorian.

I visited Brixton after he returned home from the police station. His mom was sitting on one side of his bed.

"I'm never letting this one out of my sight again," she said. She pulled him close and planted a kiss on the top of his head. "He's grounded for the rest of the summer."

Brixton rolled his eyes. "Very funny, Mom."

Heather's breezy smile turned almost as grim as the day I'd seen her at the morgue. "I'm dead serious, Brix."

"But I—but you—I mean, I nearly *died*."

"Exactly," Heather said. "You're too old to get away with acting so stupidly. Running off to a foreign country with a delusional neighbor? I liked Ivan, too, but you can't do things like that, honey."

Brixton leaned back on the assortment of pillows his mom had propped up. I had a feeling his summer of being "grounded" would consist of a fair amount of TLC from his parents and probably visits from his friends Ethan and Veronica.

"At least I haven't been keeping a secret," Brixton said, making a face at his mom. "You want to know why Mom has been disappearing lately, Zoe?"

"Brix!" Heather said, "I'm not telling people yet!"

"You said it wasn't a secret anymore."

"Not a secret to *you*, silly."

"Zoe is family, Mom."

I felt a lump form in my throat.

"You're right," she said. "I'm sorry for the secrecy. I didn't want to tell anyone, especially Brixton, before I knew if I'd succeed."

"You'll succeed," a deep voice said. Abel leaned against the bedroom door. "She's studying for her GED."

"That's wonderful," I said.

"You know I dropped out when I had Brix," Heather said. "In a year, he'll have more education then I do. That's not a great example."

"You're a great mom," Abel said. He strode across the room and gave them both a hug. "Stay for dinner?" he asked me.

"I wish I could," I said.

Heather pulled Abel to the bedroom door. "We'll let you two visit a few more minutes while Abel starts dinner."

I'd never been inside Brixton's room before, yet it felt to me like something was missing. "Your mom took away your guitar?" I asked.

He shook his head. "I sorta … sacrificed it."

"Why would you—"

"Ivan said I had to make a sacrifice for the alchemy to work. That's what we thought the sacrifice was. Giving up something I loved."

"Oh, Brix. I'm so sorry. Your heart was in the right place. Where did you toss it? The Willamette?"

"Pawn shop. I used the money for my ticket to Paris. Ivan talked about *intent* being important in alchemy. My sacrifice used my intent and got me to Paris. Wicked city, by the way." He smiled mischievously for a few seconds before growing serious again. "I'd do it again, you know. To help him not die. I mean, as long as it didn't mean dying myself. Which is totally messed up."

A happy tear slid down my cheek as I walked back to my truck. I'd leave my truck and trailer to Tobias, I thought to myself. Since Rosa was dying, he'd soon need a change. He liked my truck when he visited a few months ago. Maybe he'd like the Airstream too.

––––––––––––

At home, Leopold was still passed out, although now his hefty gray body was sprawled on my green velvet couch. I poked the bottom of his foot. He twitched but didn't open his eyes. I poked his foot again.

"'I have felt the wind of the wing of madness,'" he mumbled, then rolled over.

I felt myself roll my eyes like my young friend would have done. Leopold wouldn't be disturbing me anytime soon. I unlocked the door to my basement alchemy lab and began the preparations for my sacrifice.

I lit a kerosene lamp and walked to my main work table. A prickle made its way up my spine. Someone had been inside my lab. *Recently*. My gold leaf was gone, as were all of my salts.

But Percy was the one who'd searched my lab before, and he was long gone. Wasn't he?

Where *was* Percy?

FORTY-NINE

"THIS IS ONE OF my favorites," Leopold said. "*Un moment.*" He rubbed his jaw and opened his mouth terrifyingly wide, revealing rows of pointy teeth. Squaring his shoulders, he took a stance that made it look like he was howling at the moon.

"Or this one," he added. He moved out of the werewolf position, shaking his body as if stretching after a workout. Next he crossed his arms, held his head high, and looked down his nose at us.

"That pose does not look scary," Dorian said. He tried to make a frightening pose himself, spreading his wings wide, but he nearly lost his balance. The speed of his deterioration was quickening.

"You miss the point, *mon amie*. In this simple posture, I inch closer … and closer …. It instills fear in the hearts of men!" He guffawed.

"Er, yes," Dorian said.

"Or how about this one?" Leopold thrust out his chin, baring his bottom row of teeth, and hunched his shoulders.

Dorian circled him. "Too humorous."

"*Oui*, I suspect you are right." Leopold shook out the pose.

At least the two gargoyles were getting along better.

For the last half hour, Leopold had been showing Dorian the various ways he'd stayed hidden since being brought to life. His family of drunken artists and writers had known of his existence (though I suspected half of them thought he was a figment of their collective imaginations), but nobody else did.

Like Dorian, Leopold had learned how to live in the shadows. As we were coming to realize, though, he pushed the boundaries. He went where he wanted then simply turned to stone on the spot if he was in danger of being seen. Often in a bizarre pose, to keep people off balance.

"And nobody ever saw you?" I asked. "Truly?"

Leopold shrugged. "In the music halls and museums, the people think with their hearts, not with their minds."

We all gave a start when my phone buzzed. It was Brixton texting me that he was at the front door.

"You really need a doorbell," he said after I let him inside and we were walking up the stairs. "I've been knocking for five minutes. You're always in the attic."

"Leopold Baudelaire, meet Brixton Taylor."

"Wicked," Brixton whispered, staring at the gargoyle.

"Your servant?" Leopold asked me.

"Our friend," Dorian corrected.

Leopold rubbed his chin and nodded. Dorian prodded him to shake Brixton's hand.

"I thought you were spending time with your family," I said. "And grounded."

"Yeah, Mom is studying for her GED in the open now, but then she and Abel..." He cleared this throat. "I think they wanted to do things no mom should do. Ever."

"'From love there will be born poetry,'" Leopold recited, "'which will spring up toward God like a rare flower.'"

"My life is too weird," Brixton mumbled. "Anyway, I snuck out."

"Now that we have made introductions," Leopold said, "we have important matters to discuss. A council of war, if you will."

Finally. He'd put me off every time I tried to address the problem of backward alchemy turning the gargoyles back into stone.

"It has been brought to my attention," Leopold continued, "that you are cavorting with *un flic*. This will not do. The police are not to be trusted."

I groaned. "My love life isn't your concern. I thought we were going to talk about—"

"If you think this is unimportant, you are *assez stupide!*"

"Not cool," Brixton said. "That's so not cool."

"Why don't you play some music for us, Brixton," Dorian said diplomatically. "I see you have brought your banjo."

Skeptically eyeing Leopold, Brixton picked up the banjo he carried slung over his back. He strummed a 1960s folk song.

"This is not music," Leopold said. "This is—"

He broke off when two phones began to ring at once. Grateful to head off that argument, I picked up mine and smiled.

"Max," I said into the phone. "It's wonderful to hear your voice, but this isn't really a good time."

"I won't take long. This isn't a social call—but I hope it's a good one. Is Brixton there with you?"

"Yeah, he is." How could this be good? Brixton had answered his own phone and stood in the corner, his back to us.

"Good," Max said. "Ivan gave a confession."

"Ivan," I whispered, closing my eyes as I let out a sigh of relief.

"Not what I expected either," he said, misinterpreting my surprise. "He emailed a confession, and we know he's not lying to protect anyone, because he gave us details that led to blood evidence. The man was apparently an aggressive salesman who came to the house while Brixton was there. Grabbed Brixton's arm, which is why Ivan threw him out. I'm betting it'll be Brixton's DNA the lab finds under his fingernails when they conclude their analysis. It was an accident, so I wish Brixton had just told us what happened, but I understand that he's scared. This has been such a strange case—but now life can go back to normal."

Normal. I bit back my true reaction. Everything would be all right without me now. It was time to make my sacrifice.

FIFTY

BRIXTON USED THE INTERRUPTION of the phone calls as an opportunity to escape the rude gargoyle. I walked him downstairs.

"I can let myself out," he said.

"I need a break from those two too," I said. "You hungry? Before you go, you can grab something from the kitchen."

He turned to me, and I saw in his face the caring man he was growing into. "You're different today, Zoe. I don't know what it is. I don't think it's your frustration with Leo—even though you're gonna have to watch that dude."

I gave him a hug. I hadn't meant to, but I was overcome with emotion realizing that I wasn't going to live to see Brixton grow up. "I'm so proud of you," I said, blinking back tears.

Once I was sure I wasn't going to cry, I pulled back from the hug. Brixton was rolling his eyes. "Okay, Zoe. Whatever."

I watched Brixton ride his bike down the driveway with his banjo slung over his back. When he reached the street, he briefly glanced both ways. Catching a glimpse of his profile, I was struck by the handsome man he would soon be.

Instead of going back upstairs, I grabbed my silver raincoat. I scribbled a note to Dorian so he wouldn't worry, then set off on foot.

For the next three hours, I walked around my Hawthorne neighborhood of Portland, stopping to speak to the locals walking their dogs, browse the wares of the quirky stores, pick up a cup of tea at Blue Sky Teas, and literally stop and smell the roses.

Without realizing the route I was taking, I found myself in front of Max's house. The sun hung low in the sky. The day was coming to a close. As was my life.

I was here to say goodbye.

I stood in front of the red door with a gold dragon knocker but paused before I raised my hand to lift it.

The door swung open and a very wet Max grinned at me. In jeans and a white t-shirt, his feet were bare and he held a towel to sopping wet hair. "I thought I saw someone out here. Sorry, I didn't hear the door."

Inside, I walked through the uncluttered living room, filled with a white couch, pewter coffee table, and paintings of forests that were taller than either of us. I came to a stop in front of the sliding glass door that led to the backyard garden. Max laced his fingers through mine as I looked out at the wooden bench where we'd spent so many happy hours together.

When I'd been in a reckless mood, I'd allowed myself to fantasize about spending years with Max, sitting on that bench watching the night-blooming jasmine unfurl and the morning-blooming California poppies awaken with the day.

"You want to go outside?" Max whispered. "Let me grab my—"

I stopped his words with my lips. He didn't object. And it was a good thing he didn't have many things in the house to bump into. Only that plastic skeleton in the hallway.

An hour later, Max fixed us a pot of lemon balm tea using his grand-mother's iron tea kettle.

"Sorry about that skeleton," I said. "I can put it back together. I'm good with my hands."

"I know." He kissed my shoulder. "But don't worry about it. It's time I got rid of it. Time I moved on." He added a sprig of fresh mint to the tea, then handed me a white porcelain cup with deep blue Chinese characters. The minty steam made it the perfect choice.

It hit me that it had been selfish of me to come here. While I was here to say goodbye, Max was ready to take the next step with me.

"I'm not entirely convinced the stories about the skeleton are true anyway," Max said.

"You didn't tell me the story. Only that Chadna wanted to draw it out so you'd learn more about it each year as you grew old to-gether."

"Supposedly this skeleton originally contained some *real* human bones."

"That's how med schools used to train their students, you know."

"Apparently some of them still do. My guess was that it was a secret society type of thing. Creepy, huh?"

"Oh my God," I whispered.

"It's not *that* great a story."

"Max, I'm so sorry, but I have to go. I lost track of time."

"You're not staying?"

I kissed him hard and fast. "No, but I'll be back."

Maybe this wasn't goodbye after all.

I ran home, my silver raincoat flapping behind me and hope surging within me. I might not have to sacrifice myself. I now knew what had changed. As a true alchemist, I was looking at it the wrong way around. I was in control of my own life force, but backward alchemists weren't. They relied on the remains of other willing sacrifices.

In spite of the late hour, I was energized with hope. Too energized. I failed to notice the front door of the house wasn't as securely locked as it should have been.

Only as I bounded up the attic stairs, calling for Dorian and Leopold, did I notice something was off. The house was quiet. Yet it was too early in the night for the gargoyles to be on the prowl.

I thought to myself that I'd have to lecture Dorian about not following Leopold's lead of trying be cool. Did gargoyles even care about being cool? Never mind. I'd have years to find out. Since I now knew a better way to save the gargoyles. A way that didn't involve sacrificing my life. I knew that—

I stepped into the attic and froze. I saw not two gargoyles, but two *people*: Percy and Madame Leblanc.

Only Madame Leblanc wasn't quite herself. This woman was decades younger. Her daughter? Granddaughter?

No, it couldn't be …

The woman in my attic looked almost identical to the woman with movie-star good looks in the black-and-white photograph Percy carried in his wallet.

Madame Leblanc wasn't an innocent actor like the man who played the part of her nephew. She was the backward alchemist who'd killed him. This whole time, she was the mysterious mastermind.

FIFTY-ONE

ALL THE PIECES FELL into place. Madame Leblanc—or whatever her real name was—was the true charismatic leader of the backward alchemists. Not Lucien. Not Percy.

I should have seen it sooner. In Paris, Madame Leblanc played her role with me so lyrically it was almost theatrical, and she'd believed in my immortality all too readily. She knew I worked with Jasper Dubois, who was an aspiring alchemist, so she was able to create a believable lie. The actor who played her grandnephew policeman had looked young from afar but up close he looked tired—because he was a backward alchemy apprentice. Back in Portland, Percy had said "only three of us left" while telling me about backward alchemy. The woman in the photo in Percy's wallet had looked familiar. And when Ivan had said "*they'll* be returning soon" to the alchemy lab, as opposed to "*Percy* will be returning soon," it was Madame Leblanc he was referring to.

"Cat got your tongue, Zoe?" she said. The accent was English. "Don't look so surprised. I'm sure you've figured everything out."

"I was so gullible," I hissed, barely able to control my anger at having been so close to the truth but also so far off.

"Don't be too hard on yourself, dear. I really am an actress. Made quite a splash in the West End for a while. That's where Percy found me." I could believe it. Though her skin was pinched, her large eyes and lips were stunning. Her hair was a rich, lush black, and it flowed past her shoulders.

"You killed the actor playing your nephew," I said. "He was your apprentice. That's how you look so young again."

"Oh, do catch up, my dear. And hand over the book. *My* book."

I smiled. Now *I* had the upper hand. If she didn't already have Dorian's book, that meant Dorian and Leopold had gotten away through the hole in the roof. It also meant Madame Leblanc hadn't figured out the book was, as Dorian would have put it, a McGuffin. Everyone was searching for the damn book, but it *wasn't* the key. It was only the clue that pointed to Notre Dame.

"Why are you smiling? Percy, restrain her."

So strong was Madame Leblanc's presence that Percy had faded into the background. He now stepped forward, though the movement was half-hearted. His eyes darted between the two of us. His hair was flecked with gray, and his jowls sagged. While Madame Leblanc had grown younger, he'd grown older.

"Don't touch me, Percival," I said.

He stopped.

Madame Leblanc sighed. Theatrically. "Do I have to do everything myself?"

"You have me at a loss," I said. "I don't even know your real name."

She smiled wickedly. "I wondered if I'd gone too far there. Blanche Leblanc: White White. The embodiment of a Ms. Goody Two-Shoes."

Mentally kicking myself, I edged my way toward the attic door.

"I see you moving, Zoe. Stop right there. Don't you want to know my true name?" The look in her black eyes told me I wasn't sure I wanted to. "The name I've used since my transformation is Raven. And you don't want to mess with the Raven."

The skin on her forearm had firmed enough for me to realize that what I'd mistaken for faded numbers from a concentration camp was actually a tattoo of a raven. My subconscious had noticed it and turned it into a dream.

"You will give me that book," she said. She didn't yell. Her words were so soft that I barely heard them. Yet there was a cold forcefulness to the directive that made me shiver. "I will be restored to my former beauty for eternity."

"I don't have it," I said, matching her strong, stoic intonation.

"Wrong answer." She drew a sword from behind her back.

FIFTY-TWO

It was one of *my* swords from my collection of antiques that Raven held in her hand.

"Percy," I said, "you don't have to go along with—"

"Enough!" Raven thrust the sword into the creaking floorboards, showing its might.

"I swear I don't have the book here," I said. I knew I was convincing, because it wasn't a lie.

"I know. We've searched the house. But I have very persuasive ways of making people talk."

I nodded. Not too quickly. I couldn't let her think I was eager. I couldn't let her know I now knew more than she did. "I'll tell you where it is," I said, "if you let me understand what's happened. I need to know."

"Why?"

"I have a friend who's dying, like you."

"The gargoyle," Percy said, raising his hand in earnest like a sycophantic schoolboy. "The gargoyle I told you about."

Raven and I both ignored him.

"I don't care what happens to me," I said, "but I want you to help Dorian."

I knew she wouldn't, but there was still a chance I could, if I could think of a way out of this.

"All right," Raven said cautiously. She motioned for Percy to close the attic door. He rushed to oblige.

"I thought you would find our secret alchemy lab," Raven continued once the door was bolted. "That would have ruined our plans to sacrifice the actor. I couldn't kill you without hurting myself, so I devised a plan to get you to leave Paris of your own accord."

"Because an alchemist can't kill a person without hurting themselves."

She smirked. "Nice try. Percy convinced me it was true, long ago. But now, thanks to you, I know the truth. It's only a superstition."

Me and my big mouth...

"I never suspected that you had Lucien and Olav's backward alchemy book," she continued, "or that you could help us. It was Lucien who realized you had the book and could help solve what the rest of us could not. You aroused his suspicions, and when he asked Percy about a woman called Zoe Faust, Percy told us who you were. That's why Lucien followed you to Portland."

"I made it so easy for him. I even gave him my address."

"Most backward alchemists aren't 'friends,' so we don't keep each other's confidences. Stupid Lucien didn't tell us his suspicions that you could help us. And I didn't tell Lucien of my plan to get rid of you."

"That's why Lucien was truly shocked when I said I was leaving Paris. He was upset that you'd messed up his plans, so he followed me to steal *Non Degenera Alchemia*—which he originally planned on doing more easily in Paris, before you ruined his scheme."

"Lucien was almost out of Alchemical Ashes. He was smoking them frequently to stay young until we could permanently stop our life forces reversing. Lucien was arrogant, and thought he could get the book without much effort."

"That's why he lost his temper so quickly at my friend Ivan's house," I said, using the word *friend* automatically before I could think better of it. "Lucien was upset that Ivan refused to help him."

"I've never trusted Lucien, so I sent Percy to follow him. Can you believe Lucien once said theater was for the mindless masses? Yet it was my acting skills that fooled you. I'm the one who has outlived them all—"

Percy cleared his throat.

"Oh, yes, my love," Raven said. "Of course I meant *we* are the ones who have outlived them all. And now we are going to retrieve our long-lost book and live on forever as the beautiful specimens we once were."

Raven had to come to Portland to do her own dirty work. And she still mistakenly believed Dorian's book contained the secret to the "change" that had reversed the transformations of backward alchemy.

"You're forgetting the most important part of the story," I said. "*What was the shift that occurred six months ago?*"

She blinked at me. "What do you mean?"

"What happened six months ago?"

"We began to age and die."

"Percy already told me that much," I said. "I need to know what *triggered* the change."

"You're trying to confuse me. Percy warned me that you were overly intellectual. Half of your antiques are books. What good are books? Scripts for the theater are different, of course. The only book I need is the one Olav and Lucien created."

Was my theory right? "Who was the first to die?" I asked.

"Why does it matter?"

"Humor me."

"Olav," she said, a look of suspicion creeping onto her face.

"Percy said he wasn't very intelligent. Is that right?"

"He was a stupid, stupid, man," she agreed.

"How did he die?"

"The same as the rest of us. He began aging rapidly."

"You saw his transformation take place?"

She hesitated. "We weren't friends. Who wants to associate with a man less interesting than a rock?"

"How did you know he died, then?"

"I found him," Percy spoke up. "Inside the underground tunnels not far from the alchemy lab. The smell … I went to investigate."

"What was he doing in there?"

Percy shrugged. "It's trendy for people to go down into the catacombs and tunnels these days, so I assumed he was making sure our laboratory entrance remained hidden, as I was."

"People get lost down there," I said. "Especially people—"

"The idiot!" Raven shrieked. She grasped the hilt of the sword and paced back and forth on the creaky attic floor, her silky black hair snarling around her face. "You mean he got lost in the tunnels and starved or froze to death, like other stupid explorers have done. We're not immortal, we just don't age."

"Exactly," I said.

"Hang on," Percy said, "I don't get it."

"Olav didn't die because of a shift," I said. "His death *was* the shift. Because backward alchemy is a shortcut *tied to another person*, Olav's death broke the link. That's why you're all dying."

"The sacrifices," Raven said, comprehension sinking in. "The sacrifices aren't enough?"

"What happened to Olav's bones, Percy?" I asked. "What happened after you found him?"

"When I touched him," Percy said, "he turned to ash."

I nodded. "And the ashes?"

"I sprinkled them in the Seine."

"So it's over," I said softly. "The link is broken."

Bones and ash are our core essence. That's why relics have significance. And that's why Max's skeleton helped me see the possibility that a person's physical body was tied to the shift.

Raven's eyes locked on mine. "No. There's got to be another answer in that book."

I shook my head sadly. I didn't think there was.

I understood the truth about *Non Degenera Alchemia*. Backward alchemy was a quick fix for lazy people who were willing to sacrifice the life of another for their own unnatural immortality. To get around the core tenet of alchemy—using guided intent to transform the impure into the pure—backward alchemists had to sacrifice an innocent.

An alchemist's lab is their sanctuary and thus inexorably linked to their work. The pure intent of Notre Dame Cathedral balanced the impure intent of the two men who recorded their backward alchemy steps in *Not Untrue Alchemy*, allowing for some sort of stability. Because Dorian and Leopold were *innocents* from the cathedral, the book itself was able to bring them to life without an external sacrifice. Yet when the original intent was broken, everyone given life through backward alchemy faced the consequences.

Steps sounded beneath us. Had Dorian gone to Max to get help?

The attic door opened. Ivan stepped inside and relief washed over me. He'd had a change of heart after all.

Ivan wasn't quite as young and vigorous as he'd been when I saw him at the alchemy laboratory in Paris, but he was strong enough to help.

"The book?" Raven asked him.

Ivan shook his head. "I searched again. It's not here."

My relief turned to cold terror. Ivan was still working with the backward alchemists?

But it didn't matter. The quick deterioration of Ivan's body showed me that backward alchemy was over. And Dorian's life along with it.

FIFTY-THREE

"IT'S OVER, IVAN," I said. "We've figured out that backward alchemy is done for."

"She's lying," Raven said. "She's trying to trick us into thinking there's no solution. But her beastly friend is hiding the book that will save us."

"I'm telling you the truth," I said, wondering where my decidedly non-beastly gargoyle friend had gone. "She and Percy misled you—"

"It's because of *us* that you're healthy again, Ivan," Raven said. "Zoe would have had you die."

"And *you* would have had him kill Brixton," I said.

Ivan winced.

"I forgive you, Ivan," I said. "I know you didn't know—"

"Enough with the sentimentality," Raven said. "Do you want to survive or not, Ivan?"

He nodded silently, his jaw clenched. He refused to look me in the eye.

"How many more sacrifices will you make?" I asked. "With the link broken, it will never stop."

"Men will always willingly give me this gift," Raven said. "Jasper jumped at the chance."

I gasped. "It *wasn't* a lie that Jasper Dubois was murdered. Only it was *you* who did it."

"I'll let you in on a secret, my dear: if you want to tell a convincing lie, stick to the truth as closely as possible."

I glared at her. That was *my* secret. And she'd killed *my* shopkeeper assistant. Not that I'd been all that fond of the misogynistic Jasper, but still, he didn't deserve to be murdered.

"Didn't you wonder how I knew you wouldn't be able to trace Jasper's movements?" she continued.

"Because you knew he was already dead." I should have thought of it, but she'd thrown me off balance by appearing in my attic today.

"I can practically feel my face sagging," Raven said, feeling her neck with the hand that wasn't clutching the sword. "Percy, Ivan, stop standing there like useless lumps."

Now I was *really* angry. Not only had she manipulated me, but she'd turned Ambrose's son Percy and my friend Ivan against me. I lunged for the second sword that was part of the pair. I'd been so calm until now that she didn't anticipate the movement.

"Stay out of my way, Percy. Ivan." My voice didn't sound like my own, but I was fairly certain it was me speaking. "This is between me and Raven."

Decades ago, I'd taken some fencing lessons with a lovely German man named Anton. I hoped I'd remember what he taught me.

The men stepped back as Raven and I lunged at each other. In our rage, we weren't going for proper form. We were trying to kill each other.

Raven was already aging, so she wasn't as strong as she thought she was. She was the first to draw blood, a shallow wound to my hip. While she regained her balance, I slashed a long cut across her shoulder. She cried out, more in shock than pain, I expect. Her sword dropped from her hand and she gripped her arm.

I immediately thought of Tobias, who carried cayenne pepper with him in his role as an EMT, as an unconventional herbal remedy to stop blood loss. I kept a glass jar of cayenne on an antique spice rack there in the attic and wondered if it would help staunch the flow of blood from the wound I'd inflicted.

I knew then that I couldn't kill Raven. It wasn't in my nature.

But there was something else I could do. I grabbed the jar of cayenne, tore the lid off, and threw the spice into her eyes.

Raven screamed in pain, blinded and writhing on the floor. Since she was no longer a threat, I pressed a towel to her bleeding shoulder and looked for something with which I could tie her arms.

A piece of rope secured a curtain in the corner of the attic that Dorian kept for his private reading room. I yanked off the rope and turned back to Raven. But she was no longer sprawled on the floor. She stood in front of me, red-faced and wielding her sword.

Then the look on her face morphed into surprise. A spot of deep red formed in the middle of her chest. The tip of a sword burst through her chest. A metallic scent filled the air. She looked down at her chest for a brief moment before her eyelids closed and she crumpled to the floor.

Behind her stood Ivan, a blood-drenched sword clutched in his hands.

FIFTY-FOUR

"On my God!" Percy screamed. He repeated the words again and again until I slapped him.

Unlike Percy, Ivan stood as still as a nonliving gargoyle statue.

"Ivan?" I said quietly.

"She was going to kill you," he whispered. "I couldn't let her. I couldn't."

As we stood there, the three of us in shock, Raven's body shriveled from a woman into a skeleton, then before our eyes changed from bone to ash.

A siren sounded in the distance.

I swore. "Dorian and Leopold must have sent for help."

"Nobody will believe what has happened," Ivan said.

"Oh my God!" Percy started repeating again. Goodness, that man was tiresome. And he hadn't lifted a finger to help me.

"Percy," I said, shaking him by the shoulder. "You're not doing anyone any good. You're going to give me your cell phone number and then get out of here. All right?"

He nodded, wide-eyed.

"Ivan," I said. "Pick up Raven's ashes and then leave. The cut on my leg will explain the mess. I'll tell the police there was an intruder." The sirens grew louder. "Hurry."

I scooped Raven's ashes into a set of glass apothecary jars. After a quicker cleanup of Raven's remains than I thought was possible, I collapsed onto the attic floor. I hadn't attended to the cut on my hip. There wasn't enough blood loss for me to pass out, but it was the middle of the night. I didn't have the natural energy from the sun to draw upon.

I closed my eyes and felt the cool hardwood floor on my cheek. I'd rest for a few moments ...

"Zoe?" a distant voice called. "Zoe?"

"Mmm?"

"You're awake," a familiar voice said, followed by a sigh of relief.

"No, I'm not," I mumbled.

Max's lips found mine. "I hope you're awake now."

I opened my eyes. I was still sitting on the attic floor, but now Max had wrapped an arm around my shoulder. His other hand pressed a cloth to the wound on my leg.

"EMTs are on their way up," he said. "Hang on."

"I could hang on better if you put both of your arms around me."

He laughed. "You scared me, Zoe. You said you'd come back, but you didn't. Instead I got a call from that French friend of yours—the guy I've never met. He said you were in danger. He wouldn't give me details, but insisted I rescue you. He's a strange guy. I don't know how he knew, if he wasn't involved—"

"He didn't do this to me."

"I know. We saw Ivan Danko leaving your house."

"You have him?" What would Ivan tell them?

"No, he got away. I can see that you rescued yourself, so I'll have to play hero another day, but what exactly happened here, Zoe?"

"That question can wait, Detective Liu," a woman said. She and a man rushed over to me and examined my hip. "We're having a hell of a time getting a stretcher up here. These old houses aren't up to code. Let me check out this wound and get you downstairs."

My wound was deemed superficial, so I was treated by the paramedics but I wasn't forced to go to the hospital. Max, however, wasn't happy about my decision to stay home.

"If you won't go to the hospital," he said, "you could at least stay with me. Or I'd be happy to … "

I swept an errant lock of hair from his forehead. "I appreciate the offer, but I won't get any rest if you stay. I need to sleep."

He took my hand and kissed it. "I promise I'll let you get some sleep."

With how much my insides melted with that gentle brush of his lips against my hand, I gave him a truthful answer. "I don't trust myself to make you keep that promise."

That seemed to appease him. I sent him home and awaited Dorian's return, which was the more important reason I couldn't have Max stay.

I wasn't sure what I was going to tell Dorian, now that all hope was lost. There was no cure for the backward alchemists and those who'd been brought to life by backward alchemy's power. I could continue making the Tea of Ashes frequently enough to keep Dorian alive temporarily, but I'd be killing myself while he'd continue to slowly die. I should have accepted the truth earlier, but I hadn't been open to the possibility that I wouldn't be able to save Dorian.

I wished Dorian would return home. Everyone had left over an hour ago. A detective had taken my statement. I told him that Ivan Danko had returned to seek revenge on me after I thwarted his crazy attempt to kill Brixton. I hated that it was the lie closest to the truth. I really had wanted to save Ivan.

291

I fixed myself a chocolate elixir in the blender in an attempt to stay awake, but I fell asleep on the couch waiting for a gargoyle who never came.

———

At dawn, I awoke to the sound of singing and the scents of cinnamon and smoke.

Dorian stood at the kitchen counter, whisking batter in a stainless steel bowl. Turning at the sound of the swinging kitchen door, he hopped down from the stool and grinned at me. "*Bon*, you are awake, *mon amie*. I have only just returned from Monsieur Lake's home."

"I have so much to tell you, Dorian."

"And I you. Why do you look so sad?"

"Why didn't you come home sooner?"

"I was confident you could defeat the insane woman who was after my book, as you have. I also knew you would not be alone. I was certain Max would come to your aid. He is a good man, and he cares very much for you. I decided it was best to remain hidden and attend to pressing matters."

I sat morosely. "I have news. It's bad. I don't know how to tell you this, so I'm going to come right out and say it."

Dorian rocked back and forth on the linoleum floor and looked at me expectantly.

"There's no cure, Dorian. There's no cure for a backward alchemy transformation."

"Ah. Is that all?"

"Is that *all*?"

"I will share my news." He gave a little hop and clapped his hands. *Hopping and clapping…*

"You're moving your left arm. And your ankle. It bends again."

"*Oui*. And all the rest of me. He wriggled his horns and flapped his wings gracefully. "You see, my friend, I have discovered true alchemy. I have found the Elixir of Life!"

"But how?"

"Through cooking."

FIFTY-FIVE

"Like alchemy," Dorian said, "cooking, at its core, is about transformation."

"You truly found the Elixir?" I asked. "You're not joking? Trying to make me feel better about failing?" I'd had so much false hope that I was scared to hope again.

"*Il est trop vrai.* It is as true as true can be. This is why I returned to Julian Lake's house last night instead of coming to check on you. I knew you were safe, so I wanted to complete the transformation."

"At his house rather than your own? I'm sorry if I haven't made you feel like you belong—"

"Not *inside* his house. His backyard, you may recall, has an outdoor brick kiln. It is meant for pizza, but it is the same heat—"

"As an athanor." The fire to cook the philosophical egg.

Dorian grinned. "I cooked many foods in that oven, each of which represented a step to create the Philosopher's Stone."

"You're the one who was moving things around in my laboratory! I worried that was Lucien or Percy. I had the locks changed for nothing."

"*Oui*. I apologize for the deception. But it was necessary."

"And you weren't even bleeding the other day, were you? I knew it wasn't tomato sauce."

He shook his head. "Cinnabar."

"I *knew* someone had taken my dragon's blood."

"I am sorry, my friend. But as you know, alchemy is a personal process. That is why I roped off my own meditative space in the attic."

"Your reading space."

"Yes, only it was not a reading space. I was meditating on alchemy. Did you not wonder why I had not asked you to obtain more library books lately?" He smiled sheepishly.

"What was your philosophical egg?"

"Can you not guess?"

I smiled. "A food?"

"An avocado." He beamed at me. "It was the perfect ingredient for the first step to my Emerald Tablet: Gourmet Food Version."

I burst out laughing.

"It is perfect, no? The avocado is the shape of an egg, and it represents life and fertility. The tree lives hundreds of years. It is even green, like an emerald."

"And your last step must have been salt."

"But of course. Salt purifies and protects foods from being corrupted, as alchemy's transformations purify the impure. Salt is the truest, most natural, and most essential of all foods."

"The product of mercury and sulfur. The child of the spirit and the soul."

"You alchemists are more clever than I gave you credit for. I knew there was a reason I sought you out, Alchemist. We are a perfect balance, you and I. You claim you are not prepared to train others in the art of alchemy, yet it was your guidance that enabled me to find the Elixir."

"But I didn't—"

"You are too humble, Zoe. You are the one who showed me that a meal need not be complicated to reach perfection. You are the one who taught me that salt is the child of the alchemical king and queen. And you are the one who sacrificed yourself for me by creating the Tea of Ashes, showing me that backward alchemy was not the way I wished to live."

I hugged my friend, and he wrapped his wings around me. His wings were no longer the stiff-yet-malleable stone they once were. Now they felt like I imagined the wings of an angel would feel.

I squeezed Dorian's strong, feather-like wings, then pulled back to look at his transformation. He looked much the same as when I'd met him six months before, but his gray skin held a radiance that hadn't previously been there.

"Where's Leopold?" I asked.

Dorian blinked. "Is he not in the attic?"

"I don't think so."

Dorian ran up the stairs. I tried to keep up, but now that he was healthy again, it was all I could do to keep him in sight.

"*Merde*," Dorian said from the attic doorway. "He promised he was coming back here. I had to leave him so I could finish my transformation alone."

"It's not your fault. I'm sure he'll turn up."

"Zoe, you do not understand. He has *my* book."

"You don't need it anymore. And what could he do with it on his own?"

Dorian rubbed his chin. "I wonder."

We tromped down the stairs, me pestering Dorian about the fourteen food steps he used to create the Elixir of Life.

"To the kitchen," he said. But as soon as he opened the pantry door, he flapped his wings in earnest. He turned around, clutching a mangled note in his clawed hand. "From Leopold," he sputtered.

"He has taken the last of my wine from the pantry. And look, that is the least of the affront."

I eased the wrinkled note from his hand.

It is by universal misunderstanding that we agree with each other, it read. *You have convinced me, my friend, that I must come to understand this foul alchemy that has given us this malady of life. This is why I must borrow your book, say farewell, and accompany my new friend Ivan to the land of alchemists.*

Adieu.

L.B.

Leopold and Ivan together, with Dorian's book? That couldn't be good.

I quickly looked up the local Portland news on my phone to make sure there hadn't been any gargoyle sightings. Thank goodness for small favors.

"Zoe," Dorian interrupted. "I hate to alarm you, but your leg is bleeding."

I put my phone down and looked at my healthy friend once more. "I wasn't kidding when I said I had a lot to tell you about what happened last night."

"Let me cook us breakfast. We have much time to talk, and much grand food to eat."

THE END

RECITES

Each of these recipes is an easy dish that Dorian was able to make with only one good arm. Using simple ingredients doesn't mean sacrificing flavor.

CREAMY GARLIC TOMATO SAUCE (VEGAN)

Total cooking time: 1 hour
Makes 4 servings

Ingredients:
- 2 tbsp plus ¼ cup olive oil, divided
- 10 medium-size cloves garlic
- 24 oz. jar tomato puree or strained tomatoes
- 1 tsp salt (or to taste)
- ¼ tsp red chili pepper flakes (or to taste)

Directions:
Smash the garlic cloves, and let them rest for 10 minutes. Heat a medium saucepan on low heat while peeling and mincing the smashed

garlic. Add 2 tbsp olive oil and garlic. Cook garlic and oil slowly on low heat for 20 minutes. Add tomato puree and simmer for another 20 minutes, minimum.

Remove from heat and cool for a few minutes, then stir in ¼ cup olive oil. Use an immersion blender or transfer to a blender. Watch the color of the red sauce transform to a lighter shade of pink before your eyes, as if you'd added cream.

Once blended, stir in salt and red chili pepper flakes.

Add to 4 servings of a grain (e.g., pasta or freekeh) or use as a dipping sauce for bread.

Note:

You can skip the step of letting the garlic rest for 10 minutes, but the most health benefits will be released by letting it rest for at least 10 minutes once smashed or chopped before heating.

Note:

The trick of transforming these simple ingredients into more than the sum of their parts is *time*. For the best results, don't skip the step of letting the garlic and sauce simmer.

CHOCOLATE MOUSSE (VEGAN, RAW)

Total cooking time: 10 minutes
Makes 2 servings

Ingredients:

- 1 large ripe avocado
- ¼ cup cacao powder
- ¼ cup maple syrup (or ⅓ cup for a sweeter mousse)
- ¼ cup cashew milk (or other nut milk of choice)
- ½ tsp vanilla
- dash sea salt

Directions:

Add all ingredients to a food processor. Puree for at least 1–2 minutes, until smooth and creamy. If lumps persist, stop the food processor and stir the mixture before resuming blending.

Divide into two dessert serving bowls. Optional: garnish with fresh berries on top.

Note:

Skeptical that avocado is the main ingredient? Tasters were surprised to learn the mousse even contained avocado.

FROZEN LEMON CHEESECAKE DROPS (VEGAN, RAW)

Total cooking time: 15 minutes hands on (plus overnight soaking time, and time to set in freezer)
Makes 6 servings (approx. 24 drops)

Ingredients for the topping:
- ¼ cup dates (or up to ½ cup, if you prefer a sweeter crust)
- ½ cup walnuts (or substitute almonds)

Ingredients for the cheesecake:
- 1½ cup raw cashews
- ⅓ cup maple syrup
- ⅓ cup coconut oil
- 3 tbsp lemon juice (add an additional tbsp lemon juice for a tarter tart)
- dash of salt
- dash of turmeric (optional)

Directions:

Soak the cashews in water overnight. Or, if in a rush, boil water and soak in hot water for 4 hours.

To make the topping, chop the dates and walnuts in a food processor. Set aside in a small bowl.

To make the cheesecake drops, drain and rinse the cashews. Melt the coconut oil. Puree all cheesecake ingredients in a blender or food processor until smooth, around 1 or 2 minutes. Line a baking pan with parchment paper. Scoop heaping tablespoons of batter onto the parchment. Sprinkle with the date and nut topping. Let set in the freezer for at least 2 hours.

As with the other books in the Accidental Alchemist mystery series, *The Elusive Elixir* is a work of fiction, but the historical backdrop is real.

The façade of Notre Dame Cathedral in Paris includes several alchemical carvings, including a person carrying a shield with a salamander in flames. My addition of Dorian's alchemy book to the carving is fictional, and there aren't currently any alchemists using Notre Dame as described in the book—as far as I know.

Dorian Robert-Houdin is based on the famous *Le Penseur* gargoyle that sits high on Notre Dame. If you're ever in Paris, he's worth the long line and stairs to visit.

Nicolas Flamel's house still stands in Paris at 51 *rue de* Montmorency, and is now a restaurant. *Rue Nicolas Flamel*, a street in the 4th Arrondissement in Paris, is also named after the famous alchemist. Le Cabaret de L'Enfer was a real Hell-themed café that opened in the 1800s in Paris's Pigalle neighborhood, the red-light district famous for the Moulin Rouge.

The Death Rotation is a real concept in alchemy, but backward alchemy as portrayed in this book is fictional. I enjoyed developing this idea because alchemy is so shrouded in secrecy that it's easy to imagine what some of the codes and concepts might have meant. Alchemy is an example of a subject where the Internet doesn't reveal all. In my research I came across many old books that have not been digitized, filled with fascinating historical facts about alchemy and old alchemical drawings.

Alchemy, in reality, is both a figurative concept and a precursor to modern chemistry. As Zoe explains, alchemy is about transformation. Alchemists of previous centuries wanted to transform their bodies (seeking the Elixir of Life for immortality) or the elements (transmuting lead or other metals into gold). Their experiments resulted in many discoveries that led to chemistry as we know it today. Zoe is a spagyric alchemist, someone who uses alchemical processes to extract healing properties from plants. Spiritual alchemy is the practice of inner transformation.

I'm not an alchemist (nor am I a French gargoyle chef), but my life transformed five years ago when I was diagnosed with breast cancer in my thirties. I began writing this series steeped in alchemy and cooking transformations while I was undergoing chemotherapy. I took cooking classes and learned how to cook healing vegan foods that nourished both my body and soul. As I write this, I'm four years cancer-free and working on the next Accidental Alchemist mystery.

ACKNOWLEDGMENTS

What would I do without my critique readers? Huge thanks go to the ever-insightful and supportive Emberly Nesbitt, Nancy Adams, Brian Selfon, Stephen Buehler, Juliet Blackwell, Susan Parman, my agent Jill Marsal, and my editorial team at Midnight Ink: Terri Bischoff, Amy Glaser, and Nicole Nugent.

I'd go crazy without the support from the writers in my life. Local pals Emberly Nesbitt, Mysti Berry, Juliet Blackwell, Lisa Hughey, and Michelle Gonzales make sure I make it to the café and keep writing. Sisters in Crime, especially the Guppies, provide endless online support. And Diane Vallere, my kindred spirit on this path, is always there to bounce around ideas.

My parents always told me I could be anything I wanted to be. Without their early encouragement, there's no way I would have conceived of this series. And my amazing husband James encourages my dreams in every way.

© *Michael B. Woolsey*

ABOUT THE AUTHOR

Gigi Pandian is the *USA Today* bestselling author of the Accidental Alchemist mystery series and the Jaya Jones Treasure Hunt mystery series. A breast cancer diagnosis in her thirties taught her two important life lessons: healing foods can taste amazing, and life's too short to waste a single moment. Gigi spent her childhood being dragged around the world by her cultural anthropologist parents, and she now lives in the San Francisco Bay Area with an overgrown organic vegetable garden in the backyard. Find her online at www.gigipandian.com.

"Hamilton's story will mesmerize anyone whose identity mixes cultures or marks them as out of place in that place called home . . . an astonishing achievement . . . a masterpiece."
—*Washington Post*

"The rare quality of this memoir owes much to [Hamilton's] novelistic skills, not least his handling of the child's point of view throughout, with its luminously comprehending attentiveness to adult behavior . . . the cumulative effect is to elevate an act of scrupulous remembering into a work of art."
—*New York Times Book Review*

"An astonishing account, both delicate and strong, of great issues of twentieth-century Europe, modern Ireland, and family everywhere, as they were felt within the heart and mind of a growing boy."

—NUALA O'FAOLAIN,
author of *Are You Somebody* and *Almost There*

"A terrific achievement, thoughtful and compelling, smart and original, beautifully written."
—NICK HORNBY, *London Times*

"This is the most gripping book I've read in ages. . . . [A] fascinating, disturbing and often very funny memoir."
—RODDY DOYLE, author of *The Commitments*

"*The Speckled People* stands head and shoulders above the ruck of memoirs pouring out of Ireland . . . an accomplished work of art and a strange tale brilliantly told." —*Boston Globe*

HUGO HAMILTON was born in Dublin of Irish/German parentage. The author of several highly acclaimed novels, he contributed to the 2001 mystery collaboration *Yeats Is Dead!* along with Frank McCourt, Roddy Doyle, and other major Irish writers. He was awarded the Rooney Prize for Irish Literature in 1992, and has worked as a writer-in-residence at many leading universities, among them Trinity College, Dublin. Hamilton recently received a DAAD scholarship and currently lives in Dublin.

"I wait for the command to show my tongue. I know he's going to cut it off, and I get more and more scared each time."

— ELIAS CANETTI

The Speckled People

A MEMOIR OF A HALF-IRISH CHILDHOOD

HUGO HAMILTON

Fourth Estate

An Imprint of HarperCollins*Publishers*

The author would like to thank Colm Tóibín and Eileen Ahearn for their generous help and encouragement with *The Speckled People*. Many thanks also to Colum McCann, Joseph O'Connor, Seán Ó Riain, Hans Christian Oeser, Gerald Dawe, Leo Lecours, and John Smallwood. The author also wishes to acknowledge the financial assistance of Aosdána and The Arts Council in Dublin, as well as the financial support and hospitality of DAAD in Berlin and Künstlerhaus Schloss Wiepersdorf in Brandenburg.

Image on title page: Hugo Hamilton, left, his mother and sisters, Ita and Maria, in Connemara in 1959. By kind permission of Hugo Hamilton.

HarperCollins books may be purchased for educational, business, or sales promotional use. For information, please write: Special Markets Department, HarperCollins Publishers Inc., 10 East 53rd Street, New York, NY 10022.

First Fourth Estate U.S. paperback edition published 2004

Printed on acid-free paper

Library of Congress Cataloging-in-Publication Data is available upon request.

ISBN 978-0-00-715663-4 (pbk.)

04 05 06 07 08 OS/RRD 10 9 8 7 6 5 4 3 2 1

One

When you're small you know nothing.

When I was small I woke up in Germany. I heard the bells and rubbed my eyes and saw the wind pushing the curtains like a big belly. Then I got up and looked out the window and saw Ireland. And after breakfast we all went out the door to Ireland and walked down to Mass. And after Mass we walked down to the big green park in front of the sea because I wanted to show my mother and father how I could stand on the ball for a count of three, until the ball squirted away from under my feet. I chased after it, but I could see nothing with the sun in my eyes and I fell over a man lying on the grass with his mouth open. He sat up suddenly and said, 'What the Jayses?' He told me to look where I was going in future. So I got up quickly and ran back to my mother and father. I told them that the man said 'Jayses', but they were both turned away, laughing at the sea. My father was laughing and blinking through his glasses and my mother had her hand over her mouth, laughing and laughing at the sea, until the tears came into her eyes and I thought, maybe she's not laughing at all but crying.

How do you know what that means when her shoulders are shaking and her eyes are red and she can't talk? How do you know if she's happy or sad? And how do you know if your father is happy or whether he's still angry at all the things that are not finished yet in Ireland. You know the sky is blue and the sea is blue and they meet somewhere, far away at the horizon. You can see the white sailing boats stuck on the water and the people walking along with ice-cream cones. You can hear a dog barking at the waves. You can see him standing in the water, barking and trying to bite the foam. You can see how long it takes for the sound of the barking to come across, as if it's coming from somewhere else and doesn't belong to the dog at all any more, as if he's barking and barking so much that he's hoarse and lost his voice.

When you're small you know nothing. You don't know where you are, or who you are, or what questions to ask.

Then one day my mother and father did a funny thing. First of all, my mother sent a letter home to Germany and asked one of her sisters to send over new trousers for my brother and me. She wanted us to wear something German – lederhosen. When the parcel arrived, we couldn't wait to put them on and run outside, all the way down the lane at the back of the houses. My mother couldn't believe her eyes. She stood back and clapped her hands together and said we were real boys now. No matter how much we climbed on walls or trees, she said, these German leather trousers were indestructible, and so they were. Then my father wanted us to wear something Irish too. He went straight out and bought hand-knit Aran sweaters. Big, white, rope patterned, woollen sweaters from the west of Ireland that were also indestructible. So my brother and I ran out wearing lederhosen and Aran sweaters, smelling of rough wool and new leather, Irish on top and German below. We were indestructible. We could slide down granite rocks. We could fall on nails and sit on glass. Nothing could sting us now and we ran down the lane faster than ever before, brushing past nettles as high as our shoulders.

When you're small you're like a piece of white paper with nothing written on it. My father writes down his name in Irish and my mother writes down her name in German and there's a blank space left over for all the people outside who speak English. We're special because we speak Irish and German and we like the smell of these new clothes. My mother says it's like being at home again and my father says your language is your home and your country is your language and your language is your flag.

But you don't want to be special. Out there in Ireland you want to be the same as everyone else, not an Irish speaker, not a German or a Kraut or a Nazi. On the way down to the shops, they call us the Nazi brothers. They say we're guilty and I go home and tell my mother I did nothing. But she shakes her head and says I can't say that. I can't deny anything and I can't fight back and I can't say I'm innocent. She says it's not important to win. Instead, she teaches us to surrender, to walk straight by and ignore them.

We're lucky to be alive, she says. We're living in the luckiest place in the world with no war and nothing to be afraid of, with the sea close by and the smell of salt in the air. There are lots of blue benches where you can sit looking out at the waves and lots of places to go swimming. Lots of rocks to climb on and pools to go fishing for crabs. Shops that sell fishing lines and hooks and buckets and plastic sunglasses. When it's hot you can get an ice pop and you can see newspapers spread out in the windows to stop the chocolate melting in the sun. Sometimes it's so hot that the sun stings you under your jumper like a needle in the back. It makes tar bubbles on the road that you can burst with the stick from the ice pop. We're living in a free country, she says, where the wind is always blowing and you can breathe in deeply, right down to the bottom of your lungs. It's like being on holiday all your life because you hear seagulls in the morning and you see sailing boats outside houses and people even have palm trees growing in their front gardens. Dublin where the palm trees grow, she says, because it looks like a paradise and the sea is never far away, like a glass of blue-green water at the bottom of every street.

But that changes nothing. *Sieg Heil*, they shout. *Achtung. Schnell schnell. Donner und Blitzen.* I know they're going to put us on trial. They have written things on the walls, at the side of the shop and in the laneways. They're going to get us one of these days and ask questions that we won't be able to answer. I see them looking at us, waiting for the day when we're alone and there's nobody around. I know they're going to execute me, because they call my older brother Hitler, and I get the name of an SS man who was found in Argentina and brought back to be put on trial for all the people he killed.

'I am Eichmann,' I said to my mother one day.

'But that's impossible,' she said. She kneeled down to look into my eyes. She took my hands and weighed them to see how heavy they were. Then she waited for a while, searching for what she wanted to say next.

'You know the dog that barks at the waves?' she said. 'You know the dog that belongs to nobody and barks at the waves all day until he is hoarse and has no voice any more. He doesn't know any better.'

'I am Eichmann,' I said. 'I am Adolf Eichmann and I'm

going to get an ice pop. Then I'm going down to the sea to look at the waves.'

'Wait,' she said. 'Wait for your brother.'

She stands at the door with her hand over her mouth. She thinks we're going out to Ireland and never coming back home again. She's afraid we might get lost in a foreign country where they don't have our language and nobody will understand us. She is crying because I'm Eichmann and there is nothing she can do to stop us going out and being Nazis. She tells us to be careful and watches us going across the street until we go around the corner and she can't see us any more.

So then we try to be Irish. In the shop we ask for the ice pop in English and let on that we don't know any German. We're afraid to be German, so we run down to the seafront as Irish as possible to make sure nobody can see us. We stand at the railings and look at the waves crashing against the rocks and the white spray going up into the air. We can taste the salt on our lips and see the foam running through the cracks like milk. We're Irish and we say 'Jaysus' every time the wave curls in and hits the rocks with a big thump.

'Jaysus, what the Jaysus,' I said.

'Jaysus, what the Jaysus of a big huge belly,' Franz said, and then we laughed and ran along the shore waving our fists.

'Big bully waves,' I shouted, because they could never catch us and they knew it. I picked up a stone and hit one of the waves right in the under-belly, right there as he stood up and rushed in towards us with his big, green saucer belly and his fringe of white hair falling down over his eyes.

'Get down, you big bully belly,' we laughed, as the stone

caught the wave with a clunk and there was nothing he could do but surrender and lie down across the sand with his arms out. Some of them tried to escape, but we were too fast for them. We picked up more and more stones and hit them one by one, because we were Irish and nobody could see us. The dog was there barking and barking, and we were there holding back the waves, because we didn't know any better.

Two

I know they don't want us here. From the window of my mother and father's bedroom I can see them walking by, going from the football field around by our street and down to the shops again. They carry sticks and smoke cigarette butts and spit on the ground. I hear them laughing and it's only a matter of time before we have to go out there and they'll be waiting. They'll find out who we are. They'll tell us to go back to where we come from.

My father says we have nothing to worry about because we are the new Irish. Partly from Ireland and partly from somewhere else, half-Irish and half-German. We're the speckled people, he says, the 'brack' people, which is a word that comes from the Irish language, from the Gaelic as they sometimes call it. My father was a schoolteacher once before he became an engineer and *breac* is a word, he explains, that the Irish people brought with them when they were crossing over into the English language. It means speckled, dappled, flecked, spotted, coloured. A trout is brack and so is a speckled horse. A barm brack is a loaf of bread with raisins in it and was borrowed from the Irish words *bairín breac*. So we are the speckled-Irish, the brack-Irish. Brack home-made Irish bread with German raisins.

But I know it also means we're marked. It means we're aliens and we'll never be Irish enough, even though we speak the Irish language and my father says we're more Irish than the Irish themselves. We have speckled faces, so it's best to stay inside where they can't get us. Inside we can be ourselves.

I look out the window and see the light changing on the red-bricked terrace across the street. I see the railings and the striped canvas sun-curtains hanging out over the front doors. There's a gardener clipping a hedge and I hear the sound of his shears in English, because everything out there is spoken in English. Out there is a different country, far away. There's a cloud moving over the street and I can see the gardener looking up. I hear my mother behind me saying that there's something strange about the light this afternoon. She says the sun is eclipsed by the cloud and throws a kind of low, lantern light across the red-bricked walls and it feels like the end of the day.

'*Falsches Licht*,' she calls it, because everything inside our house is spoken in German, or in Irish. Never in English. She comes to the window to look for herself and says it again, false light. She takes in a deep breath through her teeth and that means it's going to rain. It means the seagulls will soon come in from the sea and start screeching and settling on the chimneys. It's a sign for people to run out and bring in their washing. A sign for the gardener to go inside, because large drops are already appearing on the pavement. And when all the drops are joined together and the pavement is fully wet, then my mother goes downstairs to the kitchen.

She lets us play with some of her things. My older brother Franz, my younger sister Maria and me examine everything on her dressing table – lipstick, scissors, nail clippers, rosary beads. There's a brush lying on its back with a white comb stuck into it like a saw. A bowl of hair clips and a box of powder and a gold and blue bottle with the big number 4711 written on it. We empty out a box of jewellery and find the emerald snake which my mother calls the Smaragd. Maria keeps calling out the big number 4711 as she blesses herself around the ears and on the wrists and behind the knees, again and again, just like my mother does, and the whole room fills up with scent of cologne. I look at the print that the hairbrush makes on my arm. Franz finds the crocodile-skin purse with lots of heavy silver coins inside and we're rich. The smell of rain and leather are mixed together all in one with the smell of cologne. In the drawers on each side of the dressing table we find letters, scarves and stockings. Passports and photographs, rail tickets, sleeper accommodation on night trains.

And then we came across the medals. I knew immediately that they were German medals because everything that belongs to my mother is German. She tells us lots of stories about Kempen where she grew up, so I knew that my grandfather Franz Kaiser was in the First World War and that my mother was in the Second World War. I knew that my grandmother Berta was an opera singer and that my grandfather Franz once went to listen to her sing at the state opera house in Krefeld, and because everyone else was sending her flowers, he decided to send her a bouquet of bananas instead, and that's how they fell in love and got married. Sometimes my mother puts on the radio to see if she can hear some of the songs that her own mother sang. I know how far away Germany is by the way my mother sometimes has shadows around her eyes. By the way she stays silent. Or by the way she sometimes throws her head back and laughs out loud at some of the things that her father used to do. Like the time he once asked to borrow the postman's cap and said thank you very politely and then climbed up the monument in the middle of the square to put it on top of St George's head.

We didn't have to be told that these were military medals which belonged to Franz Kaiser. When he was on duty during the First World War, his wife Berta brought him his dinner once a day by train in a straw basket. Sometimes she just put the straw basket on the train by itself and it came back empty in the evening. Then he had to go to the front one day and came back with a disease in his lungs that killed him. He was not well even before the war started and my mother says he should never have been taken into the army because he died when she was only nine years old. She says she still remembers the smell of flowers in the room around his coffin and the shadows around her mother's eyes. So I put on Franz Kaiser's medal with the cross and march up and down the bare floorboards of my mother and father's bedroom, looking at myself in the mirror of the dressing table and saluting, while my brother salutes behind me with his own medal and my sister behind him with the emerald snake.

Then the sun lit up the street outside and I thought somebody had switched on a light in the room. The cloud had already passed over and gone somewhere else and there was steam rising from the pavement. The gardener was back out, clipping the hedge, and there was no other sound anywhere except my sister Maria breathing through her mouth and sometimes the sound of a train in the station. The smell of baking was coming all the way up the stairs from the kitchen and we should have rushed down to get the leftovers in the bowl. We should have been running up to collect my father from the train. But we were too busy looking for all these old things.

At first there was nothing much in my father's wardrobe,

only cufflinks, ties and socks. But then we found a big black and white picture of a sailor. He was dressed in a sailor's uniform with square, white lapels over his tunic and a rope lanyard hanging down over his chest. He had soft eyes and I liked the look of him. I wanted to be a sailor, even though I had no idea what this sailor was doing in my father's wardrobe.

I know that my father comes from Cork and works as an engineer in Dublin and writes his name in Irish. When he was small, Ireland was still under the British. His father's family were all fishermen. His father fell on deck one day and lost his memory and died not long after that in a hospital in Cork city. But we never talk about that. I knew there would be trouble when my father came home, but I didn't think about it, not even when I saw the shape of his good Sunday suit swinging on the hanger in front of me. Not even when I heard the trains coming into the station, one by one. We continued to inspect everything quickly, pulling out drawers full of handkerchiefs and gloves and mothballs and socks rolled up.

There were boxes at the bottom of the wardrobe, full of letters and postcards, certificates and holy pictures. And at last we came across more medals. Heavy bronze medals this time, one for each of us. The medal I put on hung from a striped ribbon that was just like the faded sun-curtains across the street. We didn't know where these new bronze medals came from, except that they must have belonged to the sailor hiding at the back of the wardrobe. Whoever he was, he must have owned the waterproof identity papers, too, and the photographs of HMS *Nemesis* with sailors lined up in a human chain along the deck. And he must have got all the postcards from King George wishing him a happy and victorious Christmas.

Some things are not good to know in Ireland. I had no idea that I had an Irish grandfather who couldn't even speak Irish. His name was John Hamilton and he belonged to the navy, the British navy, the Royal Navy. He joined up as a boy of fifteen and served on all kinds of ships – *Defiance*, *Magnificent*, *Katoomba*, *Repulse*. He fell on a British naval vessel called HMS *Vivid* when he was only 28 years of age. He died because he was homesick and lost his memory. But I didn't know any of that. There's a picture in the front room of Franz Kaiser and Berta Kaiser with her head leaning on his shoulder, both of them laughing with a big glass of wine on the table in front of them. There's no picture of John Hamilton or his wife Mary Frances, alone or together, hanging anywhere in our house. Our German grandparents are dead, but our Irish grandparents are dead and forgotten. I didn't know that the bronze medal I was wearing beside the Iron Cross belonging to my German grandfather came from the British navy and was given to my Irish grandmother, Mary Frances, along with a small British war widow's pension which she had to fight for. I didn't know that my Irish grandfather, John Hamilton, and my German grandfather, Franz Kaiser, must have stood facing each other in the Great War. Or that my mother and father were both orphaned by that same war. Or that I was wearing the medals of two different empires side by side.

I didn't know what questions to ask. I heard the trains coming home one by one and I knew that we were not allowed to speak the language of the sailor. It's forbidden to speak in English in our house. My father wants all the Irish people to cross back over into the Irish language so he made a rule that we can't speak English, because your home is your language and he wants us to be Irish and not British. My mother doesn't know how to make rules like that, because she's German and has nothing against the British. She has her own language and came to Ireland to learn English in the first place. So we're allowed to speak the language of Franz Kaiser, but not the language of John Hamilton. We can speak Irish or German, but English is like a foreign country outside the door. The sailor in the wardrobe, with his short haircut and his soft eyes looking away, was not able to talk to us. Even if he was still alive and came to visit us and was ready to tell us all about his travels around the world on those ships, about all the cities and ports he had been to, I could not have asked him any questions.

There were so many boxes at the bottom of the wardrobe that we could sit on them and pretend we were on a bus. We called it the number eight bus, and Franz was the driver holding a hat for a steering wheel. I was the conductor bedecked in medals, and Maria was the only passenger apart from my father's Sunday suit hanging on the rail and the quiet sailor in the back seat looking away out the window.

'Hold the bar please,' I called and Maria got on. She was carrying her crocodile-skin purse and paid the fare with the precious coins.

'Fares please,' I kept demanding, until she had no money left and I had to let her on without paying. I rang the bell with my fist against the handle of the drawer. Then I closed the door and the wardrobe drove off in the complete darkness. Maria cried and said she wanted to get off, but it was already too late for that, because the bus was going so fast that it started leaning over. Before we knew it, the whole wardrobe was lying on its side. The only thing stopping it from crashing all the way down to the floor was my mother and father's bed. We didn't even know what happened. All we knew was that we were now trapped inside and unable to open the door. We knew there would be trouble. We were silent for a while, waiting to see what would happen next. Maria kept crying and then Franz started calling for help.

'Mutti, Ma Ma . . .' he said.

I started calling as well. My mother was far away downstairs in the kitchen baking the cake. We called and called and waited for a long time. But nobody could hear us, not even the gardener or the neighbours or anyone out on the street, because they could only hear things that were said in English. Nobody even knew that we were calling for help, because we had the wrong words. We were the children in the wardrobe and no matter how loud we shouted and knocked, they could hear nothing.

Some time later I heard my mother's voice outside saying that she could not believe her eyes. She said she had seen a lot of strange things in Germany during the war, and in Ireland, too, after she came over, but never before had she seen a wardrobe on its side, crying. She was not able to lift the wardrobe by herself, or to open the door because it was jammed shut against the bed. But everything was going to be all right in the end, she said, because even if we had to stay in the dark for a while longer, she would tell us a story until help came. We listened to her and almost fell asleep with the fog of 4711 and mothballs and the cake downstairs, until my father came home and the wardrobe suddenly stood up and the door opened. It was daytime again. I rubbed my eyes and saw my father blinking through his glasses and saying everything with a frown on his forehead.

'Who gave you the right to look at my things?' he said, because he didn't want any of us to know that he had a father in the navy who could not speak Irish and once stood with the British in a war against the Germans, when his own country was still not free.

Maria was huddled in my mother's arms, crying even more after she was rescued than before when she was trapped. She said Franz was the driver and I was the conductor and she was only a passenger, like the sailor in the back seat. My father's voice filled the room and I felt the sting of his hand, but it was nothing because soon we were all safe again and my mother was talking about the cake for after dinner. The medals were taken off and put away. The picture of the sailor with the soft eyes disappeared and we never saw him again after that. Nobody mentioned him. I had no way of keeping him in my head because he was gone, back into the wardrobe where nobody could rescue him. We didn't know how to remember him, and like him, we lost our memory.

Three

My mother's name is Irmgard and she was in a big film once with lots of war and killing and trains on fire. It's a black and white picture that happened long ago in Germany. A man trapped her in a place called Venlo where she was working and she couldn't escape. She says it was just like us being in the wardrobe because she was far away from home and couldn't call for help. She couldn't write home or tell any of her sisters what was happening. She didn't know who to talk to. The man's name was Stiegler and he would not listen to her when she spoke to him and would not let her go. Instead he told her to smile. And even though she was too afraid to smile, he just put his hand up to her lips and made her show her teeth like a big unhappy grin. She can't talk about it any more than that. She has told nobody else, not even her sisters, not even my father. One day, when we get older we'll hear the whole story. But now we're too small, and some things about Germany are not good to think about. 'That's a film you can see when you grow up,' she says.

All we need to know is that at the end of the film, when the war is over, my mother runs away to Ireland to go on a pilgrimage. She meets my father in Dublin and they talk about everything except the time she was trapped once by the man in Venlo. They go back to Germany to get married with the snow all around. They travel through the white landscape and go to a mountain along the River Rhine called the Drachenfelz, and after that my father brings her back to Ireland to another mountain close to the Atlantic called Croagh Patrick.

'And that's how the film ends,' she says, because it's time to sleep and she doesn't want us to keep calling her and asking more questions about Germany that she can't answer. 'The End. Film over.' She says the same thing sometimes when we start fighting over the leftovers of the cake bowl. Or the time we went to the strand and stayed there all day until it started raining and she said it was a pity it had to end like that. Or when something breaks, like the time the blue vase that came from her father and mother's house in Kempen smashed in the hallway and she said it was a very nice film but now it was over.

In my mother's film, she was in a building where there was nobody else living. At night when everybody was gone, she was afraid and locked the door of her room. She knew that there was no point in shouting for help, because nobody would hear her. Then she heard the man coming in and there was nothing she could do except pray and hope that it would be all over some day. She could hear him coming up the stairs as if he was counting them on the way up. She could hear him breathing outside the door. She could see the doorknob turning and she could smell cognac.

During the day, the man was always very nice to everybody. He looked very well, dressed in a suit and a clean shirt every morning, and he wore good shoes. He spoke kindly and shook hands with everyone when they arrived to work. He smiled and even remembered everybody's birthday. He brought flowers to work when somebody had bad news. Everybody said he was a good man during the day and full of compliments. He had read a lot of books and he was very generous, giving presents of theatre tickets and opera tickets.

But you can't always trust nice people. My mother says that sometimes there is no defence against kindness. It's easy to be taken in by compliments, by smiles, by nice words. But you can't let yourself be stung by things like flowers and theatre tickets and invitations to the opera. Everybody can make mistakes but there are some mistakes you can't even talk about, because you feel so stupid that you can only blame yourself. My mother wants us never to be fooled by nice words. She wants us never to have things that we regret, because everybody in Germany has things in their heads that they keep to themselves. Everybody has things they wish had never happened.

When you're small you can inherit a secret without even knowing what it is. You can be trapped in the same film as your mother, because certain things are passed on to you that you're not even aware of, not just a smile or a voice, but unspoken things, too, that you can't understand until later when you grow up. Maybe it's there in my eyes for all to see, the same as it is in my mother's eyes. Maybe it's hidden in my voice, or in the shape of my hands. Maybe it's something you carry with you like a precious object you're told not to lose.

'That film will still be running when we grow up,' she says.

All we need to know for now is that she ran away to Ireland to become a pilgrim in a holy country with priests and donkeys that had crosses on their backs. She picked Ireland because she heard there were lots of monastic ruins. She didn't expect so much poverty. But the Irish people knew how to deal with poverty, through celebration, with smoke and stories and singing. A man with a packet of cigarettes was a millionaire in Ireland. And the Irish people had never tried to hurt anyone. So maybe they would not pass judgement on a German woman. In the days before she left Germany, it was so exciting, she says, because nobody in her family had ever been that far away before. Everybody was talking about Ireland, even the neighbours, asking what the weather was like and what the houses were like inside. What she should bring and what she didn't need. She said she packed and unpacked all over again so often that it was hard to believe she was going away at all in the end.

At the station, she embraced her aunt Ta Maria and her Onkel Gerd and her youngest sister Minne, but it was hard to feel she was leaving. They all had tears in their eyes and would not let her get on the train because they thought she would never come back. They made her promise to write home every week. Even when she was sitting down in her seat, even when the train carriages jerked and the train moved out of the station, it was still hard to feel anything except fear. Everybody in Germany was used to being afraid. She waved her hand slowly. She saw the houses and the fences and the fields passing by, but she still had the feeling that she was trapped. But then, my mother says, there comes a moment when you don't care about anything, when all fear and doubt disappear. It's a moment of weakness and strength at the same time, when nothing matters and you're not afraid any more.

Sometimes she still thinks about it as though it just happened yesterday, as though the film is never over and she'll never escape. Maybe the reason why people are good at stories is that they sometimes have things they can't tell, things they must keep secret at all costs and make up for in other ways. So she tells us the story of the pilgrimage instead. She tells us how Ireland was a place where you could trust everyone, where people prayed every day, where you could go and say the rosary and make up for all the things that happened in the war.

It was a great way for a film to come to an end, cycling along the small roads with the sun slanting through the clouds like in holy pictures, lighting up the mountains like a stage in the opera house. It was flickering through the stone walls. Everywhere these stone walls and everywhere the grass combed in one direction by the wind. Trees bent like old men and everywhere so empty except for the haystacks in the fields and the monastic ruins. Once or twice along the way there were cows on the road that made her stop completely. Big cow faces looking at her, as if they were amazed to see a German woman in Ireland after the war.

Then it started raining and getting dark and she had to find a place to stay quickly. It was raining so much that the water was jumping away from her eyes when she blinked and her shoulders were shivering. She got off the bicycle because it was impossible to go any further. A man pointed to a house that didn't even look like a guest house, but it was better to stay there because you couldn't see a thing any more. There was a light on inside and the woman of the house came to the door with lots of children behind her. One girl had her dress in her mouth, all of them staring as if my mother had come in with the rain.

'It's not often we see a German woman cycling around these parts on her own,' the woman said.

My mother says you can't be sure in Ireland if people say things with admiration or not. Irish people are good at saying things in between admiration and accusation, between envy and disdain. She says the woman looked her up and down as if she liked German clothes but didn't completely trust her.

'I have come from Lough Derg,' my mother explained.

That made everything right. She was a pilgrim. A pilgrim coming to Ireland to pray for all the bad things that happened in Europe.

In the kitchen, they made her sit and eat a meal while they all watched and the man of the house kept asking questions about Germany. Was it in ruins like they said in the papers? She had to describe the cities after the war – Nuremberg, Hamburg, Dresden. The woman of the house kept saying 'You're not serious', but people in Germany wouldn't make up something like that. The children kept staring. They were so shy that they were afraid to move closer to her. It was like being a film actress. They spoke about her as if she was still in a film. She'll have some more bread, the man of the house said. She'll be needing a glass of whiskey, he said after she was finished eating, as if they had to celebrate the guest who came in with the rain.

The man of the house raised his glass with all the children looking up.

'Heil Hitler,' he said.

There was a big smile on his face, my mother says, and she didn't know what to say. Of course, he was only being friendly. It was part of the Irish welcome.

'Fair play to the Germans,' he said.

He said the Germans were great people altogether. He kept saying it was a pity they lost because they were a mighty nation. He winked at her with admiration, then left a long silence, waiting to see how she would respond.

'Fair play to the Germans, for the almighty thrashing you gave the British. Fair play to Hitler for that, at least.'

He was only being hospitable, my mother says, to make her feel at home. She could not argue with him. She was trapped inside German history and couldn't get out of it. Instead she smiled and said it had been a long journey back from Lough Derg. She thanked them for such a lovely welcome, but said she could no longer keep her eyes open.

She was given a room with a small fire going. Her clothes were still steaming. There was a smell of cabbage and damp walls. The bed sank down in the middle, but she was so tired that nothing mattered any more and it didn't take long to fall asleep to the sound of the rain. She heard the voices of children on the far side of the wall and sometimes the man of the house, too, speaking in a deep voice. But the rain was whispering and bouncing into an enamel basin outside and rushing away into a drain like the sound of the rosary being said all night.

Sometime later she woke up and saw the woman of the house standing beside the bed, holding a lamp, gently shaking her arm. The woman explained that there was an emergency. Would she mind giving up the bed and spending the night in another room? There were three men soaked to the skin outside on the doorstep needing accommodation for the night.

'I can't turn them away,' the woman said. 'Poor creatures.'

My mother says she had to get up and take her things to the family room where the woman pointed to the marriage bed. The children were all fast asleep in another bed. And the room was in such a mess, with clothes and newspapers on the floor, bits of food, too, even a harness for a horse and a hay-fork and wellington boots. She stood there looking around as if she couldn't believe her eyes.

'It's only topsy dirty,' the woman said.

'But where is your husband?'

'You have nothing to be afraid of, love. He'll stay by the fire.'

My mother says you can't complain if you're a pilgrim escaping from Germany. She says you have to offer things up. For people who are less fortunate and for all the awful things that happened. So she just got into bed with the woman of the house. She felt the warmth left behind by the man of the house. She could hear the whole room breathing, until the woman started speaking in the dark. She listened to the woman talking for a while, and then she began to talk as well, as if there were things that could only be said in the dark.

She says she never saw the men. She heard them coming in and muttering for a while to each other in the room. She never saw the man of the house again either, but she heard him in the kitchen, tapping his pipe against the fireplace. She heard the children dreaming sometimes and the cows elbowing each other in the barn outside. She smelled the rain and heard it drumming on the roof, like somebody still saying the rosary. They whispered so as not to wake up the children. They talked for a long time as if they were sisters.

Four

On the front door of our house there is the number two. I know how to say this number in German: *Zwei*. My mother teaches us how to count up the stairs: *Eins, Zwei, Drei* . . . And when you get to ten you can start again, so many steps all the way up that you can call them any number you like. And when we're in our pyjamas, we say goodnight birds and goodnight trees, until my mother counts again very quickly and we jump into bed as fast as possible: *Eins, Zwei, Drei*.

There are workers in the house and they know how to smoke. They made a mountain in the back garden and sit on it, drinking tea and eating sandwiches. They smoke cigarettes and mix sand and cement with a shovel. They whistle and make a hole in the middle where they pour in the water to make a lake, and sometimes the water from the lake spills over the side before the shovel can catch it. We do the same with spoons. The workers have different words, not the same as my mother, and they teach us how to count in English: one, two, three . . . But my father says that's not allowed. He says he'll speak to them later.

One day there was a fox in the kitchen, just like the fox in the story book. The workers were gone, so my mother closed the door and called the police. Then a Garda came to our house and went into the kitchen on his own and started banging. There was a smell of smoke and we waited on the stairs for a long time, until the Garda came out again with the fox lying dead on a shovel with his tail hanging down and blood around his mouth and nose.

'You'll have no more strangers in your house, please God,' he said.

The Garda showed his teeth to my mother and called her 'Madam'. The workers called her 'Maam'. We called her 'Mutti' or 'Ma Ma' and my father is called 'Vati' even though he's from Cork. The Garda had a moustache and said it was no fox we had in the kitchen but a rat the size of a fox. And the rat was very *glic*, he said, because he hid behind the boiler and would not come out until he was chased out with fire and smoke.

There are other people living at the top of our house, all the way up the stairs, further than you can count. They're called the O'Neills and they never take their hats off, because they think the hallway is like the street, my mother says. They are very noisy and my father makes a face. He goes up to speak to them and when he comes down again he says he wants the O'Neills out of the house. There will be no more chopping wood under this roof.

Áine came to look after us when my mother had to go away to the hospital. She's from Connemara and has different words, not the same as the workers, or the O'Neills, or the Garda, or my mother. She teaches us to count the stairs again in Irish: *a haon, a dó, a trí* . . . She doesn't lay out the clothes at night or tell stories. She doesn't call me Hanni or Johannes, she calls me Seán instead, or sometimes Jack, but my father says that's wrong. I should never let anyone call me Jack or John, because that's not who I am. My father changed his name to Irish. So when I grow up I'll change my name, too.

Áine can't speak my mother's words, but she can speak the words of the Garda. She brings us for a walk along the seafront and shows us the crabs running sideways and the dog barking for nothing all day. She says she wants to go to London, but it's very far away. And Connemara is far away, too. I said London was far away one, and Connemara was far away two, and she said: 'Yes.' She sits for a long time looking out across the sea to London. Then she takes us up to the shops to buy sweets and I get more than Franz because I'm very *glic*. She teaches us how to walk on the wall, all the way back along the seafront, and Franz makes up a song about it: 'Walk on the wall, walk on the wall . . .'

My mother came back with a baby called Maria, so that's Franz, Johannes and Maria: *Eins, Zwei, Drei*. We speak German again and my mother shows us how to feed the baby with her breast. Maria opens her mouth and shakes her head and then my mother has to change her nappy because the baby did 'A A'. After that, my mother puts Maria out in the garden with a net across the pram to stop the birds from stealing her dreams.

Áine took us down to the sea again because Franz had a fishing net and he was going to catch one of the crabs, but they were too fast. I said they were all 'two fast and three fast', and Áine said: 'Yes.' She took out a box with a small mirror and put lipstick on her lips. She took off her shoes to put her feet into one of the pools with the crabs. I started throwing stones into the pools. Franz got all wet and Áine said 'A A' in Irish. Then I threw a stone in Áine's pool. She chased after me and on the way home she would not let me walk on the wall, so I tried to walk sideways, like the crabs.

My mother knows everything. She knows that I was

throwing stones, but Áine said it wasn't 'half as bad as that', which is the same as what my mother says only in different words: *Halb so schlimm.* My mother wagged her finger and said: *Junge, Junge,* which is the same as what Áine says in English: 'Boy, oh boy', and in Irish '*a mhac ó*'.

That evening, my mother brought us up to the station to collect my father from the train. She picked us up to look over the wall at the tracks. We waved and shouted at the train rushing through under the bridge and then we started running towards my father coming out of the station. My father is different to other men. He has no moustache, but he has glasses and he has a limp, too. He swings his briefcase and his leg goes down on one side as if the ground is soft under one foot. It's the same as when you walk with one foot on and one foot off the pavement. My mother kisses him and puts her arm around him. He looks into the pram at Maria to see if she has her eyes open. Franz tries to carry the briefcase and I try to walk like my father, but that's not allowed. He hits me on the back of my head and my mother kneels down to say it's not right to imitate people. You always have to walk like yourself, not like your father or the crabs, just like yourself. At home, my father was still angry. He wanted to know why I was throwing stones at the pools so I told him that Áine said 'A A' in Irish. I mixed up the words like sand and cement and water. I used Áine's words and told my father that she said 'A A', what the baby did, in my mother's words.

'What did you throw?' my father asked.

'Stones.'

I saw myself twice in his glasses and he made a face, just like when the O'Neills were chopping wood upstairs.

'Stones,' he said again, very loud. Then he stood up.

My mother was laughing and laughing until the tears

27

came into her eyes. She said it was so funny to hear so many words and so many countries being mixed up.

'Stones,' my father said again. 'I won't have this.'

'It's not half as bad as that,' my mother said, still wiping her eyes.

'She's here to speak Irish to them,' my father shouted, and then my mother tried to stop him going up to speak to Áine. She was holding on to his arm and saying: 'Leave it till the morning. Let me talk to her.'

My father says there will be no more chopping wood and no more speaking English under his roof. I stay awake and look at the light under the door. At night, I hear my mother and father talking for a long time. I hear the O'Neills coming up the stairs and I hear my father coming out on the landing to see if they will start chopping wood. Then the light goes out. I hear water whispering. I hear a fox laughing. I hear stones dropping into the pools and I hear sand and cement being mixed with a shovel. Then it's silent and nobody is listening, only me.

My mother spoke to Áine the next day. She's not able to speak Áine's words. So in the words of the Garda and the workers, my mother tells her never to speak the words of the Garda and the workers to us again.

'You must try to speak to them in Irish,' my mother said.

'What good is that to them?' Áine said.

'Please. It's my husband's wish.'

So we have to be careful in our house and think before we speak. We can't speak the words of the Garda or the workers, that's English. We speak Áine's words from Connemara, that's Irish, or my mother's words, that's German. I can't talk to Áine in German and I can't talk to my mother in Irish, because she'll only laugh and tickle me. I can talk to my father in German or Irish and he can speak to the Garda and the workers for us. Outside, you have to be careful, too, because you can't buy an ice pop in German or in Irish, and lots of people only know the words of the Garda and the workers. My father says they better hurry up and learn Irish fast because we won't buy anything more in English.

Sometimes Áine speaks to herself in the mirror. Sometimes when the O'Neills go through the hall on their way out the front door, my mother says good morning to them, but they say nothing at all and just walk out as if they don't understand their own language. Sometimes the man in the fish shop says *guten Morgen* as if he's forgotten his own language. Sometimes people whisper. Sometimes they spell out the letters of a word. And sometimes people try to forget their own language altogether and Áine continues to say 'stones' as if there's no word in her own language for it.

'*Stone mór*' and '*stone beag*,' she says. Big stone and little stone.

On Saturday, Áine goes into the city on the bus to speak English. The O'Neills were gone away, too, and my father was in the garden digging. He said he was going to get rid of the mountain the workers left behind and grow flowers and radishes, so I watched him as he jabbed the spade into the soil and then pushed it down with his foot. The worms living in the mountain had to go away in the wheelbarrow. My father emptied it and spread out the soil in another part of the garden. Then he let me hold the wheelbarrow while it was filling up again.

Franz made a wall with a line of bricks and he was walking on it singing: 'Walk on the wall, walk on the wall . . .' My father stopped digging and told him to stop. He made the O'Neill face again. But Franz kept on saying 'walk on the wall' because that was his song and he couldn't forget it. Then my father jabbed the spade into the mountain and it stayed there, standing up on its own while he went over to Franz and hit him. He hit him on the back of the head so that Franz fell off the wall and his face went down on the bricks. When he got up, there was blood all around his nose and mouth, like the fox. He opened his mouth and said nothing for a long time, as if he had forgotten how to use his voice and I thought he was going to be dead. Then he started crying at last and my father took him by the hand very quickly and brought him inside.

'*Mein armer Schatz*,' my mother kept saying as she sat him up beside the sink and started cleaning the blood away from his face. Franz kept crying and trying to say something but he didn't know what words to use. Then my mother turned around to my father and looked at him as if she could not believe her eyes.

'His nose is broken,' she said.

There were drops of blood on the kitchen floor. They made a trail all the way out into the garden. My father said he was very sorry, but the rules had to be obeyed. He said Franz was speaking English again and that had to stop. Then my mother and father had no language at all. My father went outside again and my mother brought Franz upstairs. Even when the blood stopped, he was still crying for a long time and my mother was afraid that he would never start talking again. She sat down on the bed and put her arm around the two of us and told us what happened when she was in Germany in a very bad film. She held us both very hard and I thought my bones would crack. She was crying and her shoulders were shaking. She said she was going to go back to Germany. She would take us with her. She started packing her suitcase, wondering what she should bring and what she should leave behind in Ireland.

I looked out the window and watched my father fill the wheelbarrow and bring it to another part of the garden, empty it and bring it back to start again. I watched him digging and digging, until the mountain was gone. I wanted to go down and tell him that my mother fixed Franz's nose with a story. I wanted to tell him that I would never say 'walk on the wall' as long as I lived. I wanted to tell him that my mother was going home and she was going to take us with her. But he never looked up and he didn't see me waving. Instead, he made a big fire in the garden and the smoke went across the walls, away over the other gardens, all around the houses and out on to the street. He kept stacking on more and more weeds and leaves with a big fork, as if he wanted to send a message around the whole world with smoke. The fire crackled and whistled, and it smelled like cigarettes. My father was standing with the fork in his hand and sometimes he disappeared. Sometimes the whole house disappeared and people must have thought we were never coming back.

My mother carried Maria in one arm and the suitcase in the other. In the hallway, she put the suitcase down so that she could open the front door and escape on to the street. I knew that my father would be searching for us all over the place in the smoke. But my mother said we were not going to be trapped again. She picked up the suitcase and told us to follow her, but then I heard my father coming in from the garden. His footsteps came all the way as if he was counting the drops of blood on the ground. We tried to run away fast, but it was too late because he was already standing right behind us. I could smell the smoke on his clothes. He asked my mother where she was thinking of going to without any money. He said there was nothing left in Germany and she had nowhere to go home to with three children. He closed the front door and said she was married now, so she sat down on the suitcase and cried.

'She's just a bit homesick, that's all,' my father said. He smiled and said he would put on some German music. He kissed my mother's hand and carried the suitcase back up the stairs.

Then the big music filled the whole house. It went into every room and all the way up the stairs. Outside, the fire kept going until it got dark and I stood at the window of the bedroom again with my mother, saying goodbye smoke, goodbye birds, goodbye trees. But we didn't go anywhere. We stayed in Ireland and my mother told us to get into bed: *Eins, Zwei, Drei.*

Five

My father's name is Jack and he's in a song, a long ballad with lots of verses about leaving Ireland and emigrating. The song is so long that you couldn't even sing it all in one day. It has more than a thousand verses, all about freedom and dying of hunger and going away to some other land at the end of it all. My father is not much good at singing, but he keeps repeating the chorus about how we should live in Ireland and be Irish.

'No more shall we roam from our own native home,' is what he says when we're standing at the seafront, holding on to the blue railings, looking out at the white sailing boats. He doesn't want us to live in England or America where they speak only English and keep dreaming about going back home. So we stay in Ireland where we were born, with the sea between us and all the other countries, with the church bell ringing and the mailboat going out across the water. Instead of always going away, my father had a new idea. Why not bring people from somewhere else over to Ireland? So that's why he married my mother and now she's the one who does all the dreaming and singing about being far away from home. It's my mother who left her own native shores, and that means we still end up living in a foreign country because we're the children from somewhere else.

My father comes from a small town in west Cork called Leap and he had lots of uncles and cousins who had to emigrate. One of his uncles only sent his first letter back from America after twenty years, just to tell everybody that the rumours still going around in Ireland about a girl he left behind with a baby were not true. It was easy to say what you liked about people who went away. And it was easy for those who left to deny Ireland, to look back and say it was full of poverty and failure. Maybe they made a lot of money abroad, my father says, but they were lonely and they wanted everybody who was left in Ireland to come and join them over there. My father and his younger brother Ted were going to emigrate, too. They lived in a house at the end of the town with their mother and a picture of a sailor over the mantelpiece. They had plans to go to America to work with their uncle, but then they got a scholarship and went to school instead.

The town is called Leap after a famous Irishman by the name of O'Donovan who once got away from the British by leaping across a nearby gorge. *Léim Uí Dhonabháin:* O'Donovan's Leap, they call it. The peelers chased him all over the countryside, but he escaped over the impossible gorge and they were afraid to follow him. 'Beyond the Leap, beyond the law' is what the people of the town said. There was no freedom at that time. The whole town could hardly jump across the gorge after him, so they stayed behind where they were, under the British. They talked about it and went up there for a walk on summer days to look across to the far side. But nobody could do it. So the town was called after something that might as well not have happened at all. It was called Leap because that's what the people in the town wished they had done, what they dreamed about and sang songs about.

Lots of them emigrated after that, my father says. The people who stayed told their children that unless they wanted to jump after the famous O'Donovan and spend the rest of their lives running away, they might as well speak English, because that's all they spoke in places like America and Canada and Australia and South Africa. It was English they spoke on ships and English they spoke in films. The Irish language was bad for business, they said, so why should anyone have to risk his life across a deadly gorge for being Irish? It was madness even to think of it. Everybody in Cork started speaking English and calling each other 'boy' at the end of every sentence whether you were young or old. You'd only kill yourself, boy, they said. They started saying they could make the leap across the gorge any time they liked, no problem at all, boy. They said everything twice to make sure you believed them. They claimed they were living beyond the law and there was no need to prove it, boy.

There was lots of killing and dying and big houses on fire in my father's song, too. He tells us bits of the song, like the time the fighting started around west Cork when they tried to take down the British flag. About children hiding sweets in bullet holes along the wall of the creamery, and about a man named Terence MacSwiney, the Cork lord mayor who died on hunger strike in a London jail. He puts on the record with the song about another man named Kevin Barry who was hanged one Monday morning in Dublin. He tells us about the time when the British soldiers came to their house in Leap, threatening to burn it down because they thought the rebels were shooting from the upstairs window. They had to run away in the middle of the night to Skibbereen and on the way down the hill the cart overturned with their belongings, so the donkey ended up on his back like a beetle with his legs in the air. And then the very same thing happened again after the British had gone and the Irish started fighting among themselves, because that's what they had learned from the British. Then one day they had to leave the house a second time when Irish Free State soldiers said they would burn it down, because they were sure they saw IRA snipers in the upstairs window.

'There will be no more fighting and dying,' my father says. He wants no more people put out of their houses, because it's time to live for Ireland and stop arguing among ourselves over stupid things. He says there are too many things to do and too many places to see in Ireland like the round tower in Glendalough and the new IMCO building that looks like a white ship when you pass it by on the bus. My father pays the fare in Irish and sometimes when the bus turns around the corner you think you're going straight into a shop window. We go to the zoo and have a picnic in the Phoenix Park with a big spire in the distance called the Wellington Monument. We run across the grass, but we're not allowed to play on the monument because it's something the British left behind and forgot to take with them. Wait till we get our own monuments, my father says.

There are parts of the song, too, that my father will not tell us anything about. Some of the verses are to do with the town of Leap and things he doesn't want to remember. Like the picture of the sailor over the mantelpiece. Or the people in the town who used to laugh at him for having a father who fell and lost his memory in the navy. It was a bad thing to have a mother who was still getting money from the King of England. So they called him names and said he would never be able to jump across the gorge.

'Every curse falls back on its author,' my father says.

He promises to bring us to see his own home town, but he never does. Instead, he would rather show us the future, so that's why there are verses of the song he leaves out altogether. He lost his memory when he was small and vowed instead that he would be the first person who really leaped over the gorge since O'Donovan did it. He said they were not beyond British law as long as they were still depending on Britain for their jobs and still speaking English. So when the time came, my father jumped. He didn't emigrate or drink whiskey or start making up stories either. Instead he changed his name and decided never to be homesick again. He put on a pioneer pin and changed his name from Jack to Seán and studied engineering and spoke Irish as if his home town didn't exist, as if his own father didn't exist, as if all those who emigrated didn't exist.

There are things you inherit from your father, too, not just a forehead or a smile or a limp, but other things like sadness and hunger and hurt. You can inherit memories you'd rather forget. Things can be passed on to you as a child, like helpless anger. It's all there in your voice, like it is in your father's voice, as if you were born with a stone in your hand. When I grow up I'll run away from my story, too. I have things I want to forget, so I'll change my name and never come back.

My father pretends that England doesn't exist. It's like a country he's never even heard of before and is not even on the map. Instead, he's more interested in other countries. Why shouldn't we dance with other partners as well, he says, like Germany? So while he was still at university he started learning German and listening to German music – Bach and Beethoven. Every week he went to classes in Dublin that were packed out because they were given by

Doctor Becker, a real German. He knew Germany was a place full of great music and great inventions, and one day, he said to himself, Ireland would be like that too, with its own language and its own inventions. Until then, he said, Ireland didn't really exist at all. It only existed in the minds of emigrants looking back, or in the minds of idealists looking forward. Far back in the past or far away in the future, Ireland only existed in songs.

Then he started making speeches. Not everybody had a radio and not everybody could read the newspapers at that time, so they went to hear people making speeches on O'Connell Street instead. The way you knew that people agreed with what you were saying is that they suddenly threw their hats and caps up in the air and cheered. The biggest crowd with the most amount of hats going up was always outside the GPO for de Valera. Some people had loudspeakers, but the good speakers needed nothing, only their own voices, and my uncle Ted says the best of them all was further up the street, a man named James Larkin who had a great way of stretching his arms out over the crowd.

My father wouldn't throw his hat up for anyone, so he started making his own speeches at the other end of the street with his friends. They had their own newspaper and their own leaflets and a party pin in the shape of a small 'e' for Éire: Ireland. He said it was time for Ireland to stand up on its own two feet and become a real country, not a place you dreamed about. The Irish people spent long enough building stone walls and saying the opposite. There were no rules about starting a new country and he wasn't interested in saying what everybody agreed with either. He had his own way of bringing his fist down at the end of a sentence, like he was banging the table. Hats went up for him all right. He had the crowd in his pocket when he put his hand on his heart, and he could have stolen all the flying hats from de Valera and Larkin and Cosgrave, but he started speaking in Irish and not everybody understood what he was saying.

One day he bought a motorbike, a BSA, so he could drive all around the country making speeches in small towns. Up and down the narrow roads he went, with his goggles on and his scarf flying in the wind behind him and the music of Schubert songs in his ear. He said Ireland would soon be like Germany with its own great culture and its own great inventions. He told them Ireland could never fight with the British in a war against Germany. Sometimes he stopped to say a prayer if there was a shrine by the roadside. Or to speak to somebody in Irish. And sometimes he had to stop because of cattle on the road, until the farmer cut a passage for him through the middle and the big cow faces got a fright and started jumping to escape in all directions from the noisy new sound of the motorbike driving through.

And then my father had the big idea of bringing people from other countries over to Ireland. After the war was over he met my mother in Dublin and decided to start a German-Irish family. He was still making speeches and writing articles for the newspaper and going around on his motorbike wearing goggles. But what better way to start a new country than marrying somebody and having children? Because that's what a new country is, he says, children. In the end of it all, we are the new country, the new Irish.

So that's how the film ends and the song goes on. My mother never imagined meeting someone, least of all an Irishman who could speak German and loved German music. She never imagined staying in Ireland for good, talking about Irish schools or making jam in Ireland and picking out children's shoes. My father asked her if she was willing to accompany him on a walk and correct his pronunciation. And because Germany had such great music, he wanted to tell her something great about Ireland, about St Patrick and about Irish history and Irish freedom. He told her he was not afraid to make sacrifices. He spoke quickly, as if he was still making a speech and people were throwing their hats up in the air by the thousands and didn't care if they ever came back down again.

My mother said she had to go home to Germany because that was a country that had just got its freedom, too, and had to be started from the beginning. He would not emigrate or leave his own native shores. He said he had bought a house that was not far away from the seafront. There were no pictures on the walls yet. There was no furniture, only a table and two chairs in the kitchen and a statue of the Virgin Mary. At night, you could be lonely and you'd miss your people because it was so quiet and so empty, just listening to the radio with a naked light bulb in the room and the wallpaper peeling on the walls. But in the end of it all, you would be starting a new republic with speckled Irish-German children.

They got married in Germany at Christmas. It all happened very quickly, because you had to do things immediately, without thinking too much. She didn't get a white dress but she got snow instead, thick silent snow. They went on the train together along the Rhine. They talked about the future and he said she would always be able to speak German in her own home. She said she would try and learn Irish, too. The children would be dressed for Ireland and for Germany. She said she was good at baking and telling stories. He said he was good with his hands. He said he would buy a camera so he could take lots of photographs, and she said she would keep them in a diary along with their first locks of hair. She said she would write everything down, all the first words and the first tears and everything that was happening in the news around the world.

There were things they didn't talk about. She kept her secret and he buried his past as well. He hid the picture of his own father in the wardrobe. He didn't want to offend her, having photographs of a British sailor hanging in the house. But she had nothing against England. It was not a marriage against anything, but for something new, she said. My mother even invented a new signal so that we would never get lost. A whistle made up of three notes, two short notes dropping down to one long note, like a secret code that no other family in the world would recognise.

They went to a mountain in each country. And no two mountains could be any more different. First they went to the famous Drachenfelz, right beside the River Rhine. They stayed in the hotel at the top and had breakfast looking out across the river below them, at the barges going up and down without a sound, like toy boats. She collected the train tickets and hotel receipts, even the thin decorated doilies under the coffee cups. Everything was important and would never be forgotten. She would not forget the smell of the sea either, or the smell of diesel fuel, or the faces of Irish people on the boat coming across to Ireland. They went up to a famous mountain in Ireland called Croagh Patrick to pray. It was a much harder mountain to climb and some people were even going up in their bare feet, with sharp rocks all along the path. At one point the wind came up so quickly they had to hold on to the rocks with their hands. There was no cable car. There was no hotel at the top either, where you could have coffee and cake. But when

41

they reached the small church at the top and heard the voices of people praying the rosary together, there was a great view. They looked back down at the land all around them, with tiny houses and tiny fields and islands going out into the Atlantic.

Six

Inside our house is a warm country with a cake in the oven.

My mother makes everything better with cakes and stories and hugs that crack your bones. When everybody is good, my father buys pencil cases with six coloured pencils inside, all sharpened to a point. I draw a picture of the fox with blood around his nose. And Franz draws a picture of the house, with everybody in separate rooms – Vati, Mutti, Franz, Hanni and Maria, all standing at different windows and waving. Áine is gone away to London. The O'Neills are gone away, too, so there's no chopping wood and no English and everybody in our house is in the same country, saying the same words again.

It's Sunday and there's a smell of polish on the floor. There is a smell of baking and ironing and polish all over the house, because Onkel Ted is coming for tea. Onkel Ted is my father's brother, a Jesuit priest, and he comes to visit us after his swim at the Forty Foot. His hair is still wet and combed in lines. He once saved my father's life, long before he was a priest, when they were still at school and used to go swimming down in Glandore, not far from where they lived. My father started drowning one day so his younger brother had to jump in in his shirt to rescue him. Afterwards my father couldn't speak because he

43

was shivering for a long time. But we don't talk about that now. Onkel Ted can speak German, too, but he doesn't say very much and my mother says he's not afraid of silence. So he listens instead and nods his head. I tell him that Franz has shadows around his eyes because he fell off the wall and broke his nose, but my mother says we won't talk about that now. My mother is trying to prove how decent and polite the Germans are and Onkel Ted is trying to prove how decent and polite the Irish are. And then it's time to reach into his jacket pocket for the bag of sweets and we can have two each and no more.

Outside our house is a different place.

One day my mother let us go down to the shop on our own, but she gave us a piece of rope and told us all to hold on to it so we would not get separated. An old woman stopped and said that was a great way of making sure we didn't get lost. My mother says we're surrounded by old women. Miss Tarleton, Miss Tomlinson, Miss Leonard, Miss Browne, Miss Russell, Miss Hosford, two Miss Ryans, two Miss Doyles, two Miss Lanes, Mrs Robinson, Mrs McSweeney and us in between them all. Some of them are friendly and others hate us. Some of them are Protestant and others are Catholic. The difference is that the Protestant bells make a song and the Catholic bells only make the same gong all the time.

You have to be careful where you kick the ball, because if it goes into Miss Tarleton's garden next door you'll never get it back. She told us not to dare put a foot inside her garden. Mrs McSweeney is nice and calls you in for a Yorkshire Toffee. The two Miss Lanes across the road have a gardener who wanted to give you back the ball one day but he couldn't. He came to the gate, ready to hand it back, but then one of the Miss Lanes appeared at the window and shook her head. The gardener stood there, not knowing what to do. We begged him please to give it back quickly before she came out, but he couldn't because he was working for Miss Lane, not for us, and she was already at the door saying, 'Give that ball here.' She said she was going to 'confiscate' it. We stood at the railings until Miss Lane said: 'Clear off. Away from the railings. Go on about your business, now.'

My mother laughs and says 'confiscate' doesn't mean kill or stab with a knife. It just means taking control of something that belongs to somebody else. One day I confiscated my brother's cars and threw them over the back wall into Miss Leonard's garden, but we got them back. One day Miss Tarleton declared a football amnesty and we got nine balls back, some of which never even belonged to us in the first place and most of which were confiscated all over again very shortly after that. Miss Tarleton might as well have handed them straight over to the Miss Lanes. My mother wants to know if the Miss Lanes play football in the kitchen at night. And she wants to know what the Miss Lanes have against her, because they just slammed the door in her face.

My mother says maybe they still hate Germany, but my father says they hate their own country even more. He says they still think they're living in Britain and they can't bear the sound of children speaking German on the street and, even worse, Irish. My mother says that means we have to be extra-nice to them, so they don't feel left out. You have to try not to throw the rockets up so high because the bang frightens old women and makes them think the Easter Rising is coming back again. You have to make sure the ball doesn't go into their garden. My father says it's your own fault if you lose the ball, because their garden is their country and you can't go in there. He says our country is divided into two parts, north and south, like two gardens. He says six counties in the north have been confiscated and are still controlled by Britain. The difference between one country and another is the song they sing at the end of the night in the cinema and the flag they have on the post office and the stamps you lick. When my father was working in the north of Ireland once, in a town called Coleraine, he refused to stand up in the cinema because they were playing the wrong song. Some people wanted to put him against the wall and shoot him. And then he left his job and came back to his own country where he could speak Irish any time he liked.

So, you have to be careful what country you kick your ball into and what song you stand up for in the cinema. You can't wave the wrong flag or wear the wrong badges, like the red poppies with the black dot in the middle. You have to be careful who to be sad for and not commemorate people who died on the wrong side.

My father also likes to slam the front door from time to time. And he's the best at slamming doors because he makes the whole house shake. Lots of things rattle. Clocks and glasses and cups shiver all the way down to the end of the street when my father answers the door. He sends a message out all over the world, depending on who knocked. If it's the old woman with the blanket who says 'God bless you, Mister', and promises to pray for him and all his family, if it's the man who sharpens the garden shears on the big wheel or if it's somebody collecting for the missions, then he gives them money and closes the door gently. If it's people selling carpets he shakes his head and closes the door firmly. If it's the two men in suits with Bibles then he slams it shut to make sure not even one of their words enters into the hall. And if it's one of the people selling poppies, then he slams it shut so fast that the whole street shakes. Sometimes the door slams shut in great anger of its own accord, but that's only because the back door has been left open and there's a draught going through the house.

One day Mr Cullen across the street asked us to help him wash his car. Afterwards he gave us a whole chocolate bar each, because he works for Cadbury's and has boxes and boxes of chocolate bars and Trigger bars in the boot of his car all the time. A woman came along the street selling the red badges with the black dot in the middle, so, as well as the chocolate, he bought us each a badge and pinned them to our jumpers. Lots of people on the street were wearing them – Miss Tarleton, Mrs Robinson, Miss Hosford, and the two Miss Lanes.

We didn't know they were wrong. We didn't know that wearing the wrong badge was like singing the wrong song in the cinema. So when my father saw us coming into the house wearing poppies, he slammed the door and all the clocks and cups and saucers shivered. Franz shivered too. My father ripped the poppies off so fast that he stabbed his own finger with the pin and I thought the badge was bleeding. He ran into the kitchen and opened the door of the boiler and threw the badges into the fire. Then he ran his finger under the tap and looked for a plaster while the badges burned to nothing and I thought it was a big waste because Mr Cullen had paid money for them.

'Who gave you those damn things?' my father wanted to know.

'Not like that,' my mother said. 'They don't understand.'

'Who gave you those poppies?' I could see that my father

hated even saying the word. 'They're British army poppies. Who gave them to you?'

'Mr Cullen.'

'Mr Cullen has no right. I'm going over to have a word with him.'

But my mother pulled on his elbow again. She told him that Mr Cullen's father died in the First World War and we didn't want to offend him. My father said Mr Cullen was trying hard to offend us. Lots of good people died on the German side, too, as well as all the Irish people who died fighting against the British army instead of joining in with them. And what about all the people who died in the famine and there are no badges you can get for them. Mr Cullen was mocking us, he said, giving us the poppies on purpose because the Germans lost the war and the Irish lost the six counties. My mother says she's not offended and Mr Cullen is too nice a man to even think of something like that. Its time to be big-hearted, she says. It's not important to win. And one day they'll commemorate all the people who died in those wars, not just their own.

'They have no children,' she said.

I was afraid that my father would find out we got chocolate and that would go in the fire, too. One day when we were coming home from the shop with Smarties, Franz dropped one of them on the street and my mother told him to leave it there because it was dirty. Then he threw the rest of the Smarties on the ground as well. If one was dirty then they must all be dirty. So I thought this was the same, that we had brought home something from outside on the street that was dirty.

'Never let me see those things again,' my father warned.

'Explain it to them, for God's sake,' my mother said. She doesn't like things being taken away from us without

48

something else put in its place. She wants everything to be explained in a calm way, sitting down.

So my father sits at the table and we sit opposite him and he tells us why we can't accept poppies from anyone. First of all, he says, there was the British empire. He takes out a map of the world and points to all the pink bits that were owned by the British. Then he says the Germans wanted to have an empire, too, but the British didn't like the idea, so that was the First World War. He says millions of men died when two empires fought against each other and not even one person was killed on their own soil. It was big countries squabbling over little countries. Then right in the middle of it all the Irish decided to declare their own free state. We serve neither king nor kaiser, is what the Irish were saying to themselves and to all the other small countries around the world. But after that it's hard to understand what my father is saying any more because my mother's name was Kaiser and I don't know what the difference is between the First World War and the Second World War, and who the Nazis are and what they have to do with us. My mother says the Germans hardly behaved any better than the British, that instead of just having an empire and keeping slaves, the Nazis made slaves of their own people. The Germans turned themselves into slaves and started killing all the other people who were not German enough and my father says it's all the same thing.

'That's the end of the road,' he says, and I think there are people being killed at the end of the road and I don't want to go down there any more. My father says all we need to know is that poppies are not allowed in the house and that's the end of the story. We'll get our own badges and flags and songs. On St Patrick's day, we get shamrock and green badges and tricoloured jelly and ice cream.

At night in bed I'm afraid of silence. I can see the light coming under the door and I think my father still wants to go over to Mr Cullen, only that my mother is holding him back telling him to leave it. It's all in the past. We're in the future and we have to behave like the future. Then I hear the music coming up from the front room. Big German music spreading all over the house again, all the way up the stairs and in under the door with the light.

On Sunday, Onkel Ted comes to tea again with his wet hair combed in lines. I tell him about all the balls that Miss Tarleton gave back but the Miss Lanes took away again. I tell him that we were allowed to wash Mr Cullen's car and that we got chocolate. I tell him about the poppies and all the people being killed at the end of the road, but my mother says we won't talk about that now. I tell him that a man on the bus said Nazi to my mother under his breath, but we won't talk about that either. Then it's time to reach into Onkel Ted's pocket for the sweets and I don't know what to tell or not to talk about any more.

After that it's hard to know what's right and wrong. My mother says we've started doing a lot of things that make no sense. One day Franz put stones in his ears and he couldn't hear anything any more. Maria put a marrow-fat pea in her nose and it swelled up so much that the doctor had to come and take it out. Franz hit his thumb with a hammer and his finger went blue. Then I started burying all the silver spoons in the garden with my grandfather's initials FK written on them and my mother had to find the treasure. She laughs and says she hopes we won't do any more stupid things for a while. But then one day I started throwing the toy cars in the fire. I carried the box with all my cars into the kitchen and opened the door of the boiler by myself. I could see them lying on top of the orange coals. I watched them lighting up blue and green for a moment, until the flames disappeared and they went black and silver. One by one, I threw my cars on top of the coals until my mother came and asked me if I was out of my mind. She pulled me away and slammed the door of the boiler shut. She kneeled down and looked straight into my eyes. She makes everything better with hugs that break your bones. She tells me a story and says it's all forgotten now and we won't talk about it any more.

Seven

One day the boiler burst. It started hissing and clicking because of all the bad things that had been thrown into it. It got so hot that you could hear it cracking inside. Then there was a bang and it burst open with hot brown water gushing out all over the kitchen floor like tea with milk. My mother told my father to call the fire brigade. He frowned and sucked in air through his teeth. But then he put out the fire by himself. He carried the red coal out on a shovel and rolled up his sleeves to sweep the tea out the back door.

Then it's winter and our house starts filling up with mice. The pipes are cold and there are mice in every room because they get in under the back door. More and more of them are coming in every day until all the mice from the whole city are living in our house, my mother says. They're in the hall and on the stairs, everywhere you go. Any time you open the door and go into a room you see them running away. But mostly they're under the stairs where things are kept, like jam jars and pots and old shoes. There are so many of them that you have to watch where you walk, because one day when Franz was running down the three steps from the hallway into the kitchen, a baby mouse ran out from under the stairs and got squashed. We all crouched down to examine the flattened corpse until my mother told us not to be so interested in blood and took it away on the shovel.

It's so cold, we stay in one room by the fire where it's nice and warm, but if you go from that room up to the bedroom, it's like going out on the street and you need your coat on. My mother shows me her hands and says they will never get warm again. They've gone blue and green with the cold, like mackerel. She wants me to take pity on her hands and please let them in under my jumper to get warm. Be a good boy and give shelter to my poor fish-blue hands, she says. Just let them in for a little second or two to get warm. Then I scream and laugh and my mother screams and laughs, because the mackerel are fast swimmers and they go up under my jumper and down around my neck into my shirt and my mother says: *'Wie schön, wie schön warm'*, oh lovely and cosy and warm.

Áine came back from London, but she's so sad that she only talks to herself in the mirror now. She can't even say 'walk on the wall' in Irish or English or go down to the seafront because her legs won't carry her. She's never going back to London, but she doesn't want to go back to Connemara either, so she lives with us. Sometimes you hear her upstairs crying and my mother says something happened to her, something that can't be explained or forgotten about either, so we just had to wait for her to get her words back. Onkel Ted has to come and make the sign of the cross over her, but still she won't come out and nobody knows what to do. My mother says it's the worst thing of all to be sad for yourself. You can help other people but often you can't help yourself.

At night you can hear the mice scratching and chasing each other around. For a while we counted the number of mice we saw every day, but then we didn't know if we were counting the same mouse twice in different rooms. My father bought two traps to catch them but that wasn't enough, so he bought another one that would catch three of them at the same time. It made no difference. Even if you caught three mice each day, my mother said it would still take a hundred years to catch them all because they could have families faster than we could kill them. The only thing was to stop talking about them and then they would go away. One day, there was a dead mouse in the trap that was half eaten by his own friends, and my mother said it was time to stop talking about it. Mice have no feelings, she said, and some people have no feelings either.

Áine spent all her day sitting up in bed smoking cigarettes. My mother said the best thing was for her to find a new job, then she could buy new clothes and go out and meet new people. Áine's legs wouldn't even carry her to the front door, so my mother went around to all the neighbours to ask if anyone knew of any jobs. She spoke to people who owned a man's shop and people in two grocery shops. After a long time she found a job in a gift shop, but Áine burst into tears on the first day and the owner told my mother that a gift shop is meant to be a happy place and nobody was going to buy anything from a person with tears in their eyes. He said he would prefer it if my mother came to work for him instead. My mother said she would love to work in the gift shop, but her hands were like mackerel and nobody was going to buy anything from fish-cold hands.

My mother said she knew what the problem was. If Áine had nice shoes then she would feel better and her legs would carry her down the street with no shame. My father said it was a waste and that everyone else in our house needed shoes, too, but my mother said it would all be paid back in other ways. So Áine got new shoes, but it made no difference. At night she left the light on in her room and my father said that was a waste, too, because she was not even reading a book, only sitting there smoking cigarettes. He said he gave up smoking when he wanted to buy German records and the only way of paying for them was to take the money from the cigarettes instead. If he had a mouse for every cigarette that Áine smoked and a penny for every mouse that he caught, he would be able to buy every opera and every symphony that ever existed on Deutsche Grammophon. He said it was the cigarettes that were making Áine sad. And one morning, my mother found a black hole in one of the pillow cases and she was afraid the house would burn down.

Every day my mother sits down with Áine and tries to make her smile. She says nobody can make you smile if you don't want to. Every day my father goes to work on the train. Every day we catch three mice and every day new ones come. Every day I scream and laugh when my mother's mackerel hands go under my jumper. Every Sunday Onkel Ted comes to tea after his swim at the Forty Foot because he doesn't feel the cold. We tell him things that happened, but not about mice and not about Áine or the black holes burned in her dresses. My sister Maria pulls up her dress to show Onkel Ted her tummy and then we reach into the pocket of his jacket for the sweets. He goes upstairs to make the sign of the cross over Áine and when he comes down again, he says my mother should take her out dancing.

'Irish dancing,' my father said. 'It would have to be Irish dancing.'

Then everybody is silent for a while looking at each other. Until my mother suddenly bursts out laughing and says she's forgotten how to dance. Two silent brothers looking at my mother laughing and laughing at the idea of coming all the way over from Germany to bring an Irish woman out to Irish dancing. Onkel Ted smiles and waits for my mother to finish. He's very serious and says there are things you never forget like cycling and swimming and helping other people. So one evening, my mother and Áine got dressed up and went dancing in the city. She put on her blue dress with the white spots and Áine put on her new shoes and a dress without holes in it. My father stayed at home reading his book and we sat on the carpet playing cars and listening to mice.

My mother said Irish dancing was not like waltzing or any kind of dancing that she had ever seen before. She said in Ireland your feet never even touch the ground. Everyone was floating, except for a man who sometimes slapped his heel down with a bang to the music as if he were trying to make holes in the floor. The dance hall smelled of smoke and perfume and sweat and it was filled with people of all ages. There was a priest and some nuns as well, sitting down in the seats. An old woman with long hair was dancing as if she were only sixteen. All the men were on one side of the hall and all the women on the other. The women danced as if the men didn't exist, and at the refreshments counter there were people talking over tea and sandwiches as if the dancing didn't exist. My mother watched three boys sharing a bottle of fizzy lemonade. Each time one of them drank through the straw, the other two kept watch to make sure he didn't go past a certain mark before he passed it on to the next boy. They had tears in their eyes from drinking so fast.

All the time, men came walking across from the other side of the hall to ask my mother to dance, but she smiled and shook her head. She thanked them and asked them to dance with Áine instead. My mother says you can see a man's face drop. But once they had come all the way over, they could not just turn around and go away again empty-handed. Áine didn't want to dance either. She said her legs were gone soft. So the man had to pull her out by the hand, with my mother pushing her from behind. Then Áine tried to hold on to her seat with her foot and the chair went scraping out on the dance floor behind her, until my mother finally got it off. Even then the man had a hard job trying to make Áine dance, because her feet stayed on the floor and would not move. My mother said Áine had cement in her shoes and all the men soon stopped coming over.

She says it was funny, a German woman pushing an Irish woman out to dance against her will. She says it's hard to understand what's going on in people's heads in Ireland. She says Irish people dance with their heads and speak with their feet. Everybody knows what's inside everybody else's head, but nobody ever says it out loud. They like to keep everything inside. She says German people say what they think and Irish people keep it to themselves and maybe the Irish way is sometimes better. In Germany, she says, people think before they speak so that they mean what they say, while in Ireland, people think after they speak so as to find out what they mean. In Ireland the words never touch the ground.

After the dancing, Áine lost her words altogether. There was something inside her head that was making her sick and my mother said if she didn't speak about it, she would die. She was not eating any more either, only smoking cigarettes. Dr Sheehan had to come one day, because Áine started burning holes in her legs and arms. He said she would have to go to hospital, but then Onkel Ted came to make the sign of the cross over her once more. He spent a long time in her room talking to her very quietly and nodding his head. He gave her lots of time to remember everything that happened, until she finally spoke in her own language. She told Onkel Ted something in Irish and he came downstairs with the answer. He said if Áine was to stop burning holes in her arms and legs, if she was ever to smile again and stop being sad, then she would have to get her baby back. So one day my mother and Áine went out and they came back with a new baby. She was going back home again because she was happy now. She didn't need to smoke cigarettes and talk to herself any more because she had the baby to talk to. My mother helped her to pack her suitcase with lots of German baby clothes and they laughed because Áine said it was nearly like a German baby going home to Connemara. And the day she was leaving, it was my mother who was crying because Áine was smiling.

Men came to fix the boiler. There was some more brown tea with milk on the floor of the kitchen, but then it was all over and the pipes started heating up again. My father put lots of coal into the boiler so the house got warm. Then there was a delivery of coal. A truck stopped on the street outside and because they couldn't go around the back, the men with black faces and black hands had to come through the house. My mother was afraid the wind would slam the doors shut in anger, so we had to hold them open, Franz at the front door, me at the in-between door, and Maria at the back door. She told us to count the bags as they came in. In Ireland people count in their heads, she said, but in Germany people count out loud. Out loud we counted — *Eins, Zwei, Drei, Vier, Fünf* . . . all the way up to fifteen. The men walked in stooped over with the heavy sacks, leaving long black marks where the sacks scraped against the wall on their way through. And where they went down the three steps towards the kitchen and out the back door, they put a black hand up every time to hold on to the door frame. One of the men winked and made me forget what number I was on. I didn't know if I should be counting the sack that was coming or the sack gone by. But then I heard Franz counting the next number at the front door and I was able to catch up.

When the shed outside was full and the coal was spilling out across the path, the men got back into the truck. One of them counted the empty sacks as if he could not trust us to count right. He came back inside with a pink piece of paper covered with black fingerprints and asked my mother to sign her name. That was to make sure she agreed that there was no mistake in the counting and that nobody ran away with one of the empty sacks. But there could be no mistake because we counted out loud in German and the man counted the empty sacks in English, and it was the same number no matter what language.

Eight

My mother has to go home to Kempen and we can't go with her. She's on the phone in the front room crying and speaking in a loud voice to Germany and we're outside the door listening until she comes out with shadows around her eyes. She says she has to go away for a while. So then we have to stay in the house with the yellow door where they speak no Irish and no German, only English. My mother lays everything out on the bed for us and packs it into a bag. We get up very early in the morning when it's still dark outside and the light in the bedroom is so bright that you can't look at it. It's cold, too, and Franz is standing on the bed in his underpants, shivering and singing a long note with his teeth clacking. I'm able to put my shirt on by myself but I can't do the buttons because my fingers are soft. My mother is in a hurry and she pinched my neck when she was doing up the top button, but she said sorry and then it's time to go. It's still dark outside on the street and you can blow your breath out like smoke. It's still dark when we get on the bus and still dark when we come up to the yellow door and then I can't walk because my legs are soft. I have a limp in both legs and I hold on to my mother's coat because I don't want to emigrate and live in a different country from her.

I don't know where Germany is. I know it's far away

from Ireland because you can't go there on the bus, you can only look at it on the map. I know there was the First World War and the Second World War and the second would not have happened without the first. I know the Germans wanted to have an empire and that wasn't allowed. The goat wanted to have a long tail but only got a short one, my mother says, whenever we want something that we can't have.

I don't like the house with the yellow door. I don't like the room with the toilet and ten potties hanging on the wall. I don't like the smell of the brown rubber sheet on the bed and I don't like the smell of custard. The house with the yellow door and the yellow custard is a place where you wait for your mother to come back and sometimes you hear other children crying on the stairs because they're waiting too. Franz would not eat the custard or go to the toilet. He closed his mouth and said he would never open it again for the rest of his life. The nurse tried to pretend that the spoon was a train going into his mouth, but he shook his head and turned away. He could only eat and go to the toilet in German. So my father had to come and bring him to the toilet. I closed my mouth and refused to speak because the nurse would not say goodbye to the moon. I said she was from a different country and then my father had to come another time and give the nurse the word for moon in Irish.

I know that my mother's father, Franz Kaiser, owned a stationery shop in the town of Kempen and nobody had any money to buy anything, so he had to close it down. But that didn't stop him making jokes and playing tricks on people just to see the look on their faces. My mother says he was famous for all the funny things he did because he always made up for it afterwards. One day in the Kranz

Café he stuck his finger into a doughnut and held it up in the air to ask how much it cost, just to see the look on their faces when he said it was too expensive. But then he bought all of them, one each for my mother and her four sisters and one each for all the other children he could find on the market square.

One day he played a trick on the commanding officer of the Belgian army. I know that my mother's town was in the Rhineland but that was occupied by the Belgians and the French as punishment for the First World War. It was confiscated from the Germans by the Treaty of Versailles. So one night Franz Kaiser and his cousin Fritz planned a new trick. They filled a porcelain potty full of ink from the shop. They spread out a sheet of paper on the table and took down the big quill from over the door outside the shop. Then they invited the commanding officer of the Belgian army to come to the house for a drink, just to see the look on his face when they brought him over to the table and asked him to sign a new treaty. The officer was very angry, but then they gave him a cigar and the best wine in the house. My mother says everybody liked Franz Kaiser's jokes, even the people who were joked about, and maybe the Second World War would not have happened if there were more people like him. Then the Nazis took over and there was no more time for joking in Germany.

Then he was ill and my mother had to tell him what was happening outside on the square. He sat up in a bed in the living room upstairs over the shop, with the big alcove and the piano at the window. She had to look out and tell him who was going by. And every day, her mother played for him to make him better. She sang the *Freischutz* and all the Schubert songs she had performed at the opera house in Krefeld, when he sent her a bouquet of bananas instead of flowers. Every day, she shaved his face and played the piano, but he didn't get better. My mother was nine years old and one day he asked her to bring him a mirror so he could say goodbye to himself. He didn't want to know who was passing by the house any more. All he did was look into the mirror for a long time in silence. Then he smiled at himself and said: '*Tschüss, Franz . . .*'

My mother says she will never forget the smell of flowers all around his bed and she will never forget the people of the town all standing outside on the market square. She remembers the shadows around her mother's eyes when the coffin came out of the house. She says that maybe it's not such a good thing to be the child of two people who loved each other so much, because it's like being in a novel or a song or a big film that you might never get out of.

After that her mother was always dressed in black. Every evening she gathered all the five girls together in the living room over the shop. Marianne, Elfriede, Irmgard, Lisalotte and Minne all listening to Schubert songs and looking out at the people crossing the Buttermarkt square to go to the cinema. My mother says she can remember the soft, sad rain that blurred the sign above the cinema saying 'Kempener Lichtspiele' and made the tree trunks black. There was no money left in Germany, so her mother then had to teach the piano and put a candle in the fire to make the house look warm. They had to sell things like candlesticks and vases. The furniture began to disappear and the rooms began to look empty. Then Germany was so poor that they decided to emigrate to Brazil.

Things were happening in the town of Kempen that made people afraid. Everyone was afraid of the Communists and one night two men in brown shirts were beaten up with sticks in the street near the old school. Then it was all turned around and the Communist men were beaten up with sticks and fists by the men in brown shirts. People stayed inside their houses because of things like that. They didn't want to go outside and my mother says Germany belonged to the fist people and it was better to start again somewhere else like Brazil.

First of all it was the oldest sisters Marianne and Elfriede who were to go and marry two German boys already out there. There was a Catholic organisation in the Rhineland which matched up German girls with German boys to go and start a new life planting coffee and tobacco and looking for rubber trees. They would arrange the passage first to San Francisco and on to Brazil through missionary routes. Marianne and Elfriede went to special courses at the weekend to learn about agriculture. My mother and her sisters started laying out their things on the bed, getting ready to pack their bags, and reading books about the rainforest. They knew it would be very hot, so they bought straw hats and fans. There would be lots of insects, too, so they had to learn how to smoke to keep them away.

'Can we do the pipes now,' Lisalotte kept asking.

But first of all they had to sit by the piano and learn all the Schubert songs. In Brazil, it would be just as important to keep singing the German songs and telling German stories as it was to smoke and keep the insects away. And maybe the music would even help to bring back the good times. Maybe it was not too late and the music would help the word people to take over again from the fist people in Germany. They even sang one or two pop songs as well, swing songs that everybody whistled and sang on the Buttermarkt square.

They sang and laughed until the tears came into her

mother's eyes and nobody knew if she was crying or laughing any more. And then, at last, they took out the pipes and filled them up with tobacco from a tweed pouch. They got out the flint lighter with the initials FK that Franz Kaiser used for cigars. All the things still there from the time he invited men from the town to come over to the house and smoke until you couldn't even see the wallpaper. Now it was time for the girls to do the same. They lit up the pipes and passed them around. Each one of them had to practise puffing and coughing and spitting and holding the pipe in the side of her mouth. The smell of tobacco filled the room and it was like her father was back again.

'At last the room smells like men again,' my mother said, and they had to laugh and cough so much that they couldn't speak. They practised singing and smoking every night until they were ready to go away. But then my mother's mother Berta got ill. She was not able to live without Franz Kaiser, either in Germany or in Brazil. She died and there was another big funeral with lots of people standing outside on the Buttermarkt square waiting for the coffin to come out of the house. Then my mother and her sisters had to go to live with their Onkel Gerd and aunt Ta Maria. Then it was the end of smoking pipes and talking about Brazil, because Onkel Gerd was the lord mayor and he said he couldn't let them emigrate until they were eighteen. He said they would be homesick. They would be able to make German cakes and sing German songs but they would miss their own country. He didn't say they were not allowed to go. Instead, he gathered them all in the living room and turned the question over to them.

'What would you do if you were in my shoes?' he asked them. 'What if you suddenly had five lovely daughters, would you send them away to Brazil to be eaten by insects?'

After that there was lots of trouble for Onkel Gerd because he would not join the Nazi party. He said there was no place left in Germany for the word people to go. He said the fist people had robbed all the words, from the church, from all the old songs, from books and films. They had broken into the theatre and taken the drama out on to the streets. Everybody was excited by the new colours and the new words. But if you were not one of the fist people, you had to learn silence. You could only speak in the privacy of your own house, Onkel Gerd said. You could make jokes inside, but that's where they had to stay because it was not safe to speak outside any more. There were jokes you could not make on the Buttermarkt square any more because the fist people had taken over Germany. My mother says that if there were more people like Onkel Gerd then lots of things would not have happened.

One day my father came to the house with the yellow door and took us home on the bus. He was smiling and said we would never have to eat custard again. I know that Germany is a place full of cakes and nice things that you can't get in Ireland, because my mother came back with four large suitcases, full of chocolate and toys and clothes. There were new games, too, like the game where you throw all the coloured sticks on the floor in a big mess and then you have to pick them out one by one. My mother looked new because she had new clothes. She was smiling all the time and had new perfume on. She brought home a pewter plate and candlestick that was left over from her father and mother's house. She had pictures of the house and said we would all go there one day. My father and mother drank wine and there was big German music all around the house, maybe outside the house, too, and all the way down to the end of the street.

Sometimes my mother turns around suddenly to take us all into her arms so that my face is squashed up against Franz and Maria. Sometimes she wants to take a bite out of Maria's arm, just a little bite. Sometimes she still has tears in her eyes, either because she's so happy or because she is still sad for Onkel Gerd. He was a good man who spoke very little, only when he had something to say. It was the biggest funeral she had ever seen in Kempen, because he was a lord mayor once and he would not join the fist people. He was not afraid to resist. She hung a photograph of him in the living room so that we could see him and be like him.

My mother also brought back a typewriter and some days later she opened it up and allowed me to type my name. Johannes. The letters fly out and hit the page. *Lettetet. Lettetet.* Sometimes two letters get stuck in mid-air and my mother says we have to be more gentle, only one at a time. She holds my finger and helps me to pick out the letter. I press down on the key and the letter shoots out so fast that you can hardly see it. It slaps against the paper like magic. I want to write 'Johannes is the best boy in the world', but it would take too long. Then I ask her if I can write 'Johannes is the boldest boy in the world' instead and my mother laughs out loud. She says I'm the best boy and the boldest boy at the same time, because I get the most amount of slaps from my father and the most amount of hugs from her to make up for it. Then Franz wants to write down that he will never have to emigrate and go to the yellow house again but it's too late and we have to go to bed now.

At night, I can hear my mother downstairs in the kitchen

with the typewriter. She's *lettetetting* on her own, while my father is in the front room reading. The letters fly out and hit the page faster than you can speak. She's *lettetetting* and *lettetetting* because there's a story that she can't tell anyone, not even my father. You can't be afraid of silence, she says. And stories that you have to write down are different to stories that you tell people out loud, because they're harder to explain and you have to wait for the right moment. The only thing she can do is to write them down on paper for us to read later on.

'To my children,' she writes. 'One day, when you're old enough, you will understand what happened to me, how I got trapped in Germany and couldn't help myself. I want to tell you about the time when I was afraid, when I stood in my room and couldn't shout for help and heard the footsteps of a man named Stiegler coming up the stairs.'

Nine

On the first day of school I slapped the teacher in the face.
I knew there would be lots of trouble. I thought Onkel Ted
would have to come and make the sign of the cross over me,
but when my mother came to collect me she said nothing,
just smiled. The teacher said she had never been hit by a
child before and that I was the boldest boy she had ever
met in her entire life. My mother was so proud of me that
she smiled and kneeled down to look into my eyes for a
long time. Outside she told all the other mothers that I
slapped the teacher in the face and they shook their heads.
On the way home the bus conductor threw his eyes up and
said I would go far. She even told the man with one arm
in the vegetable shop.

'You'll have trouble with him,' they all said, but my
mother shook her head.

'Oh no,' she said. 'He's going to be like his uncle,
Onkel Gerd.'

The teacher's name is Bean Uí Chadhain and the school
is called Scoil Lorcáin. You go down the steps into the
classroom at the bottom and there is lots of noise from
all the other children and a sweet smell, like a school bag
with a banana sandwich left inside. There are toys in boxes
to play with, but some of them are broken and the cars
have bits of plasticine stuck to the wheels. There's a map

of the world on the wall and you learn to sing and go to the toilet in Irish, to the *leithreas*. And after that you get into another line to go to the yard, where the older girls are chasing and screaming, and across the wall the older boys are chasing and fighting. Then it's time to sing the song about the little red fox. Everybody who is good gets a *milseán*, a sweet, and anyone who is bold has to stand on the table to show how bold you are.

'*Maidirín a rua, 'tá dána,*' we all sing together. The little red fox is bold. Except that bold doesn't just mean bold, it also means cute and cheeky and brave and not afraid of people. The little red fox who is not afraid of anyone at all, we sing. But then Bean Uí Chadhain lifted me up on the table and said I was not going to get a sweet.

'Bold, bold, bold,' she said. '*Dána, dána, dána.*'

So then I slapped her in the face and my mother was proud of me. She's so happy that she puts her hand on my shoulder and tells everybody in Ireland what I did. They shake their heads but they should be nodding. Only Onkel Ted nods his head slowly on Sunday when he comes, but then you don't know sometimes what's right and wrong because he nods slowly even when you tell him bad things that happened. He says there are some things you can only do once in your life and most people never do at all. My father says Bean Uí Chadhain is the wife of a famous Irish writer called Máirtín Ó Cadhain who wrote a book about dead people talking. It's about a graveyard in Connemara where all the dead people talk to each other and anyone who dies brings new stories from the living world over the ground. I slapped the writer's wife, my father says, and he's proud, too, because the book was written in Irish. And dead people have the best conversations of all. Lots of people don't really speak until they're dead, because only then can they say all of the things to each other in the graveyard that they have been keeping secret all their lives.

My mother says you can't be afraid of anyone. You can't let anyone make you small, because that's what they tried to do with Onkel Gerd. He had to keep quiet and say nothing while he was alive, but now he's talking in the grave. He's talking to my mother's father and mother in Kempen, telling them that my mother didn't go to Brazil after all, but went to live in Ireland instead. Now they're having a great talk about how things were in the old days, all the jokes that Franz Kaiser made and why nobody had a sense of humour any more except for the people who were already in the grave and had nothing to lose. Now Franz Kaiser is playing all the tricks he didn't get to finish before he died. And now Onkel Gerd is telling everybody down there that Hitler is dead. There were stories brought down with the war, when the planes were all going back home to England and they dropped the bombs on the bakery in Kempen very early one morning when everybody was queuing up for bread. There were stories going down of people killed all over Europe when nobody was able to stop the fist people from taking over.

My mother says you can't keep people from talking in the grave. And you can't keep them quiet by making them stay at home or locking them up or stopping them from writing in newspapers. That's why you should never be afraid to speak. My father says that all the people who died in the Irish famine are still talking. They're whispering with dry lips and staring out with empty eyes. He says you can't go anywhere in Ireland without hearing them. You go out into the fields around west Cork, he says, and it's never silent, not even for a moment. He says a lot of the people born after the famine could not talk because they had lost their language and that's why they speak English and have to listen to the words first before they can be sure of what they're saying. But all that will be put right now that we're speaking Irish again.

You're better off dead than not being able to speak, my mother says. That's what they tried to do to Onkel Gerd. He was the Bürgermeister, the lord mayor, and they came to him every day and asked him to do things he didn't want. Ta Maria was the sister of my mother's mother Berta and she was called Frau Bürgermeister, Mrs Lord Mayor. Then they suddenly had five daughters to look after and send to school every day on the train to the convent in Mühlhausen. So when people came to the house and said the lord mayor should belong to the Nazi party, he said he was the father of five girls and shook his head every time. They were friendly and polite and spoke to Ta Maria, too, on the way across the Buttermarkt square, hoping that she would change his mind. They liked Onkel Gerd and said he was a good lord mayor, so they didn't want him to be made small like the other man Lamprecht who had to be taken away to a camp in Dachau because he kept on writing in the newspaper. They said they were hoping that would not happen to a man with five lovely new daughters.

Onkel Gerd sat in silence for a long time every evening, my mother says, because it was not easy to know what was right and wrong sometimes. My mother and her sisters kept on going to school and every Sunday they went to the graveyard to visit their father and mother. They passed by the old house on the Buttermarkt square but never went inside again because there were other people living there now. The town had changed. Everyone was poor and it was all right to beg and have a leg missing. People who had never dreamed of asking for things before were coming up to the house looking for help. So then there was an election and the Nazi party promised there would be no beggars in Germany ever again. At night, people said there were groups of men gathering around fires outside the town. People didn't know whether it was exciting or frightening or both, because on the day of the election the town was full of cars and people drinking beer in their best clothes, and when Onkel Gerd went up to vote, there was trouble.

My mother says they were very sly. They wanted to see what side Onkel Gerd was on, so they gave him a ballot paper with a special mark on it. He looked at the names of the parties and the boxes beside them to make an X in, with the Nazi party at the top and all the other parties like the SPD and the Central party below. When he held the ballot paper up to the light he found a small watermark in the corner that should not have been there. He knew they could check afterwards to see where he put the X.

'This is still a secret vote,' Onkel Gerd said and handed back the paper.

Everybody had their eyes on him and the hall was silent. He knew there would be trouble because he asked what the watermark was doing on his ballot paper, but the official just smiled and said he was making too much of it. In any case, they said, if he had a clear conscience and had nothing to hide, then the watermark wouldn't bother him because everyone else was voting for the Nazi party, too.

'What about the secret ballot?' Onkel Gerd demanded. If everyone was going to vote for the Nazi party, then wasn't it better if they did so by choice? He refused to leave. He knew it was the only way that he could be honest and not take the easy way out like everyone else. He didn't say he was against anyone or for anyone else.

He just stood and waited while the officials all whispered among themselves and wondered what to do. Until they gave him a clean ballot paper at last, because they couldn't bear to look at his face any more and they didn't want the lord mayor standing around in the polling station all day with his arms folded for everyone to see.

My mother says it's important to make a stand. Onkel Gerd won his fight in the polling station, but he went home and knew that everything was lost. Within days they heard from the other towns in the Rhineland that the lord mayors who had not spotted the watermark on the ballot paper were not so lucky. They were put out of office immediately the following day and replaced by people on the side of the Nazi party. Many of them were beaten up, my mother says. The fist people came to their houses and some of them were sick for a long time and couldn't hear properly afterwards or had trouble with their kidneys and never went to work again.

Onkel Gerd stayed on as lord mayor because nobody knew where he put his X. But that didn't last long either because they came to his office every day and asked him to do things he didn't want. And one day, when it was suddenly against the law to be a lord mayor without belonging to the Nazi party, he had to go. They gave him a last chance, but he still shook his head. Another man was waiting to take over and sit down as soon as Onkel Gerd cleared his desk. There was some handshaking and polite conversation, but then it was over quite suddenly and it was hard to walk home that day. It was hard to walk past people on the street because everybody knew he was nothing any more. And it was even harder to explain to Ta Maria and their five new daughters. She had her apron up to her eyes as they gathered together in the living room.

He stood there to tell them that even though he was not the lord mayor any more and nobody knew where the money was going to come from, he would still do everything he could to look after them. He had been made small, but he would not let them down. Some of the women still called Ta Maria Frau Bürgermeister on the street, but that was just a habit and it didn't really matter. Anyone who was not with the Nazis had nothing more to say.

After that, Onkel Gerd would sit at home for a long time without saying a word. Sometimes he played the lute in the evening and sometimes he lit a cigar and let the smoke fill the room until nobody could see him any more and it looked like he had disappeared. It looked like the Bürgermeister had vanished from the town altogether because that's what the Nazi people wanted, and even when he went for the short walk to Mass or to the library, nobody saw him. Mostly he stayed at home reading books, because there were very few people he could talk to and reading was the best kind of conversation you could have. With no secrets held back. It was as good as any conversation you could have in the graveyard.

I am the boy who slapped his teacher in the face. I'm the boy who's not afraid of anything, my mother says. One day she didn't come to collect me. I ran up to the gate of the school but she wasn't there. She was late because the bus driver didn't see her, even though she had her hand out. She says bus drivers in Ireland are blind because they don't know what it's like to be a passenger. So she didn't come and I ran all the way home in the rain. She was waiting at the door when I got back. She took off my shoes and stuffed them with newspapers. She put them beside the boiler and started rubbing my head with the towel and laughing because my hair was standing up like a hedgehog. And then it was time to make a cake. I stood beside her in the kitchen and tried to teach her Irish. She was holding the bowl in one arm and stirring with the other. I looked at her mouth as she repeated the word in Irish for milk. But it was all wrong. Her lips were still trying to speak German and it was funny to hear her say it as if she didn't know what milk was. I tried other words like the Irish for water, bread, butter, but she didn't know what they were either. Every time she tried to get it right, she had to smile and surrender, because she knew that Irish was my language.

'*Ceol*,' I said. 'That's music.'

'*Ceol*,' she repeated, but it was still not right.

She kneeled down and watched me say it again. She held her hands up in the air as if she was counting to ten with cake mixture all over her fingers. She followed my lips with her eyes but she could see no difference. Then she continued making the cake and trying the word out by herself.

'*Ceol, ceol, ceol.*'

She thought it was funny that I was teaching her how to speak. I was the teacher now and she was the schoolgirl learning to say the words and trying to grow up. Sometimes in the evening after dinner, she went back to the school on the bus to learn Irish and then we had to help her with her homework. But she can't be Irish. It's too hard.

Then I made a rule about Irish in the kitchen. I drew a line and said that anyone crossing the border into my land was not allowed to speak German, only Irish. If my mother or Franz or Maria wanted to come in, they had to stop and say something in Irish first. And if they spoke German, I expelled them. Even my mother has to cross over to Irish if she wants to get into my country. But she laughs. She says there will be no yellow cake with chocolate on top if I stop her. She says you can't make rules like that in the kitchen. It's like something the Nazis would do. I keep saying that nobody can break my rules but she keeps laughing at me. She says she's going to cross over and tickle me. She puts the cake in the oven and then says the word in Irish for music again. And even though she doesn't say it right, even though she's still saying it with German lips, I can't stop her coming across the line and I can't stop her laughing and tickling me to death.

Ten

First of all you have to mix the butter with the sugar. You have to do it hard, my mother says, but after that, everything has to be done very gently because you don't want to make an unhappy cake. If you bake in anger it will taste of nothing. You have to treat the ingredients with respect and affection. You lift the mixture and slip the beaten egg inside, the way you would slip a love letter into an envelope, she says and laughs out loud. You fold in the flour with air-kisses and you stir in one direction only, otherwise people will get the taste of doubt. And when you lay the mixture into the baking tin, you place a piece of brown paper all around the edge and another flat piece across the top to create a dome that will keep it from burning. And once the letter is posted and the cake is in the oven, you have to be very quiet and wait. You don't trudge around the house shouting and slamming doors. You don't argue and you don't say a bad word about anyone. You whisper, you nod, you tiptoe around the kitchen.

My mother likes the radio. She likes the song 'Roses Are Red, My Love, Violets Are Blue', but she's not allowed to sing it and she can only listen to it when my father is at work. When he comes home he switches on the news. The light comes on and you see all the names of the different cities like Budapest and Prague, but it takes a while for the radio to warm up and the voices to come out. After the news the radio should be speaking Irish. If you sing a song, sing an Irish song, the man says, and my father nods his head. If there's a pop song in English my father suddenly pushes back the chair with a big yelp on the floor and rushes over to switch it off. The voice doesn't take time to go away again, it disappears immediately. But even in the few seconds it takes my father to switch it off, before it gets a chance to go as far as 'Sugar is sweet, my love . . .', enough of the song has escaped and the words are floating around the breakfast room. We all sit around the table in silence, but you can still hear the song echoing along the walls. It gets stuck to the ceiling. Stuck to the inside of your head. And even though my mother is not allowed to sing it, she can't stop humming to herself in the kitchen afterwards.

In Germany, my mother says, there was good music on the radio. You had great singers like Richard Tauber and you heard some good stories and theatre if you were lucky. But it wasn't long before you got the speeches. Onkel Gerd said people thought Goebbels and Hitler had rabies because they were always foaming at the mouth. He said that having the radio on was like letting somebody into the house, somebody you thought you could trust, somebody who would pretend to be your friend and then start saying things in your ear. And once you invited them in for afternoon coffee and cake, you would be slow to argue back. Sometimes Onkel Gerd talked back at the radio, standing in the middle of the room and waving his finger, but there was no point because the radio never listens. Ta Maria said you could always tell a decent person by their shoes and their hands, but Onkel Gerd said the radio would sit there all polite and decent in your front room and, before

79

you knew it, you found yourself agreeing with the most outrageous gossip and resentment. The radio made you feel that you belonged to a great country. It made you feel safe and hurt and proud, all at the same time. Some people had no friends at all and no mind of their own, only the radio and the voice of Hitler foaming at the mouth. The radio was a scoundrel who never listens, a scoundrel with nice hands and nice shoes and nice music.

'You can't switch off what's happening,' Ta Maria said.

But Onkel Gerd preferred the silence. Sometimes they huddled together and listened to jazz music from London in secret, like my mother does when my father is out at work. But that's dangerous, too. In our house, it's dangerous to sing a song or say what's inside your head. You have to be careful or else my father will get up and switch you off like the radio.

In Kempen, the man on the radio could just walk in the front door of any house and invite himself in for coffee and cake. People threw their arms out. Sometimes they brought out their best linen tablecloth and lit a candle. Some of them got dressed up to listen to the radio. If it was a Strauss concert they clapped along with the audience at the state concert hall in Vienna as if they were there themselves. They believed what they heard. And before they knew it, they were clapping after some speech, too, because they had no idea who they were letting into their home. The town hall on the Buttermarkt square was then called the 'brown house' because it was full of men in brown uniforms. The newspaper man Lamprecht was taken away to the KZ in Dachau where he could not say another word and that's what was going to happen to Uncle Gerd, too, if he opened his mouth. They had switched him off. He had no name any more and no voice. He had no face and no hair and no eyes. Nobody saw him, even when he walked over to Mass on Sunday morning. And then one day they made a rule that the Jewish people had no names and no faces either. Everybody had to pretend they had disappeared, too. When they came to the market square you could not buy their pickled gherkins, you could not even say 'good morning' to them. They still walked around the streets but nobody could see them. It was easy enough, because once the lord mayor was gone and the newspaper man was gone, anyone else could disappear, too.

'*Unverschämt*,' Ta Maria said. It was a rule that nobody would be able to obey. Onkel Gerd said it was un-German and wouldn't last long. He said they would continue to greet Jews in the street as always. No matter what rule they made in the brown house, they would carry on recognising Jewish names and faces. But it didn't matter any more because it was like the people with no faces saying hello to other people with no faces. They might as well be like the people in the graveyard talking to each other. Nobody in the brown house cared very much whether Onkel Gerd was still saying hello to the Jews or not because he didn't exist anyway. What they did care about was my mother and her sisters. They didn't want them to disappear, so they made another rule which forced them to join the Bund deutscher Mädels – the League of German Girls. It was another rule that could not be obeyed. So they ignored it and continued to attend their own Catholic youth meetings until people came around to the house and asked questions. Three hundred other girls from Kempen and the surrounding district had all joined in the BDM rallies without question, so why not the Kaiser girls.

Ta Maria heard things at the Café Kranz on the Burgring. She went around there for coffee every afternoon because it was the place to hear what people were saying around the town, what they whispered, what you did not hear on the radio. Everybody said it was best to go along with things for the moment, see what happened. It wasn't all that serious anyway, because they were joking and giving the BDM funny new names in secret. Instead of calling it the League of German Girls, everybody was now calling it Bund deutscher Matratzen – the League of German Mattresses. My mother says her father would have laughed at that.

Onkel Gerd called them all into the living room and asked them to sit down. He waited for a long time, quietly picking out his words before he slowly looked around at each of them individually and told them they had to decide for themselves. He was always calm. He didn't trust things that were said with emotion, the way they spoke on the radio. Instead, he spoke slowly in clear sentences, breathing quietly and hardly moving his head, like a father. He said it was all right for him to make a sacrifice, but he would not force it on them. He said you have an instinct and you have an intellect and if you had to join the BDM meetings by law, then maybe there was another way out. Sometimes it's good to tiptoe around things to avoid trouble.

'The silent negative,' he said. 'We will use the silent negative.'

On Sunday the Buttermarkt square was full of colour. There were flags everywhere, flying above the trees and hanging from all the windows around the square. There were standing columns, too, with eagle wings. Loud-speakers had been broadcasting speeches and marching music all morning, and a massive portrait of the Führer had been put up outside the brown house. My mother says she looked up and saw a long red flag with the black swastika on a white circle hanging from the window where

82

her mother once played the piano and where her father said goodbye to himself in the mirror. Sometimes, she says, you have to bite your lip and not allow yourself to be hurt.

Onkel Gerd said it was only a matter of time before somebody took it into his head to play God. The BDM meeting had been arranged to coincide with Mass, so that the girls in Kempen would turn away from the church, so they would belong to the state instead, like a big family. My mother insisted on getting up for early Mass. She could hear the loudspeakers on the square as if they wanted to drown out the prayers inside. And when she arrived late on the square with her missal under her arm, the BDM leader was already foaming at the mouth. She told the Kempen girls they would never need Mass or missals, or candles or head scarves or Corpus Christi processions any more, because now they would be devoted to the Führer. One day, the men in brown broke into the convent school in Mühlhausen smashing everything up and painting swastikas on the walls of the classrooms. And not long after that, they closed the convent down altogether so the nuns had to disappear, too.

The leaves of the missal are not like any other book, they are soft and thin, easy to bend and easy to turn without the slightest bit of noise in church. But outside at the big BDM assembly on the square, my mother says they made a big noise that nobody could ignore. All the girls had to raise their right arms in salute. So when my mother raised her arm, the missal fell down on the cobbles with a clack. It opened up and the breeze rustled the pages so they could be heard all around the square, maybe even all around the town. She bent down and picked it up. She dusted off the covers and then finally raised her arm in the air towards the portrait of the Führer over the Rathaus. The entire square was suddenly tilted at an angle, like a tilted painting, like the dizzy way you can see things when you bend down to look back through your legs. It was time to be obedient, time to swear an oath of allegiance to the Führer, time for the silent negative.

'I swear under oath that I will – NOT – serve the Führer as long as I live.'

After that it was like any other Sunday. Apart from the flags and the loudspeakers left behind on the Buttermarkt square, everything was normal. The shops stayed closed, but you could buy cake and you could see people coming out of the Café Kranz with precious parcels wrapped in coloured paper, holding them flat as they walked. Like every other Sunday, they went to the graveyard to put flowers on the graves. And then it was time to prepare for visitors in the afternoon.

You have to open the doors to be sure that the smell of soup is not lingering in the hallway when the visitors arrive. A sensitive nose can detect a hint of fat in the air, my mother says. Then you let the smell of baking take over. You would commit a mortal sin any time for a decent cup of coffee, my mother says, and then she laughs out loud, because that's what her aunt Ta Maria always said. The smell of coffee and cake is like a hearty welcome, like an embrace. Your visitor will want to jump right into bed and snuggle up with the cake. And when you're serving, you have to cut the slices without touching the cake. You have to serve with the same affection that has gone into the baking, using the silver trowel that has been in the family for generations. The cake has to appear on the plate as though it had never been touched by human hands.

On Sunday we went for a walk in the afternoon. We had to put on our coats and hats and gloves because it was windy and cold outside. My father criss-crossed his scarf over his chest and we did the same. Maria's gloves were attached to an elastic band inside the sleeves of her coat so they wouldn't get lost. We walked past the station where my father gets the train every day. We came to a place where we could kick through the brown leaves with a hissing noise. Sometimes my trousers rubbed against the inside of my leg and it was sore. And sometimes when we walked around the corner, the wind was so strong that we couldn't even breathe or speak any more. We had to push hard against it until we started laughing.

Then we came to the shop and everyone got pocket money. Franz wanted a toffee pop and I wanted a bag of sherbet with a lollipop inside. We waited outside while my father and mother were still inside trying to help Maria decide what to buy. There were boys standing by the wall of the shop and they started calling us Nazis. There were lots of things like that written on the wall in paint, including a big swastika sign in red. They kept saying we were Nazis, until my mother came out and heard them.

'Heil Hitler,' they shouted.

They were not allowed to say that kind of thing and I looked at my mother to see what she would do. They said it again and laughed out loud, so there was no way that she might not have heard it. She even stopped and looked at them for a moment. But she said nothing. I knew she was biting her lip. I knew by her eyes that she was sad this was happening, but she could do nothing about it.

'Come on, let's walk ahead,' she said. She didn't wait for my father and Maria to come out, she just turned us around and walked away. Behind us we could hear them laughing and clicking their heels. I was sure my father would do something, but he said nothing either and we all walked quickly down to the seafront.

We could smell the sea and hear it because it was very rough. The waves were crashing in against the rocks, all white and brown. The seagulls were balancing in the air over the waves and we were standing in a line, holding on to the railings with brown rust marks growing through the blue paint. The dog was there, too, the dog that belongs to nobody and barks at the sea until he is hoarse and can't speak. From behind the railings you could look the waves right in the eye as they came rushing in and my mother said: 'God help anyone who is out at sea.' The waves were so strong that when they threw themselves on to the rocks, the foam sprang up like a white tree. Bits of black seaweed were flung in the air with no mercy. We had to move back so as not to get wet. Only a tiny shower covered our faces and we could taste the salt. We shouted back at the waves but it was hard to talk because of the wind. Here's a big one, my father said, but there was so much noise that you could hear nothing anyway, as if the sea was so loud, it was actually silent. My mother said nothing and just looked far away out into the waves. Bigger and bigger waves all the time, hitting the rocks and bouncing up, right in front of us.

Eleven

I like giving the wrong answer. My father sits on the far side of the table in the breakfast room and says he's going to wait until I give the right answer, even if it takes all day.

'Five plus six makes . . . ?'

My father was a schoolteacher once so he knows what he's doing. He says that he and his brother Ted both got a scholarship and now he wants to make me the best boy in Ireland at tables. I can see myself twice over in his glasses, sitting with my arms folded. He waits and waits, while I search around in my head and say to myself that I will – NOT – give the right answer. I know the answer but I frown and roll my eyes up towards the ceiling and even put my hand on my chin, because that's meant to help you with thinking.

'Nine,' I answer.

'Wrong,' he says. 'Think again.'

We have all the time in the world. It's Saturday afternoon, he says, and we have better things to be doing. He could be sitting in the front room reading any one of six books about the history of Germany or the Spanish Civil War or the lives of saints or the Blasket Islands or cabinet-making or beekeeping. I could be outside running around in the garden. Franz is waiting for me to go and play football. But we're going to stay sitting there in the breakfast room all day and all night if we have to. So then I try again, squinting and frowning and humming to myself, now let me see, five and six makes . . . ? I have given every wrong answer there is so there's none left except the right one.

I look at my father's bad ear which is flattened out of shape and purple. When I asked him once what happened, he told me that a teacher in boarding school hit him with a steel ruler. Maria said she would pray for it to get better, but then he frowned and blinked and said he didn't want us looking at his ear any more or talking about it. My mother told us afterwards that he had no father and at boarding school his ear started bleeding and lost all its feeling because he was homesick and wanted his mother. It's hard not to look at his ear and think about the steel ruler coming down like a sword. I keep thinking of things like that not happening. I try to imagine stopping it with my arm. I imagine fighting off the teacher with long brush. I imagine bending my father's ear back into shape again, like plasticine.

'Concentrate.'

He slams his hand down suddenly on the table and I jump. Then my mother comes in because she doesn't want this to go on for ever either. She says it's time to give in and then I'll be free to go. Outside, I can hear the sound of Mr Richardson hammering at something and the echo coming back across the gardens. I can hear Miss Tarleton's lawnmower and I know there's hardly any grass on her lawn but she does it anyway. Then I hear the two bangs from the lifeboat, one after the other with a long gap in between, and my mother saying 'trouble on the sea'. I can hear the Corbetts' back door closing like a sneeze. Then silence again. Everyone is waiting for the right answer.

88

My mother is nodding. My father is staring. And Franz is standing at the door with the football.

'Nil.'

It's the only answer I could think of that I hadn't given already apart from the right one. But then there was real trouble and real silence. People passing by our house would have heard nothing at all only breathing. Now I could see my father's eyes inside his glasses, and his ear was red hot, like a piece of coal out of the boiler. He pushed the chair back with a loud howl on the floor and told me to wait while he searched in the greenhouse for a good stick that wouldn't break this time.

My mother shook her head because it was out of her hands. The person who can't hear it, must feel it, she said a few times, because that's what they say in Germany. I could see that she was sorry this was happening but she could do nothing to stop it. She took Franz and Maria away and closed the door. I could hear the 'in between door' closing, too, that separates the back of the house from the front. I could hear her going up the stairs, further and further away, closing another door behind her until she could hear nothing at all any more and didn't have to think about what was going to happen. Everybody was gone, even the sound of the hammering outside, and I could only hear the stick whipping through the air. My father was breathing hard and thinking about lots of angry things in his head like the lives of saints and beekeeping and the time he was at school in Dunmanway and couldn't go home to his mother. He was thinking about all the things that he couldn't do with his own life, that he was going to make me do instead. He said he would keep hitting me all day and all night until I gave the right answer.

'Eleven,' I cried. 'Eleven, eleven, eleven.'

89

Then he stopped and asked me if I was good again.

'Yes,' I said.

'Say it.'

'I'm good again.'

I could still feel the hot red lines on the back of my legs when it was time for tea. Franz and Maria wanted to look at them but I didn't want anyone talking about me, not even my mother. My father shook my hand and said it was time to put it all behind us. It was time to smile because we all have to be friends again. But I couldn't smile. So then he held my chin and pushed my lips apart with his fingers and I had to show my teeth.

'Nobody can force you to smile,' my mother said.

She had a better idea. She offered me an extra biscuit, one more than anyone else. And then she started telling a story about the time they got married and went up two mountains, one in each country. On the train going along the Rhine together, they sat in a carriage with a young boy who looked out the window and ate biscuits from a brown paper bag. All the way to Koblenz, the boy sat eating one biscuit after the other without a word, as if he would never see a biscuit in his life again, as if he was afraid the time of no biscuits would come back. Sometimes he closed the bag and put it aside, as though he told himself he was not going to have any more, but then he could not resist starting again and again until the whole lot was gone.

After that I was sick for a long time. It started after we helped to clean the windows one day, first with soap, then with crumpled newspapers that make a squeaking sound like wild dogs barking far away in the hills, my mother says. The windows were so clean that we thought we were outside and there was no glass at all. After that it was hard to breathe, because the sound of the wild dogs got into my chest. I had to stay in bed listening to them howling all day and all night. My mother came with plasticine and cars. She bought a new colouring book and new pencils, but my fingers were soft and I couldn't draw. She came in with a tray, but I could not even eat the biscuits, so she made me sit up and drink the lemon tea, at least one sip for your mother, she said.

At night she left the door wide open and the light coming up the stairs, but I was still afraid. The window rattled and there was a large piece of wallpaper hanging down on the far side of the room which looked like a man with a hat coming in sideways through the wall from next door. At first I laughed and said he was only a piece of wallpaper. But he just looked at me with one eye and kept coming with his shoulder held forward. A light from the street shone into the room and sometimes the man stepped right into the light, then moved back into the darkness again. I was very hot and shivering at the same time. I put my back against the wall and started shouting at him to stop, until my mother came running up and sat on my bed. She said I was soaked with sweat and brought in a warm towel to wipe my chest. She said I was afraid of my own imagination. My father came up and stuck a piece of folded paper in the window to stop the rattling. He put on the light for a minute to prove that there was no man coming through the wall, then he smiled and kissed the top of my head. He listened to the howling in my chest and said it didn't sound as bad as before. Then he went downstairs again and my mother stayed sitting on my bed to tell stories.

'I don't want to be a Nazi,' I told her.

'But you're not a Nazi,' she said.

She smiled and tucked the blankets in around my neck

so that only my head was out. I told her what the boys outside the shop were saying about us.

'I don't want them to call me a Nazi,' I said.

'Ignore them,' she said. She looked at me for a while and said they were the real Nazis. She said I shouldn't worry about it so much, because it was usually people who had something to hide who called other people Nazis. 'They want to make everybody believe that they're innocent. So they call other people Nazis, as often as they can. It's the same the world over.'

She stroked my forehead. She said it was not important what the boys outside the shop said. If I was a real Nazi, then I would know it myself. Maybe you can hide it from other people by pointing the finger somewhere else, but you can't hide things like that from yourself. What's inside your head is what matters.

'But that won't stop them.'

'You can't,' she said. 'You can't go around telling the whole world what you're not. That would be ridiculous. I can't send you down the road to the shop with a sign around your neck saying "I'm not a Nazi."'

It was time to concentrate on good things. Soon I would be better again, running around like before with no dogs howling in my chest. And my father has a new plan, she said, a plan to make money, so that we can take the wallpaper down. Sometimes he is very hard, she said, but he knows what's good for Ireland. He doesn't mean to be angry, but he has a lot to worry about and he's doing his best. And the next day he was busy downstairs starting a new business that would make us rich, so we could take down the old wallpaper. He bought a desk for the front room. He put the telephone on it and a desk-light so he could sit down and have his own office. He bought lots of stationery, too, and gave the business a name. Kaiser and Co., he called it, because that was my mother's name and her family had been in business for a long time in Kempen before they went bankrupt. He got a machine that printed the name on to paper, so he wouldn't have to write it out every time. And when the business was set up, he sat at his desk waiting for phone calls and saying there should be less noise in the house, because he had to try and guess what the people of Ireland needed most at that moment.

My mother said I was getting better. She let me go downstairs to the front room to see the new office. My father was out buying stamps and I lay on the sofa with all the cushions and blankets while my mother sat at the desk with her diary, writing in all the things that were happening in our family. She glued everything in, like photographs and locks of hair and tickets to the zoo. She wrote in lots of stories, like me not giving the right answer and Franz going to bed every night, laying out his socks in the shape of a crucifix. She also put in things that were happening outside in the world, like the photograph from the newspaper of the tanks in Hungary, and a photograph of the Irishman, Ronnie Delaney on his knees thanking God for winning the race at the Olympics in Melbourne, Australia. Then she went into the kitchen and it was our turn to play office. Maria started drawing a picture on the wall and Franz found a matchstick.

'Light it,' I said. But I didn't even have to say that, because the match was saying it himself with his little red head, asking to be lit. Franz struck it along the wall and it flared up. He blew it out straightaway, but my father must have heard it. His good ear can hear things from miles away. He asked if we had lit a match. He called my mother in because she has a good nose and between them they were able to prove it. She said that's why people get married, because one person has a good ear and the other has a good nose, and hopefully we would have both and that would help us not to do anything in our lives that we would regret later.

Sometimes my mother was able to talk around trouble. Sometimes you couldn't stop things happening so you tiptoed around them instead, she said. Even when there should be real trouble and my father should be much more angry than ever before, she was able to find another way out. My father proved that we had lit a match but he had other things to get angry about. He saw what Maria had done. She had taken a crayon and drawn lines all along the wall, right around the room.

'Look at that,' my mother said, and my father was frowning hard. But then she had an idea to stop him getting angry. She clapped her hands together and said it was the most beautiful drawing she had ever seen in her life and they had to take a photograph of it for the diary. It was a drawing of my mother with her arms stretching all the way around the four walls, embracing everyone who came into the room. And anyway, she said, there should be no more anger in our house, because we had a big plan for the business, Kaiser and Co. My father thought of something that the Irish people needed most. They were going to import crosses from a famous place in Germany, hand-carved wooden crosses from Oberammergau.

I was still sick. The howling dogs came back again, and something started happening to one of my legs as well. It swelled up bit by bit, until it was twice the size of the other one. Onkel Ted came to make the sign of the cross and Dr Sheehan came too, because I was still a Nazi and I knew it. He called me 'young man' and said it was serious this time. My leg was about to explode. I had to go to hospital and an ambulance came. I couldn't walk, so the men came up the stairs and wrapped me up in a red blanket, then carried me down, through the hallway and out the door, past the people on the street standing around the gate. My mother was crying and the neighbours said I would soon be better again, please God. They would all pray for me every day and every night.

Inside the ambulance I couldn't see where I was going, so I tried to follow the streets in my head, around each corner, past the church and past the people's park. But then I got lost and I was blind with my eyes wide open and I knew they were taking me to a different country again where they spoke only English. I could smell the hospital and the doctors and nurses were standing all around me looking down. They listened to my chest and heard the dogs howling. They looked at my leg and measured it. Every day, new doctors came to examine it and stick needles into it. Some of them said it was a mystery. It made them scratch their heads, because nothing like that had ever happened before in the medical books and they had no way of making it better. And then one day, the howling stopped. The swelling in my leg started going down again, and my mother came to visit me with a new toy car and said I was getting better. The nurse showed me the measurements on the chart. The doctors were amazed and said my leg would be famous and would enter into history, if only they could explain it. The nurse said I was famous already, because I was a German-Irish boy and everybody knew me. At night I begged her to let me go home. She smiled and stroked my head and said I still had to stay in hospital until the doctors said I was fully back to normal.

'I'm good again,' I said.

'You mean you're better,' she said.

'Yes, I'm better,' I said. 'I'm too better.'

'Of course you are, love,' she said. But still she could not let me go until the doctors said so. Everybody was gone and the hospital was quiet. All lights were switched off except for the small one at the door. The nurse was tidying up all around me and not saying very much. Her white shoes were making tiny squeaks on the floor.

'I'm not a Nazi,' I said.

Then she looked up and smiled.

'I'm not German,' I said. 'I promise.'

'I know that, love. I believe you.'

Twelve

It should be easier to sell a crucifix in Ireland. My mother closes the front door and stands in the hall with her coat still on, looking up at the picture of the Virgin Mary. She throws her arms up in the air and says she can't understand it. She has been to every church and every convent and every hospital in Dublin. We went with her on the bus one day and a priest gave us a sweet each, a satin cushion. He smiled and nearly said yes to the cross, but then he shook his head at the last minute. Beautiful hand-carved oak crosses from Oberammergau and nobody wants them, my mother says. It's hard to believe, when you think of everyone in Ireland praying twice a day at least and all they still have to pray for.

'Surely somebody needs a crucifix,' she says.

That's the whole idea of my father starting a business, to sell something the Irish people really need, something you believe in yourself. We believe in crosses, so we kneel down every night and pray that we will have God on our side as a partner in business. But in the end, nobody wants them and my mother sits down in the kitchen without even taking her coat off, shaking her head from side to side and breathing out slowly as if she wants to be the best at not breathing in again until you have to. Maybe they're too expensive, she says. Maybe it's too late and there are too many crosses in Ireland already. Or maybe they're the wrong kind of crosses and Irish people only like the ones where Jesus has blood on his hands and feet and there's a gash in his side and a scroll at the top saying INRI.

She doesn't understand Ireland sometimes, because they like strange things like pink cakes and soft ice cream and salt and vinegar. They spend all their money on First Holy Communion outfits. They don't like serving people and they don't like being in a queue either, because when the bus comes, they forget about the rules and just rush for the door. The bus drivers in Ireland are blind and the shopkeepers don't want to sell things to you. The butcher has a cigarette in his mouth while he's cutting the meat, and nobody knows how to say the word no. In Ireland, they nod when they mean no, and shake their heads when they're agreeing with you. She says it's like in the films, when somebody looks up with a worried face and says one thing, it means that the opposite is going to happen. When somebody says nobody is going to come out alive and that they're all going to die, then at the last minute somebody comes along to the rescue. And when everybody at the bus stop begins to say that the buses have stopped running, along comes the bus at last and they all rush forward to get on.

Sometimes Irish people don't understand my mother either. When she's trying to be helpful, they think she's interfering and being nosy. When she tries to warn some of the other mothers about their children eating too many sweets or crossing the road without looking, they say they don't want some German woman telling their kids what to do. One day, there was a woman outside the shop with a brand new pram with big wheels. It had the word Pedigree written on the side and the woman was very proud of it, because it was like a new car. My mother admired the new pram, but she warned her to be careful it didn't fall over with the baby inside. So then the woman called her a Nazi and told her to mind her own business.

Nobody knows what my mother is trying to say sometimes. And nobody has any idea where Oberammergau is either. She tells them it's a place in Bavaria, where they have the crucifixion every ten years, a bit like going up to Croagh Patrick. They nod and say yes and look very interested, so why don't they buy hand-carved oak crosses with no blood, just nails and the rest left up to your imagination?

'It's the shoes,' she says at last.

Nobody will buy anything if you don't look half-decent. You can tell a person's character by their hands and their shoes, she says, because that's what Ta Maria always said. Even though Onkel Gerd always said the opposite, that it's only what's inside your head that makes you either a scoundrel or a saint. But when you're trying to sell something, my mother says, it doesn't matter if you're a scoundrel or a saint, because what you're wearing is all they look at. You have to be honest, she says, but you can't let people know that the wallpaper is hanging off the walls at home.

Then we head off into the city so she can get a pair of decent shoes. I swing around the bus stop and climb up as far as I can until the bus comes. We fight over the window seat, and over who gets the ticket, until my mother says that's enough, it's not important to win. Everybody on the bus turns around to look at us because we're German again. Then we have to behave and sit quietly and bless ourselves whenever we pass by a church, to prove that the Germans are decent people and we did nothing wrong. I pretend to be Irish and look at the IMCO building passing by like a white ship.

My father says the Irish people can't live on their imagination for ever. They need money in their pockets now. It's time to work hard so we can be free and so that nobody will ever starve or be poor again like all the people in west Cork were. He doesn't want the song about emigration to go on for ever, so it's time to speak Irish and make Ireland a better place to live. He tells us how his mother Mary Frances spent all her money on putting him through university in Dublin while she fasted and hardly had anything to live on herself. He tells us exactly how much he had to spend each week on food and lodgings, and how he had two pennies left over, one for the Mass on Sunday and one for a razor blade. He sent his washing home by post and cycled all the way home to Leap at Christmas because he could not afford the train or the bus. He had no way of borrowing from a bank, and if it wasn't for the Jesuits who lent him the money for the final year, we wouldn't be here now but in America or Canada maybe. He paid back the money as fast as possible when he got his first job as an engineer in Dublin, making matches with Maguire and Patterson.

Even when my father started sending money home, Mary Frances was not able to spend it on herself, because Irish people didn't know how to do that yet. All she wanted in her life was to make sure that her two sons were educated, one an engineer and the other a Jesuit. And that was the happiest day of her life, when my father came home to Leap with initials after his name. Better than that, the Jesuits even allowed Onkel Ted to go home for a day to see her for the first time in seven years. So she sat looking at her two sons together in the kitchen for a few hours at least, until

Onkel Ted had to leave again very early in the morning to get back to the seminary in the Bog of Allen.

His father died in Cork and the navy refused to give them a pension at first. His mother spent all she had on getting the body home for burial in the mountain graveyard above Glandore. After that she could no longer pay the rent and the landlord wanted her out of the house. A letter went to the local police station telling them to 'proceed with eviction forthwith', so she walked up to the church and told the priest she was going to bed. She was not a political person, and some people didn't mind all too much one way or another who was in the government, because it didn't make a bit of difference to them. Some people in Ireland had no time for guns either, only education. But everybody hated landlords. So she took her two boys upstairs and got into bed. If they were going to evict her, she said, they would have to drag them out of the bed.

It was not the first time something like that happened in Ireland either. Her uncle was put out of his home and the cottage burned down because he refused to pay rent to the landlord any more. He had nowhere to go after that and if it wasn't for the local people who built him a tiny cottage to stay in, he would have become a traveller with no place to settle any more, like all the the people on the move after the famine. We would have been travellers, too, moving around from one place to another all our lives and knocking on doors to sell carpets, my father says, so that's why he gives them money when they come to the door and say 'God Bless.' In the end, her uncle went to America. But before he left Ireland he made one great speech for the Land League on a platform in Skibbereen. He stood up and said it was time to wipe landlords off the face of this earth. Then he swung his right arm over the crowd and knocked the hat off the priest sitting down behind him as he was doing it, so that everyone laughed about that story, long after he was gone. There were lots of people put out of their homes, my father says, until Michael Collins stood up for them and started the resistance.

Sometimes my mother goes over to the neighbours for coffee mornings. Mrs Corcoran invites all her friends around for sandwiches and cakes and gossip. They think my mother is very posh and unfriendly, because she has no gossip and speaks in a German accent all the time. My mother says Mrs Corcoran has a funny accent, too, because she and her friends all speak English like no other Irish people. My father says it's the famine. Even the people with money to burn and accents that hurt your mouth are still afraid of the famine. They speak like that because they're afraid of the Irish language coming back and killing everybody in the country this time. He says Irish people drink too much and talk too much and don't want to speak Irish, because it stinks of poverty and dead people left lying in the fields. That's why they speak posh English and pretend that nothing ever happened. My father talks about people dying on coffin ships going to America and my mother talks about people dying on trains going to Poland. My father talks of evictions in Leap and my mother talks of evictions in Kempen. My father says our people died in the famine and my mother says those who died under the Nazis are our people, too. Everybody has things they can't forget.

My mother likes Irish people, but she doesn't want to go to any more coffee mornings. They talk about going on holidays all the time and about new things like cars and washing machines. Mrs Corcoran talks about where she has been in the summer and shows the souvenirs she brought back, like the black bull from Spain and a big bowl with zigzags from Greece. This time, my mother says, she was in South Africa and brought back lots of wood carvings. But that's not all she brought back either, because right in the middle of the coffee morning, Mrs Corcoran started saying that black people would never be the same as white people. They would never catch up no matter how much education they got.

In the shoe shop, we sit in a line and get a liquorice shoelace each while my mother tries on shoes for a long time. She taps the heels together to hear what they sound like. She says it's as hard to buy shoes in Ireland as it is to sell a crucifix. Sometimes you have to beg people to sell you something. At first the assistant smiled and said every pair of shoes looked gorgeous. She thought people from Germany had to try on every pair in the shop before they could make up their mind. My mother started imagining shoes that didn't even exist, shoes from Italy, great shoes she had seen in the past sometime. My mother and the assistant didn't understand each other. In the end, she went for the dark blue pair that matched her blue dress with the white squiggles, the shoes that made her feet look smallest of all. She walked up along the floor one last time, turned in front of the mirror, then came back and paid.

Now my mother can sell anything. Franz carried the box with the new shoes and we walked across O'Connell Street holding hands in a chain. When you look up at Nelson's Pillar you sometimes think the white clouds are standing still and the city is moving, running fast out to the sea. If you close your eyes you can hear the sound of footsteps and buses and cars all around you. Seagulls, too. There were seagulls on the roof of the GPO and seagulls standing on the shoulders of Daniel O'Connell.

My father took a half-day and came to meet us in the restaurant. He looked at the new shoes and said they were beautiful. He said it was a great day for us because we would soon be in business, making a profit. There was a big smile on his face. He has lots of straight teeth and when he starts talking, he sometimes sounds like he's making a speech. He starts blinking and speaking fast, as if he'll never catch up with all the things he wants to say. My mother says there are lots of men who like to turn things into a joke and make people laugh. She says it's good to laugh, but my father has a different way of doing things. He can laugh too, until the tears come into his eyes. But then he's always serious again afterwards, because he is a man with ideas. A man, my mother says, who could never live for himself, only for his children and his country. That's why he frowns, even when he's not angry, because he's in a hurry to do all the things that are still left unfinished in Ireland.

My mother said we could have a cake each, but not one of the pink ones because they're too sweet and leave nothing to the imagination. My father didn't want a cake because they were nothing like hers. He said people would fight each other over my mother's cakes, and anything else that she put her hands to. Then he took her hands and held them up in the air for everyone in the restaurant to see. My mother smiled and got embarrassed. It looked like he was going to stand up and make a speech to the whole restaurant about her. My mother says you can sometimes be overcome by the smell of coffee. His eyes were soft. He said they were precious hands. He said it didn't matter that we were left with hand-carved wooden crosses from Oberammergau all over the house, because there were plenty of new ideas. He mentioned other things that the Irish people needed very badly. Like umbrellas. And Christmas-tree stands.

And German toys. We would sell things that were so well made and so beautiful that people would fight each other to buy them.

Afterwards my father bought hurling sticks, but said he would take them off us again if we used them as swords for fighting. It was dark by the time we went home and my father showed us the glass of whiskey that kept filling up again and again on the side of the building. There was a packet of cigarettes too that kept disappearing and lighting up again slowly, bit by bit. The seagulls were not there any more, but there were men shouting the names of newspapers on the street like seagulls. Herald-a-Press. Herald-a-Press. On the train, everybody was looking at us because we were the Germans with the hurling sticks. My mother told us the story about Rumpelstiltskin, who gave away his secret in the forest when he thought nobody was listening. Everybody on the train was listening to her. They all surrendered to the story, even though it was in German. One man was already asleep and Maria was trying hard to keep her eyes open. At the end of the story my mother always says the same thing: 'and if he isn't dead yet, then he must be still alive'. So I think about that for a while and look out at the lights of the city, moving along and blinking.

Thirteen

It takes a long time for things to come to Ireland. My father and mother are waiting every day for a big box to arrive from Germany. He sits at his desk in the front room and my mother is in the breakfast room typing. Then my father gets a letter to say that the box has arrived in Dublin, but the Irish government won't let it go until he pays them lots of money, nearly as much as he already paid for what's inside. Then he collects the box in a taxi. In the front room, we sit around and wait for him to open it. It's full of party hats for policemen and sailors and firemen and doctors and nurses. There are German crackers, too, and lots of caramel walking sticks in all colours. My mother says they're beautiful, but we can't play with them because they have to be sold. They put on some music and drink cognac, because a little bit of Germany has come over to Ireland at last and my mother doesn't feel so homesick. Maybe Germany is not so far away as we thought, she says. Then it's time for my father to put some of the hats and caramel canes into a suitcase, so he can take them around to the shops the next day. It won't take long before the whole box is sold. It won't be long before these party hats will be seen in every shop all over the city and people will be fighting each other to get more.

Every night, we pray for luck in business. We pray for

people in Germany and for people in Ireland, for Ta Maria and for Onkel Wilhelm and for Uncle Gerald who drinks to much in Skibbereen. Then we pray for the new baby, too. One at a time, my mother allows us to listen to her tummy, a little brother or sister kicking and playing football, she says. Then I lie awake listening to them whispering as they go into bed. Every night I can hear my mother saying that money doesn't matter, that there are far more important things in life than money, because we'll be rich once the new baby is born. Every night, I hear her washing her feet because your feet are your best friends.

Every morning, my father walks up to the station with the suitcase in one hand and his briefcase in the other. He stops halfway to swap over the briefcase and the suitcase, then he carries on. At lunchtime he leaves the office and walks around the city with the suitcase, going around to all the different toy shops and department stores. And every evening he comes home again and stops halfway to change over, because the suitcase is getting heavier all the time, not lighter, and the handle makes a mark on his hand. He has tried every shop in Dublin, but not one single hat has been sold. He starts going to all the hotels and pubs instead, even as far away as the airport on the other side of the city. And one night he came home so late on the bus that he could not even carry the suitcase up the road any more, it was so heavy. He was limping and the suitcase was left beside the bus stop, until my mother went down to collect it with the pram. Then it was my father who took off his shoes and socks one by one to wash his feet, because your feet can be your worst enemy, too.

There is nothing wrong with the party hats and crackers and caramel canes. Everybody says they're just lovely. The people in the shops and pubs and hotels say they would

love to buy them but they can't. It has nothing to do
with them being German or Germany losing the war or
what the Nazis did. And it's got nothing to do with the
Irish famine either, or the people of Ireland not having the
money to spend on themselves and celebrating and having
parties. The problem is not the party hats and crackers. It's
the name, our family name. My father will not sell anything
to anyone unless they say his name properly in Irish.

It's the name that causes all the trouble. The Irish name:
Ó hUrmoltaigh.

People jump back with a strange expression and ask you
to say it again. They don't really trust anything Irish yet.

'What's that in English?' they ask.

But you can't betray your family name. My father says
we can't give the English version, Hamilton, no matter how
often they ask for it. We can't even admit that an English
version exists. If they call us Hamilton, we pretend it's not
us they're talking to. Our name is proof of who we are and
how Irish we are. We have to be able to make a sacrifice,
even if they laugh at us. They can torture us and make
martyrs of us and nail us to the cross and still we won't
give in. It would be a lot easier to let them have their way,
to give the English name, just to be friendly and make it
simple so they'll buy things. But my father says there can
be no compromise. It's hard for business, but you can't
betray your own name, because if the cheque is made out
to Hamilton, he will send it back and not accept it until
it's paid in Irish.

Your name is important. It's like your face or your
smile or your skin. There's a song at school about a man in
Donegal who once wrote his name in Irish on a donkey cart.
It was the time when Ireland was still under the British and
it was forbidden to write your name in Irish. Every cart had

to have the name of the owner written on it in English. So when a policeman saw the name in Irish, the man was arrested and brought to court. The bobby argued that he saw no name on the cart, because Irish was not a language that he could read. It was a famous court case with Patrick Pearse as the lawyer for the cart owner. And even though the law was still British and the cart owner lost the case and had to pay a big fine, it was still a big victory for the Irish, because after that, all the cart owners in Donegal started putting their names in Irish on their carts and there was nothing the police could do because there were too many of them. So that's why we have our name in Irish, too.

My mother said she would try and sell the party hats with a smaller suitcase. Every evening she went out to the local hotels and clubs, while my father stayed at home to look after us. The Royal Marine Hotel, the Royal Yacht Club, the Royal Irish Yacht Club, the Crofton Hotel, the Pierre Hotel, the Castle Hotel, the Salt Hill Hotel and the Khyber Pass Hotel. She walked so much that the new shoes were hurting. She went all the way up the hill a second time to meet the manager of the Shangri-La Hotel, the man who could not say no.

The Shangri-La was an old hotel with long blue-velvet curtains hanging in the windows, full of old smoke. The man who couldn't say no asked her to sit down in the lounge so he could look at what was in the suitcase properly. At first he shook his head from side to side and she thought she had come for nothing. But then he said they were absolutely beautiful. He praised them so much, my mother says, that she suddenly thought she had sold them all in one go, without even saying a word. She had dreams in her head of running home with an empty suitcase and ordering more and more of them to come over immediately. The problem was how fast they could get the Irish government to let go of the boxes when they arrived in future. The Shangri-La manager didn't have to be told they were German-made, because anything that was really well made had to be German, he said. He knew that she was German, too, by her accent, but then he asked for her name and all the trouble started again.

'Ó hUrmoltaigh,' she said. Irmgard Ó hUrmoltaigh.

'Good Lord, I'll never remember that,' he said.

He pulled out a packet of cigarettes and offered her one, but my mother doesn't know how to smoke yet.

'Would that be Hurley in English?' he asked.

'No,' she smiled. He picked up one of the sailor hats to admire it and she waited for him to make up his mind, to say how many of the party hats he was going to take, how many of the caramel canes and crackers. The people in all the other hotels and shops would soon be kicking their own backsides for not taking them while they had the chance.

'Hermon, Harmon? What about Harmon?'

My mother repeated her name in Irish, because you can't betray your skin. He tried again and again to get it out of her in English. And when he ran out of guesses, he finally tried to pronounce it in Irish, but it was such hard work.

'Ó Hermity, Ó Hamilty, Ó Hurmilly . . . Ó Himmel.'

My mother could not help laughing. It was her feet, she says. Her feet were tired and singing and begging to be washed and put to bed. So when the manager scratched his head and blew out smoke and called her 'Ó Himmel', she could not help laughing out loud.

Mrs O'Himmel – Mrs O'Heaven.

Nobody had come up with that one before. The party hats and caramel sticks were lying all around and she was laughing at her own name. It was the hardest name in the world. Nobody in the whole of Ireland got it right, not even those who spoke fluent Irish. Most of the neighbours and people in the shops made a complete mess of it, so that after a long time, my mother didn't mind what way they said it as long as it still proved how Irish she was and it didn't get her in trouble with my father. The postman called her Mrs O'Hummity, and the man in the fish shop called her Mrs O'Hommilty, and the man with one arm in the vegetable shop did his best and called her Mrs O'Hervulty. If only they could have agreed on one version. But it was different every time. And there was always something funny about it, too, that made people smile, or try not to smile. Some people could only manage Mrs O'Hum. The butcher with the cigarette in his mouth just called her Mrs O . . . And sometimes she came home with no name at all and wished things were still as plain and simple as they once were long ago when her name was Irmgard Kaiser.

'Ó hUrmoltaigh,' she tried once more, because you can't hate your own name. 'It's a Cork name. My husband is from County Cork.'

'That explains everything,' the manager said.

He wanted to know what brought her over to Ireland, and how she had married a man from Cork of all places. She said she loved the sea. She loved the smell of the sea and the sound of the waves crashing on the rocks. He asked her if she got homesick. He knew that she was only trying to sell these German things because she was so far away from home, because she could not go back to Germany herself and wanted instead to bring a bit of her country over here to Ireland. He asked her did she want a drink. He said she had a lovely accent and a lovely voice. He said he would love to hear her speaking a bit of German, anything at all, but then he wasn't even looking at the hats any more, only at her and her shoes. He said he would love her to come back and have a drink some other time when she was not so busy. And when she asked him finally straight out about the hats and crackers, he threw out his arms and couldn't say no. He couldn't say yes and he couldn't say no either. He said he would love to take them all, every last one of them, but he couldn't.

'I'm sorry,' he said.

It was all for nothing. It was even harder putting them back into the suitcase. It looked like there were more than she started with. Instead of any of them being sold, my mother says it looked like they were starting to reproduce. On the bus home she fell asleep and only woke up after she had gone way past her stop. She walked back and when she arrived in the door she had to sit down with her coat still on and take off her shoes first because her feet were on fire. She had to close her eyes and wash her feet until they were friends with her again. She was very quiet. She could not speak and she would not let us listen to the baby in her tummy. She had no name any more.

One day, a man with a car came to take away the box with the party hats and crackers. We were allowed to choose one hat each, but the rest were sold off all around County Cork for nearly nothing and my father said it was a mistake to try and bring things over from Germany. He said it was better to produce things at home, so then my mother started a sweet factory instead. For weeks and weeks there was a smell of caramel and chocolate all over the house. Every night she was mixing and baking. Sometimes the sweets came out too hard or too soft, but my father said that's the way any business started out, by experimenting. If they were not like shop sweets it was because they were far superior to shop sweets. My mother put them all in little jars with labels and ribbons. Soon there would be people queuing up outside our front door, my father said. But the problem was that nobody wanted home-made sweets. So the jars kept piling up, waiting and waiting on shelves under the stairs, until they eventually had to be given away or eaten by us. My mother laughed and said we were our own best customers, and when the last of the jars were gone we didn't talk about the sweet factory any more either.

My father says the only way to make money in Ireland is not to spend it in the first place. So then he started switching off lights and using as little coal as possible. He made new rules. We would make our own bread and our own jam. He found a supermarket where groceries were cheaper than anywhere else, so he went there on the bus to bring home what was needed. When my mother ran out of butter one day and had to buy it in a local shop, he wanted to know why she was breaking the rules. She explained that to get the cheap butter, she would have to spend more money on the bus fare, so if you worked it out, the local butter was cheaper and quicker. She said you couldn't save what you didn't have in the first place. Anyway, there was nothing to worry about because we would be rich when the baby was born. But he frowned and slammed the door because everybody was breaking his rules.

After that my father sat at his desk in the front room on his own every night, until at last he came up with the right idea. Then he came running out, telling us that he had found it, what Ireland needed most. He was blinking again and talking very fast, trying to catch up with all the ideas in his head. How had he not seen it before? One Sunday afternoon when we were out walking he discovered that all street names were still in English. He stood by a sign that said Royal Terrace and wondered how any Irish speaker could walk around these streets without getting lost. So then he started writing letters to the government and to the corporation. The machine printed the address at the top of the page every time and my mother typed out the letters for him. Now things were working at last. Every morning he took a stack of letters with him to the post office. He had tried so many different things like crosses and hats and crackers and sweets and savings, but now he was in business, changing the names of the streets.

De Vesci Terrace, Albert Road, Silchester Road, Neptune Terrace, Nerano Road, Sorrento Road. He had them all changed into Irish, one by one. Royal Terrace became Ascal Ríoga, because money and profit were not everything, he said. On Sundays we walked everywhere to make sure that we covered them all. He told us about the great Irish poets and scholars who once lived in Munster where he came from, among them his own grandfather who was known as Tadhg Ó Donnabháin Dall, or Ted O'Donovan Blind. When the names of people and places all over Ireland were changed into English, all those poets and Irish speakers lost their way and suddenly found themselves in a foreign land. He told us how they all went blind overnight, stumbling around in the dark with no language. And now it was time to change the names back to Irish so the people knew where they were going again.

Then my mother was sick and had to stay in bed. We were allowed to go up to her room for a while and talk to her. Maria stroked her arm and I was the doctor. Until the real Dr Sheehan arrived and we had to wait outside the door. We could hear her crying because the baby had stopped playing football. It was still inside her tummy but it would not come out alive. I knew she was crying for other things, too, because Germany was so far away, because nobody in Ireland wanted party hats, and because she had no name any more, and no face and no feet in Ireland. Onkel Ted came and made the sign of the cross. There were shadows around her eyes when we were allowed back into the room, but she was trying to smile and she put her arms around us and said she was rich because she had three children.

Downstairs in the kitchen, my father tried to bake a cake. He wanted to help and make everything better again, so he put on the apron and mixed the ingredients the way my mother told him to. Now and again he sent us back up the stairs to ask her what to do next and my mother smiled and sent us back down again to tell him to switch on the oven. He did everything he was told, step by step. He held his hands up in the air, quietly counting to ten with cake mixture on his fingers, repeating all the German instructions from above in his Cork accent. And when he was finished he put the cake in the oven and there was a smell of baking all over the house and everyone went around on tiptoes. But when it came out it was all wrong. There was a frown on his forehead and he blinked quickly when he saw the cake had sunk down in the middle. My mother didn't laugh. She said it was fine. He had done his best, but there were some things that could not be translated into Irish.

Fourteen

There's a man who comes to our house to see my father. His name is Gearóid and he's not very tall, but he smiles a lot and has a strong voice, like the radio. In the hallway, he shakes my hand with both of his and then pats me on the shoulder and looks into my eyes in a very friendly way, because he likes hearing Irish. He is my father's friend and when he comes to visit everything in the house changes. Everything is translated into Irish – the tables, the chairs, the curtains, even the teacups and saucers turn Irish. The music on the radio has to be Irish. We have to go and play and be happy and not fight in Irish. My mother has to sit down in the front room and listen, even though she doesn't understand a word. There's not much laughing either, or drinking cognac, only Gearóid and my father talking and foaming at the mouth about all the things that are not finished yet in Ireland.

Gearóid has a car, a blue Volkswagen full of newspapers on the back seat written in Irish and English. The newspaper is called *Aiséirí*, which is the Irish for resurrection, and there is a photograph of corporation men taking down an old English street sign and putting up a new bilingual one, with the Irish on top and the English below in second place. There's an article in the paper, too, about my father and a letter from Mullingar. One day at work, my father

116

refused to answer a letter because it was addressed to John Hamilton. He kept sending it back because that was not his name. He told them there was nobody by the name of John Hamilton working at the Electricity Supply Board in Dublin. He pretended there had been a big mistake and the letter was for somebody in a different organisation, maybe even in a different country, at the electricity board in England or America or South Africa maybe. There was a lot of trouble with this letter going back and forth for weeks and weeks, because the people of Mullingar had to wait all that time for their electricity masts to be repaired. My father didn't care if the whole country was left in darkness. And in the end, the people of Mullingar got their electricity back only when they learned to respect his proper name. But then the boss at the ESB refused to give my father promotion because the Irish language was bad for business.

In the front room, Gearóid smiles and claps his hands together with a bang. He says my father is a man who does what he believes in, not just for money. He's a real fighter who wrote articles for *Aiséirí* and made great speeches on O'Connell Street once. He says people will still throw their hats up in the air these days for a good speech. Ireland is far from being finished and there is a lot of de-Anglicisation still left to be done. My father says he loves his country as much as ever, but he has a different way of fighting now, through his children. From now on he's going to use his own children as weapons, he says, because children are stronger than armies, stronger than speeches or articles or any number of letters to the government. One child is worth more than a thousand guns and bombs, he says.

'You're the lifeblood,' Gearóid says to my mother in Irish. He says the Irish language is dying, day by day. It's choking to death slowly with everybody speaking English on the radio and in the government. But he means the opposite, like in the films. He holds his fist up in the air and says the language is not dead at all, and there's a few shakes left in the animal yet, as long as there is one family like us in the country. Even if Irish is not our mother tongue and we speak German, too, we are still more Irish than many others. *Teaghlach lán-ghaelach*, he calls us, a full-Irish fireside. Then he has to leave again. He doesn't stay for tea because he has to go to visit some more families and deliver the paper to them, too. We stand at the door and watch him getting into the car. We hear the car starting with a big growl and then we wave goodbye, the full-Irish family on the doorstep.

Afterwards, my father tells us about the time he made a speech in Dublin, with thousands of people looking up at him. He can still hear the sound of them cheering every time he walks up O'Connell Street. It's something you never forget, something you carry with you, like the sound of the sea in your ears. He takes off his glasses and starts making a speech at the dinner table. His face looks very different, like a different man in the house, a man I've never seen before. There are two red marks, one on each side of his nose. His eyes look smaller and darker, and his voice gets harder and stronger, like the radio. It looks as if he has never seen us before either, as if he's surprised to be here in this house. And he talks so fast that he has a little white blob of spit on his bottom lip. Every time Gearóid comes to the house he's like this afterwards. Happy and proud one minute, sad and angry the next, because not everybody in Ireland is doing what he told them to do.

He tells us about the time he went all over the country on his motorbike, frightening the cows as he drove past. He saw cows shaking their heads to try to get rid of the noise, like a bad dream. He tells us about a time when the police tried to stop one of the articles he wrote. They came to the offices of *Aiséirí* and said they would close down the paper, but Gearóid wasn't afraid of them. They weren't afraid of going to prison for what they believed, even if the whole country was against them. So they printed the paper with the article in it, because you have to do what's right, he says. My mother nods, because she's thinking of the time when Onkel Gerd refused to be a Nazi. I want to be proud of my father, too, so I asked him what was in the article and why they tried to stop it, but he wouldn't say. My mother doesn't know either, so we all wait for him to tell us.

'Explain it to them,' she says.

It's not something he wants to talk about. I know it's all in the wardrobe upstairs, but I'm not allowed to go near anything. I know there are piles of old newspapers and things from the time he made those speeches, hidden away in boxes. So I ask him again, why the police tried to close down the newspaper. But then he slams his fist down on the table and all the cups and spoons jump in the air. Maria shivers.

'I won't be interrogated by my own family,' he said. Then he walked away to the front room and slammed the door. My mother sits with us for a long time and tells us her stories about Germany instead. She doesn't mind being interrogated. And sometimes she says things that we don't understand. She looks far away and says we will be putting our parents on trial one day and asking what they did.

'You are the fathers and mother now,' she says. 'And we are the children.'

She is starting to clear the dishes without thinking. She's not even looking at what she's doing. It doesn't make sense stacking up plates and unstacking them again. I know she's thinking right back to when she was a girl in Kempen. She says things were different when she was small in Germany and my father was small in Ireland. We will soon be adults, she says, and they will be the children. We will grow up and look back at all the things they did in their lives, like trying to sell crucifixes and party hats and sweets. We will go over the secrets, too, that are hidden in the wardrobe.

'You'll say we're children and we didn't know any better.'

Then she starts clearing the dishes all over again, stacking up the plates and collecting the knives and forks. We start asking her more questions. I want to know if she's Irish or German now.

'What country do you love?' Franz asks.

'Ireland,' she says, because that's where she's living now and that's where the postman brings her letters and where her children are going to school. But what about Germany? And then she says she loves Germany, too, very much, because that's where she was born and went to school herself and where she remembers the postman coming to the door.

'You can't love two countries,' I said. 'That's impossible.'

'Why not?'

'What if they start fighting against each other?'

'I don't just love one of my children,' she says. 'I still love all my children, even when they start fighting.'

In school, they teach us to love our own country. They sing a song about the British going home. The *máistir* takes out a tuning fork and taps it on his desk. It rings, and when he stands the fork up on the wood it makes a long note. We hum the note and sing about the British getting out of Ireland.

Ó ró sé do bheatha 'bhaile . . .

It's a funny song and very polite. It says to the British that we hope they'll keep healthy and have a good trip home. When you sing this song you feel strong. You sit in your desk with all the other boys singing around you at the same time and feel strong in your tummy, right up to your heart, because it's about losing and winning.

The master says Irish history is like a hurling match in Croke Park with his team, County Mayo, losing for a long time, right up until the end of the match when they start coming back and win the game at the last minute. He says that's the best way to win, to lose first. He tells us the story of a man named Cromwell who was winning and sent the Irish to Connaught or Hell. But they made one big mistake, leaving lots of dead people in Ireland to keep talking in the graveyard. The fools, the fools, he says, because then the Easter Rising happened and there was lots of fighting and dying and the British had to go home, even if they didn't want to. Then the game was over and the British flag had to be taken down in Dublin Castle. Michael Collins arrived late and kept the viceroy waiting, but he said the British had kept him waiting for eight hundred years so a few minutes wouldn't make much difference. The master taps the tuning fork and we sing again. Even when we're not singing the song in our class, you still hear it coming from another class somewhere else down the corridor.

My brother gets in trouble because he writes with his left hand and the master wants everyone in Ireland to write with the same hand. Franz can only eat with his left hand and write with his left hand. He's a *ciotóg*, the master says. My mother has to go into school and tell the master that

Onkel Ted was a a *ciotóg*, too, and now he's a Jesuit. But that makes no difference and the master ties Franz's hand behind his back to make sure he can only write with his right hand. All that comes out on the page is a scribble. I want to help him, because the master laughs and says it looks like a snail has crossed the page with ink.

I know what it's like to lose, because I'm Irish and I'm German. My mother says we shouldn't be afraid of losing. Winning makes people mean. It's good that the Irish are not losing any more. It's good to love your country and to be patriotic, but that doesn't mean you have to kill people who belong to other countries. Because that's what the Germans did under the Nazis. They tried to win everything and ended up losing everything. Like a hurling match? Yes, she says slowly, like a very brutal hurling match.

The master says I'm a dreamer and that's worse than being a *ciotóg*. He says I'm always disappearing off to some other place. He wishes he could tie my head down, but that isn't possible, because no matter what happens, you're still free to go anywhere you like inside your own head. You can travel faster than the speed of light to any place you want in the universe, but now it's time to be here in the glorious Republic of Ireland, he says. He bangs his stick on the desk and asks me what blasted country I'm in at all. Germany? So then he has to come down to my desk and drag me back home to Ireland by the ear. The only way that he can stop me from emigrating again is to tie my head down with a poem after school. I have to stay behind and learn a big poem about a priest who was hanged long ago in the town of Ballinrobe where the master comes from in Mayo. We sit in the classroom alone when everyone else has gone home and learn all the verses about the priest being hung, drawn and quartered because he spoke against the British.

I can see that the master has hair growing in his ears, like grass. I think of blood on the grass in Ballinrobe.

There are gangs in the school. At lunchtime, they fight each other in the yard and it's all about winning and losing. One of the gangs is called the cavalry and they are looking for Indians to kill. When you're in a gang, you feel strong in your tummy. You run and shout and everyone else is afraid. But they don't want me any more because I'm a dreamer, so it's best to stand with my back against the wall and make sure they don't get my brother. One day, I saw them running through the yard and they punched a boy right in the stomach. The boy was eating lunch and when they hit him, he dropped his sandwiches and opened his mouth. There was no sound, only a piece of sandwich that came out and dropped on the ground, too. He stayed like that for a long time, leaning forward with his mouth wide open and a dribble coming down. I could tell they were jam sandwiches because the white bread was coloured pink. I thought of his mother making them and now they were wasted. Somebody came and picked them up but he didn't want to eat any more, only cry. Then you could hear his voice coming out loud, like a high screech with lots of pain.

Back in class, the master said there would be no more gangs. The boy who was hit by the cavalry had gone home and the master made a big speech about the potato famine in Ireland. He said the people had green mouths because grass was all that was left to eat. He said it was a disgrace to hit anyone in the stomach while they were eating. I looked out and saw the sandwiches still lying on the ground. The yard was empty. I stared at the seagulls screeching and fighting over the jam sandwiches.

And then the master bangs the desk again, as if he wants

the stick to be a tuning fork and give a long humming note. He says he's fed up with me dreaming and not knowing what country I'm in, so now there's trouble and I feel like going to the toilet quickly. He's going to punish me, but not with the stick, and not with a poem about Ballinrobe or a song about the famine. Instead he's going to send me over to the girls' school and that's the worst punishment of all, to go over there with ribbons in your hair. He takes me by the ear and we travel at the speed of light over to the girl country. I sit at the back of the class and see the girls looking around and giggling, until it's time to go home.

At home, my mother says we have started doing strange things again. When it was nearly dinner time, she told us to put the bowl of mashed potato on the table. My father was talking to her in the kitchen and she was listening and cooking at the same time, so I carried the mashed potato up to the room where we play and took the lid off. With the spoon, I threw a bit of the mash at the wall. It stayed there and we looked at it for a while. I threw another spoonful at the ceiling and it stuck as well. It made a strange sound each time, like a click. It made a different shape each time, too, sometimes like a little cloud, sometimes with a spike pointing downwards.

Maria said she was going to run and tell on me. But I told her that we had to make a sacrifice. I closed the door and said it was our duty to do this for Ireland. We had to make as many shapes as we could. Franz took lumps out with his hand and together we tried to cover the whole ceiling. Sometimes a lump came unstuck and fell down again and Maria screamed. We laughed and threw more and more of it up, until it was all gone and the whole room was covered. My mother came in and saw the glass bowl, empty on the floor. She said we were going out of our minds. My father rushed into the room and looked at bits of mashed potato on the ceiling and said they would never come off. They would be there for ever. We were in real trouble. But my mother wouldn't let him hit us. Instead of getting angry, she said you couldn't punish a thing like that because it happened only once in a lifetime. My father was still frowning, but then she put her arm around him and said it didn't matter going without mashed potato for one day. She said they were lucky to have children with such imagination. She smiled and said you had to have an imagination to do something as mad as that.

Fifteen

I was sick again. The dogs were howling in my chest. At breakfast time I could not even eat the porridge. I looked at the ring of milk around the rim and smelled the warm steam coming up into my face, but my eyes were blurry and I couldn't breathe. My father said I was trying not to go to school. He was a schoolteacher once and he knew when people were making things up, he said, and if I was really sick I wouldn't have to prove it. But when it was time to go to school, my legs were soft and I couldn't walk. I heard Franz say that my face was white, so then my mother and father had to help me up the stairs, one either side. And halfway up my head dropped down on the step in front of me and I felt the cold wood on my forehead. I heard the sound of buzzing in my ears and the sound of my mother calling me from far away. Then I fell asleep.

When I woke up again my father was gone. Only my mother was there sitting on the stairs waiting for me to come back. She asked me if I was ready to go on and then she helped me the rest of the way up to bed. She stayed with me and sat on the bed repairing a jumper, pulling a blue woollen thread across the elbow. Some boys in school had leather elbows, but we had dark blue elbows. She told me stories to make the howling go away. So I lay there watching her, and sometimes I fell asleep and woke up again later, only to see that she was still mending the same spot and telling the same story, as if no time was going by.

She told me about the time there was a big fire in Kempen. She was afraid of fire, she said, because her sister Lisalotte's hair once caught fire on a candle. When you see something like that happening with your own two eyes, when you see it happen to somebody else it's much worse and you remember it more than when it happens to yourself. She can't forget the time people came to set fire to the synagogue and she hopes I never have to witness something like that with my own two eyes. That was the time Germany was sick and took a long time to get better.

My mother had to leave school early and go to work. Onkel Gerd had no more money once he lost his job as lord mayor. She got a job in the Kempen registry office and had to learn typing and filing names in alphabetical order. She remembers people coming in to find out if their grandfathers or grandmothers had ever been Jewish. She remembers how happy one old woman was, how she had tears in her eyes and put her hand on her heart when she found out that she was one of the lucky ones. Other people were not so lucky. Every day, they came to make sure they were not Jewish. Every day, Ta Maria wondered if the Catholics would be next. It wasn't long afterwards that the Nazis closed down the convent in Mühlhausen and wrote dirty words all over the classrooms.

My mother had long plaits at that time, down to her waist, like two dark ropes. But Ta Maria said it was time to cut them. It was time to grow up and look like an adult. So one day she stopped being a girl. She asked the hairdresser to give her the Olympia Roll, because that's what all the women were wearing in the films, but, by then, her hair had already been cut too short and she had to wait for it to grow again. She says it's funny how you can get so upset about something like that, how important those things can be and how you can sometimes cry more about little things than all the big things put together. She had to wear a hat and Ta Maria promised to go down to Krefeld with her and make up for it with new shoes.

My mother says she was at work when the trouble happened and saw nothing herself. She only heard about it later from her youngest sister Minne. But she smelled the smoke in the streets that afternoon. The synagogue was on fire and the fire brigade was standing by, doing nothing. Men in brown uniforms had gone around to the Jewish houses and Minne saw them going by with red batons. She said the curtains were flapping out through the broken windows and there were books lying on the pavement. Somebody's private letters were flying around in the street like litter and there were children walking around the town with black and white ivory keys that belonged to a piano.

Onkel Gerd said they could not be part of this. You couldn't watch something like that. People in Kempen blew their breath out slowly and thought how lucky they were not to be Jewish. That same evening, they all went to the big Catholic procession in the town where hundreds of people quietly passed through the Buttermarkt square with candles and torches, praying and singing hymns as if they needed to be especially close to God from then on.

The next day Ta Maria brought my mother to Krefeld, but you couldn't buy anything that day. When they entered the shopping street they saw shoes thrown out on to the ground. The Germans would regret this one day, Ta Maria said. It was not so long ago that they were wearing newspapers around their feet. And now there were shoes lying everywhere on the ground and people stepping over them. You could smell the leather. For a moment it even looked like a shoe paradise where you could just pick them up and try them on. This was the city where my mother's mother sang at the state opera house. Now people were stopping to look through the broken shop windows. A man with a clapper board was walking along the pavement advertising ladies' stockings as if nothing had happened. It made no sense. Expensive shoes. Brand new. Some of the best quality. Some still in their boxes, or only half out, on display. Some other boxes trampled flat, and the thin, blue-grey paper that goes to wrap new shoes blowing up and down the street as if nobody cared, as if nobody needed footwear any more, as if they hated shoes.

I couldn't breathe very well. My shoulders were going up and down trying to get air. My mother stroked my head and listened to the howling in my chest. She prayed that I would get better. She smiled at me and said everything would soon be fine again, because her oldest sister Marianne was coming with her daughter Christiane. And Tante Marianne was very good at helping people breathe. She helped people in Salzburg when it was hard to breathe.

For days and days my mother was cleaning the house. She polished the stairs and every piece of wood in the house was shining. She put fruit in a bowl on the table and baked a cake. Tante Marianne was going to get my room. It had no wallpaper any more, only pink plaster and some long cracks, but my mother said it looked clean and friendly, and that's all that mattered. And as soon as Marianne walked in the front door, she would see the old oak trunk that came from their house on the Buttermarkt and think she was at home.

My mother put on her blue suit with the big white collars. She put the big number 4711 on her wrists and wore the green Smaragd snake. We put on our best clothes, too, with no blue elbows, and kept looking out the window until Tante Marianne and Christiane arrived in a taxi with suitcases. Then my mother dropped her apron on the floor of the kitchen and ran all the way along the hallway smiling and crying at the same time. Tante Marianne was smiling and crying, too, as they embraced and stood back to look each other up and down.

'Ja, ja, ja,' they kept saying. And then, 'Nein, nein, nein.'

They could not believe their own eyes. They shook their heads and wiped their tears and embraced each other again. Ja, ja, ja, and nein, nein, nein, and ja, ja, ja, until Tante Marianne turned around to look at us. She knew our names from letters and photographs, but she had to kneel down and look at us properly, one at a time. She knew everything. She knew about Maria's picture of my mother with the arms going all around the walls. She knew that I slapped the schoolteacher. And she knew about the mashed potato on the ceiling.

My father carried in the suitcases and smiled at everyone. Christiane talked to us and Tante Marianne talked to my mother as if they couldn't waste a minute. They went through each of the names one by one – Ta Maria, Elfriede, Adam, Lisalotte, Max, Minne and Wilhelm, and all the children, as if they had to travel around Germany in their heads until every question was asked and every story was told. My mother had to hear everything twice and clapped her hands around her face as if she could not believe what she heard.

Tante Marianne brought new perfume into the house. Everyone wanted to be close to her all the time and sit beside her at the table. Maria followed her everywhere. My mother and Tante Marianne could not be separated either, because they kept talking, even when they were not in the same room. Even when Tante Marianne was upstairs and my mother was in the kitchen, they kept remembering things out loud, calling up and down the stairs as if they were at home again in the house on the Buttermarkt square. Tante Marianne called her Irmgard. We still called her Mutti, and it was like having two mothers in the house, because they had the same teeth and the same eyes and the same hair. They had the same words and the same way of laughing out loud until the tears came into their eyes. They had the same way of peeling an orange in strips along the side and the same trick of cutting the peel into the shape of teeth. Two mothers playing the monster with big orange teeth while my father was out getting coal for the boiler.

'Vooo, vooo, vooo, vooo . . .,' they both said. Then they started laughing so much that they couldn't stop any more. Laughing and shaking, so that my father stopped pouring coal into the boiler to come and see what was happening.

Tante Marianne's suitcase was full of toys and books for everyone. There were lots of gummi bears and chocolates and biscuits that you would never get in the shops in Ireland. She brought a spirit level for my father, and a toy train for me and Franz. Some other presents were wrapped and put away immediately, for Christmas. There were biscuits to be eaten now and biscuits to be kept for later. One by one, Tante Marianne took things out with great care, explaining where they came from. We were allowed to read the *Mecki* books immediately, about a hedgehog who travelled all over the world in a hot air balloon with his crew – Charlie Penguin, and a cat called Kater Murr. Nobody in Ireland knows about Mecki, and they laugh at us because we don't know who Red Riding Hood is and we don't realise it's the same as Rotkäpchen.

Everything in our house was German again. Around the table every evening, all the stories were German. Tante Marianne's daughter Christiane had plaits tied up over her head and she wore a dirndl like in fairy tales. Maria got a dirndl as well. Tante Marianne said it was lovely to see Franz and me wearing lederhosen and Irish sweaters, German below and Irish on top. She said it was remarkable that we could speak three languages. My mother told her how we sometimes got things wrong and how Maria came home one day and said: *Ich kann es nicht believen*, which is a mixed up German and English way of saying: I can't believe it. Tante Marianne said our German was different, softer, more like the old days. And she wanted to hear some Irish spoken, so we said a prayer and she said it sounded different too, not a bit like English.

I wanted Tante Marianne to stay in our house for ever. I went with her down to the seafront. I showed her all the street signs that had been changed into Irish. I showed her where the doctor lives and where the shops are. I told her that when you pass by the shoemaker's shop you get an echo, because when you shout in, the shoemaker shouts back without looking up. She laughed and said it was just like something her father would do. People stopped to speak to her. The man in the fish shop recognised her immediately and said: 'You must be the sister.' He talked to her for a long time and Tante Marianne had to explain that she was from Germany, too, but that she was now living in Austria, in Salzburg.

'Salzburg,' he said. 'I know the place you're talking about.'

We went with her on the bus to Glendalough to see the round tower. We had tea and cakes in a hotel and helped her stick stamps on lots of postcards. She said Ireland was so beautiful. She envied my mother living in a country where the people were so friendly and spoke English all the time. But my father didn't like her saying that. He tried to stop himself being angry at the table that night. He didn't want to make any trouble while there was a visitor in the house, but there was something Tante Marianne didn't understand yet about Ireland, something that had to be explained.

'One day, the man in the fish shop will speak his own language,' he said.

Tante Marianne said there was nothing wrong with speaking English. But my father shook his head. He said we were the new Irish children and soon the whole country would be speaking Irish in the shops. He said children were the strongest weapons, stronger than armies. But then Tante Marianne had an argument with my father. She said all the things that my mother can't say. She said it was wrong to use children in war. She kept her arm around Maria all the time as if she was going to protect her for the rest of her life.

'In Germany,' she said, 'they used the children, too.'

That was the only argument in our house while she was there. On the last evening, before she was going away, she showed us a photograph of the house where she lived in Austria. It was a house with a small wooden fence outside, near the castle on the hill called the Mönchberg. One day we would go and visit her. And then they talked about all the other well-known visitors that came to stay there every summer. People like Oskar Kokoschka, the famous painter. People like Ernst Rathenau, whose cousin Walther was assassinated by the Nazis in Berlin. My mother looked at the photograph and said it was a good place to breathe in deeply. She said you could look out the window and see the castle above you every morning, as if it had just grown out of the rock overnight.

When Tante Marianne was gone home again, Christiane stayed with us so that she could go to school in Ireland and learn English. My mother told me the story of going to visit her sister Marianne in the snow. It was during the war, when nobody had much food. My mother took a train all the way to Salzburg and walked up the Mönchberg in winter with a bucket of sauerkraut, because Marianne had nothing. She says she remembers the thick snow all around and the silence. Tante Marianne was always very strong, even though sad things happened in her life and her husband Angelo never came back from the war. My mother and Marianne met Angelo on the same day, when they were out in the country one time, on holiday. And afterwards Angelo sent a parcel to each of them with the exact same gift inside, a book by Thomas Mann. But it was Marianne who married him while the war was still on. They married by proxy, my mother says. One day Marianne sat in the house in Salzburg with a picture of Angelo and a glass of wine in front of her, while Angelo sat around with his friends in Split and a picture of Marianne in front of him. They got married miles and miles apart. And that's why they're still so close, even though she heard nothing more and no more letters came home. She waited and waited, but he never came back from the war. And then one day, Marianne started up a guest house. And that's why all the famous guests like Ernst Rathenau and Oskar Kokoschka are coming to stay in her house on the Mönchberg, because

Marianne was kind to people with bad lungs who couldn't breathe very well in Germany and now they're being kind back to her.

I was better again. The howling stopped. But there was trouble for us on the street. Everybody knew that we were German again. In the fish shop, the man leaned over the counter to look at us and say the word *Achtung*, as if all the people in Ireland were going to speak German from now on. Everybody in the shop turned around. He tried some more German words and I know he's only joking, because he's a nice man with a red face and who laughs so loud that it echoes around the fish shop. Other people are the same, they keep asking us to say things in German. But we're afraid. I pretend I don't know any German. I pretend I'm Irish and speak only English. But the boys outside the shops can see us wearing lederhosen, so they call us Nazis.

'*Donner und Blitzen*,' I hear them shout. With one arm up in the air they keep saying: '*Sieg Heil*.'

I know they get all those words from reading comics in the barber shop. My mother says that's all they know about Germany. My father says there's always somebody laughing in Ireland. He doesn't let comics into the house because they are in English and have Germans dying on every page.

Then it's time to talk about Christmas. Because Christmas is something German, too. My mother tells us that pink skies are a sign of the angels baking. The angels leave sweets on the stairs. My mother sings '*Tannenbaum*' and then, as if she asked for it, the snow started falling. Thick flakes coming down silently and we hardly even noticed it. We ran into the street and looked up at the snow falling past the street light. One or two flakes fell on to my eyes and gave me white eyelashes. Franz opened his mouth and tried to eat some of the snow as it came down and he said it was like free ice pops. My mother came out and said we should all wash our faces. She scooped up the snow from the wall with her bare hands and rubbed it against her face. Wonderful, she said, and we all did the same after her, even my father, cleaning our faces with the new white snow.

Sixteen

It was a new snow country. It snowed right through the night and by Christmas morning, when I woke up and looked out the window, I could see Germany. Everything was covered over and swollen with snow. The roofs of the houses, the cars, the trees, the garden walls, even the rubbish bins were white and clean. On the way to Mass the street was like a silent room and Maria said the snow was talking under our feet. There was a lost glove which somebody had stuck on a spike in the railings so that the person who owned it could come back and find it again. But now it was covered in snow like a big white hand saying stop.

I knew that snow was not just for children, because my mother said it turned everybody into a child, even my father. He didn't want to let on that he was excited. He didn't want to make snowballs or anything like that, but I could see that he was happy because when they got married at Christmas in Germany, they travelled all the way down along the Rhine together in the snow. Snow was something German, he said. Normally the winter was too mild in Ireland and the only snow that you would see was in pictures on biscuit tins, or else as cotton wool on the crib or as icing sugar on cakes. It was the Gulf Stream, he explained. He laughed and said that Ireland would rather belong to a different climate because people had started growing palm trees in their gardens. Guest houses along the coast were called Santa Maria and Stella Maris, and there were lots of streets like Vico Road and Sorrento Terrace that made you feel like you were in a warmer country. But on Christmas morning all the streets should have had German names because everything was wrapped in white, even the palm trees.

The only thing different was the Christmas lights blinking on and off in the windows. I knew that my mother and father would never have fairy lights on the tree. Instead we had candles, because that's what they did in Germany and my mother even had special candleholders that clipped on to the branches. We had hanging chocolate angels and lots of other things that had come in a big parcel from Germany. I knew that other children had Santa Claus and they knew what he was going to bring them. Sometimes people in the street would ask us what Santa was going to bring and we didn't know. We never talked about that. One of the neighbours once brought us to see Santa in one of the shops, but I could see his brown fingers from smoking. He was coughing a lot and I saw him afterwards having a cup of tea with his beard off. I knew who he was, too, because I saw him coming out of the Eagle House another time and he wasn't able to walk very well and had to hold on to the wall.

We had Christkind instead and everything was a secret anyway until the very last minute. We were not even allowed into the front room for Advent, because some of the gifts were already laid out in the corner behind the sofa under a big brown sheet of paper. We were only allowed in to help with the Christmas tree, and once, when my mother had to leave the room to get something, I wanted to look under the brown sheet, but I was afraid the Christkind would take all the presents away again. My mother said it was not the gifts that would be taken away but the surprise, which was worse. I knew that other children were getting guns and cowboy suits, but we never got guns or swords or anything to do with fighting. Instead, we got a surprise, as well as something made by my father and something educational, like a microscope.

It was hard to wait. We stood in a line in the hallway, the youngest first and the oldest last. My father was in the front room lighting all the candles and we could smell the matches. When everything was ready, he opened the door wide and the candles were reflected in his glasses. My mother started singing 'Tannenbaum' as we slowly walked into the room and found all the gifts and sweets laid out on the chairs. There was even a trail of sweets on the floor as if the Christkind had been in a hurry at the last minute. Then everything was a surprise. There were toys and games and books from Germany and I knew I was so lucky that we were German at Christmas. We kneeled down to say thank you, and then my father put on the record of the Cologne Children's Choir so that the whole house filled up with the bells of the Cologne Cathedral ringing out across the sea to Dublin. We might as well be in Kempen, my mother said, with the taste of *Pretzel* and *Lebkuchen* and marzipan potatoes rolled in cinnamon.

Later on, we went out to play in the snow. We built a snowman in the front garden, and it was only when we saw other children on the street that we realised where we were. There were marks where they had scraped snow off the pavement or off the walls and you could see Ireland underneath. A car had skidded, too, and left two black streaks on the road. We went from one garden to the next looking for new untouched sheets of snow, where the ground was still under a dream. And when all the other children had disappeared inside for Christmas dinner, we went as far as the football field to see how deep the snow was there.

But then we were ambushed by a gang of boys. We had never seen them before and it looked like they had been waiting for us. We were trapped in the lane and couldn't get home again. Maria and I ran away into the field through an opening in the barbed-wire fence, but they chased after us. The others had already caught Franz and pushed him up against the wall, holding a stick across his neck. They twisted his arm up behind his back and made him walk towards the field where Maria and I were caught, too, near a line of tall eucalyptus trees. One of them was forcing snow up under Maria's jacket and she was starting to cry.

'Leave us alone,' she said, but they just laughed.

Franz said nothing. He just stood there and waited in silence. He was doing what my mother always said we should do, to pretend they didn't exist. I did the same. I tried to pretend that standing in that spot in the football field was exactly what I wanted to do at that moment. I remembered what my mother said about fighting. Maria stopped resisting, too, and they gave up putting snow under her jumper because it was no fun any more. They were not afraid of anything. They pushed us back against the wire fence of the football field with sticks. The leader of the gang was not even afraid of the cold, because he picked up snow and caked it into a flat, icy disc while the other boys all blew into their cupped red hands for warmth.

'Nazi bastards,' he said.

They made a circle around us and whispered among themselves. One of the boys was pushing a dirty piece of brown snow towards Franz with his shoe, saying that he was going to make him eat it. But Franz ignored him. I knew Franz was saying the silent negative in his head. Then Maria started crying and I wanted to cry as well only Franz stopped me.

'Don't indulge them,' he said.

They repeated it a few times in a German accent. And for some of them it was a sign to start speaking in a kind of gibberish that made no sense. *'Gotten, Blitzen, fuckin' Himmel.'* One of the boys started dancing around, trampling a circle in the snow with *'Sieg Heils'* and I suddenly wanted to start laughing. I thought they were very funny and I wanted to be Irish like them, to laugh and make up some of these stupid words, too, all the stuff they had collected from the comics and from films where the Germans were always losers. One of them tried to speak German by himself with his face all contorted with pain.

'Rippen schtoppen . . . Krauts. Donner und Blitzen, Himmel, Gunther-Schwein . . . Messerschmidt . . .' he said in one long burst. Then he suddenly died in the snow, falling back and shaking as if he was riddled with bullets. *'Aaargh . . .'*

I couldn't help laughing. I could see myself as part of the gang, joining in and walking around the streets with them, laughing at everything. It made me feel soft in my tummy to think that I could be friends with them. But the leader didn't like it. He wanted me to be the enemy and to see how tough us Germans really were. So he flung the snowball and it hit me in the eye with a flash of white, like a hard lump of icy stone. I couldn't see anything and I rubbed my eye, but I didn't let myself cry because I didn't want to let my brother down. I showed them that nothing could hurt me and that Germans didn't feel pain.

They continued to talk among themselves, trying to

decide what to do with us. I heard one of them say that we should be put on trial.

'Yeah, put them on trial,' they all agreed.

'Guilty or not guilty?'

I knew that whatever they said about us we could never deny it. Whether it was true or not didn't matter any more. They said things about the sinking of the Bismarck or the gas ovens but we didn't know anything like that yet. I wanted to tell them what my mother said about the silent negative, but I knew they would only laugh at that. It was no use. We were at the mercy of their court in the snow. There was nobody else in the world to say who was right or wrong. Everybody was inside on Christmas day and we were alone on the white football field with a breeze pushing the tops of the trees behind us. Above the tall goal posts, the sky was grey and green again and it looked like there would be more snow. Low on the sky there were flashes of white or silver seagulls and I knew we just had to wait.

'We have to go home now,' Maria suddenly said, as if she could just bring this whole thing to an end by acting like an adult. She tried to move forward, but they only pushed her back again.

'Execute them,' one of them shouted.

They didn't even have time for a trial. Maybe they were numb with the cold like us and wanted to go home to eat sweets and play with toys, so they decided to get on with the sentence and started to make snowballs. One of them said to pack them hard and another one of them included the discoloured piece of snow in his armoury, and when they all had heaps of white cannon balls ready beside their feet, we waited for the order and watched the leader of the gang raise his hand. It seemed like an endless wait. I thought of all kinds of things that had nothing to do with being a Nazi. I remembered that the words in Irish for grey and green are the same. I thought of marzipan potatoes. And the peculiar skull-shaped design of plum pudding. I thought of the bell on the wall of my father and mother's bedroom that didn't work any more, and I thought of the three little dials on the gas meter under the stairs, until the hand eventually came down and a shout brought with it a hail of blinding white fire.

'It's only snow,' Franz said.

He had his hands up over his eyes. Even after they were gone and the football field was empty and silent and it was already starting to get dark, he still had his hands up.

We might as well have been in Kempen, sitting in the front room eating Christmas cake, while my father lit the candles on the Christmas tree one more time. We sat on the carpet and played a game of cards where one person was always left with a picture of the black crow and had to be marked on the nose with a piece of charcoal, until everybody was a loser once and had a black nose. My father stood up and opened the door of the big bookcase to take out the bottle of Asbach Uralt. He took out the cork with a tiny, high-pitched squeak that sounded like a hiccup and poured two glasses so that the room filled up with a smell of cognac, along with the smell of pine needles and matches and candle wax.

'A cognac-een,' my mother called it. She liked to make things sound smaller than they were, like they did in Irish, too, because everything was better when it was small and harmless and less greedy. She sipped slowly and closed her eyes so she could think about what she was drinking. She said it was like a little kiss from God above. She laughed and said it again, like a tiny, little kiss from God.

My father then put on a record. He took it out of the

sleeve and made sure not to touch the music with his fingers as he placed it on the turntable. He frowned as he did it, but I knew that nobody could be angry, because it was Christmas. When he dropped the needle down lightly with his index finger, you could hear a crackle before the woman began to sing in German, a high voice that was so beautiful, my mother said, it was like silver coins falling down the stairs. And at the end, there was a single note that rose up so high in the air that it stayed in the room long after the song was over.

Sometimes a candle crackled and spluttered. And outside it was dark. I knew the football field was empty now and there was nobody out in the world. More snow was covering the footprints and it was easy to forget what happened. We had been executed but we were warm and there was a nice smell of the Christmas tree in the room, so it was easy to forget how cold and numb your hands could be outside. We had orange juice to drink and chocolate angels to eat. My father was putting on another record and my mother sniffed the cognac-een. Everybody was safe now and we were lucky to be German, but I knew it wasn't over yet.

Seventeen

I keep thinking of things not happening.

If you lie in bed and think hard enough, you can pretend that lots of things don't happen. I can pretend that I'm floating above the bed and that my feet are miles away across the sea. I can pretend that I can't use my left arm, that I only have one arm, like Mr Smyth in the vegetable shop. I can pretend that my father has no limp. And I keep thinking there was no such thing as Hitler, or the Nazis, because then my mother would not fall on the ice and break her teeth. The day we go down to Mass early in the morning, when it's still dark and there's ice on all the roads and we have to hold her hand, I keep thinking that didn't happen.

My mother says I'm a dreamer and it's true what they say about me in school. I'm the boy who lives a million miles away in outer space. She smiles at me with all her new teeth and says goodnight. But she's the one who is dreaming and still hoping that some things didn't happen at all, because she stays in the room after she's switched off the light, just to stand at the window for a while before she goes downstairs again. The light from the street outside makes the branches of the trees blow across her face. It's very quiet and she doesn't say a word for a long time.

'Nobody can force you to smile,' she says.

'What?' I ask. But I know she's not even talking to me, only to herself, as if she's the last person left in the room.

'They can make you show your teeth, but what good is that? Nobody can make you smile against your will.'

It's hard to find out what she means sometimes, but I know that she's talking about the bad film in Germany when the houses and trains were on fire. She's standing there with the black and white branches moving across her face and across the wall behind her, as if she's stuck on the screen, standing under the light waiting for somebody.

I know that she had lots of men who wanted to go out with her in Germany, but they were all 'brown', which meant that they were Nazis and she had to wait for something better. Ta Maria kept saying that it wasn't a good time for men. I'm glad I'm not looking for a husband myself, she often said. I'd rather a soldier with a missing leg any day than one of those young house-devils in brown uniform. So my mother said no to them all. And then she always laughs and sings the song about the man kissing the dog.

Ich küsse Ihre Hand Madam, und denk es wär Ihr Mund.
Ich küsse Ihren Mund Madam, und denk es wär Ihr Hund.

I kiss your hand, Madame, and wish it was your mouth.
I kiss your mouth, Madame, and wish it was your hound.

So she waited and carried on working at the registry office in Kempen, until one day when she went on holiday with Marianne to the Eifel mountains and they both met Angelo.

He was a good man. He was serious and had great humour. It was hard to know which of them he was more interested in at first, because he paid them both the same amount of attention. He had read the same poems by Rilke that they had also read. He was polite and eager not to leave either one of them out of the conversation. If he spent a morning walking through the fields with Marianne, then he would make up for it in the afternoon coming back with her younger sister. At night in their campbeds, they whispered about him as if he was the last good man left in Germany.

I know they were the best two weeks that my mother ever spent in her life, because she still likes to talk about them. And sometime later, she received a parcel from him with a scarf inside and a book. She was so excited about the gift that she went around and told everyone, even all the old people working in the registry office, until Marianne wrote to say that she too had got a scarf, and the same book. So then it was time to give way, my mother says, because that was Angelo and he married Marianne later on and never came home from the war.

And then she's gone. The branches are still waving across the screen, but she's downstairs again, clacking on the typewriter, putting down all the things that she can't say to anyone, not even my father. Things you can't say in a song, or a story, only on the typewriter for people to read later on sometime, on their own, without looking into your eyes.

She got a new job in Düsseldorf, working in the central employment office. She was glad to be in a city at last where things were happening and you could go to the theatre and meet new people. The office was run by an energetic man named Stiegler who arrived every morning smelling of aftershave, dressed in a lovely suit with the newspaper already read and folded under his arm. He wore good shoes and always had his hair combed. He greeted everyone by name and shook everyone's hand, clasping it in both of his with great warmth. She was the youngest and the older women in the office said he was a good boss who liked a joke from time to time, unlike the crusty old boss that went before him. Herr Stiegler was human, they said, and not bad looking at all. He was modern, too, because even though he was married himself, that didn't stop him flirting harmlessly now and again, just for the fun of it. And whenever it was somebody's birthday, he made sure that it was remembered.

I know that she didn't like the work very much, but Herr Stiegler praised her and said she was intelligent. He was good with compliments. And if she made a mistake in her typing, he would not shout or humiliate her in front of the other women, but instead just point to the misspelling so that she could quietly go and do it again. It was a matter of being obedient and efficient, however boring and senseless the work was. Even when she once made a big mistake and he should have been really angry, he just smiled and said quite honestly that it was pigs' work. He expected more from her. And the way he said it was so inspiring that you could only vow to do better in future.

There was little contact with the other workers outside the office hours. They all went home to their families. So one evening, Herr Stiegler invited her out to the theatre to meet his wife. And Frau Stiegler was so kind and kept the conversation going afterwards over a glass of wine at a nearby café. They were cultured people, she discovered, and some days later, when Herr Stiegler noticed a book of

Rilke poems in her bag at the office, he was able to discuss them with her and even went on to suggest that she should read a poet named Stefan George, a real German master. He said the greatest poets were also the greatest patriots.

In Düsseldorf she didn't feel so much like an orphan any more. She was a grown-up now. At nineteen years of age, her other sisters envied her because she was able to do lots of new things, like going to concerts and watching the latest films that would take years to arrive in a small town like Kempen. She bought new clothes and changed her hair. The Olympia Roll didn't quite suit her any more and she decided to wear it more casually, in natural curls that other women in the office said they would give their right eye for. Everyone admired her, even Herr Stiegler, though he didn't comment openly. He waited until he found a big mistake in her typing and then he came right over to her desk and informed her that he was a little disappointed with her work.

'But the hairstyle,' he whispered, 'that's a big success.'

My mother says if we could all see into the future and tell what's coming then it would be a wonderful world altogether. Lots of things wouldn't happen at all. If you could tell the future then you could stop trains crashing into each other. She says the Germans are very good at finding out what's going to happen and being ready for it because of all the things that have gone wrong before. But lots of things in this world still happen for the first time and sometimes people just don't expect it.

Everybody must have known that there was another war coming. Herr Stiegler was away a good bit after that, setting up new recruitment programmes in various towns and cities in the region. It was all in the newspaper, too. The women in the office cut out a picture of Herr

Stiegler, smiling and saluting along with leading figures in the Nazi party.

And then one day, he picked her out to set up an office in the town of Venlo, on the Dutch border. The whole thing had to be restructured and he would need a dynamic assistant. Out of all the women in the department, he chose her for this important job. She was very happy and a little embarrassed to think that the others in the office were giving her jealous glances. She got ready and took the train to Venlo and started working immediately with energy. There would be no more typing errors, she vowed. She got a small room at the top of the administration building where she would stay and it was nice to have the whole house to herself at night.

On the second night, Herr Stiegler came back to the office because he had forgotten something important. She heard him downstairs. He was very polite and came up to her room, just to make sure that she didn't get a fright, hearing somebody in the office below. It was only him, he assured her. When he tried the handle of the door and found that she kept it locked at night, he laughed and said she had nothing to fear. But even then she didn't open the door, because it wasn't right to let a man into her room at night.

Herr Stiegler went downstairs to look for what he needed. And afterwards he came back up once more to speak to her again through the door. He said he had forgotten to mention it before but that he had brought something for her, just something small, a book of poetry. It was Stefan George. She said thank you very much, it was very kind of him, but that she had already gone to bed and she hoped she wasn't being rude by waiting for it until the morning in the office. So then Herr Stiegler said he just quickly wanted to point out a line or two in the book.

'My wife is downstairs,' he said. 'I better not keep her waiting.'

'She's here, in Venlo?'

'Of course,' Herr Stiegler said.

So then she had to get dressed quickly and open the door. And before she knew it he was in the room, reading out one of the poems and telling her what it meant. She was nervous and didn't like the way he talked about the poetry. He was breathless. She was afraid that Frau Stiegler would suddenly come upstairs and there would be trouble.

'I must ask you to leave now,' she insisted, but he just smiled at her and asked what she was so afraid of.

'Come on,' he said. He put the book down and stepped towards her. She could smell the cognac on his breath as he put his hands straight on her waist. She tried to push him away. She tried to remind him that his wife was downstairs waiting.

'Frau Stiegler . . .,' she kept saying, but that didn't stop him.

'Come on, Fraülein Kaiser, don't make such a big fuss,' he said. And then she was afraid because she knew what was coming but she couldn't stop it.

I can see the branches dancing across the street light outside. I can see them swinging from side to side along the wall in my room. I can hear my mother clacking downstairs on the typewriter, putting everything down on paper for later. She can't stop what's happening, but she can write it down instead, how she struggled to keep Herr Stiegler away from her. All she could think of doing was to call through the open door, down along the empty corridor.

'Frau Stiegler,' she shouted. 'Upstairs.'

But that made no difference, because she realised at last that his wife was not there at all. He had come alone. The whole building was empty and there was nobody she could call for help. Herr Stiegler had planned it. Maybe he had even planned the whole office expansion for this. She said she was an honest woman. She threatened that she would go to the police, the Gestapo, but he didn't seem to care. Nothing would stop him, not even when she started screaming and she could hear the echo of her own voice going through the whole building. There was nobody to hear it. Then he just slapped her across the face, twice, very hard, for making such a big pantomime out of it all. Her face was stinging and she got the salty taste of blood.

'You have to be able to make a sacrifice,' he said.

And that was the worst thing of all, that he accused her of not being able to make a sacrifice. So then she started crying helplessly, because she knew that he was much stronger and that she was trapped now and could not stop him doing what he wanted. There was nothing more that she could do to resist. She repeated the silent negative in her head again and again until it was over. Then Herr Stiegler said she should smile.

'Give me a little smile,' he kept saying afterwards, but she couldn't. And then he forced her to smile. He ordered her to smile. He put his fingers up to her mouth and pushed her lips apart so that she had to show her teeth.

There was lots of ice on the road and it was still dark as we went down to Mass. The street lights were still on and I could see a shine on the road where the ice was slippery. My mother told us to hold her hand, Franz on one side and me on the other. And when we were crossing the street, my mother suddenly pulled her hand away and fell forward. I heard her falling and I heard a click when her mouth hit the ground. Franz fell, too, at the same time and he was sitting down in the street. I tried to help my mother to get up, but she stayed there on her knees, looking around as if she didn't know where she was, as if she had just woken up in Ireland for the first time. She said nothing. She was looking for something, feeling the ground with her hand in the dark as if she was blind. She took out a small white handkerchief that she sometimes wipes my face with at the last minute before going into the church. She started picking things up and putting them into the handkerchief.

'Mutti, are you all right?' Franz asked, because he was the only person who could speak. My mother nodded and put her hand on his head. But when she stood up I could see that there was blood in her mouth. I could see that she had no front teeth and no smile. She put her hand over her mouth and we started walking again, very slowly this time. And when we got to the church we didn't go to Mass at all. We just blessed ourselves and said a quick prayer and then a man came to take us home in his car. All the way home the car was skidding over to the side and the man said it was lucky there were no other cars on the road.

My mother smiles at me with her new teeth and says it's all forgotten now. Everything can be repaired, she says, except your memory. A lot worse happened to other people, things we should not forget. The Germans broke their teeth, she said. But you can't be thinking about things not happening. You can be careful to make sure it never happens again, but you can't be still trying to stop things after they've happened. She laughs and smiles again, with her eyes, too, this time. And then she starts singing the song about the man kissing the dog.

Eighteen

My father took over the *Kinderzimmer*. That's the room we play in and keep our toys in, the room most people call the dining room. It's the room with the mashed potato still on the ceiling. Now my father says he's going to start a new factory and he needs a place where he can make things. First of all he built a workbench in one corner that's so heavy it can never be moved again. It has a vice at one end and lots of space underneath for spare pieces of wood that might be needed later. Then he made a press on the wall where he could hang up lots of tools like chisels and a saw and a wooden mallet. And before you start buying anything like wood or glue or screws, before you even start measuring and sawing, you have to have an idea. You have to draw a plan.

My father has great ideas for things that are badly needed in Ireland, like *Wägelchen*. They have lots of them in Germany, my mother says, but none in Ireland. So he drew a picture of one that looked just like a box with lots of measurements. He can see it in his head. He can see exactly what it will look like when it's finished, a German boxcar with stickers of forests and mountains and fairy tales stuck on to the sides. He calls it the prototype and we're allowed to watch while he works every evening after he comes home.

'Is it for us?' Maria asks.

'Yes and no.'

'Is it for Ireland?'

'Yes and no.'

He keeps frowning as he works. He has to concentrate hard and you can see the tip of his tongue coming out the side of his mouth. He says you have to measure everything twice because you can only cut once. Then you see the sawdust falling on the floor like snow. You see wooden curls falling like blond hair. There are some thin, cut-off pieces of wood, too, that look like swords for us to fight with. Sometimes you can hear him whistling a tune as he works every night until it's very late. Even long after we go to bed you can still hear the sound of the hand-drill squeaking and sometimes the mallet banging, until my mother goes into the *Kinderzimmer* to put her arm around him and tell him the world wasn't made in one day either and there's plenty of time tomorrow. But he still wants to finish one more little thing and after that it's quiet again with everyone asleep.

One night he was working so late it was after midnight. You could hear him sanding all the time and it sounded like he was telling everyone to be quiet.

'Shish . . . Shish . . . Shish . . .' he kept saying.

Then there was a smell of paint in the whole house that was nicer than any other smell in the world. And in the morning when we got up, the first *Wägelchen* was standing all ready in the hallway, painted red with black wheels and a rope for pulling tied at the front. My mother clapped her hands and said it was beautiful, just like one of the toy trolleys she had when she was small. There was a new baby in our house called Ita and everybody was always gathering around her and trying to make her smile. My mother took the baby and laid her in the new red *Wägelchen* so that we could make her smile and my father could take a photograph. And then it's time for him to go to work with the trolley under his arm and a list that my mother typed up of all the things that went into it, how much everything cost, from the wood to the wheels, down to the cheapest thing which is the glue.

In the shops in Dublin, they kept saying it was beautiful but too expensive. Even when my father told them it was made in Ireland, even when he showed them the list of materials and explained how long he spent working on it, they still shook their heads and said nobody in Ireland had the money to spend on a boxcar. A boxcar is not something people buy in shops, no matter how beautiful it is. When he walked around the city at lunchtime every day with the *Wägelchen* under his arm, people stopped to ask him where he got it. Which doesn't mean they want to buy it or that the shops want anything that's handmade. But that doesn't stop him either. Every night after he comes home on the train he goes into the *Kinderzimmer* to work on the next one. Because one day, he says, Irish people will stop buying only things that are made in Britain. One day Ireland will have its own great inventions.

Everybody in our house is busy working and inventing things. Franz is making a bridge with Meccano and Maria is learning how to knit. If my father is not busy making more trolleys, then he's in the greenhouse sowing trays of seeds so that he can plant as many different flowers as possible when the summer comes. There will be lots to eat as well like cabbage and peas and tomatoes from the greenhouse. My mother is busy all the time, too, trying to make the new baby talk and eat up, but Ita just keeps moving around and my mother has to chase her. She sits on the potty all day and my mother is still trying to make her eat the last spoon. Ita knows the fastest way of getting around the house, sitting on the potty and pulling herself along by the heels of her shoes without saying a word because she still hasn't swallowed the last spoon and her mouth is full. My mother is trying not to spend money, and one day she bought a big tongue from the butcher, a cow's tongue which she said was very cheap and tasty. We got up on the chairs to look at it curled up in a big jar on the kitchen windowsill, beside Our Lady. It was purple and grey, with lots of little spikes and cracks. Maria stuck her own tongue out to look at in the mirror and I thought of what it would be like to put your tongue in the vice, because that's what my mother said she would have to do with the cow's tongue. She said she would boil it and press it in the vice.

Some days when my father is at work, I go into the *Kinderzimmer* and make my own inventions. I put lots of things into the vice and squeeze them as hard as I can until they change shape. Franz, too, likes to crush down the hard-boiled sweets to dust. I have some English words in my head that I want to keep saying out loud because I like them. Don't forget the fruit gums, chum. I get bits of wood and spare buttons to see how long it takes before they bend or break. And all the time I say my secret words, don't forget the fruit gums, chum.

One day I got a splinter in my foot from running on the floorboards in my bare feet. But my father knew what to do right away. He got a needle and told me to put my foot up on the table. He took off his glasses and started to sting me with the needle, until I pulled my foot away. I thought it would hurt, but he said nothing hurts except what's in your head. Then he slowly lifted the skin with the needle and got it out without hurting, and afterwards he showed me the tiny splinter that caused so much trouble and everybody was smiling because there was no pain at all.

'There's no such thing as pain,' my mother said. 'The only pain is when you're ashamed. When you're ashamed, everything hurts.'

It's true because one day when I stole money out of her coat pocket, she brought me into the front room and tried to hit me on the legs with her hand. It didn't hurt because she's not very good at it. But I was ashamed and I had nothing say. I just felt sorry and that was much worse. My father is better at punishment, and one day when he heard that I brought English words into the house, he was very angry. I couldn't stop saying 'don't forget the fruit gums, chum' and hitting other people like Franz and Maria because the words were stuck to my mouth and I had to keep hitting people even if I didn't want to. My father knew what to do. He picked out a stick in the greenhouse and said we had to make a sacrifice. He brought me up the stairs and my mother closed all the doors in the house so that nobody would hear anything. When we got up to the landing, my father said we would kneel down and pray that he was doing the right thing for Ireland. We kneeled down and asked God how many lashes he thought was fair and my father said fifteen. I was hoping that God said no lashes, because I didn't mean it and maybe it was better for Ireland to give me a last chance. But my father heard God saying fifteen and not one less. So then he brought me into a room and told me to lie down on the bed and take down my trousers. I heard the stick whistling through the air, but it didn't hurt at all because I knew I was making a sacrifice. My father told me to count up to fifteen to make sure that he didn't forget what number he was on or leave one out. I wish I never learned to count in Irish and when it was over we had to kneel down again and say thanks to God. I was ashamed because I thought everybody in the world was laughing at me now. That's worse than anything that can happen with a stick, when everybody is laughing. Even if you squeeze your finger in the vice, even if you squeeze your tongue in the vice, it's not as bad as when you're ashamed and can't speak.

I know that people laugh at our family. I know that we are funny people because we don't speak English while we're eating our dinner or playing with cars on the granite steps outside the house. We are funny because my father goes into a hardware shop to buy wood in Irish from a man who can also speak the language. We're funny because we're German and my mother just closes the doors and keeps saying the same things over and over again and telling everybody that it's not good to win and it's better to pretend that there's no such thing as pain and nobody can make you smile and you should keep saying the silent negative all the time. On the street I feel ashamed because they know I got the stick on the backside and I can't speak English. My father says we don't care about the people outside, because we'll show them how to be Irish. We have to be as Irish as possible and make a sacrifice.

Then my father sits down and tells me the story of his grandfather again, Tadhg Ó Donnabháin Dall, Ted O'Donovan Blind. He was called O'Donovan Blind, not because he was blind himself but because he was the son of somebody who was blind. He was an Irish speaker with a beard who wrote books, a land-surveyor by profession and he travelled a lot around west Cork all his life and loved poetry in the Irish language.

In Munster where my father comes from, there were lots

of poets who spoke and wrote their own language. But that was long ago when people still spoke Irish all over and poets were welcomed in every house and treated like kings. If a poet came to the door of a big house where the noble people lived, my father says, they were offered food and a bed for the night. If you were nice to them, if you had a party and made them feel welcome, then they would write long poems telling the whole world how generous and how cultured you were. But if you were mean and turned them away, they'd write bad poems about you that would put you to shame. They were called the bards, and what happened one day was that the people who looked after the poets, the earls and all the other noble people, lost the war with the British and had to leave their houses and flee to France. There was no place for the poets to go, so they disappeared as well and Ireland was left without any poetry for a while.

After that, the Irish people didn't know where they were going any more, because the names of the streets and villages were changed into English. People lost their way because they didn't recognise the landscape around them. Léim Uí Dhonnabháin became Leap. Gleann d'óir became Glandore and Cionn tSáile became Kinsale. People's names were changed, too. Ó Mathúna became O'Mahony and Ó hUrmoltaigh became Hamilton. My father says the Irish were all stumbling around, not knowing who they were or who they were talking to. They could not find their way home. They were homeless. And that was the worst pain of all, to be lost and ashamed and homesick.

And that's how my great-grandfather became blind, because he was descended from a poet who had lost his way and went blind. Ted O'Donovan Blind got a job as a surveyor and travelled around west Cork all his life, speaking Irish and reciting some of the old Gaelic poems to make people feel at home. But it was too late, because most people were already speaking English and following the English road signs. And nobody wanted their children to speak Irish any more for fear that they would not be able to find their way in places like America and Canada and Australia.

Gaelic in Ireland is called Irish, so that Irish people will remember what country they're living in. Some people say that the Irish language reminds them of the big famine when they had nothing to eat except the old poems in Irish. My father says people transferred everything they owned into English, their stories and their songs, even all their memories and their family photographs. They deny that Irish has anything to do with them any more, but some of their ways of saying things come down from the old bards, even if they don't know it. Time didn't just begin in Ireland with the English language, he says. And just because they all speak English so well doesn't mean the Irish are not blind any more or that they know where they're going. There are some things you can only remember in Irish.

'One day the Irish people will wake up and wonder if they're still Irish,' he says.

And that's why it's important not to bring bad words like fruit gum into the house. That's why it's important to work hard and invent lots of new things in Ireland and fight for small languages that are dying out. Because your language is your home and your language is your country. What if all the small languages disappear and the whole world is speaking only one language? We'll all be like the Munster poets, he says, lost and blind, with nothing to welcome them only doors banging in the wind. We're living on the eve of extinction, my father says. One day there will be only one language and everybody will be lost.

'The world will be full of homesick people,' he says.

In the evenings, my father stays outside in the garden as long he can because it's still bright. It's time to plant all the flowers and vegetables, and to get rid of flowers like dandelions that he doesn't want. There are pink and white flowers growing out of the granite walls, too, that look beautiful but everybody hates them, because they're wild and wreck the walls and make a good hiding place for snails. There are bushes that only grow by the sea with purple flowers, too, and leaves that keep growing from the inside so that when you peel off the outer leaves it's never-ending, until you get to a tiny green bud inside. My father says all plants were wild once and he's growing sweet peas. And then he always lights a fire that crackles and whistles. You can't see any flames, but you can see lots of smoke going all over the garden, as if he's sending a message all around the world.

Inside, my mother is boiling the cow's tongue and there is a strong smell all around the house. That evening we watch as she wraps the tongue up in a white cloth and puts it into the vice. She winds the lever around and presses the tongue as hard as she can. Then she leaves it there for a whole night.

The next day we sit down to dinner and my mother brings out the tongue on a plate, all pink and pressed into a square shape by the vice and some glue around it as well. My father takes the knife and begins to cut. Everybody gets a slice along with cabbage. Franz wants to know if you eat a cow's tongue, will you start saying moo. My mother laughs, but now it's time to stop the jokes and eat. I don't like the taste of tongue. It's like eating rubber. I look around at Franz and Maria and they have stopped chewing as well. Maria is allowed to spit hers out on the plate because she's going to get sick, but we have to keep eating until it's finished and learn not to be afraid of new tastes.

'It's just exactly like ham,' my mother says.

She eats it and my father eats it and they nod to each other.

'Excellent,' my father says.

But I don't think they like it either. I think they're just pretending because they don't want it to go to waste and people to know they're wrong. We have to keep chewing, even though I nearly want to get sick, too, and I can't stop thinking of biting my own tongue and all the glue coming out from inside it. Everything comes to a standstill. There's a big lump in my mouth and I'm like Ita on the potty, not swallowing the last spoon and not saying a word, until my mother says it's all right, we don't have to eat any more as long as we finish all the cabbage.

'I suppose you don't want to eat something that somebody else had in their mouth already,' she says.

And then I can see her shoulders shaking. She starts laughing so much that she can't even eat any more either. My father is laughing, too, and he has to take off his glasses. He has tears in his eyes this time and they keep laughing for a long time, until my mother tells us to clear the table and promises that we will never have to eat tongue again as long as we live.

Nineteen

The reason my father has a limp is that when he was a boy he got a very bad disease called polio. And that's the end of it, he says. Except that it's not true. It's not a lie but it's not the truth either, because he never told us about going to the doctor or staying in hospital and getting sweets. He never had polio, because Onkel Ted told me once that my father had a limp when he was born. So maybe his mother only made up that story about polio, because people were afraid of anyone who was deformed at birth and it was better to say you had a disease like everyone else. Or maybe my father made it up himself because they were always laughing and limping after him on his way to school and saying that he had a father in the British navy.

Sometimes on Sundays we go to visit our relations. Tante Roseleen smiles at me all the time with her eyes. Onkel PJ has a wristwatch with a silver cover on it to protect the glass from breaking if you go to war. Tante Lilly has two sons called Jimmy and Pat who toss coins up in the air and show us how to play cards. And sometimes they all come to our house and bring red lemonade, then Tante Kathleen comes up from Middleton and Tante Eileen comes up from Skibbereen with Geraldine and Carmel. Then the house is full of smoke and English. I'm still afraid to bring bad words into the house, but then my father starts telling stories in English, too, and everything is all right as long as the visitors are still there. They say that nobody in Ireland can bake a cake like my mother. They say nobody can build a wooden toy trolley like my father and there are no children as lucky as we are with three languages, because we'll never be homeless. They sit around the table and talk until it's very late, but nobody ever says anything about my father's limp. We don't know what questions to ask, until one day when I told Onkel Ted that the worst disease in the world was polio because it makes your legs shorter and you get a limp.

'Polio,' he said. 'Is that so?'

My mother says some things are hard to talk about, some things are private.

'You remember the stick in the water,' she says. 'You remember the day we were down at the sea where the dog was barking and there was a stick in the water that was crooked. You know it's not crooked or broken. It's an illusion, but that doesn't mean it's a lie.'

There is nothing in the whole world that my mother hates more than lies. She wants us to be honest and to tell the truth when you're asked, because lies are worse than murder and nobody will trust you. You won't even trust yourself any more. She wants no more lies, not even a small one, not even an Irish one. Irish lies or German lies, it makes no difference to her, it's always wrong. And anyway it's impossible to tell a lie in our house because my mother has a good nose and she can smell something burning. My father has a very good ear for music, too, and he can hear the creaks in the floorboards from miles away, even in the office in Dublin where he works with the ESB. One day I started looking in his wardrobe again. I was on my own this time and I found the picture of the sailor that he

165

didn't want me to see. I found the photographs of HMS *Nemesis* and all the medals from the British navy. When my father came home from work that evening and we all sat down at the dinner table, he knew it and had a frown on his forehead.

'What did you do today?' he asked.

'Nothing,' I said.

'Nothing,' he said in a loud voice. 'That's the oldest answer in Ireland.'

He knew every answer in Ireland because he was a schoolteacher once. I could see myself twice in his glasses, but I couldn't see if his eyes were soft or hard. He was waiting for me to talk, so I told him that when I grow up I want to be a sailor. I told him I want to have a uniform and go all over the world on ships.

'Have you been looking in my wardrobe?' he asked.

'No,' I said.

I knew that nobody would ever trust me again because I said a lie. My father asked me the same question once more. He said I was the champion of wrong answers and he told me to think hard because he wanted the right one this time.

'Never be afraid of the truth,' my mother said.

I thought she was able to smell burning. And my father was watching the way I was buttering a slice of bread with hard butter, tearing big holes and making a mess of it.

'No, I didn't,' I said again.

'We have to believe him,' my mother then said, but after dinner when everything was cleared away from the table, I had to stay behind with my father looking at me. He can hear what's inside your head. He waited for a while and then asked me if there were any questions I wanted to ask him.

'No,' I said.

'Then why were you looking in my wardrobe?'

I wasn't sure which questions would make him angry and which questions would make him smile. He sat facing me for a long time until he had to get up and go outside into the garden because it was starting to get windy. He told me to sit there and think. I could hear him in the greenhouse rattling with sticks and I thought it was for me again and that we would be going up to pray for Ireland. I heard the back door banging in anger. But then I heard him outside in the garden with the sticks, tying down the new trees. I could hear the wind blowing. I could hear my mother talking to him and it was dark by the time he sat down at the table again. Then he looked at me and just smiled. He wasn't angry any more. He said it was wrong to tell lies and it was wrong to be more interested in the past than in the future. It was no use looking back all the time and he would show me something else instead.

'I'm going to show you the future,' he said.

I waited for him to say what it was but he just smiled.

'It won't be long, wait till you see. We'll be going there soon.'

That night there was a big storm. The window was rattling and the rain was tapping on the glass. Sometimes the wind pushed so hard that even all the rattling stopped and I thought the glass would break. I could see the shadow of the trees on the wall, shaking so much that they sometimes disappeared altogether. It was so wild and angry outside that I thought the roof would lift off the house. I thought the front door would blow in and everybody would be able to walk inside and see us. I heard my father coming up the stairs with one hard foot and one soft. My mother came to say goodnight and told me to pray for all the people out on the sea, and then I thought the house was moving like a ship.

I know that when my father was small he was called Jack after his own father John. He didn't know anything about his father until his mother told him he was a sailor with soft eyes. The sailor had a soft voice, too, she said, and he always called her 'baby' because she was the youngest in her family. He was away at sea all the time, even at Christmas, and the only thing that my father could remember seeing was the sailor's uniform, laid out all ready one night on the kitchen table. The next morning he was gone again and there was nothing left only the picture over the mantelpiece and all the letters he wrote home that were kept in a tin with roses on the lid.

Every time there was a storm she stayed up all night praying for all the people out at sea. And then she knew everything was all right when she got a postcard from Gibraltar with a short message.

Dear Mary Frances,
Rough crossing. More homesick than seasick,
all my love, John.

It was the last card he sent. He must have put it in the mailbox before he went out to work on deck. A wave must have come from the side and caused the ship to lurch, they said, because he fell over the railing down on to the lower deck. He would have fallen overboard and drowned if not for his friends pulling him to safety and bringing him inside to lie down on his bunk to sleep for a while. But when he woke up, he could not remember anything. He didn't look ill or have any broken bones and there was nothing wrong at all until he walked off the ship in

Gibraltar and got lost. He was like the Munster poets and kept going around and around the town in circles with no idea where to go, until the captain realised that he was missing and sent a search party out to arrest him for being a deserter.

The first thing that Mary Frances heard was some weeks later when she got a letter from Manchester saying that her husband was in hospital there. He had fallen and lost his memory on HMS *Vivid*, they said. She wasn't able to go and see him so she asked a cousin who was a nun in Liverpool to go to see him instead. And after a long time he was allowed to come home to Leap. He never wore the sailor's uniform again and he would never be seasick again because he was invalided out of the navy. There was no money coming from the British navy either to anyone who was invalided and he couldn't work at anything else in Leap. So Mary Frances looked after him and went up to Mass with him every morning to try to bring his memory back. He remembered her face and her name, but then after a while he started forgetting even that much, so that he could do nothing at times, only hold his head in his hands and say that he wanted to go home. He was a stranger in his own home. And then he lost his mind altogether one day, because he took a knife in his hand. My father was still a small child and he was crying so much that the noise went into the sailor's head like a nail into the wall, so he stood up and said he would kill him if he didn't stay quiet. Everybody in west Cork knew it wasn't like John Hamilton to do a thing like that, but his head wasn't right after falling on a British ship. He stood in front of his own picture in uniform, holding a kitchen knife in his hand and shouting, until Mary Frances had to stand in front of him, in front of the man she loved more than anyone else in the world and tell him to kill her first.

Sometimes it's a mistake to be born the son of people who love each other too much. Mary Frances went to see him at the hospital in Cork as often as she could. Once, after Ted was born, they all went up to visit him together, but he didn't recognise any of them any more and just turned away in the bed. Then a priest had to come and he died alone. Onkel Ted says it was a very cold day in winter when his body was brought on the train to Skibbereen and from there in a carriage to the graveyard on the hillside in Glandore. After that there was only the picture of the sailor over the mantelpiece and the box with the last card he sent home. After that Mary Frances had nothing in her mind only to pray and fight for a pension from the British navy, no matter how long it took, so that she could educate them and make sure they didn't have to go into the navy or emigrate to America. It was the biggest day of her life when her two sons came back to visit her in Leap, one an engineer, the other a Jesuit.

'It's no good looking back,' my father says. He is sitting across the table from me at breakfast time again and smiles. 'You should be looking forward. You're like a blank piece of paper and you should only look forward.'

Maybe that's why he had to put the picture of the sailor with the soft eyes in the wardrobe, along with all the medals and the box with the homesick postcard. Maybe that's why he doesn't want anyone to know that he has a limp, because we're living in a new country now and we can never go back again to the past. And maybe that's why he changed his name to Irish, so we'll never be homesick.

'Ten more days and then we'll be in the future,' Maria says.

The storm was gone. There was no wind at all any more and the sun was shining, but when my father went out to work he saw the broken slates on the ground and said there was a hole in the roof. There were fallen branches all over the road, too, and he told us never to touch any wires. Down at the seafront, the waves had thrown lots of sand and seaweed on to the road as if it were part of the sea, as if Dublin were going to be living underwater soon.

The man came to fix the roof. His name was Mr McNally and when I came home from school I saw the ladder in the house going up to the skylight. My mother said he had been up there on the roof for a long time and if he was any longer it would be infinity. I knew that infinity was even further away than the future, but I didn't know that infinity was in the past as well. She said she could not wait for him to come down, so she stood at the foot of the ladder and called up to him.

'Mr McNelly,' she called, because she says everything with a German accent. 'Mr McNelly, I have a cup of tea ready for you.'

In Ireland, you can't ask people anything, she says. It's not like Germany where a question is just a question. In Ireland people get offended by questions, because it's a way of saying what you're thinking. The only way to ask Mr McNally something politely was to offer him a cup of tea. My mother was not able to go up the ladder herself, so she kept calling up through the skylight. She said that the longer Mr McNally stayed up there, the bigger the hole in the roof would get and the more money we would have to pay.

Now and again, the phone would ring and it was my father calling from the office to ask where Mr McNally was now and how big the hole was. He could not come home early and go up the ladder himself, so my mother had to go back up the stairs and call up into infinity, saying the tea was already made and was now going cold. As well as that, there were homemade German biscuits, too, just out of the oven, covered with icing and hundreds and thousands. And when Mr McNally still didn't come down, she called him from the back garden, and after that from the gate in the front garden as well. Everybody on the whole street knew the tea was ready and my mother was getting worried because nobody had ever failed to come down for her biscuits before. When the phone rang again she told my father that maybe Mr McNally had a problem hearing things. And all the time the hole was getting bigger and bigger, the longer he was up there, so my mother said the next time there was a problem with the roof she would have to get two people to fix it, one man to do the work and the other to go up and call him down for tea and biscuits.

In the end she took off her apron and told us all to hold the ladder while she tried to climb up herself. The sun was shining down through the skylight and she didn't go very far because the ladder started shaking, so she came back down again. She said I had nothing to be afraid of, because she was holding the ladder herself and nothing would happen. So I climbed slowly up into infinity and put my head out over the roof, but it was so bright out there that I was blind, and I could see nothing. All I heard was the sound of snoring.

My mother could not understand why Mr McNally would not prefer to lie down and sleep on the sofa instead of sleeping on the roof. She likes things to be done properly, in the right place, and the roof is no place to fall asleep.

Mr McNally was very friendly. He smiled and said the hole in the roof was not half as big as he thought it was. It could have been much bigger. Some of the damage he had seen on other roofs was shocking, he said. He sat down at the table with the newspaper and looked at a list of horses' names. Then he rolled the paper up and put it away in his jacket pocket and drank the tea. He ate some biscuits and then lit a cigarette. He was talking to my mother all the time and he asked her if she knew what the feeling was like not to be able to remember something, like the name of a horse or a football player. My mother nodded her head as if there was something she could not remember either. Sometimes, Mr McNally said, he thought he was losing his memory. He said it was the worst thing of all, not knowing what you couldn't remember. Then it was time for him to go and he said he hadn't eaten biscuits as nice as hers before. He said he was hoping there would be another storm soon, so he would have to come back and fix the roof again. My mother smiled. He hit me on the head with the newspaper and said I was a lucky devil, and after he was gone we counted the biscuits that were left over.

My mother smelled the blue smoke and looked out the window for a long time to see if she could remember what it was she had forgotten. But it was only something that she could not put out of her head. Something from the time in Germany that she had almost put away by writing it down in a diary for her children. Still, it came back again and again. Sometimes it was there at the back of her mind and she didn't even know what was upsetting her, until she sat down and remembered. She smelled the smoke and thought about when she was trapped in the past, as if she were still unable to move on and she would never see the future. She would live her whole life in the same moment, when Stiegler was coming up the stairs, and it felt like helpless infinity. At first she tried to resist. She said she would go to the police, but Stiegler said that it wasn't a good idea for her to contact them because he had too many friends in the Gestapo. They would never believe her.

'I'll tell your wife,' she said, but he wasn't even scared of that.

'I wouldn't advise that,' he said.

He had power in his words and she had none. Every night he came up the stairs and she would hear the sound of his breathing outside. She would see the door handle turning. Then he stood inside her room and she could not stop it or help herself. Sometimes she tried to believe that it was right and that this was the sacrifice she had to make in her life. There was somebody she knew who had joined the Nazi party just so that the rest of the family didn't have to. So maybe she was going through this so that nobody else in her family had to endure it. It was all her own fault and she had brought it on herself. This is what she had wanted, she thought, what she had dreamed of so often. Maybe it wasn't quite what she had imagined, but if you're weak and stupid and have been misled, it's still your own fault and you can only blame yourself for what happens next. If you can't stop something at the beginning, then you may not be able to stop it later on either and you deserve everything that follows. So she was in a trap, with Stiegler coming to her room every night. He took off his clothes and placed them neatly on the chair. He even folded his tie. He even put each sock neatly into each shoe. He took off his watch and looked at it briefly before he hung it on the back of the chair. It was never too late to resist. She still felt that she could threaten to go to the police again. But he put that out of her head and closed off the last escape route that she had.

'A lot of people are being taken away these days,' he

said. 'You don't want to go with them, now do you? Nobody comes back, you know.'

Afterwards, when he put his clothes on again, he seemed to do everything in reverse order. The watch was first, the tie last. Then he lit a cigarette, every time, as if he wanted to keep her company for a while longer. He smoked his cigarette and sometimes he would tell her to smile. Where were all the smiles, he would ask, and then he looked at his watch and said he had to go. My mother sits in her chair and smells the smoke and stares out the window as if she will never escape.

Twenty

I keep asking my mother questions about the future. What language do they speak there? Do they have cars and buses and streets like here? Will you have to walk any more or will people have legs like wheels? Will people be able to live without breathing? Will there be shops with machines outside where you put in a penny and twist the handle for chewing gum? Will there be money or will people just be able to draw things and sprinkle salt on the picture to make it come true? She stretches her hands out in the kitchen and says she can't look into the future, only saints can do that. All she knows is that the future is far away and it will take a whole day to get there, first on a bus, then a train and then another bus. It might rain there a bit, she says, so she has to go out and buy a rain mac for each one of us.

Everybody is busy preparing for the journey. I watch my father making the last of the trolleys, concentrating hard with his tongue out the side of his mouth and saying nothing, only yes or no. Then I go upstairs and watch my mother laying everything out in rows on the beds first before she puts it all into the suitcases. We'll be sleeping in new beds, she says, so we'll need new pyjamas. Maria keeps counting and saying that there's only one more sleep and one more bowl of porridge before we go. Ita keeps mixing up words in every language in her mouth, like *bye bye Baümchen* and *go go maidirín*. She is very kind to everybody and always wants to give you things, even things that you didn't ask for. But you have to say thank you and then she goes off again to get something else. She goes around the house and comes back with a pencil and a cup and a broken umbrella. And those things have to go into the suitcase as well, my mother says, it's all coming with us.

Then everything was packed and ready in the hallway. My father lined up the trolleys one by one – blue for Franz, green for me, red for Maria, and the pram at the back for Ita. Each trolley had a rope at the front and pictures on the side. Each trolley was packed with a colouring book, a box of crayons, plasticine, sweets, biscuits and a grey, plastic rain mac. Behind the trolleys and the pram were the suitcases all in a single line, like a long train ready to move out of the station. And before we went up to bed for the last time, I felt strong in my tummy because we looked back from the stairs and saw how close we were to leaving.

The next morning we got up and had breakfast very early. When it was time to go we all kneeled down in the hallway first to pray for a good journey, then my father carried each trolley down the granite steps, followed by the pram and the suitcases. My mother stood with us on the pavement, while he went back in to lock the front door from the inside. We heard the big bolt sliding across and waited while my father closed all the windows and doors in the house and made his way out the back door, across the garden wall and all the way around the lane to meet us again on the street. There was nobody up and nobody there to see the Irish-German train heading off into the future, nobody to hear us squeaking and rattling down the street with my father out front carrying the suitcases, wearing his tweed cap and his own grey, plastic rain mac and with the umbrella hanging around his neck.

It took a long time to get down to the bus stop because one of the wheels came off Maria's trolley and had to be fixed. But there was no shortage of time, my father said. The bus conductor stacked the trolleys carefully one on top of the other under the stairs, and then we were moving at last with a long ticket flapping like a white flag out the window. On the train we had a table where we could take out the colouring books and draw. In Galway we sat by the river and looked at swans while we were eating our lunch. Then we got the bus to Connemara and my mother said it was more like being on a roller-coaster because the driver had a cigarette in his mouth and drove so fast it was impossible to see around the next turn or over the next hill. She said the bus drove itself. Chickens were scattering off the road. Sometimes a dog ran alongside, barking and trying to bite the back wheel, and my mother called them *Reifenbeisser*, tyre-biters. People waved at the bus and one time an old man sitting in the long grass held his cap in the air without even looking up to see, as if he knew it was the bus passing by and everybody on the bus knew it was him. Once or twice the bus had to stop because there was a cow in the middle of the road that wouldn't stop chewing. But then we were off again, going further and further into the empty brown land, full of rocks and stone walls that my mother said looked like a place on the moon.

It was the evening by the time we arrived and there was a man waiting for us. It was Seán De Paor, the postman, and we were going to stay in his house. He smoked a pipe and there was a smell of turf all around and sometimes you didn't know which was which. The place was called

An Cheathrú Rua, which was true because that's the Irish for 'The Red Quarter', the land that's brown red all around. There were no road signs because everybody knew the names of the streets in Irish. We followed him up the road past the handball alley, up Bóthar an Chillín to his house, and all the way the trolley train rattled so much that people came out of their houses to tell the dogs to stop barking.

My father was speaking Irish all the time and laughing and I knew he would never be angry again. There was Fear an tí, the man of the house, and Bean an tí, the woman of the house. There were two boys called Seán and Máirtín who had never seen plasticine before. Everybody said lederhosen were the best trousers they had ever seen and wanted to know where they could be got. All the men wore caps like my father and asked you what story you had. Some of them even wanted to learn German, so my mother had to give them German lessons on the road through Irish.

It was like being at home in the place where we all wanted to be for the rest of our lives. Every day we went for long walks down to the sea, down to the beach beside the graveyard with all the Irish names. We met the old people who could remember as far back as infinity and didn't even know any English, my father said. We didn't understand them either because they spoke very fast with no teeth, but my father took photographs of them outside their houses with thatched roofs, to make sure they wouldn't disappear. Sometimes we walked further up to Pointe, to the little harbour where the lobster pots were stacked up and where you thought you were standing on the furthest piece of land, looking right out across the bay to the Aran Islands, like black whales coming out of the sea.

This really was the future, my mother said, because

when we were playing on the rocks, there was lots of seaweed that looked like the tails of crocodiles and some like the tails of lions. We laughed and dragged the lion tails across the sand behind us. It was the future because sometimes the tide went out so far that you thought the sea had run away and disappeared altogether. The water drained away and left the land behind, silent and deserted, with black seaweed draped across the rocks like hair. As if everything had gone to sleep. As if we were the first people ever to discover this place. Sometimes there was nobody out under the sky and we didn't see anybody for hours. It was the future because when we climbed up the hill it was like walking on the moon, with nothing but grey rocks and rusty brown colours all around. And behind us the black line of the coast going in and out as far as your eyes could see.

It was a place where you could live on your imagination, my mother said, a place where everything was simple and you didn't need possessions, not like some of her sisters in Germany who had to own more and more things all the time, until they could only talk about what they didn't have and what they still wanted. It was a place full of things you could not pay for with money, a place where you could be rich with nothing but silence and landscape. All you needed was sandwiches and milk and the wind at your back, she said, and my father repeated the same thing in Irish, only the other way round, with your backside to the wind.

'*Tóin in aghaidh na gaoithe,*' he said.

So we laughed with our backsides to the wind and nobody ever thought of going home again. When it rained we got out our macs and sheltered behind the stone walls. The best shelter of all we learned from the sheep, when we were so far away from any house or any walls and the rain came so quickly that we just copied them and crouched down behind the rocks. Sometimes we found shelter in a doorway and stood watching the rain coming down at an angle. There was nothing to say and I saw my father going into a dream as he stared out into the rain without a word. My mother, too. All of us dreaming and sheltering from the words, speaking no language at all, just listening to the voice of the rain falling and the sound of water gurgling between the stones somewhere behind the barn. Then afterwards you could see the steam rising on the road when the sun came out again as bright as ever and the water continued to whisper along the roadside like the only language allowed.

One day my father met a man at the harbour whose name was De Bhaldraithe, and he had invented a dictionary of English words in Irish. It was a great book, my father said, as good as the book about people talking in the graveyard, because now at last everybody could learn Irish again. And that night they were invited over to a house where people gathered around to drink whiskey and sing songs. My father told lots of stories in Irish and my mother had to sing a song in German. The man who made the dictionary knew some German, too, so he was able to speak a few words to her, because nobody could speak any English.

And after all the singing and talking, there was a discussion about the state of the Irish language and everyone agreed it was still alive, more alive than ever before. They said people were putting the Irish language in a coffin and bringing it to the graveyard, but they didn't realise that people can still talk in the grave. One man said Irish speakers in Ireland were being treated like people from a foreign country, from another planet. But as long as there were people like De Bhaldraithe and my father who made their own children speak it, the language would never die out. They drank whiskey and smoked pipes and passed around plates of ham sandwiches. It was a great night because nobody was laughing at the Irish language, except one woman who disagreed and said nobody could live on their imagination for ever. It was no use being poor, the woman suddenly said, and everyone in the house went so quiet that you could hear the turf hissing in the fire and somebody's stomach murmuring. The woman said she was sick to death of seeing people coming down from Dublin for their holidays and all they wanted was the people in Connemara to stay living in thatched cottages with no toilets inside. What was the use in speaking Irish if you couldn't put food on the table? But then my father made a speech in Irish that made everybody hold their glasses up in the air to him. He said he could see the woman's point of view and it was no fun to be poor, but that's why people in Dublin were busy working hard and making a sacrifice, too, so that Ireland could live on its own inventions and its own imagination. And in the end, he turned the argument around to say that toilets inside the house and food on the table were no good if you lost the language. Your stomach could be full but your heart would be empty.

They came home along the road in the dark when all the lights in the houses were already gone out. My mother says you could not even see your own shoes it was so dark. And one time, they stopped and whispered to each other because there was somebody standing right in front of them on the road just breathing and staring at them and not letting them pass by, but it was only a donkey that suddenly got an even bigger fright himself and ran off.

It was the best night of all, my mother said, except that

in the middle of the night something funny happened. My father had to get up and go to the *leithreas* outside. The toilets in Connemara were all outside in a small wooden house with lots of flies and a bad smell of newspapers that always made me want to get sick. Inside there was a big box with a wooden lid and a hole in it. Underneath there was a bucket that Fear an tí sometimes brought to a field nearby where he could empty it out and bury it all underneath the soil. That night my father had to feel his way along the walls to go out the back door into the darkness. He found the *leithreas* and locked the door shut behind him. But then, as he turned around, there was no wooden board and he fell right down with his backside in the bucket.

At first everything was silent. It was dark all around and everybody in Connemara was asleep. My father couldn't lift himself out. He was stuck in the bucket with his legs hanging out over the wooden box and his pyjamas around his ankles. He had his shoes on, but no socks, and his laces were undone. He thought he would be stuck like that for ever, so he started calling for help in Irish. Nobody came and all he could do was to keep shouting and banging on the side of the shed, until there was so much noise, they said the dogs were barking as far away as Casla. Everybody in the house woke up and Fear an tí went down at last to rescue my father from the *leithreas*. He first had to break down the door to get in. Then he had to put his arms around my father to lift him out and get the bucket off his backside and tell everybody, even the neighbours across the road, to go back to bed, it was nothing at all. He offered him a cigarette and a pipe and some whiskey, but my father just said he was going back to bed and after a long time the dogs stopped barking and everything was quiet again.

In the morning we could see the door of the *leithreas*

lying on its side and the lock broken. Nobody said a word about what happened. Maybe Fear an tí was afraid that my father had hurt himself and wasn't saying anything. Maybe Bean an tí was even more embarrassed, because if they all spoke English and had a proper toilet inside the house, it would never have happened. Maria kept saying that she was never going to the toilet again as long as she lived. She was holding her knees together and we started pretending that we were falling into the *leithreas* all the time. Going down the stairs or walking around the house, Franz just suddenly said 'Oh' and fell down into an invisible toilet. We did it again and again and kept laughing.

Even at breakfast around the table, it was hard not to think about the *leithreas*. It was Sunday and my father came down all ready for Mass in his best suit. Nobody said a word. Franz was trying not to laugh and had a very cross face with his mouth closed tight. We knew my father couldn't be really angry because all the people in the house would be watching him. Every time I looked at Franz I couldn't stop myself from making a snort with my nose, until my father looked at me with hard eyes and my mother told us it was not nice to laugh at people's misfortune.

'It's not fair,' she said. 'Because your father made such a good speech last night . . . and then he fell into the toilet.'

That was the end of it and everyone was silent again, until my mother's face went completely red. I saw her shoulders starting to shake and then she made a big snort with her nose, too, and suddenly had to run upstairs. We were left at the table with my father looking at us. We were afraid to laugh any more and everything was so quiet in the house, until my father spoke up at last to make conversation. There was a sign near the door with a well-known phrase in Irish that said: *níl aon tinteán mar do thinteán féin*: there's no fireside like your own fireside. So my father turned it around and tried to make a joke of it. *Níl aon tóin tinn mar do thóin tinn féin*, he said, which meant that there's no sore backside like your own sore backside.

Then everybody in the house suddenly laughed out loud at that. Even though it was an old joke that everybody had heard a hundred times before, they still thought it was the funniest thing they ever heard in their whole lives. My mother came back down again and said the best thing is to laugh at yourself before anyone else does. My father says that if you laugh against yourself the whole world will laugh with you, and if you laugh at other people, you laugh alone. But my father is not good at laughing at himself. And he never laughs at other people either. He's much better at making a sacrifice. After Mass, we met the dictionary man and all his friends again outside the church. My father was afraid that he would be famous all over Connemara for falling into the *leithreas* rather than for his speech. But there was no mention of it and everything was forgotten, because there were too many other things to remember and Irish people don't say everything that's inside their heads.

We were going back home to Dublin the next day, so my mother asked us what we wanted to do most on the last day. We went back to the sea and played with the lion tails and then up the hill behind the house to be the last people to look out over the sea to the Aran Islands. We sat on the grass with the sheep all around us, waiting for the sun to go down. We looked out along the coast where the sea was just mixed in with the land, with inlets and islands and peninsulas as far as you could see. The sun went down and An Cheathrú Rua was even redder than it ever was before. My father said it was time to go, but my mother said we would wait until the very last minute, until it was completely dark, until all the colour had disappeared and there was nothing left except the lights in the houses and the smaller twinkling lights further away along the coast that told you where the land was.

Nobody was sad to go home the next day because my mother said we would remember this place for ever. Nobody was sad because my father said we would be coming back again soon. Nothing would change, he promised, not one rock, not even one stone wall. We would come back and see that everything was still there in the same place as it was before. Nothing was going to be in the past.

Twenty-one

That summer the garden was full of flowers. There was so much fruit, too, raspberries and blackcurrants and plums, that my mother started making jam again. And there were so many tomatoes in the greenhouse that we had to give lots of them away to the neighbours. There were flowers on the table every day and my father said we should keep bees. He started buying books on beekeeping and said it would make sense to put a few hives on the roof of the breakfast room where they could fly straight out to collect the honey and pollinate the fruit trees.

The same things were forbidden in our house as always. There was a song on the radio that said we had all the time in the world in the deepest voice in the world. My mother liked the song too, but only when my father was out at work. Ita started saying 'good morning' to all the people on the street, and when there was nobody else to say good morning to, she said it to the lamp-posts and the gates, all day until she was back in the kitchen saying 'good morning' to the cooker and the washing machine as well. My father said the rules had to be obeyed even though she was still a baby. So then there was trouble because Ita went on hunger strike and wouldn't eat or speak any more, and my father had to hold her head with one hand and try to force her mouth open to push the spoon in with the other. All the time she was shaking her head and I thought it was funny because Ita was winning. But my mother didn't want us to see what would happen next, so she closed the doors and brought us outside and told us to run down to the shop to buy ice cream until it was over and Ita stopped crying.

My father said he couldn't understand why the stick wasn't working any more. He said he was doing his best. Everything was for us. He made the trolleys, he made a wooden see-saw, he was even building a real puppet theatre, and if we kept on breaking the rules he would have to find new ways of punishing us that would hurt more. Sometimes I tried to punish Franz and Maria to see if they would feel pain, so my father said anything I would do to them he would give me back a hundred times, and I said anything he would do to me I would give back to Franz and Maria a hundred times, until nobody could feel any more pain. He brought me upstairs and we kneeled down again to pray in front of Our Lady that he was doing the right thing. But that didn't work so he had a better idea, something that would make me ashamed. He confiscated the braces on my lederhosen and I had to go down to the barber to get my hair cut, holding my trousers up with my hands in my pockets.

In the barber shop we sat on the wooden bench reading the comics. Most of them were torn and falling apart, but it was good to see them, even the ones I had read before. I didn't like the comic called *Hotspur* as much as the *Dandy*, and I didn't like it either when somebody was punished and put across the teacher's knee. There were lots of other boys waiting and reading comics, too, but none of them noticed that I had no braces and couldn't walk around without my hands in my pockets. The barber kept clicking the scissors all the time, even when he was not cutting hair, and there was a huge pile of hair swept into one corner on the floor. We waited and read as many comics as we could and pretended that we were Irish and spoke English like everyone else, even though everybody could see that we were from a different country.

When we came out I tried to speak English to Franz but he was afraid. The barber, Mr Connolly, always gave every boy back a penny, so you could buy a toffee bar. But that day we put our pennies together, along with other pennies that Franz still had from Tante Lilly, and we bought a brand new comic called the *Beano*. We took turns reading it and spoke Irish to each other in between. My mother said it was good to buy something that lasts longer, not like a liquorice pipe that's gone within minutes and can't be remembered, but there would be trouble if we brought the *Beano* into the house. So we pretended it wasn't our *Beano* and hid it in the hedges of Miss Hart's garden.

At night I thought of Mr Connolly still clicking his fingers, even when he was having his tea and there were no scissors in his hand. I thought of all the hair mixed together in a large wig, like the mane of a buffalo. I thought of Mr McNally reading his paper with crooked glasses held up only by one stick over his right ear, and I thought of Mr Smyth from the vegetable shop getting undressed and going to bed with only one arm. Downstairs my father was building the puppet theatre and my mother was making the costumes and the curtains. Outside it was raining and I thought of the *Beano* getting wet and all the colours washing out.

After that, my mother said we were all starting to go crazy because one day I told Maria to climb up on the wall in the front garden and show her backside to the wind. She did it because she trusted everything I said, even things she didn't want to do, even things she knew were not right. I promised that we would do the same after her, but she had to go first because she was younger and everything in our house was always done from the youngest to the oldest. So Maria stood on the wall and laughed with her backside to the wind for everyone to see. Then one of the neighbours came over and told my mother it was not very nice to do that in front of Irish people, Catholic or Protestant. So we all had to stay inside for a day and my mother said we were living on our own imagination too long and we needed friends to play with.

My father said we could only play with children who could speak Irish. He contacted lots of people and first of all we played with a boy nearby whose name was Seán Harris, the son of a painter and decorator, but their Irish wasn't good enough. Then one day my father brought us across the city on the bus to Finglas and we played with a boy called Naoise. Once or twice, children were brought over to our house by bus from other parts of the city, and there were some older boys who came to play in German but didn't say much. They stood around looking at our things and not even playing with them, just eating the biscuits that my mother made. There were some boys from our school who came over, too, but even they thought it was stupid to play in Irish and didn't want to come back again, even for the biscuits. You couldn't be cowboys in Irish. You couldn't sneak up behind somebody or tie somebody up to a chair in Irish. It was no fun dying in Irish. And it was just too stupid altogether to hide behind something and say 'Uuuggh' or 'hands up' in Irish, because there were some things you could only do in English, like fighting and killing Indians. My father was no good at making friends, so my mother took over and told us to join the altar boys. But they only wanted to kill Germans, so we served Mass and just went home again.

One day I was playing with the umbrella in the hallway, trying to kill all the coats with one arm behind my back, and Franz was outside on the street with his scooter. He was listening to the trains pulling into the station, waiting for my father to come home. But then he saw some other boys playing on the street with sticks and guns. They ignored him and didn't call him any names, so he stood there with one foot on and one foot off the scooter, looking at them from a distance, even though he couldn't join in. They were cowboys fighting and killing Indians. Franz was pretending that his scooter was a horse and that he had a real gun in the side pocket of his lederhosen, until my father came around the corner with his limp and his briefcase swinging. Then Franz turned around and tried to scoot back to the house as fast as he could, but it was already too late. I heard the key in the door and I saw Franz coming in with nothing to say. I saw my father turning around to look at the boys on the street before he closed the door and put his briefcase down. My mother came to kiss him, but that didn't stop him saying that Franz had to be punished for pretending to be with the other boys on the street.

'Now why is that?' my mother asked.

'He was listening to them in English,' my father said.

'My God,' she said. 'Are you not taking this too far?'

My father shook his head. She tried everything she could to stop it. She tried to distract him by saying it was the feast of St Brigid and that the curtains were finished for the puppet theatre and that she got a letter from her sister Marianne. She tried to say that we should phone Onkel Ted and see what he would say. And when my father still shook his head she tried to put her arm around Franz to stop him from feeling pain.

'Not with violence,' she begged him. 'Please, not with violence.'

So instead, my father confiscated the scooter and carried it upstairs. That meant there were now two scooters in my father and mother's bedroom. My scooter was there for days because I was listening to songs on the radio.

'Two horses up there eating grass,' she said to us afterwards.

I knew she was making a joke because there was no other way out of it. But I knew it wasn't over with the scooters either and after dinner, when we were gone to bed already, my mother tried to get my father to put on some music and pour a glass of cognac. They were talking for a long time and he said he was not going to be tricked into changing his mind, because that was like going backwards and letting the strongest languages win over the weakest. She said that punishing the innocent and confiscating things was going backwards. Then she laughed and asked how anyone was going to be able to sleep with two horses in the bedroom. But he just got angry again and she asked him to go up and give us a sign that everything was still positive in our family. She wanted him to go up and kiss us on the forehead.

'I love each one of you,' he said, and I could smell the cognac on his breath. 'You are like no other children in the world.'

And some time in the middle of the night, my mother got up and brought the scooters back down the stairs, one by one, because they were there in the hallway the next morning waiting for us. It didn't mean everything was all right again, but at least we had our horses back and soon we would be starting swimming lessons.

After that my mother kept asking people in the shops if there were any children that we could play with and one day she met Dr Sheehan and he had a boy called Noel who had red hair and glasses that were wrapped around his ears. So she brought us down to his house to play in a huge garden beside the church with bulldogs and apple trees. He was our friend and his house was the best place in the world to live. There were bicycles that we could ride around the path like a racetrack, and we could reach up from our saddles and pick apples from the trees above us any time. Sometimes the bell from the church rang and you could hear nothing at all except one of the dogs howling. One time Franz found a tap in the garden and drank some water, but then his mouth was full of earwigs and he thought he would die. And one time we found a wasps' nest and started throwing stones at it until they got very angry. We played in English all day until Noel's mother asked us to stay for tea. She had trouble with breathing and spoke very gently to say that she had phoned my mother. There was nothing my father could do to stop it. Even when we were walking up the road on our way home at the end of the day, Franz and me still kept talking English as far as we could, until the last lamp-post.

Then my father wanted to know if Noel could speak Irish. Before he could come and play in our house, he would have to sit an exam first in the front room. Next Saturday, my father asked him lots of questions in Irish, like what his name was and how old he was and what his father did for a living. We stood around watching and hoping that Noel could answer them, wishing that we could whisper and help him, but he knew no Irish at all. He just kept smiling and blinking behind his glasses and repeating the only thing he remembered from school.

'*Níl a fhios agam,*' he said. 'I don't know.'

That was the oldest answer in Ireland and my father started shaking his head. It was not good enough, he kept saying. But then my mother had a great idea.

'He wants to learn Irish,' she said. 'Dr Sheehan wants him to learn. It's his only chance.'

My father looked very cross, but my mother kept trying. She said Noel was not so good at Irish yet, but he would soon become a native speaker if he was allowed to come to our house. And then who knows, maybe his family would then become a full-Irish fireside and maybe even Dr Sheehan would begin to speak Irish to his patients and then everybody in Dublin would love their own language. It would be a pity to miss this opportunity.

So then we had a friend for life. We learned swimming and diving and went down to the public baths every day for the whole summer. We saved up and bought goggles so that we could dive down underwater and have contests picking up pennies from the bottom of the pool. We would throw the penny into the deep end and watch it turning as it sank out of view. Then we dived down to reach it underwater, where there was no language only the humming bubbles all around. We timed each other to see who could stay down for the longest and I was nearly always the winner because I could stay under until my lungs were bursting, until I nearly died and had to come up for words. I was the champion at not breathing. Sometimes the three of us went down together and shook hands, and it looked like you could live down there, just sitting on the bottom of the pool signalling to each other. When we got out of the water, our knees were purple. We had purple hands and purple lips and our teeth were chattering. Then it was time to go home and we bought chewing gum. Noel found there was still water in one ear and he had to lean over on one side to let it pour out like a jug. We were friends for life and walked home with our towels around our necks, slapping the swimming trunks against the walls and leaving wet marks behind, like signatures all the way home. Then we waited till we got to the last lamp-post before we stopped speaking English.

Twenty-two

You stand behind the puppet theatre with the puppet in your hand, completely hidden. Nobody knows you're there. Then you pull on the string to open the curtains and make the puppet walk out in front of the audience. You can say anything you want. You can change your voice and make up any story. You can hide behind the story, and it's a bit like being underwater because everything you say goes up like bubbles to the surface.

'Have you seen the dog?' Kasper the puppet asks.

'What dog?' the puppet man answers.

'The dog that has no name and belongs to nobody and barks all day until he's hoarse and has no voice any more?'

My mother helps us to make up a story. She goes upstairs to get the hairdryer. She takes out a thin blue scarf from her dressing table and when she comes back down she goes in behind the puppet theatre with me. She plugs in the hairdryer and the blue scarf starts crashing on to the beach and the dog starts barking and biting at the waves because he doesn't know any better.

Everybody has a story to hide behind, my mother says. In the vegetable shop one day, Mr Smyth started talking to her about a wall in Germany. He doesn't normally talk very much, but that day he was talking about a wall and that nobody had any courage left to stop it. Then he asked her when she was going back home to Germany, but she gave the oldest answer in Ireland and said she didn't know. Missersmiss, she calls him, because of her accent. He asked me if I had ever been to Germany. The little German boy who has never been to Germany, he said, and even though he only has one arm, he's able to keep talking and put the potatoes in a brown bag and take the money all with one hand. I wanted to know why he only has one arm and what story he was hiding behind, but we can't ask those questions. Sometimes he uses his chin to hold things like an extra hand. He picks up the bag of potatoes against his hip and slips it into my mother's net shopping bag. He said Germany was very far away. He spoke as if he had been there once himself, but couldn't say any more because of his missing arm. And my mother just kept looking at the Outspan letters hanging in the window, until Mr Smyth said 'please God', it would not be long before she could go back to Germany. He said he had brothers and sisters in America who would give anything to come back to Ireland even for a day.

Other people started talking about the wall and asking the same questions. After Mass one day, a woman whose name was Miss Ryan asked my mother about going home and she said she wasn't even dreaming about it. But that's not true because, later on, she said it felt as though people in Ireland knew what you were thinking, long before you even thought of it yourself. Before you opened the door to go outside, they knew what was on your mind, even something you had already put out of your head for good. She made up a story to hide behind and said she was nowhere more at home than in Ireland with her family.

Everybody knows how far away Germany is by looking

at our family. They know that my mother is homesick. They can see it in her eyes. They could see her dreaming again that morning. They could see us all from the back, standing at the seafront, looking out at the waves, until my mother heard the bells and remembered what time it was and what country she was in. On the way back, my mother was trying not to step on the cracks in the pavement. I was hiding in doorways and she was pretending that she didn't know where I was. Maria was talking to herself and stopping to point at a spot on the wall. Ita was smiling and saying 'thank you' to all the lamp-posts and gates. Franz went ahead and waited at the corner for us with his scooter, one foot on and one foot off, while Maria was still trailing far behind. Maybe we look like the children who are always thinking of home. The homesick children.

Outside the church the next day, Miss Ryan stopped to speak to my mother again and asked if she wanted to borrow the money to go back to Germany. There would be no rush in paying it back, she said, but my mother shook her head. They were whispering for a long time until all the people had left the church, until Miss Ryan told my mother to go home and have a think about it. But my father didn't want that. He says you can't borrow money from the neighbours and he doesn't want my mother to go home on her own because she might never want to return.

My mother said it was time to stop dreaming. Instead, she asked her sisters to send over lots of books and magazines about Germany so that she could tell us what was happening there. She showed us the pictures of people running through the streets with suitcases. She explained how the Russians had put up a wall right in the middle of Germany and there was nothing the British or the Americans could do except watch. There was lots of barbed wire and tanks in the middle of the streets. There were people climbing out the window and letting children down slowly on ropes. And when the wall was built, people still tried to escape to the other side but they were shot and there were pictures of them lying on the ground bleeding to death and nothing anyone could do to help.

Onkel Ted came to talk to my mother because she didn't know what to do. She told him that Miss Ryan offered her money to go back to Germany and that she would not have to pay it back or ever mention it again. There were two Miss Harts and two Miss Doyles and two Miss Ryans, and they always went to Mass in pairs on Sunday. The Miss Ryans said they had set aside the money as a gift, but my father didn't want money from the neighbours. After dinner and after the sweets in Onkel Ted's pocket, we went to bed and they sat in the front room until there was nothing more to say about it. I heard my father taking out the cognac and putting on some music. It was the record of the two women doing a duet in French. I could hear the sound of the two high voices, like two sisters singing together. I thought it was like the two Miss Ryans going up the stairs together, arm in arm, up one or two steps and then back down two steps, then up three or four more and back down two, until they finished on the landing at the top with their arms around each other, saying goodnight and lying down softly in their beds.

After that, Onkel Ted was only afraid that my mother was homesick so he started sending her more books and pieces about Germany cut out of newspapers. He wrote long letters, too, in German and she wrote letters back, but my father said that had to stop, because he didn't want Onkel Ted to be her friend for life, only himself. He didn't want anyone to know more about Germany or to read any more books than he did. He was able to read five books at the same time with a bus ticket sticking out of each one, but Onkel Ted was able to read so fast that he didn't need a bus ticket and a book still looked brand new when he passed it on to my mother. My father didn't like my mother reading books that he didn't read first himself. He didn't like her talking too much to the neighbours either or getting friendly with people in the shops or going to coffee mornings and getting ideas from other people, only Catholic ideas. He was afraid she would not listen to him any more. He started slamming all the doors in the house because he didn't like anyone else calling her Irmgard. And one time there was a French woman living on our street who kept dropping in and talking to my mother. Even though they were from different countries, they had the same questions and the same answers when they talked. She wanted to become my mother's friend for life, but my father stopped all that because she was talking about going back to France to get a divorce from her Irish husband who was friends for life with other women. That was the worst thing that could happen, if Irish people started getting French ideas. That would be the end of the family. That would be the end of Ireland, he said.

Then Onkel Ted sent Eileen Crowley out to talk to my mother instead. Her father PJ had a good business in Dublin, but his shop had to close down when he lent a friend some money and never got it back. They went into debt and had to sell everything and move house. My mother knew how bad that was, because her father had to close his shop, too, in Kempen. It was bad luck. My mother saw it as a failure, and Eileen would never call it that. They had different ways of seeing things. Even different words that led to misunderstandings. Maybe there was no failure in

Ireland, only bad luck, and maybe there was no bad luck in Germany, only failure. They were friends, and Eileen was good at helping people out of trouble. My mother didn't want our family to be a failure, because this was the last chance she had in her life. It would be her own fault if she was back on the streets of Germany with suitcases and children, like the people running away across the Berlin Wall. The family was a good story to hide behind and so she said it was time to stop dreaming. She went over to the Miss Ryans to put an end to it once and for all. She told them it was very kind of them to offer the money, but there were other people who might need it more, people who had nothing even to dream about, people who had nowhere even to be homesick for.

After that, everything was back to normal. The doors stopped slamming and my mother started writing in her diary every day because that's your only real friend for life. She collected lots more pictures of what happened in Germany. In some places, she said, the wall went right through the middle of a house, so that the back of the house was in one part of Germany and the front of the house was in the other. She showed us pictures of all the planes bringing food to Berlin and pictures of John F. Kennedy in the city. She said it was great to hear John F. Kennedy saying that he was a Berliner, because most American people were afraid to be German and changed their names from Busch to Bush and Schmidt to Smith and maybe you can't blame them.

Every day we played with the puppets and my mother said we would put on a play for our relatives and invite all the neighbours, too. We stayed inside to practise the play about the dog barking at the waves. There was even a book in our house about staying indoors. It was about what to do if an atom bomb fell anywhere near us like it did on Hiroshima. There would be nuclear radiation all around the streets. The radiation was always shown with red dots, like a disease in the air. It explained how to build a nuclear shelter, how to put sandbags in all the windows so you could stay inside living on tins of beans for a few years until the red dots were all gone again.

One day, Eileen brought Franz and me up to the top of Nelson's Pillar and my father said nothing, even though it was something the British left behind. When we came home, Onkel Ted was there with sweets in his pocket and we told him that we were going to put on a play for relatives and neighbours. He said it was a very fine idea and Eileen said we were full of talent. At the dinner table that night, my mother told a story about a family who had a puppet theatre under the Nazis. The father was afraid to say anything against Hitler. He was afraid that the children would go out and there would be trouble if they repeated what he said on the street. So every day they put on a puppet show in the evening after dinner, just for themselves. He would go in behind the puppet theatre with his children and make up story about a very bad man named Arnulf. And at the end of every play they always had to find a way to kill Arnulf, so that the other puppets were safe again.

'Remarkable,' Onkel Ted said.

He nodded his head slowly and said it was a great sign that people had courage. He had read lots of books about people like that, books that make you feel strong. There are no German songs that make you feel strong in your stomach but there are stories like that. Eileen was nodding because she was chewing a toffee in her mouth and my father had nothing to say either. They all just quietly swallowed the story and the room was silent.

My mother tells stories like that because there are other stories she can't tell. When it's silent, she thinks of all the things she has to keep secret. She wishes that she could have resisted more. For a minute, she sits there and everybody is waiting for her to tell another story. She is thinking about how she is trapped in Ireland now and how she was trapped in Germany once, and how nothing has changed. She wishes that she had thought of the puppet show killing Arnulf.

My mother was back in Düsseldorf, back in the same office, working as if nothing had happened. Nobody asked questions and she had no idea who to talk to now. One night, Stiegler even invited her out to the theatre again with his wife, as if it was all fine, as if the world could just go on as before. Frau Stiegler kissed her on the cheek as always, and it was like a cosy family, with everybody very happy not to say a word that might make things uncomfortable. My mother can't remember what the play was. She can only remember the lip biting and the helpless anger. She was thinking only about what happened in Venlo and how she wanted to go away and work somewhere else in a different place. She wanted never to see Stiegler again. She wanted a new life, maybe even in a new country. She even thought of running away and going into hiding because of the shame she might bring to her family if the story came out. She sat in the theatre with Stiegler in the middle and Frau Stiegler on the far side, dressed with a scarf made of fox, with fox eyes and fox paws hanging down. It was only at the interval, when Herr Stiegler left them alone for a moment, that my mother had the courage to say something.

'I think there is something you should know,' she said. 'About your husband.'

So then Frau Stiegler stared and listened to what happened in Venlo. It was hard to describe it in words, but my mother said Herr Stiegler must have planned it all and she could do nothing to stop it.

'What?' Frau Stiegler said, and it was like a little bark that the fox on her shoulders was making. She had angry eyes and my mother thought at last that there was somebody on her side again. Everything was going to be put right again. But, instead, Frau Stiegler looked at her with vicious eyes. The fox, too, as if they were not angry at Herr Stiegler at all, but at her. Maybe my mother was too polite. Maybe she didn't have words bad enough in her head to describe what happened to her. She didn't have a way of telling things that was ugly enough to describe Herr Stiegler and what he did, because Frau Stiegler just turned on her instead. It was as if she had started it all and Herr Stiegler was innocent. As if she had brought it all on herself and he could do no wrong.

'If I hear another word of this,' Frau Stiegler said, 'if you say a single word to me or to anyone about this, I will call the police instantly. I will not have my husband's reputation destroyed like this before my own eyes. Herr Stiegler is a good man, a respectable man, and how dare you even think up such a thing.'

They even sat through the end of the play and afterwards had the usual drink in a nearby café, but there was nothing more to say.

My mother is a dreamer and sometimes she just sits and stares, hoping that she will still find a way out, something she can say, some clever way that she can escape even now. She stays in the past for a few minutes and doesn't hear you sometimes when you speak. She's still thinking of running away.

Very late one evening, an envelope was dropped in the door. It was addressed to my mother and, when she opened it, she found it was full of money. There was no note going with it to say who it came from, but my mother knew immediately. She also knew that my father would not allow it and the trouble would start again and all the doors in the house would be banging. So she put the envelope away and said nothing. Next day she went straight over to the Miss Ryans to give the money back. She said it was so generous of them, but she could not accept it because that would be the end of the family and the end of Ireland. Then the Miss Ryans both stood at the door and shook their heads.

'What money?' they said.

They looked at each other and said there was some kind of mistake. Money in an envelope didn't automatically mean it came from the Miss Ryans. They don't go around dropping money into people's letter boxes before they go upstairs and lie down softly in their beds. My mother asked if it wasn't the Miss Ryans who dropped the money into her door, then who was it? So the Miss Ryans scratched their heads and thought about it for a moment and said the money probably came from God.

There was no way out but to bring the money back home again and there was nothing my father could do about it. My mother told him the money came from God and you couldn't give it back, unless he wanted her to put it into the poor box in the church, but he didn't want that either. There was no slamming doors this time, but he said she was still not allowed to go back home to Germany on her own. He said he had lots of cousins in America and South Africa who couldn't come home to Ireland any time they liked. So she put the money away and said she would wait until there was enough for all of us to go to Germany together.

Then everything was all right again and everybody in our house was dreaming and saving up money in jars.

My mother helped us to get everything ready for the puppet show. My father said we could use his desk-lamp as a spotlight. Onkel Ted came and Tante Roseleen and Tante Lilly, as well as Eileen Crowley and Kitty from Cork. Tante Eileen came up from Skibbereen with Onkel John this time, because he was attending the Fianna Fáil Árd Fheis and he knew all about politics. Anne was there and so was her brother Harry, and everybody was afraid of him going to the Congo, because the only thing the Irish army was good at was keeping the peace. Lots of the neighbours came, too, like the Miss Ryans and the Miss Doyles. There was a whole table full of sandwiches and cakes. People brought lemonade and there was even wine and whiskey and bottles of black beer.

All the chairs and seats in the house were brought into the *Kinderzimmer* and lined up in rows. My mother helped Maria to tie a box of sweets around her tummy as a belly tray, so she could go around offering them to the audience. Ita was sitting on Harry's knee trying to comb all his hair forward, and Tante Eileen from Skibbereen was showing everybody how to light a new cigarette from the old one. And when they were all sitting down, my mother closed the big wooden shutters on the window and switched on the spotlight. It was like a real theatre with people coughing in the audience and trying to stop making noise. My mother got in behind the puppet theatre with us and when everybody stopped talking and coughing, Franz pulled the string to open the curtains.

'Have you seen the dog?' Kasper said.

Then Ita suddenly started talking back to the puppets, because she believed everything they said and my mother had to put her head out and tell her to be quiet and not give away the ending. We continued and it was all in German, so nobody could understand what was going on except Onkel Ted and my father. Everybody else was in the wrong country and couldn't rescue us.

There was a man called Arnulf, like the story my mother heard about in Germany, and he would not let any of the other puppets speak. All the time, Kasper was walking along and meeting other puppets like Hansel and Gretel and the grandmother and the queen and the king and other puppets that we made up ourselves with papier mâché. But none of them could say a word to Kasper, because Arnulf said they were not allowed to speak to him. Kasper asked them where the dog was, but they were all afraid to say anything in case Arnulf would come and punish them. So then Kasper had to find a way of killing Arnulf so that all the other puppets could speak again. And when Arnulf was dead with his head over the side of the theatre, my mother switched on the hairdryer and the blue scarf started blowing across the stage. Then Kasper came to the seafront and found the dog barking at the waves. That was the end and when Franz pulled the curtain closed, the audience clapped for a long time.

Twenty-three

It's a long way to go to Germany. You have to go on two different ships and five different trains. My father shows us the tickets and my mother counts the luggage lined up in the hallway, six suitcases and four children. She laughs and claps her hands because we're going home and everybody is so excited that you feel nearly sick in your stomach. First you go on the ship to Holyhead. You go across the gangplank and my father laughs at the sign over the door that says 'Mind your Head' because it's like a warning to anyone who leaves Ireland to be careful, not to forget where you come from or do anything stupid. Outside on deck you can see the lighthouse going by and the land moving further and further away until it's out of sight. Maria wants to know if we're going to get seasick, because the ship is moving from side to side and you can't walk straight. The seagulls keep following us even though it's dark now and there's nothing more to see except some yellow light from the ship on the water. At night you take the train to London to see the black taxis. And the next morning you take another train and another ship to Holland and three more trains after that until you're in Kempen and we're back in my mother's film.

They were waiting for us at the window. Ta Maria came out and threw her arms around my mother for a long time

208

without a word. Then it was Tante Lisalotte's turn and she wouldn't let go. They stood outside on the street, hugging and looking at each other up and down, again and again, and they just kept saying '*ja, ja, ja*' and '*nein, nein, nein*' as if they didn't believe their own eyes. The suitcases were forgotten on the ground. They shook hands with my father and called him Hans, as if he was going to be German, too, from now on. They knew all our names, but they kept saying '*Ach, Du lieber Himmel*', as if they thought my mother had only gone away to Ireland for a few days and come back with four children.

Then it was time for coffee and we were sent over to the Kranz Café to get cakes. The smell of baking was like a warm pillow in your face when you walked in the door. All the women in the Kranz Café asked us questions and said we had soft voices, like German children long ago before the war. They said we were the long ago children with good manners and straight backs and no chewing gum. The cake was wrapped in the shape of a church so that the paper didn't touch the icing on the top. They told us to hold the parcel flat so that it would arrive on the table the way it left the café, and Ta Maria even had the same silver trowel that my mother has, so you could lift a slice on to the plate and make sure it had never been touched by human fingers.

My mother walked around the town with us to look for all the things that had not changed. The church with the red steeple was there, just like it was in the photographs, as well as the cinema with the name Kempener Lichtspiele and the windmill on the Burgring. The shops had everything laid out in the windows just like the day that she left. The only thing that was missing was the house on the Buttermarkt square where she lived when she was small. The fountain was still there outside, but the house was gone. There were new doors on the houses and new windows. My mother said everyone had new kitchens and new cookers, and that's what happens when you lose the war and you never want to look back at old things. Everything has to be new. The streets and the people still had the same names in German, but she was sometimes lost and couldn't find things she remembered.

It was like being six years of age again and maybe she was homesick in her own home town. Or maybe we had been away too long, she said, and we were getting used to living by the sea, because she was expecting to see a bright blue glass of water at the end of every street. And late in the afternoon when we walked so far that we were nearly in the country, there was a high breeze in the trees that sounded like water. At the edge of the town we stood looking at the flat land going out for ever and watched a car travelling all the way across the horizon behind a line of tall trees.

There was lots of talk about making the evening meal and who would be eating what. Did Irish children like *Wurst*? Was there anything we didn't eat? They had black bread and black jam, and plates made of wood. They kept tidying up even while they were eating because nobody likes the table to be '*abgegrasst*', like a field where the cows have already eaten all the grass. Then there was lots more talk about who would be sleeping where. Everyone was counting heads and spaces in beds. In between, they would sometimes remember a story and laugh so much that they had to lean on something to stop themselves from falling down. '*Zu Bett, zu Bett wer ein Liebchen hat, wer keines hat geht auch zu Bett*' – 'To Bed, to Bed if you're in love, to bed if you're on your own.' The soap was different, and so were the basins and the toilets. The pillows were square and there was a big duvet instead of blankets. I was allowed to sleep on the sofa with the curtains moving slowly and the light coming in from the street outside like my mother's film on the wall, and when I woke up the next morning I found that I was still in Germany with my arm hanging over the side.

It was like being at home because they were always talking about things to be cleaned. There was a smell of washing and the white sheets were hanging out on the line outside so that you could run through them with your eyes closed, like running into the smell of baking in the Kranz Café. Tante Lisalotte kept checking through our things, examining the collars, picking up shirts and asking if they had been worn, as if she wasn't happy until she found something to wash. And then we had to help with the sheets and everyone picked a corner each and walked in towards the centre like Irish dancing, until they were folded and ironed and counted and put away again.

Tante Lisalotte was the aunt with a cravat-making factory in the house, so we got a coloured cravat each. She was married to Onkel Max and they had two boys called Stefan and Herbert who showed us how to throw water bombs out the window. They had a box of matches and a cigar in the basement, but Tante Lisalotte could smell trouble and came down before they had a chance to light it up. Four boys in lederhosen, she said, like *Max und Moritz* multiplied by two. Tante Minne was a doctor who wanted to collect lots of valuable antiques and Onkel Wilhelm was an optician who had hundreds of guns and antlers covering all the walls of the house. He was the uncle who kept a bottle of schnapps hidden in the aquarium of his surgery, behind artificial plants and the two lazy carp swimming back and forth. They had two children called Mathias and Ursula who also wore lederhosen and taught us new words in German. Ursula had blonde plaits, too, and knew how to whistle with two fingers in her mouth.

All our aunts in Germany had the same nose, so they could sniff what was going on anywhere, even things that had not happened yet. My mother said it was a gift that the Kaiser girls inherited down through the generations and that maybe all the Germans had. They could sniff every warning signal, every danger and every possible misfortune. My mother could sniff a lie from a million miles away and Tante Lisalotte could sniff trouble around the corner. Tante Minne could look at you for a long time and sniff what was inside your head. They knew if you had brushed your teeth or whether you had washed your hands. They knew if you had said your prayers or not. They could walk into a room and tell what you were talking about. They could sniff where you had been and they knew if you were wasting your money on chewing gum. The Irish aunts and uncles gave you money but the German aunts never gave you money, only clothes and toys. The German aunts and uncles told you not to spend any money, even the money that the Irish aunts and uncles gave you.

My father was different in Germany. He wore a cravat and a new suit, and he also got a new pair of glasses from Onkel Wilhelm that had a brown tint and made him look more German. He stopped wearing his tweed cap and his face was brown from the sun, right down to the collar of his shirt. He smiled a lot and one day Maria even made him eat chewing gum, just to try it. He liked talking to people about technical things, about all the new inventions in Germany. He had lots of new friends, like Onkel Willi, the priest who drove too fast with a cigar in his mouth and played chess with a box of cigars on the table beside him. I watched them one afternoon playing quietly until the room filled up with smoke and my father won and they shook hands like friends for life.

My father drank beer and sometimes he was nearly as German as any of the uncles, telling stories and laughing. With his brown face and his new cravat he looked so German that I thought he was going to buy a car and start smoking cigars as well. We didn't need to be Irish and there was no point in speaking Irish to people on buses in Germany. Tante Minne knew that Ireland was full of monastic ruins and valuable antiques, and Onkel Wilhelm knew it was full of rivers with salmon and trout. Onkel Max said it was a small country with lots of big writers. Onkel Willi knew it was full of priests and sheep and holy shrines along the road, and Tante Lisalotte knew it was full of rainbows and lots of trees bent over by the wind. They said Irish people were very friendly and very generous, but my father said that was because they didn't know how to own anything or keep money in their pockets. The poorer you were the more generous you were, he said. Irish people were so afraid of being poor that they spent all their money, while German people were so afraid of being poor that they saved up every penny.

My father said Irish people lived like there was no tomorrow and Onkel Wilhelm said the Germans lived like there was no yesterday. Onkel Max said that's why Germans were busy trying to invent lots of new things like cars and tinted glasses and the Irish were busy inventing stories and literature instead. My father said the Irish invented lots of other things, too, like the hunger strike and Irish coffee. Tante Minne said it was a pity nobody in Germany thought of going on hunger strike against the

213

Nazis. Onkel Wilhelm said it was a pity the Germans weren't more like the Irish and my father said it was a pity the Irish weren't more like the Germans. He said it was a pity that Ireland wasn't closer to Germany and Onkel Max said it was a pity that Germany wasn't surrounded by water. My mother said Ireland was a place where you still needed luck and prayers, and Ta Maria said Germany was a place where you made your own luck and deserved everything you got. They all agreed that the Irish never hurt anybody. They said the Germans tried to drive everybody who wasn't German into extinction, unlike the Irish who were nearly driven into extinction themselves. Would you rather kill or be killed, my father asked, and nobody knew how to answer that question. Would you rather trample or be trampled, he said, because one language always goes into extinction in the end and nobody knew how to answer that either. Instead they agreed that Ireland and Germany were both still divided countries. The only difference was that the Irish won the war and still hated the British, while the Germans lost the war and had nothing against the British. And then there was an argument because Tante Minne wanted Mathias and Ursula to practise speaking English to us, but my father said that wasn't allowed. So Tante Minne said my father was a welcome guest but he couldn't start making rules in her house.

'If you hate the British so much,' Tante Minne said, 'then why don't you teach your children the most perfect English.'

My mother didn't know how to fight back like that any more, even though she was in her own country. She had other ways of going around trouble. And anyway it was soon forgotten because it was time to start visiting more people and travelling around Germany. We took the train to Neuss to visit a bishop who had a large bowl of fruit on the table and a painting of a fruit bowl on the wall. He asked me if I preferred the real fruit or the painting of fruit, so I pointed at the bowl on the table and his housekeeper packed it all up in bags for us. He gave me his name too, Hugo. Then his driver drove us all the way to Cologne on the autobahn that went straight for ever. You could trust that there would be no cows chewing on the road and no 'Reifenbeisser' dogs running out to try and bite the tyres. We saw the Cologne Cathedral and the railway station and the bridge that once fell into the river during the war and the big number 4711 lighting up at night.

Then we all had to split up. My mother took Maria and Ita on the train to see Tante Elfriede in Rüsselsheim and, after that, all the way up to Salzburg to see Tante Marianne and to meet all the writers and artists who came to visit there. My father took Franz and me to see the Drachenfelz and he was happier than he had ever been in his life before because it was like being on his honeymoon. We sat on a boat going down the Rhine and he talked a lot, much more than ever before, pointing at the mountains and telling us about how he met my mother. He wanted to explain everything and we had to listen. We drank lemonade called Miranda and had our dinner on the boat, watching other boats passing along beside us, some of them flat with lots of coal heaped up on them. The river was so wide it was like an autobahn with boats going up on one side and down the other.

It was evening by the time we got off the boat and started climbing up the Drachenfelz. We went up the steps and then walked along the path. My father was limping and it wasn't long before we slowed down, because it was very steep. We stopped to take a rest and turned around to look at the river below us with the ships still going up and down slowly without a sound, almost like toy boats. After a while, we continued back up the hill again but we were hardly moving at all. My father took off his cravat and put it in his pocket. He opened his shirt and you could see his white neck inside. He took off his jacket and carried it on his arm instead. But then he stopped to ask us if we still wanted to go all the way to the top. I knew how much he wanted to see the hotel again where he stayed with my mother. I knew it was a place you could not talk about, only see with your own eyes. He wanted to go back and see if it was still the same. And maybe then he was afraid to go back and find that it was not the same.

'Are you hungry?' he asked.

'No,' we said.

We carried on for a while, but then he stopped again and sat down on a bench as if his legs couldn't carry him any more. There wasn't far to go, but instead he started talking and telling us things that he had never told us before. He said it was not true that he had rescued my mother because it was the other way around. If it wasn't for her he would have joined the priesthood like his brother Ted. He said he once went to Rome to pray and ask God whether he should be a priest or get married. He went to see an Italian doctor who could hardly speak to him and used his arms a lot. The doctor said he should get married, because getting married and having children was the only way of getting rid of a limp. My father thought it was like God talking in broken English. He even cried and the doctor had to put his hand on his shoulder. Then my mother came to Ireland and rescued him from the priesthood. And that's why he could not go up to the top of the Drachenfelz without her. After that he was

216

quiet and said nothing all the way back on the train to Kempen.

That night, back in Ta Maria's house, I was trying to get to sleep and I thought of what it would be like if we all came to live in Germany instead and all had the same language. Nobody would ever call us Nazis. My father would have lots of friends and my mother would have all her sisters to talk to. My father would be more German and my mother would learn how to argue and make the rules, like her youngest sister Tante Minne. I lay there and saw different shadows on the wall. I was back in the black and white film that made my mother so afraid.

'Please God, help me to get out of this,' she wrote in her diary.

She didn't know what to do any more. At night she prayed on her knees and walked up and down in her room. She was afraid of what was going to happen to her now. She was back in Düsseldorf, but she had nobody to speak to. She wanted to go home to Kempen, but she was afraid to make trouble for Ta Maria and Onkel Gerd. They had no money and they couldn't support her. She was afraid of being a beggar with no work. She saw Stiegler in the office every day in his suit and she could smell his aftershave. She had not learned the words to describe what happened to her in Venlo. She could not trust any of the women in the office and she didn't know how to go to the police either, because Herr Stiegler had lots of friends in the Gestapo and the Waffen SS. He could accuse her of not helping Germany and then she would be taken away instead. In the end, the only person she could go to was Stiegler himself, because she was only nineteen years old and sometimes you think the person you're most afraid of is the only person who can help.

One day, she had the courage to go straight up to his desk after work. The typewriters were all silent. Herr Stiegler sat looking out the window while she spoke.

'I'm glad you told me this,' he said.

Then he asked her to go home, back to her apartment room. He told her to wait there for him and not to say a word to anyone. He would come and discuss it with her there. He said there was nothing to worry about because he would personally see to it that everything was all right. She was afraid it would start all over again. She could not let him come near her. But he was so calm and so confident that she began to think everything was fine. She knew everything was going wrong but she wanted to believe it was right. As if it was easier to believe a lie. She went back to her apartment and paced up and down the room that night, wondering if she should just run away, just go and start again in a new city where nobody knew who she was.

It was about midnight when Stiegler came to her apartment. She heard his footsteps on the stairs. He was very quiet because there were neighbours living in the other apartments. He entered her room carrying a pouch under his arm that was black and shiny, with a rubber band around it. He told her to lie down on the bed and sat beside her. He held her arm and asked her where all the smiles were gone. He held her chin with his thumb and forefinger and told her to relax, it would only take a minute and then everything would be all right again. This was the solution. He would give her a small injection that wouldn't hurt at all. It might make her feel a little nauseous afterwards, but that would all pass over and she would be full of smiles and dimples and going out to the theatre again. She wanted to know what was in the injection and he said it was a simple preparation, made of purely natural ingredients like vinegar and alcohol. He was already rolling up her sleeve and rubbing a little swab of alcohol on her arm. He said he had received it from a very good doctor that he was friendly with. It would make her strong. It would wipe away all the sickness and disgust. It was an injection against disgust.

'There we are,' he said, like a real doctor.

He was very kind and very polite. He sat with her for a while stroking her forehead and there is no defence against kindness, my mother says. He kept saying he admired her strength and her courage. He said she was very brave and very beautiful, a real German woman. She could smell the cognac on his breath. Then she fell asleep and when she woke up, he was gone. She felt dizzy and sick. She tried to stand up, then she kneeled down, and then she lay on the floor as if nothing mattered any more. Even though she vomited everything up and her stomach was empty, the pain kept getting worse. She left the room and staggered to the bathroom in the hallway, holding on to the wall as if she were on a ship. She tried not to draw any attention to herself, and then she started bleeding and crying silently at the sight of her own blood all around her. She was afraid that one of the people in the other apartments would come out and find her there.

Stiegler came back some hours later. He found her lying on the floor of the bathroom. Her face was white and he could hardly wake her up any more. He was worried that something might go wrong, that she might die maybe and then he would have to explain himself. He had to do things quickly now. There was no time to clean up the blood in the bathroom. He dragged her back to her room very quietly so as not to wake anyone up. He left her on the floor and packed her belongings quickly into a suitcase. He lost no time on this and went straight out to arrange for a car to come and take her away. He had already discarded the needle and the doctor's pouch in various bins around Düsseldorf. When the car arrived, he got the driver to come up and help carry her down the stairs.

She woke up once or twice and saw that she was dribbling on to Herr Stiegler's jacket and there was a white mark on his collar like a new badge. Then they put her into the back of the car with her suitcase beside her and Stiegler handed the driver some money. She heard the engine starting with a growl. And as the car drove away she looked up and saw Herr Stiegler taking out his handkerchief to wipe his suit.

Twenty-four

Then it was the time of the bees.

My father had been preparing for a long time, talking to other beekeepers on the phone and planning everything like a new business. He worked out how much he would have to spend on one side of the page and how much the bees would pay him back with honey on the other. He bought a jungle hat with a wire cage around his face and leather gloves that reached all the way up his arms, past his elbows. He bought the hives and the frames and a smoke gun where you could put in a piece of rolled-up sackcloth on fire and shoot smoke out through the spout to calm the bees down. Everything else was free. The bees would fly out from the roof of the breakfast room from morning till night and nobody could stop them collecting pollen.

On the evening they arrived, my mother got out her special tablecloth, as if the bees were coming to tea like relations from Germany or west Cork. It was like having a party because she put flowers on the table for them and bought lemonade, too. From now on we knew we would never be the same as any other family, because we had friends who were bees and everybody on our street thought the bees were sitting at the table with us eating bread and jam. We even said a special prayer for them, and when the bell rang we all jumped up from the table together and ran to the front door. There was a tall man standing there with a straw skep in his hand. He smiled and spoke to my father in Irish. Then they both went up the stairs and through my bedroom, and we watched from the room above as my father stepped out the window on to the roof of the breakfast room with the cage around his head.

My mother had a picture in the diary of a man named John Glenn who was dressed like a beekeeper. He was the first man to go into orbit, but then he lost his balance in the bath one day and broke his middle ear and stayed in orbit for the rest of his life after that. My father looked like he was in space for ever when he came out in his overalls and his long gloves and with his heavy boots on. The tall man said there was no need to shoot smoke because the bees were very happy to come to our house. He banged the skep and threw them all out on a board where they marched into the new hive with their white tails up in the air.

My mother and father are not afraid to be different. Other families are getting a car and a TV and we want those things as well, but we're German and Irish and have bees as friends. They say we're lucky to be so different because bees were better for the world and better for us. Most other children don't even know the difference between a bee and a wasp. The TV kills your imagination and makes you stupid. But I know the other boys are not stupid, they just don't care if there's a difference between a wasp and a bee. They don't care about the famine either. They don't care about coffin ships and they don't care about concentration camps.

All they care is whether we can fight. They call us Hitler and Eichmann and they want to see if we can fight like Germans. They want to hear us saying aaargh and uuumph like they do in comics and films. We try and run away. One day when they came after us, I ran one way and Franz ran a different way. I got home first through the football field, back along the lanes and in the back door. I didn't know where Franz was. He came home later and stood at the front door with blood on his face and blood on his shirt.

'*Mein Schatz*, what happened?' my mother asked.

There was nothing we could do about it. She could not tell us to stop being German, so she brought Franz into the kitchen and began to clean up the blood on his face. She got some chocolate out of the press to make things better. She said it was good that we didn't fight back because we are not the fist people. We are the word people and one day we will win them over. One day the silent negative will win them all over.

When my father came home he was very angry, because nobody is allowed to hit Franz except him. He examined the shirt with the blood on it and said he could not let it go. I thought it was great because he was going to pay them back for what they did to Franz. Maybe he would get the boys who did it and make them kneel down to ask God how many lashes. He put his cap back on again and went straight down the road to one of the small houses and my mother tried to hold him back by the elbow at the last minute to make sure that he would stay friendly.

'I'm not going down with fists,' my father said.

Instead, he took the bloody shirt and brought Franz with him. When they got to the house and rang the bell, a woman answered the door and pretended that they had come to the wrong house. It was a funny thing to say, because the boy who hit Franz was hiding behind the banisters right beside her. My father smiled and said he didn't come with fists, but he wasn't leaving until somebody listened to him making a speech. So the man of the house had to come out in his slippers and his sleeves rolled up and a tattoo of an anchor on his arm. He was very tall, almost twice the size of my father. He had twice as many children as my father and their house was not even half the size of ours. He was tired and he had a stubble on his face, and it looked like he had no time to listen to speeches from people in bigger houses. The television was on in the front room and he was missing half the football match. My father didn't care how big the man was or how small his house was or if he watched TV all day. He wasn't looking for revenge. He just held up the shirt with the blood on it and let the tall man look down at it for a long time.

'This is your own blood,' my father said.

Then he recited pieces that he remembered off by heart from books he had read. He said it was time to fight for the rights of small people and small nations. He said the reason we were all on our knees was that others thought they were so great. He said it was no use fighting each other all the time because then Ireland would never have its own inventions and its own language.

The man with the tattoo started scratching his belly. He thought he was back at school. He had no idea why my father was coming down to his house to start reciting things from books and saying a few words, too, in Irish with a bloody shirt in his hand. Maybe he thought it was like a new religion or a new political party looking for money. Maybe he thought my father was a Communist. And that was even worse than being a Nazi, that was like the nuclear thing, when the air is full of red dots and everybody stays inside for the rest of their lives watching television. The man with the tattoo started looking down at the sour sallies that were growing beside his slippers at the door. Then my father said goodbye and insisted on shaking hands. He didn't even mention the boy who hit Franz. He just left it at that. He even closed the gate after him, the gate that was never closed in its life before because the man with the tattoo and his whole family just left it open all the time and didn't care how many dogs came into their garden to lift their leg and scratch the grass. As they walked away, my father told Franz not to look around.

'Did you win them over?' my mother asked.

'They laughed,' Franz said.

My mother said it didn't matter because they were the fist people and you were right not to fight back, otherwise you would become just like them. My father didn't even mind that they laughed and ignored his speech.

'What matters,' he said, 'is that a small man was able to walk up to a big man and not be afraid.'

I knew it wasn't over yet. I knew they would come looking for us again because I was Eichmann and I could do nothing about it. I wanted to be one of the fist people so that I could defend myself and not be afraid on the streets. From then on I wanted to be a real Nazi. I wanted to be so cruel and mean that they would be scared of me instead. In bed at night I thought of all the things I would do. I thought of bashing their heads against the wall. I thought of smashing a rock into some boy's teeth. I would be famous all over the place. People would be afraid even to go swimming when I was out. I thought of them running away and hiding in doorways when they heard me coming, shivering at the sound of my name. Eichmann.

I started practising on my own. I learned how to do the evil smile. I learned to laugh like the Nazis do in films, slowly, while I was getting ready to torture somebody. I spoke English to myself in a German accent. I kept saying things like 'my friend' and being so polite that people would be even more frightened when they realised that I was going to kill them. I stuck knives into puppets and grinned into the mirror. I threw rocks at cats. I practised torturing Franz and Maria. And one day, I even threw a chair at my mother and there was nothing she could do about it. So she left the chair there where it fell and said nobody else would ever pick it up again and it could stay there for a hundred years.

'Why do you want to be one of the fist people?' she asked.

'It's boring to be good,' I said.

I wanted to be as bad as possible. When you're bad you get a good feeling because people look shocked and worried and that makes you want to be even worse. If you're good nobody looks at you.

'I'm Eichmann,' I said. 'I'm going to kill people and laugh about it.'

She brought me into the front room and showed me a book where there was a picture of a boy in the street with his hands up in the air saying don't shoot. She told me about a place called Auschwitz and how Eichmann was the man in charge of the trains for getting people there. She could remember Jewish people in Kempen. They were called '*die Jüdchen*: the little Jews' because they lived in the small houses. She never saw any of them being taken away, but she said there was only one Jewish man who came back to Kempen after the war and he didn't stay. He just came to look around once and then he left again and now there are no Jews in Kempen. She said they were our people. Our people died in concentration camps.

I wonder what it's like for my cousins in Germany and if they still have to think about it every day like me. Is anyone calling them Nazis on the street? Here I have to be careful where I walk, because if they catch me then I'll go on trial and they'll execute me.

'I don't want to be German,' I said.

She had tears in her eyes and said the Germans would never be able to go home again. Germans are not allowed to be children. They're not allowed to sing children's songs or tell fairy tales. They cannot be themselves. That's why Germans want to be Irish or Scottish or American. That's why they love Irish music and American music, because that gives them a place to go home to and be homesick for.

'It's like a birthmark,' she said.

It was time for us to go down to the sea and look at the waves, because she had to carry on with her work. She stood at the door to watch us going across the street until we disappeared around the corner. I knew I was in the luckiest place in the world with the sea close by. The sun was shining and you could smell the dust in the air. There were tar bubbles on the road and further along you could see a shimmer, as if the ground was rising up in the heat. Some of the shops had canopies that were flapping in the breeze. The boats were out on the bay and there was a haze over the harbour. We went swimming, Noel, Franz and I. We dived under the water for as long as possible. I knew I could stop breathing longer than anyone else. I could stay down there until my lungs nearly burst. I was the champion at not breathing and not speaking. I could hear the voices around the pool, but they were muffled and far away. Down there it was blue and calm, like being inside a cool drink.

Sometimes the bees come into my room at night. They go after the light because they think it's daytime and they want to get as close to the sun as possible. They go mad and whirl around the light until they crash into the bulb in the middle of the room and fall down. Then they pick themselves up and start again, whirling around and getting more and more excited and impatient, until you switch off the light and they move to the window instead. Then they buzz up and down the window for ages trying to get out to the light in the street, until they get so tired they drop down on the floor and crawl around in circles. They always go in circles when they're dying, as if they're trying to make themselves dizzy. You can't let them out, and I have to sleep with my head covered up in case they come over and sting me in the middle of the night.

I know it's the smallest things that hurt most because I got stung in the garden one day when I put my hand down on a bee in the grass. He had been hit by a drop of rain and was going mad in circles. When I put my hand down he stung me and after that nobody wanted to play on the grass any more. My father says that stings are good for you and we'll never get rheumatism. If you want to reduce the pain, he says, you should take the sting out quickly to stop the poison going in. He explained that a bee sting is very different from a wasp sting, because a bee has a hook at the end of it and he showed it to us once under the microscope. He says we'll soon get used to bee stings and won't even feel them. And my mother says we shouldn't howl so much every time a bee stings us because the neighbours will think we're being tortured to death.

Sometimes when I'm inside the house I hear somebody screaming outside and I know it's a bee sting. Maria or Ita or Franz, everybody has a different scream. And sometimes they scream before they're even stung. If a bee goes near them they start shouting and running inside, as if they're going to die. It's not even the bee's fault. They fly out over the garden and come back with pouches so full of pollen, like heavy suitcases. And when the wind suddenly blows around the corner at the back of the house, they get pushed back down into the garden and find it difficult to pick themselves up again. Sometimes the wind blows them into somebody's hair and it's not their fault because they just want to get back up and carry the pollen home to the hive. Then they get tangled up in hair. You hear Maria or Ita screaming and running into the house even though the bee hasn't stung yet and is only trapped and buzzing like mad, trying to get back out.

One day it happened to my mother and we invented a way of stopping the bee from stinging. My mother came running inside and shouting that there was a bee in her hair. She held her hair tight to try and stop it from getting closer to her head. The bee was probably lashing out and stinging everything it could touch because it was trapped in a prison of hair, like a spider's web with no chance of getting out alive. But as long as it didn't get close to the skin, then there was still a chance of stopping it from stinging. She told me to get a tea towel and put it on the place where the bee was. I could feel the buzzing under my fingers and I pressed hard until the buzzing went up to a high pitch, like a motorbike far away. Then I pressed even harder until I felt a crack under the towel and the bee was dead. Nobody said anything about it afterwards, in case my father would get angry that we were killing all his bees. After that I was the expert at stopping stings. I was the sting stopper.

Twenty-five

After that we tried to be as Irish as possible.

There was a new baby in the house named Bríd. Onkel Ted came out specially to our church to say Mass in Irish and we were the altar boys, Franz and me. Some people coughed and walked out because they thought they were in the wrong country and couldn't pray to God in Irish. But Onkel Ted carried on without even looking around once. He baptised Bríd and poured holy water over her head, and afterwards there was a big cake in our house with a Celtic spiral made of Smarties. It didn't matter who walked out of the church with a bad cough because my father said Bríd was born and baptised now and those people would soon be outnumbered. My mother wanted to know why they were more afraid of the Irish language than they were of the bees, and Onkel Ted said maybe the sting is worse. Franz said Irish speakers don't sting and then everybody laughed and ate the spiral cake.

Then we went back to Connemara for three months to be as Irish as possible. We got new caps and new rain macs and went on a train with a group of boys who were all going to live in a full-Irish fireside. We were going to school in the Gaeltacht and we would come back like native speakers. At the station, a photographer came to take a picture for the newspapers and my mother kept it in the diary. Franz and me and the other boys waving goodbye on the platform, because we would not see or speak to anyone in our family until we came home fully Irish.

Franz went to An Cheathrú Rua and I went to a new place called Béal an Daingin, but I was sick again and the howling started up in my chest every night. The people in the house were very nice to me, but sometimes I wanted to go home because I couldn't breathe. I had lots of trouble with the dogs howling in my chest. The local doctor came and he said I would soon get over it. But I was coughing all the time and had to stay in bed. Then Bean an tí gave me cigarettes that were good for asthma. She bought a packet of Sweet Afton and put them beside my bed with a box of matches. She told me that if I felt short of breath I should light up a cigarette and smoke away like a good man, because that would help me to cough up all the bad stuff and not be afraid of the dark. Then I got better again and forgot that I was German and started learning how to live in Irish.

There was a boy named Peadar in the house who showed me how to get water and how to milk the cows. Bean an tí taught me how to find all the places where the hens laid eggs. I helped Fear an tí to stack turf against the side of the house and I learned how to say 'go dtachtfaidh sé thú' which is the Irish for I hope it chokes you. I learned how to turn English words into Irish and to say 'mo bhicycle' and 'mo chuid biscuits'. I learned how to walk to school backwards to stop the hailstones stinging my legs. I watched men gathering seaweed and putting it on big lorries to be taken away to Galway and turned into cough medicine. I saw people laying out salted fish on the stone walls to dry them in the sun. I saw the tide going out every day as if it was never coming back, and I saw donkeys with their feet tied together to stop them running away and laughing at everybody.

There was a curly piece of brown sticky paper hanging in the middle of every room with dead flies stuck to it. There was a dog beside the fire who had his chin on the floor and his eyes closed and only lifted one ear to hear if anyone was coming. Every day a man named Cóilín came to visit and sit by the window. He was a cousin belonging to the woman of the house and he would look out at the road and tell them who was passing by. There was a radio in the house but there was no TV and no need for one, because the man at the window was the man who said the news. The woman of the house could carry on making the dinner and the man of the house could sit with his pipe by the fireside without looking up. That's Joe Phait going west now with his new coat on, Cóilín would say. Here's Nancy Seóige making her way back from the east now with biscuits for her sister. There were four different directions you could go – west, from the west, east and from the east. Sometimes they came in to visit and then the whole house was like a television programme, with the man at the window keeping everybody talking. Nancy Seóige came in to smoke a fag out of the wind and explain that the biscuits were for her sister, because she was ill in bed for a long time and the Sweet Afton were doing her no good any more. She came in from the east and when she finished her story she went back out to the west.

There's Tom Pháidin Tom going east now with his bicycle and his dog behind him, the man at the window said. Sometimes the woman of the house would ask questions, too, like what Tom Pháidin Tom was thinking about, and she was told that he was thinking he had spent long enough in his own company on the bog for one day, and he was going east up to Teach Uí Fhlatharta to buy pipe cleaners and tobacco for himself. The man at the window knew who was going by and who was not going by. He knew what everybody was saying in Connemara, and all the conversations that were going on in England and America even, as far away as Boston. I see the *sagart*, Father Ó Móráin has not gone up to see the Johnson family yet about their son in Birmingham. Páraic Jamesey must have gone up to Galway on the bus for the day, because they say he's great with a nurse from Inishmore working in the Galway regional hospital. They say that Patricia Mhuirnín Leitir Mochú is getting married in the spring in America, to a stranger.

The man at the window could tell who was up at Teach Uí Fhlatharta and what stories they all had. He knew that Tom Pháidin Tom was buying more than pipe cleaners because his dog was coming back from the east already and that meant Máirtín Handsome was surely up there as well and Tom Pháidin Tom would not be going home until it was late, unless Peigín Dorcha went up after him with her dark hair. He knew what all the living people were saying and also what all the dead people were saying in the graveyard. He knew that Tom Pháidin Tom's brother Páidin Óg was calling out from the grave, saying that his throat was like a dry stick and that if he was still alive and hadn't drowned out of Ros a Mhíl one day, then he'd be up there in Teach Uí Fhlatharta and nobody, not even the priest or the Pope in the Vatican or Éamon de Valera himself would get him out until he had sung '*Barr na Sráide*' and the 'Rocks a Bawn'.

One night I had to go up to Teach Uí Fhlatharta with a blue and white milk jug. The man of the house was not allowed to go up himself because the priest had told him

never to go east or he would never come back west again
if he did. So then I had to go east for him and he told me
to be careful on the way back not to spill a single drop.
It was dark and as I walked along the road towards the
lights of Teach Uí Fhlatharta, I knew that the man at
the window was telling the man of the house about me.
There's Dublin Jack going in the door now carrying the
jug with the blue and white stripes and there's Dublin Jack
taking out the money and buying sweets instead, but that
was only a joke.

Teach Uí Fhlatharta was a big shop with everything you
could buy, like jam and sweets and things like cement and
wood, too. There was lots of smoke and lots of tall men in
wellington boots standing at the counter, all talking at the
same time. They were telling all the stories in Connemara
as far away as Boston. I saw Tom Pháidin Tom laughing
and smoking a pipe that had a lid on it for the rain. I
stood behind them waiting for a while and looking at the
new brushes and buckets hanging from the ceiling, until
one of the men turned around to take the jug from me.
He told the man behind the counter to fill it up to the top
because Dublin Jack was very thirsty. I put the money up
on the counter and, when the jug was full, they passed it
down to me and told me to hold it with both hands. There
was cream on top to stop you from seeing what was inside
the jug, but you could smell it. Then one of them came
over to open the door, and I walked back slowly in the
dark without turning the jug upside down or meeting any
ghosts or falling down in the ditch or getting swallowed
up by the ground and never seen again. I didn't spill a
single drop. But when I got back, the man of the house
looked into the jug for a long time. He asked me did I
drink half of it myself, but the woman of the house told

him I didn't. The man at the window wanted to know if I saw anyone with a tweed cap turned backwards and that was Máirtín Handsome. Then the man of the house drank from the side of the jug and started telling a ghost story that happened to himself one time when he was coming home from Teach Uí Fhlatharta in the dark.

When I was going back to Dublin again, the woman of the house went out and caught a chicken for me to take back with me on the train. She put it into a bag and tied it with a ribbon so that the chicken was looking out at one end and some feathers were coming out the other. I knew that the man at the window was still talking about me long after I was gone. There's Dublin Jack on the train now with the chicken beside him looking out the window at the stone walls going by. There's Dublin Jack going home more Irish than anyone in Connemara, talking to the chicken in Irish and giving it a bit of his sandwich.

After that we started going to a new all-Irish school in Dublin with the Christian Brothers. Every day we had to get a train into the city and walk past Nelson's Pillar and Cafollas and the Gresham Hotel. Everything at the new school was done through Irish – Latin, algebra, hurling and even English. The Christian Brothers wore black with a white collar and white chalk marks around their shoulders. One of them had brown fingers and smoked a piece of chalk all day in class, until his lips were white from talking. He asked me to read out a piece in a book and the whole class had to listen. He said it was a miracle how a Dublin boy could become so Irish. He escaped out of the classroom and took me by the hand, flying down the stairs three at a time and leaving all the other boys behind fencing with rulers. He said I had to go around and read in front of the whole school. I had to go to every classroom and show them what a native speaker was like, and the principal said I should be on television as an example of how history could be turned back.

Everybody was proud of me and I liked being Irish. But I knew all the boys in the school were laughing at me. Nobody really wanted to be that Irish. If you wanted to have friends you had to start speaking to yourself in English, so that nobody would call you a mahogany gaspipe or a sad fucking sap or think that you were from Connemara long ago. You'd never get into the Waverley Billiard Hall speaking Irish. You had to pretend that you had no friends who lived long ago like Peig Sayers. You had to laugh at Peig Sayers so that nobody would suspect you were really Irish underneath. You had to pretend that Irish music and Irish dancing were stupid, and Irish words smelled like onion sandwiches. You had to pretend that you were not afraid of the famine coming back, that you didn't eat sandwiches made by your own mother and that you had an English song in your head at all times. You had to walk down O'Connell Street and pretend that you were not even in Ireland.

There were celebrations everywhere in Dublin for the Easter Rising. It happened fifty years ago and my father said it should happen again because Ireland would never be free until we had more of our own inventions. He said the Irish people were forced to repeat their history because of all the things the British left behind. And one day we saw the Easter Rising happening again in front of our own eyes. They were making a film of it and I saw Patrick Pearse coming out and surrendering with a white flag before he was executed by the British. There were pictures of Patrick Pearse in the windows of shoe shops and sweet shops. The shops had Irish flags, too, and copies of the proclamation which we all learned off by heart. We sold Easter lilies and there was hardly a single person in the city who wasn't wearing one. In school a man came from the Abbey Theatre to put on a pageant and we got parts as croppy boys or redcoats and died every night. On the buses there were little torches and swords and all the lamp-posts in the city had flags so that everybody would remember how great it was that the Irish were free to walk down any street in the world, including their own. Nobody was telling the Irish when to get off the bus. Some people still thought it was the British empire coming back every time a bus conductor asked them for their fare. And some people thought it was the Nazis coming back every time an inspector came on to ask for their ticket. But the flags and the special stamps and the pictures in all the shops were there to remind everybody that the Irish were not the saddest people in the world any more, they were laughing now and nobody could stop them.

One day the whole school was brought out to see a film called *Mise Éire* which is the Irish for 'I am Ireland'. Some of the boys in the class were asking was Sean Connery in it and was there a woman smoking and blinking and wearing nothing under her dressing gown. But it wasn't that kind of film. There were no horses either rising up and whinnying. It was mostly about the Easter Rising, with black and white pictures of windows smashed and bullet holes in the walls. There was lots of big music that sounded like big country music from the end of a Western film and made everybody feel strong in their stomach. There were two boys standing guard and protecting the grave of O'Donovan Rossa with hurling sticks. There were people marching through the streets with hurling sticks on their shoulders and a deep voice saying 'Ireland unfree shall never be at peace.' It didn't matter that James Bond wasn't in it because Patrick Pearse was in it instead, and even though he got killed in the end, he put up a good fight.

I had new friends in school and one of them had a brother who worked in a gardening shop. One day he brought a bag of green dye into school that was used to mix with fertiliser, so that everybody would know it was not to be eaten. At lunchtime, we were not let into the Waverley Billiard Hall yet, so we brought the bag of fertiliser over to the new garden of remembrance across the road from the school. Then I had the idea to throw the dye into the fountain for Ireland. It turned green before we even got a chance to get back out of the garden again and the guards were sent for. The problem was that anyone who touched the dye had green hands and green faces, so it was easy to tell who did it. I tried to wash my face in the public toilets near the GPO but every time I put water on my face it turned even more green. There was a lot of trouble at school because I walked into the class late with my face all green, and I thought I would be expelled, but nothing happened because they said it was the right colour at least.

On the train home everybody thought it was part of the Easter commemorations and that every boy in Ireland was turning green. I wanted to be as Irish as possible so that I would never have to be German again. I wanted to belong to the saddest people and not the people who killed the saddest people. At home I tried to speak Irish to my mother again but she didn't understand a word, so then I sat at the window while she was working, and I pretended that I was the newsreader, like the man at the window in Béal an Daingin. I waited for my father to come home from the station and told her all the people going by.

There's Miss Ryan going east now to get minced meat

for herself and her sister. There's Miss Hosford going east, too, on her bicycle and nobody knows where she's off to at this time of the day with a rucksack on her back. They say that Mrs MacSweeney's niece is getting married soon in Dublin. They say that one of the Miss Doyles nearly got married to a stranger once, but she's happier now living with her sister till death do us part, and reading to each other every evening after dinner from an indecent book by James Joyce. Here are the Miss Lanes coming out and looking up at the Irish flag hanging from the front window of our house, and they think they're in the wrong country altogether. They look around the garden to make sure that nobody has kicked a football into their country and say that it's a shame more Irish people didn't die fighting the Nazis. They say the Irish were cowards because they didn't fight against the Nazis, but they forget that the Irish fought against the British. There's Miss Tarleton coming out now picking up bits of paper in her front garden and wondering why my mother didn't die fighting against the Nazis. But she doesn't know that my mother lived against the Nazis instead. They say that Miss Tarleton hates the bees more than the Irish language, except that they're good for the loganberry harvest. They say that Miss Tarleton went into the butcher's shop one day and asked Mr Furlong what the picture of Patrick Pearse was doing in the window beside all the meat. He said it was time to die for Ireland and she said that meant it was time to kill for Ireland, but my father says they're both wrong because it's time to live for Ireland and be Irish. They say that Mrs Creagh once went over to England for horse racing at Cheltenham and somebody asked her if the Irish still kept pigs under the bed, and she said it wasn't half as bad as having the pigs in the bed like they do in England. Here's Mr Clancy going down to the Eagle House and he once had a big argument with my father in the street. My father told him we were trying to be as Irish as possible. Mr Clancy said he was just as Irish as us and didn't speak a word of Irish. He said Irish was the 'aboriginal' language and no bloody use to anyone any more. So then my father told Mr Clancy he would soon be outnumbered and Mr Clancy said my father better have a lot more children. Here's my father coming around the corner saying that nobody is going to stop us speaking Irish or make us take down the Irish flag from the window until we feel like it. My father and Mr Clancy are going towards each other on the pavement and you think there's going to be a big fight and blood on the ground, but my father is not one of the fist people and neither is Mr Clancy, and they both nod to each other politely as they pass by.

One morning my father woke me up early and showed me the newspaper. He still had shaving cream on his face and he was breathing fast from running up the stairs. He opened the paper wide and pointed at a picture of Dublin after a bomb. It was a bomb for Ireland, he said. I rubbed my eyes and looked at the picture, but I didn't know what was happening until he read it out to me. It said that Nelson's Pillar had been blown up during the night. I remembered going up to the top of Nelson's Pillar once with Eileen and now it was gone and nobody would ever go up again. My father slapped the paper with the back of his hand and said the empire was crumbling. At last all the things the British left behind are disappearing, he said. At last we're living in our own country and telling our own stories and speaking our own language. When I went to school I saw hundreds of people standing around looking at the remains of Nelson's Pillar. There were no buses going up and down the street any more because there was rubble all over the place. The windows were broken and there was glass everywhere. People couldn't go shopping that day or pass by to get into the GPO either. I saw a shoe shop with glass all over the new shoes. I looked up and saw the stump of Nelson's Pillar like somebody's arm cut off. Nelson's head was on the ground and the dust of the empire was all around.

Twenty-six

I keep thinking this didn't happen.

One day I had to collect Bríd from school because she was homesick. The wind was howling in her chest so I had to go into the girls' school and bring her home. I had to go up the stairs past the glass cage with the stuffed birds and knock on the girls' classroom. They opened the door and I saw Bríd sitting down with three girls and the teacher around her. Her face was white and she was breathing with her mouth open. Her hair was wet from sweating and they were wiping her face with a towel, but she was happy and she smiled because I was there to take her home. I picked up her schoolbag and took her by the hand and we walked down the stairs very slowly. She was holding on to the banisters and sitting down sometimes to take a rest with her head down and her hair in her face as if nothing mattered any more.

When we got outside I had to carry her because she couldn't walk. She was leaning forward and stopping all the time to hold on to the railings, so then I hung the schoolbag around my neck and gave her a piggyback up to the bus stop. On the bus I got her to lie down on the seat like a bed with the schoolbag as a pillow, but she got up again, because she was coughing and crying for air with her arm around me. I knew she wouldn't be able to walk home from the bus, so I asked the conductor if he could get the bus to bring her home. He was clicking the money in his hand and said he wasn't allowed to do that, but then I told him that my sister was going to get sick and he talked to the driver. So the bus turned up at the Eagle House and all the people were lost because they had never been up that street before on a bus. The conductor explained that the bus was an ambulance now. He was still clicking the money in his hand to see if anyone hadn't paid their fare, but then he sat down like a passenger himself, until the bus got to our street with the red houses and the driver stopped because it was impossible to go any further. I told him it was all right because we lived in number two and that wasn't too far. Then the bus conductor carried Bríd as far as the front door and afterwards everybody was talking about the lost bus, because it took so long before it turned around and drove back down to catch up with the main road again.

The doctor had to come and we went down for the red medicine and twisted glucose sticks. Bríd took only one spoon because she wasn't able to swallow and the second spoon dribbled down her chin, down the outside of her neck instead of inside. My mother tried to make her go to sleep with a song about a donkey who said he was better at making noise than the cuckoo, but she kept sitting up in bed and trying to run away. So then we carried the bed down to the kitchen to make sure that she wouldn't be lonely upstairs. She fell asleep for a while and we walked around the house very quietly as if there was a cake in the oven. When my father came home he knew what to do. He sat on the bed and stroked her head. He got her to swallow another spoon of medicine inside her neck, and even when we were going to bed, he was still sitting there with her, trying to make her smile and asking her puzzles like the one about the man who came to a fork in the road and had only one question to ask. He gave her lots of clues, but she still didn't know the answer and he had to tell her in the end. We could hear her breathing up and down all through the house, and sometimes she was crying and putting her arm around my father to beg him to help her breathe.

'It's all right, *Tutti*,' I can hear them saying all the time. 'It's all right, *mein Schätzchen*, it's all right.'

The man named Gearóid still comes to our house sometimes on Saturdays and he says the only thing that would help Bríd is goat's milk. He comes in his Volkswagen and says we're a true Irish fireside and we should be drinking goat's milk anyway. He wants my father to start making speeches again and to write for the newspaper *Aiséirí*, like he did long ago. Everybody knows that the *Aiséirí* office is on Harcourt Street because you can see the blue Volkswagen outside every day with all the newspapers on the back seat, and sometimes you can see a goat tied to the railings as well to show the people of Dublin that the Irish are not afraid to be different. Gearóid keeps a goat in the city and we keep bees in the city, to remind people not to be so afraid of the country. My mother thought the goat was coming out to our house in the back of the Volkswagen but Gearóid said it would only eat up all the copies of *Aiséirí*, so the next time he came out he brought a canteen full of goat's milk instead and my father gave him a jar of honey in exchange.

The goat's milk didn't help Bríd. She spat it out all over the bed clothes because it looked grey and tasted like pee-pee. Some people said Bríd should not be drinking milk at all. Some said she should be living in the mountains in Switzerland, not by the sea in Ireland, because it's damp and sometimes you can't even look out the window. Miss Tarleton said Bríd would grow out of it because she had a really bad chest herself when she was a little girl, and look at her now, she's 78 years old and she can't remember the last time she had a cold or even a cough. But Bríd doesn't want to be like Miss Tarleton when she grows up with two different shoes on. The Miss Ryans said Bríd should go on a pilgrimage to Lourdes or Fatima but you have to be in a wheelchair for that. A German woman, who was not allowed to come to our house because she was divorced, gave my mother eucalyptus oil. And Mr Furlong told my mother it was good to have asthma, because then you would never get malaria. But Bríd is still sick all the time and getting thin because she doesn't want to eat anything any more, not even glucose sticks or cakes that my mother makes.

In the middle of the night the doctor had to come back again because she was trying to open the window and get air from outside. I woke up and heard her crying, begging my father for air, and my mother still saying 'it's all right, *mein Schätzchen*, it's all right. Come back to bed now.' Everybody was afraid because nobody in our house ever cried that much before. I got up and saw Bríd reaching forward with her mouth open. My mother and father were holding her arms on each side. I asked if I could help but my father told me to get back to bed. Franz and Maria were standing on the landing as well, and they ran back into bed as soon as they heard his voice. My mother came and told us to pray hard, so I listened to Bríd in the dark and prayed that the bad chest would come back to me instead. Then I heard Dr Sheehan's voice downstairs in the hall. He said Bríd was an angel and a saint and he gave her an injection to make her go to sleep. The next morning she was still going up and down all the time, but she was smiling again and my mother got her to eat some toast with jam.

Gearóid came again the next Saturday with the new *Aiséirí*. He's always dressed in a brown tweed suit. His knees are bent even when he's standing up, and, one time, me and Franz laughed because his trousers looked like they wanted to stay sitting down. He has bits of hair growing on his cheeks, too, where he stopped shaving, and a big smile when we answer him in Irish. He says Bríd is a *páistín fionn*, a blonde child, and really Irish underneath. She's a fighter, he says. Then they go into the front room to talk for a long time about all the things that are not finished yet in Ireland, like still only one pop song in Irish about a goat that went mad and had to be stopped by the priest, and lots of other things like street names still in English and no parking fines in Irish. What if somebody wanted to break the law in Irish? Gearóid said they were going to put him in jail for not paying motor tax on the Volkswagen in English. They were going to put my father in jail, too, because he was waiting to pay a fine in Irish. My mother brings in the tea and we can hear Gearóid's voice coming out under the door. He says he can't keep writing all the articles in *Aiséirí* on his own, and he wants my father to write something big instead of just writing letters to the papers.

One day my father wrote a strong letter to the papers to prove that what they were saying about Cardinal Stepinac was wrong, that he wasn't a Nazi at all and that he didn't even hate any Jewish people, even though he was a Catholic. It was a big mistake to believe Radio Éireann, he wrote, because they only repeated the rubbish that the Communists in Yugoslavia were saying. They locked Cardinal Stepinac up in his house and put him on trial because they felt guilty themselves. People who feel guilty point the finger, my father says, and they're just putting the blame on Cardinal Stepinac for everything that happened in the concentration camps. There were lots more letters in the paper after that and a Protestant man named Hubert Butler from Kilkenny once insulted the Papal Nuncio, saying that Cardinal Stepinac was guilty because the Catholic priests in Yugoslavia baptised children before they were killed in concentration camps. Nobody in Ireland could ever believe that priests helped the Nazis to kill children and save their souls. Nobody could ever believe Catholic priests helped a big SS man named Artukovic to escape to Ireland after the war and live in Dublin for two years before he emigrated to Paraguay. My father says Cardinal Stepinac should be made into a saint, and Gearóid said it was a pity my father didn't take up writing again because he was so good at making speeches and lighting matches and going around the country on his motorbike.

'His speeches had passion,' Gearóid said to my mother. 'He had them throwing their hats up.'

It's good to hear people saying that. It's good to think about my father standing up on a platform with crowds of people around him in the street throwing their hats up and not caring if they ever came back down again. It's good to like your own father otherwise you won't like yourself very much either. You want to believe that everything your own father says is always right.

'Aiséirí,' Gearóid said. 'Resurrection. What about the daily uprising?'

My father smiled and said he was still waking up for Ireland every morning, but he was very busy with other things, too, at the moment, like beekeeping and making German oak furniture and reading about how to cure

247

asthma without listening to doctors. He was starting to translate a German book as well that Onkel Ted gave my mother about training children without sticks. He was also trying to write more letters about Cardinal Stepinac not helping the Nazis to kill children, as well as trying to write an article about Guernica to say that the painting of screaming cows and legs in the air by Picasso might be a masterpiece, but maybe it wasn't the Germans who did it. Gearóid says the Irish spent a long time building stone walls and saying the opposite and pretending the British were not there, and my father is a real Irishman with a gift for being against. He holds his fist up in the air and says my father could make anyone believe that day is night. He turns to my mother and winks at her because she is the audience and she says it's good that people in Ireland can't be kept quiet.

'Remember the article they tried to ban,' Gearóid said.

'What article?' my mother asked.

Gearóid punched his fist down on the side of the armchair and told her that my father once wrote a great article about the Jewish people in Ireland. He said they tried to stop them from printing it. They threatened to close down the office in Harcourt Street. The police came and took away lots of documents, but they were not afraid of going to prison and they went to confession and printed the article on the front page, because *Aiséirí* is the Irish for not sitting down.

'Did you never read it?' he said. 'It was very well written. Very balanced and fair-minded. Maybe it didn't even go far enough.'

After that my mother was very upset and she didn't even do the washing-up. She was using the silent negative all the time. She told Bríd she was going back to Germany. She said she was going to pack her bags and take Bríd with her to a place where she would be able to breathe.

There were lots of doors slamming in our house after that. Bríd jumps in bed when the door of the front room bangs shut. Sometimes we get a fright as well when there's a draught and the back door bangs shut in anger of its own accord. I know where my father is by the sound of the last door banging. One day I started slamming doors as well, but he said that wasn't allowed and it's not too late for him to get the stick and take me upstairs and close all the doors so that nobody will hear. My mother reminds him that he's translating a book about punishing children without sticks, so then he puts on his coat and slams the front door, and everybody thinks he's gone away and never coming back. Everything in the house rattles and then stays quiet for a long time. Then one day I told everybody I was leaving and slammed the front door from inside. It was a joke just to annoy them. I hid behind the oak trunk in the hall so that everybody thought I was gone for ever, but then Bríd started crying and my mother said she would start banging the doors, too, one day, then we would see how funny it was. And one night she did it. It was very late but she did it really and truly. My father came back and slammed the door of the front room without eating his dinner. He sat there staring at all the patterns in the carpet. My mother didn't want him to feel sorry for himself, so she went in to sit beside him and put her arm around him like a friend for life. She wanted him to say that he made a mistake, but he just pushed her away. Then she stood in the hall and put her coat on slowly. She went out and closed the front door very, very quietly, as if she was leaving us and going back to Germany for ever.

'Jaysus, what the Jaysus,' I said. Nobody ever heard a

door closing so much before in their whole lives. It was so quiet that you could hardly even hear the click of the lock, and this time we were really afraid that she would never come back. This time the silence was bigger than after the loudest bang. I ran to the window upstairs and looked out, but she had already gone around the corner out of sight. I thought I should run after her. But then I waited. The whole house waited for her to come back. And when she came at last, everybody was happy, even my father. He said he would never slam doors again as long as he lived.

My mother says it's the hardest thing in the world to say that you're wrong. She wants us not to be afraid to make mistakes, and, when we do our homework, never to use a rubber or tear a page out of the copy book. She wants everybody to honest and Onkel Ted comes out to the house specially because he's a priest and he's heard all the mistakes that have ever been made in Ireland. He always brings a book in German for my mother and you wouldn't think he's read it because it looks new. This time he brought a book about Eichmann and a book about a priest named Bonhöffer. They sat around the table in the breakfast room and didn't come out because they had so much to talk about. We went into the front room instead to listen to the radio and there was a song we liked called 'I Heard it Through the Grapevine'. We listened to the radio with one ear and listened out for my father with the other, to hear if he was coming with one soft foot and one hard.

The next day, when my father was at work and we were at school, my mother went upstairs very quietly to her bedroom with lots of clean laundry. Bríd was still breathing up and down, so my mother sat her up in the big bed where she could look out and tell her everything that was happening outside on the street like a newsreader, who was going east and who was going west. She put the light on because it looked like it was getting dark outside and the red houses on the far side of the street said it was going to rain. Bríd said there was a man from the corporation slicing the weeds off the path with a shovel. Miss Tarleton came out and threw some more weeds out on to the path while the man wasn't looking. And a dog came walking into our garden because the gate was open, but he just scratched the grass and went out again.

My mother opened up my father's wardrobe and put away lots of clean shirts and rolled-up socks. She left the doors open and started looking at all the things that belonged to him before they got married. She found the picture of the sailor with his soft eyes looking away that my father never wanted anyone in our house to see again. She found other pictures of my grandfather when he worked on ships that belonged to the British navy. She found the last postcard he sent home to his wife saying: 'More homesick than seasick.' There were rosary beads belonging to my grandmother Mary Frances and a box full of letters and lots of medals she got from the navy after he died on his own in a Cork hospital. There were more boxes of letters from people in America and South Africa who couldn't come home again. There were letters that Mary Frances wrote to my father when he was going to university in Dublin so that he would never have to leave Ireland and get seasick or have to work in America. Letters that my father wrote home to Leap to say that he got the money and a list of all the things he had to spend the money on, like the rent and razor blades and a penny for Mass on Sunday. Letters from his mother asking him to send home his clothes to Leap to be washed. Letters to ask him if he had heard anything from his brother Ted.

Bríd said it was raining and the man from the corporation left the shovel leaning against our wall. She said he was standing under the tree across the road taking shelter and smoking a cigarette. She said Mrs Robinson opened the door to hold her hand out and see if it was really raining, because there's a clock in her hallway that tells the weather, but it's not always right and you have to tap it with your finger. Bríd said it was raining hard now and there were big drops on the pavement and nobody on the street at all any more going east or west.

My mother sat on the floor and looked at photographs of my father before he was married. She found pictures of the time when Onkel Ted was becoming a priest and my father was becoming an engineer. She found German language lessons from Dr Becker and homework my father did. There were lots of things from the time during the war, when my father met Gearóid at university in Dublin and started the party called *Aiséirí*. There was a picture of my father walking down O'Connell Street at the head of a big march, holding a poster with the words: 'For whom the bell tolls, *Éire Aiséirí*.' There was another picture of my father and Gearóid in his tweed suit walking down Harcourt Street, smiling as if they were not afraid of the police.

There were boxes full of green leaflets to say what *Aiséirí* was going to do with Ireland if they were in control. They were going to stop people being greedy and getting rich on their own without sharing. People would not have to pay rent if they had to live with rats and not enough clothes or food for their children. Irish people would no longer have to go away and get seasick. They would get rid of all the things the British invented like county councils and slums and postboxes with the crown. They would take back all the things that belonged to the Irish, like the rivers and the big houses and the six counties in the north. It was time that the Irish took back the factories and the shops and put up the Irish word *Amach* on the doors in the cinemas instead of Exit. They were fed up with Irish people changing their minds all the time and not knowing how to start up a new country from the beginning. They said it was time for Irish people to stop sitting down and staring out the window as if they got an awful fright. What they needed was a big strong leader, not like Hitler or Stalin, but more like Salazar, because he was a good Catholic and Portugal was a small country like Ireland with stone walls and poor people living on their imagination.

My mother doesn't understand very much about politics so she can't tell the difference between the things that people say before elections. She knows they have nice hands and nice shoes and make lots of promises. She doesn't understand what difference *Aiséirí* would have made if more people had thrown their hats up in the air for my father and not kept some of the things that the British left behind, like the trains and the courts and elections. She found notes for all the speeches on O'Connell Street, written in tiny handwriting on cards. But they made no sense. There were notes about laziness and blindness and immoral practices. Notes about greediness and money lending. Notes about bringing horses to the water and making them drink. About biting the hand that feeds you and rubbing salt into the wounds. There were notes about how silly it was to live in Ireland and not be Irish, notes about people still calling themselves British. People calling themselves Jewish, too. Notes about Jewish people giving Irish people carpets and making them pay for the rest of their lives. Leaflets about an international conspiracy of Jewish bankers. One of the cards quoted a man named Belloc, asking if anybody had ever heard of such a thing as an Irish Jew. And then my mother found the newspaper that Gearóid was talking about. It was so old it was gone yellow and almost brown. The headline on the front page said: 'Ireland's Jewish problem'. The date on the top was 1946. There was a note in handwriting, too, from Gearóid saying: 'doesn't go far enough'.

When you're small you know nothing and when you grow up there are things you don't want to know. I don't want anyone to know that my father wanted Jewish people in Ireland to speak Irish and do Irish dancing like everyone else. I don't want people to know that he was foaming at the mouth. That the Irish language might be a killer language, too, like English and German. That my father believes you can only kill or be killed. It's the hardest thing to say that you're wrong.

One day when I was coming home from school I saw my father in the street. He was on his way home, too, buying a newspaper on O'Connell Street. He looked like a different man when he was outside, more like an ordinary Irishman going home from work, with his cap on and his briefcase in his right hand. I was standing beside a newspaper stand looking at all the books and the magazines. There was a book with a gun and a dead bird on the cover and I wanted to know what the story was inside. All the time the man was shouting 'Herald-ah-Press', with the newspapers under his arm. There was an echo coming from across the street where another man was doing the same thing, shouting 'Herald-ah-Press' back. When somebody asked for a paper, the man quickly took one out from the bundle under his arm and held his hand out flat so that people could give him the money. They could take the paper out of his fingers and walk away home quickly without wasting any time. The man's hand was black from the papers and there were black marks on his face.

Then I heard my father speaking right beside me. I got a fright because I thought he was coming to get me, but he was just asking for the *Evening Press*. He didn't know I was there at all. I looked up and saw him standing beside me, putting the money into the man's hand. I knew it was my father's soft Cork accent. It was my father's briefcase and I even knew what was inside – his flask and his rain mac and his book on Stalingrad, with the train ticket halfway through to show how much he had left to read.

'Vati,' I said. 'It's me.'

I waited for him to look down, but he didn't see me. He was thinking of all the things he had not finished yet and all the things he was still going to do when he got the time. He put the paper under his arm and walked away. I wanted to run after him as if he was my father. I wanted to tug him by the sleeve of his coat. I wanted him to talk to me about things like films or football. But he didn't know anything about that. And, anyway, I would have to pretend he was my friend and go all the way home on the train with him. We would have to talk Irish together, as if there was no other language in the world. Everybody would look at us. They would know that we were homeless and had nowhere to go, because we lost the language war. They would know that we were still locked in the wardrobe and didn't know any better.

I didn't move. I didn't run after him. I knew I was doing the same thing as he had done to his own father, the sailor. I stood still and heard the brakes of the buses screeching. I saw the people in a long queue waiting. I saw the windows of the buses steamed up and the places where people rubbed a circle clear to look out. I heard the man shouting 'Herald-ah-Press' and the echo still coming back across the street over the traffic. I watched my father walking away towards the train station like one of the ordinary people of Dublin. I watched his limp and his briefcase swinging, as if I had never seen him before in my life.

Twenty-seven

One day a man put a bomb in a briefcase and went out to work, like my father. He looked at his watch because he had an important meeting to go to and he wanted to be there on time. It was a hot day and he brought a clean shirt with him as well. Before the meeting, he asked everybody to wait a few minutes so he could change his shirt first. They told him to hurry up and waited outside while he went into a room and clicked open the briefcase with the bomb inside instead of his lunch and his flask. He took out the shirt and started getting the bomb ready straightaway. It was two bombs really, but he could only fix the fuse on one of them, because he had been injured in the war and only had one arm, like Mr Smyth in the vegetable shop. He could only see with one eye, too, because there was a patch over the other one, but he was not afraid to die and he took out a small set of pliers and did his best. Everybody knows how long it takes to change your shirt, even if you only have one arm. He was taking so long that somebody came to the door to ask what was keeping him and then his hand started shaking, so he decided, in the end, that one of the bombs would be more than enough. He changed his shirt quickly and came out again with the briefcase in his hand. The empty sleeve of the missing arm was tucked into the pocket of his jacket, like Mr Smyth. He didn't have to shake hands with anyone and nobody knew what he was thinking either, because he was like Onkel Ted and not afraid of silence. They didn't know that there was a bomb inside the briefcase for Germany, and when he got to the meeting where they were all standing around a table and looking at the map of the world, he gave the briefcase to another man and told him to put it as close to Hitler as possible. Then he walked away and heard the explosion right behind him. He thought Hitler was dead and everybody was free again, but that was a big mistake because, after all that trouble, Hitler wasn't even hurt and came out with only a bit of dust on his uniform.

'Make sure of it,' my mother says. 'For God's sake, don't just walk away and leave it to somebody else.'

The man who planted the bomb was arrested in Berlin very shortly afterwards. His name was Claus Schenk Graf von Stauffenberg and he was immediately taken out into a square to be executed by firing squad, along with some of the people who were on his side. Later on, his brother and all his friends were arrested, too, and put on trial for planning a puppet show against Hitler. They were put to death in a very cruel way and their children were taken away and given new names so they would forget who they were. One of the boys wrote his real name on the inside of his lederhosen, but they were all sent to a special school so that they would grow up as Nazis, and none of the puppets would ever try and speak against Hitler again.

Afterwards, Hitler went on the radio to tell everyone in the world that he was alive and still had two eyes and two ears and two of everything. In case there was a mistake and some people might not have heard the radio, they collected everyone together in halls and theatres and schools to tell them that Hitler never felt better. My mother says that she was on a platform waiting for a train when she heard the news that he was not dead yet and the war was still on. Her sister Marianne was working in Salzburg and had to go to a big meeting in the opera house to be told what happened, as if they were about to hear some music. When everybody was sitting down in their seats and all the coughing and whispering stopped, an SS man came out on stage to make a speech. He said there was some bad news. Somebody had betrayed Germany and tried to kill Hitler with a bomb. But there was nothing to worry about, he said, because Hitler was still alive and could never be killed, not even by a bomb in the same room. Then Marianne stood up.

'*Leider*,' she said out loud for everyone to hear. 'What a pity.'

The audience turned around to look at her standing up with her arms folded against the Nazis. Everybody in the whole opera house was waiting for her to be taken away and maybe even executed immediately. But then at the last minute, an older woman she had never seen before stood up beside her and spoke very calmly.

'*Ja, leider*,' the woman said. 'Yes, what a pity such a thing can happen.'

Then everybody thought it was just a mistake. Maybe Marianne wasn't a woman against Hitler with her arms folded, but a woman so much for Hitler that she was not afraid to stand up and say it out loud. Before Marianne could say anything more, before she could say that she really wished Hitler had been killed by the bomb and that his two of everything had been blown to bits, the woman pulled her back down quickly into the seat and told her to stop trying to get herself killed.

My mother says it's hard to tell that story, even it it's

true. Nobody will believe it any more, because lots of people made up things like that after the war. Everybody wanted to prove they were against the Nazis and never said a word against Jewish people in their lives and even saved lots of them from being killed. If all the stories were true, then how come Hitler was alive for so long and there weren't more Jewish people found all over Germany when the war was over. People who are guilty usually point the finger. It's the people who really were against the Nazis who don't want to boast about it. Most of the people who were against the Nazis disappeared and can't speak for themselves.

In the book she got from Onkel Ted about Eichmann, there is a story about a German man who helped the Jews in Poland. He gave them guns against his own country, against Germany. When the Nazis found out what he was doing, they killed him straightaway. And afterwards he was forgotten by everybody because what he did was not enough to stop what happened in the end. He might as well not have bothered. Nobody wanted to know. All the books and films are about the bad people, my mother says, not the good people. It was the same with the man who changed his shirt and brought the bomb in a briefcase to meet Hitler. He was forgotten and he might as well not have bothered either, because so many people were murdered by the Nazis that it's hard to think of anything else. He was not very good at making a bomb, because he was not very good at hating people. And it's hard to start boasting about somebody who was not very good at killing Hitler or giving away guns against the Nazis or standing up with your arms crossed and saying it was a pity Hitler wasn't dead.

There was fog everywhere outside that day. I looked

out the window of my mother and father's bedroom and I thought it was like net curtains hanging down. The fog was waving a little. I could hardly see the houses across the street. I was listening to my mother and I didn't know what country I was in any more. She was feeding the new baby on the bed, my small brother, Ciarán. When there was nothing more to say and she was finished telling about the bomb for Germany, we just listened to the foghorn for a long time and said nothing. Ciarán was smiling and shaking his head from side to side, trying to make himself dizzy and drunk. Ita and Bríd were playing with him and sometimes copying the voice of the foghorn until Ciarán laughed. Mrs Robinson pulled back her net curtains and looked out across the street at me and I waved, but she couldn't see through the fog. She lets us watch the television in her house sometimes and I know what her house smells like. Everybody's house has a different smell and some smells make you feel lonely and other smells make you feel like you're at home. Miss Tarleton's house smells like a greenhouse and boiling cabbage, and Miss Hosford's house smells like a chemist. Mrs McSweeney's house smells like toffee and shoe polish. The Miss Doyles' flat upstairs always smells of beans on toast. The Miss Ryans' house smells like washing and ironing and a bit of liquorice mixed in, and Miss Brown's house smells like the mixture of soap and cigarette smoke and the smell you get at the back of the radio when it's been on for a while. I don't know what makes the smell of each house so different, but our house smells of being happy and afraid. Our friend Noel's house smells like nobody ever gets angry because his father is a doctor and his mother never raises her voice and they have a dog. Tante Roseleen's house smells of red lemonade and the place where Onkel Ted lives smells like a different country, like the house with the yellow door and the custard, the place where you always feel homesick.

My mother said we would go down to find the foghorn when she was ready. We waited outside and you could not see the end of the street, only up to number six. She cleaned all the crumbs and bits of mushy biscuits out from the bottom of the pram and when she came out Ciarán was sitting up with a serious face and a hat on over his ears that has a big furry bobble on top. We walked down to the sea with Ita and Bríd holding on to the pram as if they were driving it. The cars and the buses had their lights on, even though it was daytime, and sometimes you could only see the yellow lights like a ghost coming through the fog. Everybody was travelling so slowly that you thought they were afraid of where they were going and what they might find in the fog.

It was like a new fog country where everybody was quiet and saying nothing. There were no more far away countries like Germany or England or America, because you could not even look out across the sea. There were no waves at all and the ceiling was very low. It was like a small room with net curtains. Like a bathroom with the bath filling up and seagulls floating on top and the mirror steamed up and funny voices echoing around you. When we looked back we could not even see the road or the cars or any houses either. Nothing was moving. Not even a piece of paper. The trees were pretending to be dead and the foghorn kept saying the same word all the time.

'Rooooooom . . .' You could hear the word very clearly now. The same word all the time, as if it had only one word to say.

'Rooooooom,' we shouted back. 'Room the rooooooom.'

I ran across the green park in front of the sea until my

mother and all my brothers and sisters disappeared behind me. I heard them calling and I walked back slowly, like a ghost walking out of the fog. My mother looked different. I thought it was somebody else and I had come back to a different place. She had her back turned, looking out towards the sea, like somebody from a different country that I didn't know the name of and couldn't talk to. There was a ship coming in very slowly with the lights on. There was no wind and no language, and the only word left was the word 'room'. She stood at the blue railings with the brown rust, like an ordinary German woman.

We walked on towards the harbour and the foghorn kept getting louder and louder. We saw the lighthouse coming closer, too, and the light coming around every few seconds to point the finger at us through the fog. My mother said it was like a man carrying a yellow lantern. Bríd was afraid to go any further, so my mother changed her mind and said it was just the lighthouse winking at us. We counted the time in between each word from the foghorn and in between each wink from the lighthouse. We came to the place where you can shout into a hole in the wall and hear the echo. 'Jaysus, what the Jaysus,' Franz shouted and everybody else had to do it after him in a line, except my mother. 'Room the room and Jaysus what the Jaysus and down you bully belly,' we shouted. We walked all the way out along the pier and my mother said we had to be careful not to walk straight off the end into the sea.

We came to the place where there was a granite monument for the lifeboat men who were drowned while trying to rescue people from a ship, not very far away from the land. My mother said it was very sad to think of them getting up on a stormy night and leaving the house and

263

saying they would be back soon. We stood looking at the names of the men written up and thought of them going down into the dark water so close to home without saying goodbye to anyone. When we came to the place with the wind gauge on top, the cups were stuck and not even moving at all, just waiting for the wind to come back so it could start spinning again. Any of the boats we could see in the harbour were not moving very much either and the foghorn was talking so loud that we could not say a word any more. Bríd and Ita had their hands over their ears and we could not go any closer because Ciarán started crying. We sat down on a blue bench and my mother took out a bar of chocolate. There was nobody else on the pier. We were like the last family in Ireland, listening to the silver paper and waiting for the chocolate to be shared out.

If Hitler had been killed, then everybody would have said it was a good bomb, a bomb for Germany. Instead, they said the people who planned the puppet show against the Nazis were liars and betrayers. They were bad Germans who were not very good at hating people. It was a bad bomb, they said, a bomb against Germany and they might as well not have bothered, because nobody would even remember it. Sometimes a good bomb can be a bad bomb and sometimes a bad bomb can be a good bomb. But this was a useless bomb and everybody had to wait until all the good bombs started falling on Germany. Then the trains were on fire and the streets were full of people running. That was near the end of the black and white film that my mother was in. She had to work for the German army like her sister Marianne. Her other sisters didn't have to, my mother says, because they already had children and Hitler didn't want mothers fighting in the war. That was the time when all the good bombs were falling on the cities and people were burned alive in their sleep, to make sure they learned how to hate the Nazis.

After the bomb that didn't even hurt Hitler, Marianne thought somebody was following her all the time. She was afraid that what she said in the opera house put her in trouble and that everybody knew she was against the Nazis. When she walked through the streets of Salzburg she sometimes had to look around and check to make sure that nobody was behind her. Sometimes they're after you because they think you're a Nazi and you feel guilty and you can't trust yourself any more. And then one day on her way home from work, she found out who was after her. It was the woman who stood up in the opera house and stopped her from killing herself.

'*Leider*,' the woman said and smiled.

My mother says everybody was afraid to smile and afraid to speak about things that didn't have to do with getting enough food and making sure that everybody in your family was safe from the bombs. The woman started talking about where to get butter and where to get eggs and how difficult it was to make a good cake these days. Marianne said it was impossible to get any meat at all. The woman was very friendly and asked her where she lived. Marianne told her that she lived on the Mönchberg, up high, the last house before the castle. So then the woman said how nice it must be to live up there on the mountain, away from everything, with clean air and no noise and plenty of tranquillity. They kept talking for a while, because nobody was afraid of talking about good air and bad lungs and living away from other people coughing.

'It would be a great place for a guest house up there,' the woman said.

Marianne said she had never dreamed of it. She was

expecting a baby and working every day with the German army and looking after her mother-in-law, too, who was very old. She was not afraid of work, but her husband was away in the war and she didn't know where she would get the food for the guests. And not only that, she didn't think anyone could afford to go on holidays any more.

'I know people with bad lungs,' the woman said. 'They would love it up there.'

'It's a long way up,' Marianne said, 'without a car.'

But that would even be doing them a favour, the woman said. It would be good for them to get the air even as they were walking up. And that's how Tante Marianne got the idea to open a guest house, my mother says. That's how people started coming to visit her from all over the place for clean air and tranquillity, that's how she has a name for keeping one of the most beautiful guest houses in all of Austria today, a place that has a long waiting list and you would never hear about from the tourist board, only by word of mouth.

It was thanks to the man with one arm and one eye who put the bomb in a briefcase. The bad bomb was good for one thing at least. It started a guest house on the Mönchberg where there never had been one before. It was strange that nobody had thought of it already, my mother says. It didn't start as a big business, not like a big hotel. Just one guest at a time, or two at the most. They could stay up there and breathe in deeply and pretend that there was no war on at all.

Tante Marianne didn't have to think about it for long, my mother says. She went home and got the place ready. And some days later, the first of the guests arrived, a Jewish woman who had no name and no face and no address. She didn't stay for long, only two or three days at a time, and then she moved on again to another house somewhere else.

My mother says you can't boast about things like that. You can say it to yourself. You can be proud that somebody had courage. But you can't go around telling the whole world your aunt helped to harbour Jewish people and made a safe haven out of her house on the Mönchberg. You have to remember all the people who were not saved, too. You have to remember all the voices speaking from the graves. I want to tell everybody that I had an aunt who was not afraid to lose and stood up against the killing. I want to run out and tell the whole world that she helped people to breathe in Germany.

'Maybe they won't believe me,' I say.

My mother says you know when something is true sometimes by the way nobody is boasting about it. Nobody is trying to turn it into a big story on the radio and asking people to clap. You know it's true that Tante Marianne kept the silent negative in her head until she could do something about it, because nobody is talking about it much. Because it's not written about in any newspaper.

The first Jewish woman to visit the guest house was not killed by the Nazis and went to America after the war. She never came back. But she told people what a wonderful guest house she stayed in on the Mönchberg. And later on, when other Jewish people like Ernst Rathenau started coming back from America after the war, they went straight to the Mönchberg on their holidays, as if there was no other place in the whole of Austria that had clean air. They came back to the guest house again and again, year after year, and they brought other famous people with them who were also against the Nazis, like the painter Oskar Kokoschka and the sculptor Giacomo Manzú and the singer Elisabeth

Schwarzkopf. You know it's true because why else would a Jewish man named Ernst Rathenau bring friends like that all the way up to the Mönchberg just for the air. And why would Ernst Rathenau, the cousin of Walther Rathenau who was assassinated by the Nazis before the war even started, come back from America and go straight up to visit a German woman who had lost her husband in the war? Marianne never heard from her husband Angelo again, but she had one daughter named Christiane. Ernst Rathenau even paid for Christiane to go all the way through university and become a doctor. Because Tante Marianne once did a favour to Jewish people and now they were paying her back.

My mother says you can only really be brave if you know you will lose. And the silent negative is not like any other silence either, because one day you will say what you're thinking out loud with your arms folded, like Marianne. You can't be afraid of saying the opposite, even if you look like a fool and everybody thinks you're in the wrong country, speaking the wrong language. Everybody thought the man with the bomb in the briefcase was an idiot and they only wanted to laugh at him. And Tante Marianne must have looked like a fool standing up in the opera house in Salzburg, trying to get herself killed and saying what a pity Hitler wasn't dead yet.

My mother remembers the steam from the trains like fog on the platform. She remembers the sound of the whistle echoing through the station. She remembers seeing people crying all over Germany. She shows me the photographs of cities in Germany that were bombed. She heard once of a woman carrying her dead child with her in a suitcase. Sometimes you can't think of anything else but the people you know. Sometimes people are afraid to look any further than their own family. That's when you have to be brave.

When the winter came, my mother was told to go to

Hamburg, to join a big camp full of women. From there they were sent mostly to the east to fight with the German troops. People were saying that it made no sense to go to the east because the war was lost already. Some people got a chance to go home one more time to say goodbye to their family as if they were never going to come back. My mother got letters from Tante Marianne asking for food and she wrote back to say that she would do her best. But it was nearly impossible to find anything, unless you were with the army going out to the war. My mother managed to get a bucket full of sauerkraut and instead of going back home to Kempen, she decided to try to get to Salzburg instead. She asked for a ticket to a different town called Kempten which sounds the same, and isn't in the Rhineland at all, but somewhere in Bavaria. She carried the last bucket of sauerkraut with her all the way and it was snowing heavily when she arrived to deliver it.

Nobody wanted to go back to the war. My mother says she wanted to stay on the Mönchberg and hide until it was all over. She thought of staying and helping Marianne, because she was expecting her baby and had a husband in the war and a mother-in-law who was ill. But then she would only have to eat some of the sauerkraut that she had brought and that would make no sense any more. Marianne would be worse off. So at least, my mother says, she helped her with the washing before she left. She got all the clothes and the sheets together and boiled up lots of hot water. There was enough soap and starch to do it properly, and because it was so cold outside they dried everything inside. My mother hoped it would all take longer. She hoped it would take so long that somebody would say on the radio that the war was over. When the sheets were dry, my mother helped to iron them until they were like new.

She laughed and helped Marianne to fold them together, taking one corner in each hand and dancing towards the middle like Irish dancing. The smell of the laundry made my mother think that she was a little girl again. She didn't want the dancing with the sheets to stop. It was only when it was over and all the washing was finished that my mother realised how many sheets there were. She counted them in her head and thought there were too many just for three women.

'Are you thinking of starting a guest house?' she asked, but that was a joke and Marianne didn't know how to answer. They didn't know how to talk about it. Everybody was afraid to say anything that didn't have to do with things like washing and ironing. And then it was time for my mother to leave. They looked at each other for a long time and said *ja, ja, ja* and *nein, nein, nein*, until my mother put on her coat and stepped out into the snow.

The walk down the Mönchberg was harder than the walk up, she says. It was icy and you had to hold on to the fence sometimes to make sure you didn't slip and break your teeth. At the station, the guards checked her papers and she was in trouble because she was very late and should have been in Hamburg ages ago. She was told to take the next train to Nuremberg, but there she was arrested and taken into a police station. They accused her of not following orders like everyone else in Germany. They asked lots of questions and she said she was just trying to bring some food to her sister who had a husband in the war and mother-in-law who was sick. They didn't believe her. They didn't think she looked eager enough to go back to the war. They said she was a deserter. *Fahnenflucht*, they called it, running away from the flag. They put her on a train to the east and locked the carriage door. They didn't tell her where she was going, but she knew it was to the east, that's all. She was locked in the carriage with a young soldier who was not much older than fourteen, my mother says, and he was chained to the seat by his ankles.

The fog is starting to disappear, but the foghorn keeps going just in case. It has begun to rain a bit, just a few drops on the window. It's dark now, but it's clear enough to see across the gardens to the next street. From my bedroom I can see the light and the branches in front of it. There is a bit of a breeze and the branches are dancing across the wall behind me and across my face, too. If anyone saw me, they would think there was something wrong with me. They would see spots all over my face from the raindrops on the glass. They would see a speckled face and say that I was diseased. Nobody would want to touch me. The foghorn is still going, but it sounds more tired, as if it's been saying the same word all day and now it's getting fed up with it. In my room I have some books that my mother gave me and that Onkel Ted gave her. I have some books about Irish history and some magazines that my father gave me, too, about geography, with stories about people in other countries like South Africa and Tibet that are still not free. Sometimes I read them and sometimes I just look at the pictures because I don't like any more words. I just want the one word from the foghorn to go to sleep with. 'Roooooom . . .'

I looked at the books and noticed that the picture of the man who put the bomb in a briefcase for Germany looked a bit like the picture of the man who started the Easter Rising for Ireland. I had to bend the books a little bit, but when I put the pictures together they looked alike. And they were facing each other, as if they were talking. Patrick Pearse was looking to the right and Claus Schenk Graf von

Stauffenberg was looking to the left. They seemed not to be even surprised to be in the same room together. Patrick was saying to Claus that he thought he was in Germany. Claus looked back over and said he was only here in Ireland for a short visit. There was a lot of trouble in Germany and he wanted to know if anyone in Ireland could help. He heard that the Irish were good at saying the opposite. And Patrick Pearse said he was having a lot of trouble with the British at the moment, and the only thing to do was to make a sacrifice. You can't be afraid of looking stupid.

They looked like brothers. Claus and Patrick. I sat up in bed and held the two photographs together. Claus was planning a puppet show against the Nazis and Patrick was planning a puppet show against the British. Claus knew that people might laugh at him in Germany and Patrick knew that people would surely laugh at him in Ireland. They both knew that people would say they might as well not have bothered. Patrick said that Ireland unfree shall never be at peace and Claus said long live the real Germany. Before they had to leave, they wondered if there was time to go for a walk down to the sea. Or maybe even a drink in the Eagle House. But they were in a hurry and there was no time to waste. They were not sure their plans would work either, because they were not very good at hating anyone yet. But they were not afraid to lose. They were not afraid of being put up against the wall and executed. And that's what happened to both of them in the end in different countries for the same reason. They met for one last time in my room with the foghorn still going outside. They shook hands and said 'Down you bully belly.' They laughed because they were not afraid to be Irish and not afraid to be German. I told them that Tante Marianne was going to save Jewish people who could not breathe very well and that my father was going to help people who wanted to breathe in Irish. When they were gone and the light was out, I lay back and listened to the foghorn going on and on, saying the same word over and over again until it was hoarse and had no voice any more.

Twenty-eight

Everything keeps happening again. Now I'm going down to the seafront and holding my little brother Ciarán's hand. We're going to look at the sea and throw stones at the big bully waves. I help him to walk on the wall and hold his hand to make sure he doesn't fall. He sings the same song that Franz sang when we were small and we didn't know any better. He says good morning to everyone that we pass by in English and sings 'walk on the wall, walk on the wall . . .' I'm Ciarán's big brother now, so I have to make sure he doesn't fall off and break his nose.

The dog is still there every day but he doesn't bark as much any more. Sometimes he just sits on the steps and says nothing, as if he's fed up fighting and he knows there's no point in trying to stop the waves. He still keeps an eye on them and maybe he's waiting for a big one, or waiting for somebody else to come and throw stones and then he'll start again, barking as much as ever before. He still has no name and belongs to nobody and follows anyone who pretends to be his friend for life. So we decided that he would belong to us from now on. We clicked and he came after us. We had a dog now that would protect us and we gave him a name, Cú na mara, which is the Irish for seadog. But that was too long so we tried Wasserbeisser instead, water-biter. But that was even harder, so in the end we just called him nothing and said: 'Here boy.' Every time we looked back he was still there. Even when we went into a shop to buy chewing gum and an ice pop for Ciarán, he stayed outside and waited. But then we met a gang coming towards us.

'Hey Eichmann,' one of them shouted.

They were not scared of the dog at all. They came across the street and asked if I had any cigarettes. I told them I didn't smoke yet. They called me a Kraut and wanted the chewing gum instead. They started kicking me and Ciarán was crying. The dog said nothing, but there was a man working in a garden nearby who stood up and told them to stop.

'Leave them alone,' the man said. 'Off you go about your business.'

They didn't have any business because they were the fist people. Instead, they tried to pretend that we were the best of friends. One of them put his arm around me and whispered into my ear.

'Listen, Eichmann. We're not finished with you.'

Then they walked away, laughing and eating the chewing gum that I bought. One of them whistled and the dog followed them instead of us. The man in the garden saved us and we were lucky. We were free to go home now, but I knew that wasn't the end. I know they're still after me.

Everything is happening again. My mother cuts out a picture from the newspapers of a man who set himself on fire because he couldn't live in the wrong country. She puts it into her diary, as well as pictures of Russian tanks on the streets of Prague. She remembers Prague with German troops. A new war started in Vietnam and my mother was cutting out pictures of a new kind of bomb there. She also has a picture of a black man named Martin Luther King who was assassinated in America. Now they want civil rights in Northern Ireland, too, and she cuts out pictures of people with placards and blood running down their faces. Some people even had to leave their houses because they were in the wrong country and had no names and no faces any more. So now the diary is full of pictures of Russian troops in Czechoslovakia and British troops in Northern Ireland and American troops in Vietnam. My mother says it's hard to believe how anyone thinks they can keep people quiet that way. Homesick people carry anger with them in their suitcases. And that's the most dangerous thing in the world, suitcases full of helpless, homesick anger.

In school, some of the boys made an effigy of Nelson's Pillar out of cardboard and blew it up on O'Connell Street with sodium chlorate and sugar. They made a little speech called 'Up the Republic'. The fuse was coming out the door where you used to go up the winding stairs to look out over the city. They lit it and there was an explosion that knocked the toy soldier with the sword off the top and set the whole thing on fire. Everybody going home from work in Dublin thought things were happening again. On the radio you can hear a song about people with the foggy dew in their eyes and another song called 'Up went Nelson'. On TV you can see a man in Northern Ireland foaming at the mouth about a spider inviting the fly into the parlour. You can see people marching with big drums that make so much noise none of the other puppets can speak. A boy at school told me that his mother came from Derry and she had her Holy Communion dress torn when she was a girl and never forgot it.

Up in the north the Catholics are called Fenians and the Protestants are called Prods. The Fenians are afraid to be British and the Prods are afraid to be Irish because they can't breathe very well in Ireland. People call each other names because they want to kill each other. People learn how to hate each other because they're afraid of dying out. In school they call you a Jew if you don't have any chewing gum to share. The British are called Brits and the Irish are called Paddies and the Germans are called Krauts and that's worse than being either British or Irish, or both together. They still call us bloody Krauts even though we're bloody Paddies. Sometimes they tell us to fuck off back to where we came from, but that doesn't make any sense because we come from Ireland. One day they called Franz a fuckin' Jew Nazi and held him against the railings of the Garden of Remembrance. He had no chewing gum, so they banged his head until it started bleeding. Brother Kinsella punished them all for it, including Franz who did nothing, and everybody was laughing about that for a long time, punishing the guilty and the innocent together. Brother Kinsella said it was the only way to stop things happening again, to hit the victims and the perpetrators equally.

My friend at school has stopped being my friend. I like him. I like the way he looks and the way he talks. And sometimes I want to be him instead of myself. He never called me names, but one day he stopped talking to me. He just walks past me in school without a word. Maybe he's punishing the innocent and the guilty, too, because he tells everybody that the Nazis turned people into soap and you can't deny that. He won't be my friend for life any more because he thinks I'm going to make chairs out of people's bones and I can't deny that either, even though I haven't done it yet. I know I can't have friends for life. It's better to be on my own from now on, because they'll find out sooner or later what I've done.

At home my mother wants to stop things happening

again. She says we're not the fist people, so one day she took all the sticks from the greenhouse and broke them over her knee in the kitchen until they were all in bits and my father had nothing to hit us with any more. He was still able to smack the rubber gloves into your face and give you the foggy dew. And he was able to throw pots, too, because he always did the washing up. But he was not able to take me up the stairs and pray that he was doing the right thing for Ireland, so then I started arguing with him at the table until he was blinking and I could see myself twice in his glasses. I like giving the wrong answers. One day, my father said there was nothing outside infinity. He said the universe was like a cardboard box with God sitting outside surrounded by light, but I wanted to know if maybe God was sitting inside another cardboard box with the light on, and how could anyone be sure how many cardboard boxes there are? My mother says I was driving him mad with wrong answers. He knew there were no sticks left, but there was a bowl of *Apfelkompot* on the table instead. He looked at it for a minute. Then he picked it up and threw it over my head. It was still warm. I felt it running down my face into the collar of my shirt. But I was smiling, because I knew that my father was losing the language war. My mother cleared everything up and tried not to laugh. She said you had to have an imagination to throw *Apfelkompot* over somebody's head and maybe she should make it more often if we liked it so much. But later on she told me never push people into a corner. She says there's too much fighting in our house and how can Ireland ever be at peace if we go on like this.

One day I ran away from home with another boy from school called Evil. We stayed out all night until it started raining and the only place we could find to shelter in the whole city was in the cab of a truck. It was so cold in the truck that we were shivering. In the morning we went into a church to get warm, and I knew that I never wanted to be homeless again. Homeless people are always hunched up with the cold and warm people stand up straight. I knew there was a boy living rough under the Top Hat. There's a dance hall called the Top Hat Ballroom that we pass on our way to school. It had a huge black top hat on the roof until it was blown off in a storm one night and the hat fell down into the laneway beside the dance hall. Now there's a homeless boy living under it and I don't want to be like him, hunched up with no language to go home to.

Instead, I went home and told my father that I would kill him. I said I would not speak any dying language any more, only killer languages, and then I asked him how would he like to be killed by his own son. He took off his glasses and told me to go ahead. But then I did nothing. I just said what they say in school when they're afraid. I said it wasn't worth wasting my energy. In any case, my mother said I would have nowhere to go home to if I did something like that. Once you kill somebody, you can never go back. So now she tries to keep us away from each other in different parts of the house with at least one or two doors slammed between us. She helps me to run away. Sometimes she lets me stay out of school and go to the cinema where it's dark and nobody knows who I am. Then I talk to myself in English. I pretend that I'm not German or Irish at all. But one night my father found out and he came up to my room when I was already asleep. He started punching me in my sleep and I woke up with him foaming at the mouth and my mother pulling him back by the elbow and Franz standing at the door calling peace. My father had lost the language war and everybody knew it. My mother says the people who lose become ugly and helpless with anger. Nobody wants to be a loser. Nobody wants to be left in the train station with a suitcase full of helpless anger.

Sometimes I argue with my mother as well. I start twisting around all the things she said and making no sense out of them. I ask her why she was trying to bring me up to live under the Nazis. We have to behave as if the British are still in Ireland and the Nazis are still in Germany. I tell her the silent negative is useless. She can't argue with me any more. She has other children to look after as well, she says, and so I tell her that she had too many children. Then she looked at me for a long time and waited for a moment to search for what she wanted to say next.

'Maybe I should have skipped you,' she said.

Then I threw an egg at her. I picked it up and threatened her with it, but she pretended that she didn't care. Go ahead, she said. I didn't want to hurt her. I didn't know how to hate very well yet, so I threw it softly so that she could catch it without breaking it. And then she threw it back to me and I caught it as well. So from that day on we started throwing eggs to each other every day and catching them, until we laughed and nobody ever had so much fun with eggs before without eating them.

I stand alone at the seafront a lot. Sometimes I throw stones at the waves. Sometimes I just sit on one of the rocks and think I'm in the luckiest place in the world, with the blue sea out in front of me and the sun stinging me in the back. Sometimes I think of escaping away to another country where nobody knows where I came from. And sometimes I am trapped, full of helpless anger. Sometimes I still hate everything, even the dog that had no name and no owner. He just followed the fist people when he felt like it. He was a betrayer. One day I found him near the harbour so I pushed him in and told him to drown.

There was nobody around and nobody to see what I was doing. I threw stones at him because I was Eichmann. I was the most cruel person in the world. I smiled as I watched him trying to rescue himself. I laughed like the Nazis in the films and would not let him up the steps again. I knew I was punishing the innocent instead of the guilty. He swam away to try and rescue himself somewhere else. I watched him scraping against the side of the boats, but it was no good. He swam helplessly around in circles looking for anywhere to survive and not die out. He was getting tired and then I started feeling really sorry for him, because he was an old seadog now. I wasn't angry any more, just ashamed. I said this was the worst thing I ever did in my life and I tried to save him. I ran over to the next steps and called him, but he wouldn't trust me any more and I could never trust myself again either. I was one of the fist people now. I didn't know any better. The dog had his mouth open, trying to get air and not drink any more of the seawater. He was starting to go down under and I couldn't look any more. I had to run away. I was sick of what I had done and I knew that I would never have any friends. My knees were shaking and I wanted to disappear and drown myself as well. I was so sick of what I had done that I ran home and scraped my hand on the wall so the skin came off and there were little black stones mixed in with the blood.

My father knows he's lost the language war because he's behaving more like other fathers now. He bought a television set and started watching programmes in English like the detective who pretends he knows nothing. He got a car, too, and buys petrol in English and even eats biscuits that are not made by my mother. Sometimes he looks like he's tired of fighting and tired of making sacrifices all his life, and he's sad because he might as well not have bothered. There's no point in keeping the waves back any more. He says he made mistakes. It's not easy to say that you lost, but he came to me one day and shook hands and said he wished he could start all over again because he would make different mistakes this time. Sometimes if you lose, everything is wrong. If you win, everything is right.

Then one day British soldiers shot people dead on the street in Derry. They had lost the language war, too, and shot straight into a crowd of people marching for civil rights. On television we saw a priest crouched down waving a white handkerchief and maybe the British people are afraid of dying out. My father watched it all on television and couldn't speak. He sat for a long time staring at all the things that happened in Ireland for hundreds of years and were happening all over again. Later he came upstairs and said he didn't want me to make the same mistakes again. He said he had never held a gun in his hand and there was no point in me doing it either. He said it was better to use the typewriter, because if you make mistakes, you can still correct them without killing anyone. I knew he wanted to make up for all the mistakes he made.

Onkel Ted came out and gave me a book called *Black Like Me*, about a man who changed his skin from white to black, just to see what it was like for other people. He said you have to be on the side of the losers, the people with bad lungs. You have to be with those who are homesick and can't breathe very well in Ireland. He said it makes no sense to hold a stone in your hand. A lot more people would be homeless if you speak the killer language. He said Ireland has more than one story. We are the German-Irish story. We are the English-Irish story, too. My father has one soft foot and one hard foot, one good ear and one bad ear, and we have one Irish foot and one German foot and a right arm in English. We are the brack children. Brack, homemade Irish bread with German raisins. We are the brack people and we don't just have one briefcase. We don't just have one language and one history. We sleep in German and we dream in Irish. We laugh in Irish and we cry in German. We are silent in German and we speak in English. We are the speckled people.

Twenty-nine

After that my father was killed by his own bees.

Every year in May the bees swarmed because they wanted a new place to live in, not just the same gardens and the same flowers and apple trees every time. Whenever there was a swarm, you could see it like a cloud in the air all around the house, with bees zigzagging like needles against the sky when you looked up. It was always a fine day, too, with the sun out and no rain. And they would never sting when they were swarming. My father said they were happiest when they were going off to find a new home because for them it was like going on their holidays to Connemara or Germany. You could stand underneath without any protection and not be afraid. You could watch the cloud until it started moving away from the house like a whirlwind. They would not go far at first, only up to a nearby tree where they would settle down and wait while the scouts went out to find a new address for them to live in. Then you still had a chance to catch them and bring them back before they emigrated and disappeared for ever. My father taught me how to do it. You could see the swarm like a black beard hanging in the tree and you could climb up with a straw skep and not be afraid to put it on top. You didn't need to have gloves on or anything. The bees would think it was a new home and move in. Either that or you could hold the skep underneath and shake the branch until the beard fell straight in. Then you put it on the ground and all the bees would settle down again. You had to be quick and calm at the same time. You had to do all this before the scouts came back with the new address and sometimes, when you thought you had caught them, the cloud would start swirling up in the air again and fly away over the roofs of the houses.

I was very good at catching the swarms when my father was out at work and he was good at making them move back into their old hives again as if it was a brand new home. But after a while the bees started getting very angry and they always wanted to go back to the country. My father said that maybe they were getting aggressive because of inbreeding. And one day, when he was out on the roof of the breakfast room checking the hives, they attacked him. I wasn't there to stop it. I wasn't there to do the sting-stopping trick with the tea towel and cracking the bees before they could do any harm. I was away, walking on my own all day, hanging around by the sea and thinking of going for a swim.

Nobody could stop what happened. My father was dressed for going on the moon with the cage around his head and the big gloves going up past his elbows. He was taking out the frames and trying to make sure they weren't thinking of running away again, so then the bees all went mad. They zigzagged all around him like an unhappy cloud. My mother knew there was something wrong so she closed all the windows and told everyone to stay inside. Maybe my father was not meant to be a beekeeper. Maybe he wasn't calm enough to be a father. Maybe the bees knew he was still fighting and thinking about the time when he was a boy and nobody liked him except for his mother. Maybe they could feel anger in the air from the time when Ireland was still under the British, or when Ireland was free and could remember nothing but being under the British. Maybe they could smell things like helpless anger, because they kept trying to kill him. And then one of them finally got in under the cage around his head and stung his ear.

My father thought he would never hear music again as long as he lived, so he began to panic and dropped the frame in his hands. The bees jumped up in the air like a black cat. They were humming like a furious engine now. He tried to get the bee out of his ear but they were already stinging the leather gloves. Every time he tried to stop them from getting under his cage, he was only letting more of them in. He nearly fell off the roof trying to beat them off. He shouted for help and climbed back in through the window to get away from them. My mother heard him calling and ran up the stairs with a towel, but there were bees all over the house by now. Everyone ran away to hide. Ita got into bed and covered herself up with the blankets and didn't come out again. Bríd took Ciarán into the bathroom to play with water and locked the door for ever. The whole house was full of bees. They were in every room, buzzing at the window, trying to sting anything they could find, soft things like curtains and pillows and coats that smelled like us.

My father was running through the hall with bees on his back and his arms. My mother was behind him trying to beat them off with the towel and getting stung herself as well. He was shouting and trying to get the cage off his head. They were both shouting, which is the worst thing of all because the bees know when you're not calm. That makes them even more aggressive. They stung him around his neck and close to his eyes and on his lip. They stung him inside his shirt, even under his arm, even in the other ear so that he couldn't hear anything any more. Then my mother just flung open the front door and ran out of the house, out on to the street, with the bees still following. They escaped from the house and left the front door wide open. She pulled my father across the road and waved at the cars passing by. Neighbours ran back into their houses because they were scared of bees and scared of the Irish language. In the end, a woman stopped her car to take them down to the hospital. But even then the bees got in with them and kept stinging my father. Even when he got into the hospital they came after him and kept stinging until he stopped fighting and couldn't say anything more. They were buzzing at the frosted glass of the hospital windows and around the neon lights. They were still trying to sting anything they could find, things like rubber tubes and plastic gloves. When the doctors and nurses started taking his clothes off they found bees underneath who were trying to sting him even though he was not moving any more. They found a bee right inside his ear. They counted 38 stings in all and that was more than anyone could live through with a bad heart.

When I came back I saw the front door open for anyone in the world to walk into our house. I knew there was something wrong because there was a hum in the hallway. Bees were at all the windows. They were dying on the floor and walking around in circles, making themselves dizzy. I knew there was something wrong because Ita was still under the bedclothes afraid to come out. Everybody was crying and you don't want your father to die. You still want to be friends with him, otherwise you won't like yourself very much either. I didn't want to have a father who was killed by his own bees before I could talk to him.

My father worked all his life with the ESB. He helped to bring electricity to lots of places in Ireland like Connemara and Mayo and the Aran Islands. It was called rural electrification. My father was responsible for all the wires hanging between the lamp-posts all around the country. He was respected with his long Irish name, the name that nobody could pronounce but that everybody remembered. And then he had one last job to do before he died, he had to buy some high tension cables in Germany. He was the only one who could speak German in the ESB, so he was sent over to get the best value. He visited factories and admired all the German inventions. He travelled all around the country and said the Germans were great people. And that's where he died. The bees followed him all the way and on the last day at Frankfurt Airport, when he was on his way back home again, they killed him. He was sitting down, ready to say goodbye to one of the men he was buying the cables from. Then he just fell over into the man's lap, stung to death.

The phone call came in the afternoon. My mother came out of the front room with shadows around her eyes. She walked around the house as if she was lost and didn't know where to go. His coffin came back to Ireland some days later. His suitcase, too, full of things that he had bought for us, presents from Germany to make up for all the mistakes.

I had seen other funerals before but I never thought it would be our funeral. At the church my mother looked so different. She's my mother, but when I saw her crying, she was a child again. She was thinking of all the things that happened in her life after she was nine years old and her own father died. Now she's an orphan again and everyone has to look after her. She was weak coming out of the church, so

Eileen and Tante Roseleen had to help her and hold her arms. There were lots of people outside the church that we didn't know. People shook hands with me that I never saw in my life before and I never knew my father had so many friends. Everybody was looking at us and whispering with the foggy dew in their eyes. People said there was nobody like my father left in Ireland now. They said he was the last person to be killed by his own bees and Irish people were only interested in things like cars and televisions from now on. Onkel Ted was there to help my mother into the black car for all the family because she had nowhere to go home to any more. It looked as if she had just arrived in Ireland and didn't know where she was.

After that it's sometimes hard to talk to my mother. She says she should have fought back earlier. She says she was trapped by my father and could not escape. If she had the choice she would still be born in Germany and she would still come to Ireland, but she would have changed things and made different mistakes this time. People sometimes come to visit her and ask her if there's anything they can do. Gearóid comes in his Volkswagen and his tweed suit, but she doesn't want to see him. Some of the neighbours invite her over but they don't always understand what she says in her German accent. Sometimes people come from Germany to visit and then the house fills up with the smell of cake again. But most of the time my mother prefers to sit in the front room and read books and write her diary, because that's your only friend for life. To my children, she starts off again. When you grow up I don't want you to say that you knew nothing.

My father is gone and our house is very quiet. The tall man came to take the bees away one day and there's nothing on the roof of the breakfast room now. My father's bee hat and his bee gloves are in the greenhouse. All the things in the house that belong to him are still there. Nothing has changed. His books are on the desk with a train ticket halfway through to let you know how much he has left to read. His tools are there in the *Kinderzimmer* and there is a dining-room cabinet waiting to be finished. Everybody is afraid to touch anything. Upstairs, his shirts and his Sunday suit are hanging in the wardrobe. I can walk out of the house now any time I like and go down to the seafront. There's nobody telling me what to do any more and what language to speak in. But sometimes I still think he's going to burst in the door any minute. I think he's back in the house and I can hear his voice full of anger.

You can inherit things like that. It's like a stone in your hand. I'm afraid that I'll have a limp like him. I'm afraid I might start sticking the tip of my tongue out the side of my mouth when I'm fixing something. I know I have to be different. I have to listen to different music and read different books. I have to pretend that I had no father. I have to go swimming a lot and dive underwater and stay down there as long as I can. I have to learn to hold my breath as long as I can and live underwater where there's no language.

I know they're still after me. One day when I was swimming on my own, they found me pretending that I was not a Nazi or an Irish speaker who was dying. They knew it was Eichmann gone swimming and diving underwater. There was a big gang this time and I couldn't run away. There was nobody else around either to save me. No gardener. No old man swimming with pink skin as if the water was not cold. It was Sunday morning with the bells ringing and rain coming. They started throwing stones at me, every time I came up for air. So then I had to come out of the water and they put me on trial.

I stood in the shed where you change. But I couldn't get dressed because they started kicking my clothes around. They laughed and asked me questions I couldn't answer. One of them had a knife and said he had ways of making me talk. They stood around, punching and kicking me to see if I was guilty or not.

I knew that was the reason why my mother came to Ireland in the first place. One day in the front room she told me that after the war she got a job in Wiesbaden with the American army. She worked in the de-nazification courts, she said, where they examined people to see if they were really Nazis or not. Before they could start working again and behaving like normal decent people, some of the Germans had to be put on trial and asked lots of questions to see what they had been up to in the war and if they had helped the Nazis. She had to make all the notes of what people said and then type them up afterwards. It was a good job and everybody said she was so lucky. Maybe she would even meet an American and get married. But one day, there was an old man before the court, a gynaecologist. He said he had no time for Hitler because he was only helping women with babies getting born. He said he didn't care if babies were German or not, they were all good babies to him. But they didn't believe him. In the end, a Jewish woman came home to Germany from England to speak up for him. She said he was always very friendly to her and that he helped her when it was difficult to have a baby. That should have settled everything, but afterwards when my mother was typing everything up, they came and asked her to change the words around. They wanted the Jewish woman to say he was always very angry and that he only wanted Nazi babies. But my mother couldn't. So then she wrote a letter to say that she would not work there any more. Everybody said she was mad giving up a great job like that with a flat in Wiesbaden and American food when everybody in Germany was hungry. But she could only think of the old gynaecologist sitting in court very quietly and not even trying to defend himself. He said he liked German music and German books, but that didn't make him hate other people. He was one of the last good men in Germany and they were trying to turn him into a Nazi.

She left her job and went away, on a pilgrimage to Ireland.

My mother says there are enough guilty people and we don't need to invent them. There are enough murderers left in the world today and we don't need to make up Nazis that didn't exist. And there's no point in turning the Nazis into big film stars either, because then everybody will be blind to all the other things that are going on now.

There's no point in telling any of that to the gang at the seafront. There's no point in saying that they're kicking the wrong person and that I'm not really Eichmann, that I was brought up to live against the Nazis and I don't want to kill anyone. There's no point in telling them that they're making a mistake and they don't know any better.

I had no cigarettes and no chewing gum to give them either, so then I thought the best thing was to try to be funny and Irish like everyone else. I tried to put on the slow grin that Nazis have in films. I stood up and shouted: 'Sieg Heil, Donner Messer Splitten, Himmel Blitzen.' Some of them laughed a bit, but they didn't want me to start being their friend. They stood around, trying to decide how they would execute me. All I could do was stand under the shed and wait. There was a pool of water around my feet and I felt the cold stone under my heels. I tried to stop myself from shivering. There was rust on the blue railings and green seaweed on the rocks. There was a mist on the sea and the water was licking the steps, going up two steps and back down one, down two steps and back up three like a song. The seagulls were standing around on the rocks, just watching and listening, only one of them occasionally lifting his wings and screeching as if he was the judge.

I tried to talk to them. I tried to tell them my story but there was no point. I asked them did they not trust me? But they just laughed. And there was no point in trying to be innocent. My mother says you can only be innocent if you admit the guilt. You can only grow up if you accept the shame.

Then they started the execution. One of them kicked me so hard that I had to bend over. There was a black pain spreading up into my stomach and I thought I was going to get sick. I couldn't stop the foggy dew in my eyes, but I tried to look up as if Germans didn't feel any pain. One of them punched me in the face and I saw blood on my towel. I knew that they were learning to hate and that you're allowed to hate Germans. They wanted me to surrender.

I looked up to show that I was not afraid to be silent. And then I saw the dog. I nearly forgot about the execution when I saw the dog behind them, the dog that barks all day until he's hoarse. I couldn't believe it at first and I had to wipe my eyes to make sure. The dog with no name was coming down to bark at the sea as if nothing was wrong and he never drowned.

'Jaysus, what the Jaysus,' I said. 'It's the dog.'

They looked around as if I was trying to play a trick on

them and get away. They said all the Germans were gone mad because I was calling the dog over to save my life.

'It's the dog with no name,' I said again.

He didn't drown after all. He must have rescued himself. He must have got up the steps and shook the water off his back and forgotten it even happened, because he came right over to where we all were standing in the courtroom by the sea. The courtroom in the forty-foot gentlemen's bathing place. He started sniffing around my clothes and socks scattered on the ground. He came right over and sniffed at me, too. He didn't blame me for anything and I was able to pet him as if we were friends for life. I heard them laughing and saying that the Kraut has lost it completely now. I heard them saying they were going to execute me even more after that for being so stupid, but I didn't care and they could say it until they were hoarse and had no voice any more, because the dog was alive and I didn't kill him.

'Jaysus, what the Jaysus,' I kept saying. 'Jaysus what the Jaysus of a bully belly Jaysus.'

There was nothing they could do to hurt me now. So I picked up one of my shoes and threw it into the sea. It was the only thing I could think of doing, because I grew up being good at saying the opposite and giving the wrong answers. I was not afraid any more. Laugh at yourself and the world laughs with you. Execute yourself and nobody can touch you. I heard them say that I was out of my mind and the Nazis were mental. So I picked up the other shoe and threw it out as well, and then the dog with no name ran after it and started barking. My shoes were floating on top of the water and there was nothing they could do. They didn't know how to execute me any more. They couldn't touch me because the dog was alive and barking. He was trying to go down the steps and get my shoes back, barking and barking as if he never drowned.

On the way home I walked along the wall with the dog behind me. My shoes were squeaking all the way. There were white salt marks where they were already beginning to dry. The sun was starting to come through the mist and it was not going to rain after all. I looked back and saw the sun coming out. The water was so white and so full of bouncing light that I could see nothing at all. It made me want to close my eyes and sneeze. When I looked into the shadows under the trees it was so dark that I could see nothing there either. When you're small you know nothing. I know the sea is like a piece of silver paper in the sun. I can see people walking along the seafront with ice-cream cones. I can hear the bells and I'm not afraid any more of being German or Irish, or anywhere in between. Maybe your country is only a place you make up in your own mind. Something you dream about and sing about. Maybe it's not a place on the map at all, but just a story full of people you meet and places you visit, full of books and films you've been to. I'm not afraid of being homesick and having no language to live in. I don't have to be like anyone else. I'm walking on the wall and nobody can stop me.

Thirty

We're trying to go home now. We're still trying to find our way home, but sometimes it's hard to know where that is any more. My mother went back to Germany one more time after my father died, just to visit everyone there and see where she grew up. But she was lost. She couldn't recognise anything. Now she wants to find a place in Ireland that she can remember. She says we're going on a trip to find things. She makes a big cake and we pack our bags with sandwiches and rain macs and get up early in the morning for the bus. We travel around the country to see places she went to before she got married, when she came over to Ireland on a pilgrimage, when Ireland was a holy country, full of priests and donkeys with crosses on their backs.

We came to a town where there was a carnival, with lots of people and loudspeakers playing music on the main street. There were vans selling things and a stall where you could throw wooden rings around a bottle of whiskey and win it. You could smell sweet things like candy floss and sometimes a mixture of things like chips and vinegar and diesel from the trucks. We went on the big wheel and I saw my mother and Ciarán getting smaller, waving at us below on the ground. We sat down on a bench outside the town to have the last bit of cake, with the music from the carnival still coming up and down on the wind. Then it's great to see my mother laughing and laughing, because I threw an apple at her and she caught it. And when it was time to move on and she was trying to get up from the bench, we pushed her back down until she was laughing and laughing so much with tears in her eyes. How do we know if she's happy or sad? It was getting late and she started looking for the place she remembered. She wanted to find the house that she stayed in once when she was a pilgrim after the war, coming back from Station Island.

'It must be here,' she said again and again.

We walked for a long time and she kept seeing lots of thing that she remembered, like stone walls and fields full of cows. Sometimes the cows stopped chewing to look at us as if they were surprised to see us in Ireland, so far away from home. It was the summer and we kept walking to keep ahead of the flies. We passed a house with a dog barking. One time, my mother spoke to a man to ask directions and we knew we were on the right road again. We just had to walk around another corner and find a gate where you could see the mountains, my mother said, with the sun going down like holy pictures. She wanted to speak to the woman of the house again where she stayed and the rain was praying the rosary all night. But we never found it. The night came up right behind us. We searched until it got dark and the colour was gone from the land and we could not see a thing any more. You could only smell the hay and the cow dung. It was so dark that you could only see with your nose, my mother said. Maybe she got the wrong road or the wrong mountains in the distance. She said Ireland had changed a bit. Or else it only existed in your imagination.

'Maybe I dreamed it,' she said.

We could see the lights of the next town in the distance. My mother took out a cigarette because she was free to smoke after my father died. We stood on the road and watched her face lighting up with the match. We smelled the new smoke in the clean air and waited. She said she didn't know where to go from here. We were lost, but she laughed and it didn't matter.